STORMRAGE

WORLD OF WARCRAFT®

STORMRAGE

RICHARD A. KNAAK

GALLERY BOOKS

New York   London   Toronto   Sydney

Gallery Books
A Division of Simon & Schuster, Inc.
1230 Avenue of the Americas
New York, NY 10020

Copyright © 2010 by Blizzard Entertainment, Inc. All rights reserved. Warcraft, World of Warcraft, and Blizzard Entertainment are trademarks and/or registered trademarks of Blizzard Entertainment, Inc., in the U.S. and/or other countries. All other trademark references herein are the properties of their respective owners.

First Gallery Books hardcover edition February 2010

GALLERY BOOKS and colophon are registered trademarks of Simon & Schuster, Inc.

For information about special discounts for bulk purchases, please contact Simon & Schuster Special Sales at 1-866-506-1949 or business@simonandschuster.com.

The Simon & Schuster Speakers Bureau can bring authors to your live event. For more information or to book an event contact the Simon & Schuster Speakers Bureau at 1-866-248-3049 or visit our website at www.simonspeakers.com.

Manufactured in the United States of America

10   9   8   7   6   5   4   3   2   1

ISBN 978-1-4165-5087-7
ISBN 978-1-4391-6066-4 (ebook)

For the twelve million and more
who have breathed life into Azeroth

Acknowledgments

Special thanks go to those involved in this project and my other forays into Azeroth! Here's to the folks at Blizzard in no particular order—Rob, Gina, Evelyn, Micky, Tommy, Jason, Glenn, Samwise . . . and everyone else I may have missed!

At Gallery Books—my hardworking editor Jaime, Anthony, Marco, and more!

And, with the utmost appreciation, Chris Metzen, who's been there from the beginning!

Again, thanks, everyone!

"I understand that I must find out the truth wherever that truth leads . . . even if in the end it costs me my very life . . ."

—Malfurion Stormrage, *The Well of Eternity*

PROLOGUE

BLOOD QUEST

Thura stood at the end of the great jagged chasm. The young orc's powerful hand instinctively tightened on the ax as she sought in vain a way across. Thick and muscular of limb and torso, the orc was a skilled fighter despite barely being of adult years. Yet now her broad, rough-hewn features twisted into something more childlike, more fearful, as she ran back and forth without success in her search. Her wide, tusked mouth frowned. Thura shook her head and murmured a wordless protest. Her heavy brown mane of hair, generally bound in a tail but at the moment set loose, spilled over the left side of her face.

On the other side, a tremendous battle took place, the focus of it a single, brawny male of her race and someone she knew mostly from childhood memories and tales spoken by the great orc ruler, Thrall. Facing her was a graying warrior, with a stern visage and powerful arms. Like her, he was clad in the leather kilts and harnesses of a fighter. His body was covered in old scars from other battles, other wars. Even though surrounded, the male bellowed his contempt for his monstrous foes.

And monstrous they were indeed, for they were demons of the Burning Legion . . . fell creatures far taller than the brave lone warrior. They were armored and burning from head to foot with virulent yellow-green fire whose intensity vied with the fierce determination in the brown orbs of the single orc. With wicked blades and other vile weapons, they slashed again and again, seeking to break through his guard. But ever he kept them at bay with his ax, a stunning weapon that was made more fantastic in that it was *carved of wood*.

No . . . not carved. Thura recalled that a shaman had once inspected it and declared that great magic had *shaped* the twin-edged ax into being, magic rumored to be that of the demigod Cenarius. Cenarius had been a keeper of nature, a protector of the forest.

Whatever the amazing origin of the ax, though, it clearly had magic of its own, for it sliced through strong blades and thick armor with the ease of passing through air. Great flashes of sinister yellow-green fire sparked from the deadly wounds inflicted on them as they fell one after another to the orc's sure hand.

A deep, almost hazy emerald aura that had nothing to do with the flames of the Burning Legion draped over all, even the solitary champion. The aura itself was touched by a slight blue hue that added a sense of surrealism to the moment. Thura paid little mind to the aura, though, her anxiety rising as she continued to fail to find a crossing.

Then a new, arresting figure materialized just behind and to the left of the male orc. He was an astounding being whose tall, violet-skinned race was known to Thura. A night elf. Yet this was no ordinary representative of that people, for thrusting from his head were a pair of mighty and elaborate *antlers*. Moreover, he was clad in a striking outfit that marked him not only as a druid—one of the revered keepers of nature—but clearly one of high standing, perhaps even an archdruid.

The night elf had a broader, more mature visage that gave him more individuality. He also wore a thick, green beard. His glowing, golden eyes—almost as arresting as his antlers—were plainly visible even from far away.

The coming of the night elf caught Thura's breath. Unarmed, he leaned close to the male orc to whisper something and his very presence seemed to assure the battling champion. Already the victor over many demons by himself, the older orc looked confident that he and the night elf would surely be able to stand against the bloodthirsty throng still converging on the spot.

Behind the orc, the night elf's hands suddenly filled with a long, wooden staff. He raised the staff high and as he did, the closest end suddenly sharpened to a wicked point. In front of him, the orc slashed at yet another impetuous demon, slicing off its long, narrow head, curled horns and all.

The night elf touched the point of the staff in the back of the male orc's neck.

Thura saw too late the duplicity. She shouted in vain, her words smothered by distance and the clash of arms.

From the back of the male's neck there burst a small growth. It resembled a weed, such as Thura might have trod upon a thousand times a day. Yet that weed sprouted rapidly, growing and growing within a single heartbeat.

The other orc finally sensed it. He reached back, but several dark green leaves wrapped around his wrist. The weed continued to spread, pouring over the hapless warrior's body. As it did, the leaves began sprouting terrible thorns, all pointed inward. They jabbed into the orc and wherever they did, they drew blood.

With a smile, the duplicitous night elf stepped back to admire his handiwork. Rivers of blood poured from every thorn.

The male orc shivered. His mouth gaped and he fell to one knee. The weed's tendrils covered his body until they completely bound him. Blood continued to gush from the monstrous wounds as the night elf watched with amusement.

Thura called out the male's name even though it was already too late to save him. *"Broxigar!"*

Suddenly, the demons faded to mist. There was only the night elf, his victim, and Thura. The night elf stepped back farther, his mocking gaze turning to her.

The golden orbs turned utterly black. They became deep pits that coldly pulled at the orc's soul.

Then from those dark pits poured forth monstrous, ebony carrion bugs. Beetles, millipedes, roaches, and more flowed forth from the night elf's eyes in horrific streams that spilled to the ground. The vermin spread in all directions and as they did, trees and other flora materialized in their path. Yet the lush wildlife barely appeared before the vermin swarmed it. Bushes, shrubs, even the tallest trees became enveloped.

And as they were, they withered. *Everything* withered. Thura's world became a twisted, hideous vision.

The night elf laughed. From his mouth spilled forth more fiendish vermin—

He vanished.

Thura shouted out Broxigar's name again. With effort, the dying warrior managed to look her way. One hand broke free of the strangling weed, then stretched forth, the magical ax held out.

His mouth whispered a name—

Thura awoke with a start.

She lay there for a time, still shivering despite the fact that the woods in which she currently traveled were of a comfortable temperature. The dream played over in her mind, just as it did whenever the orc was not reliving it in her sleep.

With some effort, Thura finally rose. The small campfire that she had built earlier had long died out, only a few faint wisps of smoke left in memory. Momentarily setting down her weapon, Thura used some dirt to smother what remained of the fire, then looked around for her pack. Seizing up the small, leather sack, she retrieved the ax and started off.

It was always like this. Walking until she was dead on her feet, catching her supper, then sleeping until the dream woke her up and left her in such a state that she knew it was better to move on. In a macabre way, that suited the orc just fine. Not only was there risk of late for any who were merely sleeping, but each step took her closer to her goal, closer to avenging her blood kin.

And even more, she had come to realize, she was spurred on by another mission: to prevent a catastrophe that would not only engulf her own people . . . but *all else.*

The male orc, Broxigar, had been brother to her father, although their own fathers had been different. She knew of his legendary stand with his comrades against the Burning Legion, a stand which had resulted in Broxigar—or Brox—as the only survivor. Even as a child, Thura could sense the guilt he had felt at living when his friends had not.

And then Thrall, the great orc leader, had sent the veteran warrior on a mysterious mission with another. Neither had ever returned, but then, as rumor had it, an old shaman had brought back the wondrous wooden ax from the dream and left it with Thrall. That shaman had also spoken of Brox becoming a hero who had helped to save not only the orcs, but *all* else. Some there were who said that the shaman had then sprouted wings and flown off into the night, transforming into a gigantic bird or dragon.

Thura knew not whether all the last was true, only that when she had come of warrior age and proven her skills, Thrall himself had given her the fabled ax. She was, after all, the only left of Brox's kin save for her sole remaining uncle, Saurfang the Elder, who had himself recently lost his son in battle. The ax might have previously gone to either of the other pair, but Thrall's most trusted shaman had seen in a dream that it should go to Thura. Why, no one knew, but Thrall had listened.

Thura felt honored to wield such a weapon, an irony, she knew. Years ago, under the influence of the demon lord Mannoroth's blood-curse, orcs under the legendary Grom Hellscream had invaded the forests of Ashenvale and slain Cenarius as he came forth to resist them. That had been in the days before Thrall had returned to his people their respect for nature. The death was regrettable . . . but Thura had not been part of it and so, with orcish practicality, she assumed that the spirit of Cenarius would have understood that, also.

The moment that Thura had placed her hands on it, it had felt *right*. But the ax had brought with it something else. Not at first, not even through the initial seasons after she had been given it. No, its secret had not revealed itself until later, and at first she had ignored it. A dream was just a dream . . .

Or not.

It had not taken the same shaman to finally make Thura see the truth. The spirit of her lost kin had been trying to reach out to her to demand vengeance. The dream was a hint of the truth, of that she felt certain. She had been shown how Brox had actually perished . . . betrayed by one he believed a comrade.

The night elf.

And although she could not say how she knew, Thura also understood that the night elf still lived and that he could be found. All she had to do was pay attention to the dream. Each time she awoke from it, she sensed the direction that she had to walk.

The direction in which she would find the brave Brox's treacherous slayer.

Brox had spoken his name, which had rung in her head from the very first dreaming despite her never having heard it said out loud by the male orc.

Malfurion Stormrage . . . Malfurion Stormrage . . .

Thura hefted her ax . . . once Brox's ax. The female orc had sworn an oath to her dead uncle. She would find Malfurion Stormrage, no matter how far she had to journey and no matter what her blood quest demanded she face.

She would find Malfurion Stormrage . . . and then not only would the ax mete out long-overdue justice, but perhaps Thura would be able to save Azeroth before it was too late . . .

1

TELDRASSIL

Asense of foreboding that the sleek night elf priestess had not felt since the fall of Zin-Azshari shook her to the core.

Tyrande Whisperwind tried to settle into her meditations. Darnassus, the new night elf capital, had been built to honor the survival of the race, as was appropriate, and not to honor a mad queen. While it was far smaller than its predecessor, Darnassus was in its own way no less spectacular, in part due to its location high in the western boughs of Teldrassil . . . the World Tree. So huge and mighty was it that the night elves had been able to build upon it such imposing edifices as the Temple of the Moon—crafted much of stone brought from the mainland and transported by magical means up the incredible height of the trunk. Indeed, greater than even the fact that the capital sat nestled in Teldrassil's boughs was that it was the largest of a handful of settlements existing among the foliage.

And much of all of that could be credited to the druids, who had raised up the tree.

Tyrande tried not to let even the slightest of thoughts concerning the druids interfere with her need for peace. She respected their calling, for nature had been and always would be an integral part of the night elf existence, but thinking of them even in passing always brought to the forefront thoughts and concerns of her childhood friend, of her lover, Malfurion Stormrage.

The soft light of the moon goddess shone down through the

rounded, stained-glass skylight into the vast central chamber, temporarily turning from silver to a soft purple as it did. Yet silver it became again of its own accord as it draped upon the glistening pool surrounding the statue of Haidene—the first high priestess who had, as a child, heard the blessed voice of Elune. As she was wont to do, Tyrande sat cross-legged at the edge of the pool upon the massive stone steps before Haidene's upraised arms, desperately seeking from both her predecessor and her goddess the blessing of comfort and guidance . . . and to help her shake off her growing feelings of anxiety. Though the chamber was often a place where priestesses and novices came for their own meditations and peace, Tyrande was this hour alone.

Eyes pressed shut, she sought unsuccessfully to force any thought concerning Malfurion from her mind. Their tumultuous bond stretched back to the beginning of the War of the Ancients, when she, Malfurion, and his twin brother, Illidan, had lost the innocence of their youth and become seasoned fighters. She still vividly recalled Illidan's betrayals and her own imprisonment in Azshara's palace. And though the tale of her unconscious body's transport there was something she had learned after the fact, Tyrande occasionally relived how she imagined it to have been—captured by the servants of the queen's foul counselor, Xavius—himself transformed by the Legion's master into a monstrous satyr. Also burned into her memory was the near loss of her dear Malfurion at the very end, just when he had managed to cast out most of the demons from their world. Her heart ached at the memory of him summoning his last shred of might to save her.

But, most of all, most persistent, she recalled the hopes and dreams the two had shared after the conflict. There had been talk of truly beginning a life together, of Azeroth no longer demanding great sacrifices from the two of them.

But to Tyrande's utter disappointment, Malfurion's calling pulled him away yet again. He began training other druids, for Azeroth itself had required much healing and they would be among its most ardent tenders. And when Malfurion chose to leave Tyrande behind for years at a time to walk the Emerald Dream, she had sometimes come to wonder if he had ever truly loved her.

Tyrande, meanwhile, had been thrust into the role of high priestess of Elune against her desire, and then, through circumstances and necessity, the ruler of her people. Only in that latter role had she been able to make such major changes in night elf society such as disbanding the traditional—and often flawed—system of military command based on bloodline and create the Sentinels, whose officers rose on their merits. Becoming leader was not a destiny she would have chosen for herself, but neither could she give it up, so much did she wish to help protect the night elf race.

Mother Moon, grant me calm, the high priestess silently pleaded. Although she was millennia old, the night elf physically appeared little older than that day so long ago when the mantle of leadership had been thrust upon her. She still had the lush head of midnight blue hair that flowed over her shoulders, its streaks of silver with her since her youth. Her face was that of a young maiden, and although some fine lines had begun to crease the edges of her silver eyes, even they were more the result of the last six or seven years of true aging, and not a mark of the ten harsh millennia she had lived.

But trying to rule wisely for some one hundred and more centuries took its toll within, which was why the high priestess on occasion sought respite through meditation. Tyrande only asked an hour once in a while, surely no tremendous request of Elune. Here, bathed in the ever-present light of the Mother Moon, she was generally able to find her focus with little trouble. However, this time a sense of peace continued to evade her. Tyrande understood the reasons why but refused to give in to them. She focused deeper—

Tyrande let out a gasp. The soft moonlight blazed, growing both blinding . . . and, for the first time ever, painful.

Her surroundings transformed. No longer did she sit in the security of the temple. Instead, the night elf stood in a darkened place whose earthen walls immediately marked it as a barrow den. Details of the underground chamber illuminated for her as if the pages of a tome turning. Tyrande saw the pouches of herbs, the gathered feathers, teeth, and other objects from many of Azeroth's fauna. There were markings, too, some of which were familiar to her while others remained incomprehensible.

A chill ran up and down her spine. She knew where she was but still sought in vain to deny it.

Then another priestess of Elune stepped into view. Tyrande knew her by name as well as by her thinner, unlined face. Merende. Far younger than the high priestess, but a well-respected acolyte of the Mother Moon.

A second priestess followed Merende, this one also known to their leader. That priestess was followed by a third. All wore somber expressions and kept their heads bowed. They were clad in simple silver robes with hoods. The plain garments were worn in respect to their surroundings, for these priestesses were not among their own kind, but rather in a domain under the watch of the druids. Indeed, this was the barrow den—a home, so to speak—of one of their kind.

And even as Tyrande thought this, her view shifted, following not by her choice the gazes of the troubled priestesses. A body, laid flat on a mat of woven grass, a faint, silver light—Elune's light—draping over the still form. Her heartbeat quickened at this solemn sight, even though from the past she should have long been used to it.

Even in repose, his proud visage bore the marks of time and effort even more than hers. His long, green hair had been set by the priestesses so that it lay atop his chest, where it seemed to meld with his lush, lengthy beard. He had a thick, angled brow that made him appear serious, contemplative.

He was clad more elaborately than most druids—a choice not his own but determined by his great station. Massive armor with jutting thorns protected the shoulders, while matching guards did so for the forearms and shins. Although made of wood respectfully harvested from dead trees, the spell-crafted armor was more durable and resilient than metal. The sleeveless robe stretched down all the way to his sandaled feet and bore on the sides of the legs the color and pattern of draping leaves. Near the bottom, a layer of blue marked by what seemed to be crescent moons perhaps gave some bit of honor to Elune.

Malfurion Stormrage stared up at the ceiling, his golden orbs vacant.

Tyrande drank in the sight of him, her lover. Her legs felt weak as she studied him—how could a being so bright and bursting with spirit be rendered utterly lifeless and hopelessly lost? She smiled weakly as she gazed at Malfurion, who looked so regal, so distinguished. As noble as the male night elf looked, ever one aspect about him demanded foremost attention. Sprouting from his forehead and thrusting forward were two proud *antlers*. More than two feet in length, they were no defect of birth, but rather the gift and the mark of Cenarius. Few there were of the druids who bore the four-legged, hooved demigod's blessing and of that few, the first and greatest was he who lay here.

Tyrande had not been taken aback when first the antlers had begun to grow. She had only seen them as recognition of the greatness she had always known existed in Malfurion.

"Malfurion . . ." she whispered to the body, though no one there, especially him, could hear her at all. "Oh, my Malfurion . . . why did you have to leave me again?"

She watched as her followers knelt beside the still body and placed their hands over his head and chest. Tyrande knew what they were doing, for she had given the orders herself.

Only through the blessings of the Mother Moon did Malfurion Stormrage still survive. Her faithful kept the archdruid's body alive and healthy, hoping against hope for the day when Malfurion would stir again. Hoping against hope that his dreamform would return from wherever it had become lost in the *Emerald Dream* . . .

The high priestess wanted desperately to leave. Of what purpose was there in Elune revealing this scene? All it did was stir up more anxiety, more terrible reminders. She couldn't stand to see him like that, lost to her . . . perhaps forever.

Malfurion's tenders stepped back. They looked somber. They had been at this task day after day and knew their duties well.

The archdruid's skin suddenly darkened.

The three priestesses gave no reaction to this transformation, almost as if they could not see it. Tyrande, on the other hand, leapt to Malfurion's side, paying no attention to the fact that her body glided through those of her followers as if they were but a mist. All that mattered was her beloved's horrific transformation.

And as she watched, helpless and unable even to touch him, the archdruid's body continued its macabre change. As his flesh darkened, it also crusted over, like the bark of a tree. His legs and arms grew gnarled. Jagged, ebony leaves sprouted throughout his hair and beard, quickly overwhelming both. At the same time, the leaves began slowly waving back and forth, as if a wind from somewhere far beyond this underground place blew upon them.

The golden orbs paled back to the silver of their birth, then, more horribly, they sank in, turning into black pits.

The rhythmic fluttering of the leaves seized the high priestess's attention from the awful eyes, although she at first could not say why. There was a familiar movement to the fluttering. And then a faint sound accompanied the movement, a steady, pulsating beat that swelled in intensity as it filled her ears.

A heartbeat.

She glanced around wildly—it was as though the other priestesses could not hear it. It became louder and stronger still. The sound became deafening; the leaves flickered in concert, and then . . .

The beat began to slow. Only by a minuscule rate at first, but it was slowing, as if the wind were ceasing to blow.

And as if a heart were gradually beginning to still . . .

Panicked, Tyrande thrust a hand toward Malfurion—

The barrow den vanished. Darkness and a stark silence greeted the high priestess. She discovered that her eyes were shut.

With a gasp, she opened her eyes and adjusted to Elune's glow, finding herself once more seated in the temple. Haidene's statue stood poised over her. All was as she recalled it and Tyrande knew that what she had experienced had taken place in perhaps the space of a single short breath.

But her own situation did not concern her in the least. Only the vision mattered. She had received only a handful of such gifts from her mistress over the centuries and all of them had been messages of great import. Yet this one . . . this one was the most troubling of all.

Despite the best efforts and tremendous vigilance of his tenders, it was now clear that Malfurion was dying.

The storm crow's wide, powerful wings beat hard as the avian neared the vicinity of the island. Woodland brown with tinges of silver gray at the edges of its feathers, it was large, even for one of its kind. A sloping silver crest crowned its head and twin tufts of like-colored feathers hung from both sides of its skull, giving it an almost elder, scholarly look. Deep silver eyes peered out from under the brow, drinking in everything.

Although a thick mist enshrouded the night sky, the storm crow soared through the air with a swiftness that suggested familiarity with its surroundings. Lightning flashed some distance further out at sea, and the bird took advantage of the momentary illumination to search for some sign of the island.

Suddenly, the lone traveler was forced to brace itself against an oddly cold gust of wind that seemed determined to drive him back, as if warning that only a fool would continue on. But continue the storm crow did, struggling hard against the icy current. It sensed that it was very near its goal.

And, in fact, as if curtains parting, the mists finally gave way. The island came into view at last, dwarfed beneath that for which it was both known and named. From a distance, those who beheld the great sight for the first time might have thought they were viewing some grand mountain with sides markedly perpendicular and rising so high that the clouds themselves were forced to gaze up at its majesty. But if they were able to peer up during daylight and weather far more agreeable than that through which the storm crow flew, they would discover that it was not a mountain at all—or even, perhaps, some great edifice built by hand—but was, in fact, a thing yet more remarkable.

It was a *tree*.

It filled most of the island, no small patch of ground. In the tree's very roots lay the port village—called Rut'theran by the night elves who inhabited it. It was clear the island existed purely to house the leviathan for which it was named and for which all knew it.

This was the home of Teldrassil . . . the second World Tree.

Ten thousand years earlier the original World Tree, Nordrassil, had been raised up on Mount Hyjal after the destruction of the night elves' original fount of power, the Well of Eternity. Set atop the second Well created through Illidan's duplicity, Nordrassil had served two purposes. Not only had it been designed to keep others from abusing the magic of the new Well, but also to prevent the second fount's power from growing too great over time. Blessed by three of the great Dragon Aspects—Alexstrasza the Life-Binder, Nozdormu the Timeless One, and Ysera the Dreamer—the vast tree had not only watched over Azeroth but been bound to the night elves' immortality and power.

But less than a decade ago venerable Nordrassil had suffered terrible damage during the titanic struggle against the same demons—the Burning Legion—whose initial invasion had first caused its raising. Its weakened state had left the night elves bereft of much of their vaunted power and, worse, their very *immortality*. And though Nordrassil's roots were slowly regrowing, that immortality had not yet returned.

And so eventually the druids—their apprehensions put at ease by their new leader, Fandral—had raised up Teldrassil, its successor.

The storm crow banked as the tree continued to spread before its gaze. If Teldrassil was not quite as overwhelming as its predecessor had been at its greatest majesty, none could deny that the new World Tree was a wonder of the world, a phenomenal nurturing of nature through the world of Azeroth's own magic as wielded by the druids. The width and breadth of Teldrassil's trunk were vaster than some lands. Yet, incredible as that was, it compared little to its massive, green crown, which seemed to spread along the horizon forever.

Something briefly caught the avian's attention, and it cocked its head slightly to observe it. Within the huge boughs, the storm crow sighted movement among what appeared to be not only one stone structure, but several. Indeed, protruding above the branches were the tops of several buildings.

As the flyer soared on, other smaller settlements whirred by. Even a lake momentarily glimmered among the leaves, so wide and furrowed were the gargantuan branches. And well ahead there jutted the tip of a mountain.

The storm crow approached the higher branches. There it glimpsed another wonder atop the highest of the great boughs. From that shadowed wonder came illumination not only in the form of torchlight, but also what appeared to be bits of living moonlight.

The magnificent city of Darnassus, capital of the tree-dwelling race, beckoned. Even from a distance, it was clear that Darnassus rivaled fabled places such as the humans' Stormwind City or the orcs' Orgrimmar.

The World Tree collected enough dew to create and feed many rivers, streams, and lakes among its boughs—one of the last so wide that part of Darnassus had been itself raised up on it. The night elves further manipulated the waters here to maintain the splendor of the Temple Gardens and the stunning waterway coursing through their city. Further north and on the other side of the water, the druids had set up their own sanctum, the woodland-shrouded Cenarion Enclave.

But the bird veered away, not just from Darnassus, but from the rest of the incredible cities nestled atop the crown. Inviting though the sight was, the storm crow's destination was far below.

The huge avian dropped until only a dozen yards or so from the dirt, then, with innate ability, arched its wings to slow its descent. It extended its talons out as it prepared to land.

Just before the storm crow touched ground, it swelled in size, in only a single breath growing to a height greater than any human. Its legs and talons shifted form, the former becoming thicker and longer and the latter now turning into feet that were sandaled. At the same time, each of the wings melded and stretched and fingers blossomed. The feathers vanished, replaced by thick hair of forest green that was bound tight in the back and flowed down in the front in a lush beard that extended to what was now a cloaked chest.

The beak had receded into the face, becoming a separate and still-prominent nose and a broad mouth bent into what was almost a perpetual frown. Ebony feathers had given way to flesh of a dark violet hue that marked the shapeshifter as of the race that lived in this land and above it.

Broll Bearmantle, being a night elf, looked much akin to most druids. True, he was brawnier and seemed much more like a warrior than the others. His less-than-peaceful, troubled existence gave him fuller, more weathered features, but he still passed among his fellow druids as close kin to any of them.

He peered around. There were no immediate signs of other druids, though he sensed them near. That suited him. He had wanted a moment of solitude before joining the others.

There were many thoughts swirling around his head, most of them concerning his shan'do, his teacher. Each time Broll came back to Teldrassil, the broad-shouldered night elf thought of his shan'do, knowing that without him, he would not be who he was—even if Broll considered himself a sorry excuse for a druid. In fact . . . *none* of those gathering for this sudden convocation, not even Fandral, would be here at all if not for the legendary Malfurion Stormrage.

Malfurion had not merely been their leader; he had been the first of Azeroth's mortal druids, trained in his calling by the demigod Cenarius himself. The woodland deity had seen in the then-young night elf a unique quality, a unique link to the world, and had nurtured it. And before Malfurion's mystical training had even been completed, he was thrust into that first titanic struggle against the demons and his own traitorous kind . . . including the night elves' very queen, Azshara, and her treacherous advisor, Xavius. If not for Malfurion's efforts, so many believed, Azeroth itself would surely have ceased to exist.

The tales of his extraordinary feats stretched through time. Malfurion had sacrificed the considerable centuries of his life for the sake of his world and his people over and over. When others had fallen, he had taken up their battles and added them to his own. For a master of the ways of nature, Malfurion had also become a champion in war.

Yet, most recently, with lasting peace once more perhaps possible,

Malfurion had reorganized his fellow druids and tried to set them on their original, destined path. The past was the past; the future a fascinating enigma to be quietly and calmly explored. Indeed, Malfurion had said they were better off as they were now—without their immortality—for that forced them to become more a part of the vibrant life of Azeroth rather than some staid, unchanging element merely observing the passage of time . . .

"Malfurion . . ." he muttered. But for two others in his life, no one had affected Broll like his shan'do. He owed a great deal to Malfurion . . . and yet, he, like the rest, felt helpless to do anything to save the archdruid from his dreadful fate.

Broll blinked, returning to the moment. He had sensed another coming up behind him. Even before turning, the night elf knew who it had to be. The scent alone marked this one particular druid.

"The blessing of the forest upon you, Broll Bearmantle," rumbled the newcomer. "I felt you near. I had hoped to see you."

Broll nodded. While he hadn't expected to see the newcomer, he was glad for it. "Archdruid Hamuul Runetotem . . . you made swift passage from Thunder Bluff."

Where Broll looked akin to his fellow druids, his new companion did not. The torso of the newcomer somewhat resembled that of a night elf or a human, albeit one even broader of shoulder than the powerfully built Broll. Unlike the other druids, he was clad in the loose, tanned garments of his tribe. Two long, red straps fastened his leather shoulder armor to his red-stained leather kilt. Striped bands of red, gold, and blue adorned each forearm near the wrist.

But what marked Hamuul as different, not only from Broll but the rest of the night elves was that he was a *tauren*. Thick, cloven hooves carried his massive body, and his head resembled that of a bull—as was characteristic of the tauren race, though none ever said so to their faces without risking life and limb. He had a great snout in which he wore a ceremonial ring, and long horns that curved to the side first before thrusting outward.

Hamuul stood over eight feet tall, even with the characteristic humpback of his kind. His fine, gray-brown fur tended more toward gray these days than when Broll had first met the tauren. Hamuul also wore two thick braids, also graying, that hung down over his chest. He had come late to the druidic calling, brought to it in great part, naturally, by Malfurion Stormrage's encouragement. The tauren had been the first of his race to join the ranks in almost twenty generations, and although there were now more, none was as accomplished as him.

"The journey was uneventful, if oddly quiet," the tauren remarked. His light green eyes narrowed under the thick brow ridge, as if he wanted to add something but chose not to.

The night elf nodded, his thoughts briefly turning to how he himself would be received by the others. So much had been expected from Broll, so much since birth . . . and all of it stemming from a singular feature that he shared with Malfurion, a singular feature that, to Broll, was also the ever-present sign of his lacking.

The antlers thrusting out of his temples were nearly two feet long, and if they were not quite as impressive as those that adorned the famed archdruid, they were certainly something arresting to behold. They had marked Broll even as an infant, the then-tiny nubs seen as a sign of future distinction. Even as a child, he had been told that one day—someday—he would be the stuff of legends.

But where others had seen the antlers as a gift of the gods, Broll had quickly come to consider them a bane. And in his eyes, his life had thus far proven him all too correct.

Of what use had they been, after all, when he had needed aid at the most critical moment of his life? When Broll had stood facing an onslaught of demons and undead under the vile mastery of the pit lord Azgalor, it had seemed that at last all the predictions might have borne truth. Wielding the Idol of Remulos, his druidic powers had expanded. The enemy had been pushed back while Broll's comrades had made use of his sacrifice to pull back toward the main army.

But, once again, he had proven insufficient to the task. Exhaustion assailed him. Azgalor's malevolent blade, Spite, wielded expertly, finally overcame the night elf's weakening defenses. Broll lost his grip on the idol as Spite's edge cut into it.

The demon blade's power instantly corrupted the figurine's own energies, and it erupted with a warped magical force—one that enveloped the last remaining defender at Broll's side.

There had been many times, especially since then, that the night elf had considered cutting his antlers off and burning the nubs to prevent future growth . . . and yet he never managed to take the final step toward doing so.

Broll realized that Hamuul had been silently and very patiently watching him.

"She will always be with you. The spirits of our beloved kin ever watch over us," the tauren rumbled.

"I wasn't thinking of Anessa," the night elf murmured, lying.

Hamuul's ears flattened. "My humblest apologies for bringing her up."

Broll waved off the tauren's regrets. "You've done nothing wrong," he muttered. "Let's move on. The others will already be gathering at the portal as per custom—"

Hamuul's brow knitted. "But we are not to go up to Darnassus and the Cenarion Enclave. Fandral intends our convocation to take place down here . . . in fact, on the side opposite from where we now stand! You did not know that?"

"No . . ." Broll did not question the archdruid's decision. After all, as leader of the druids, Fandral Staghelm had their best interests at heart. If he thought it wiser to meet down here than in Darnassus, so be it. There was surely a good reason why—

And then it came to him. Perhaps Fandral had found a way to save their shan'do.

"Let's get going," he said to Hamuul, the night elf suddenly impatient to be there. Spurred on by the deep, unswerving hope that consumed him each time he returned to Teldrassil, Broll was certain that Fandral had some answer to Malfurion's dire situation.

And if not . . . the night elf shuddered to think what course, if any, would be left to the druids . . .

2

Convocation

L ucan Foxblood had not slept in days. That was by both choice and necessity. He even tried to keep his moments of rest to a minimum, for every pause in his endless flight meant risk of slipping into sleep. Yet there always came the point when the sandy-haired cartographer could go no farther, when his legs buckled and he fell to the ground, often already unconscious and dreaming.

And suffering nightmares . . . the same nightmares that had taken so many others in places through which he had traveled, such as Goldshire, Westfall, and his own Stormwind City . . .

Lucan bore the semblance of one who might have once been a soldier and, indeed, had briefly been one, though he had never served in any conflict. But now, a little more than three decades old, he looked as if he were in the very midst of war. His once-deep brown tunic and pants had turned the color of mud, and the fine threading at the rounded shoulders and along the sides of the legs had begun to fray. His leather boots were stained and cracking.

The cartographer fared little better than his garments. While there still remained evidence of his patrician features, the pallor of his skin and the days of unkempt growth on his face made him appear almost like a slowly decaying creature of the undead Scourge. Only his eyes, nearly as green as a cat's, showed any spark whatsoever.

During his dazed wanderings, he had lost all the tools of his trade and even the pack in which he had kept his meager supplies and a

blanket for sleeping. Lucan could not recall the name of the last settlement in which he had found lodging. He could barely even recall his
life before the dreams and nightmares had taken over and sometimes
he was not certain if those memories were real . . . or remnants of the
nightmares themselves.

The region through which he traveled was thickly wooded, but it
might as well have sprouted mountains of pure diamonds for all he
noticed it. Lucan Foxblood wanted only to keep moving.

He blinked, the first time he had done so in several minutes.

The landscape around him abruptly turned emerald green with
hints of a soft blue, and the misty air seemed to wrap around the staggering figure like a thick blanket. Many of the distinctive markings
vanished, making the cartographer's surroundings look like a drawing only half-completed. Yet, despite this remarkable change, Lucan
stumbled along without interest.

He blinked again. Around him, the land returned to a normal
hue . . . but details had changed. It was no longer the region through
which he had been journeying. True, there were still trees, but in the
distance there now arose a settlement that had not been there before.
Moreover, the scent of the sea now wafted past his nose, though it
went as unnoticed as the dour shadow over the entire landscape.

Lucan passed a stone marker, one with script that would have
proven illegible to him, had he even noticed writing at all. But that
script would have been very legible to a night elf and in reading it,
they would have known exactly where they were about to arrive.

Auberdine . . .

A colder, harsher wind confronted Broll and the tauren as they wended
their way to where Hamuul said the convocation was to meet. Both
druids bent their heads down, thrusting against that wind as if it were
an enemy. Hamuul made no remark, but the tauren did unleash a
grunt at one point that seemed to echo the night elf's growing dis-
quiet.

A great rustling of leaves arose. Curious, Broll glanced up.

The druid froze. His eyes widened in horror.

Teldrassil stood changed. The great branches above were filled with leaves, yes, but many had abruptly turned dried and wrinkled, while others now grew black and curled. All of them, even those that were still green, were covered with sharp thorns.

Broll heard Hamuul's voice, but it was as if the tauren were miles away. The leaves continued to twist and blacken and now the fruits the great giant bore were changing, too. Among gnarling branches there sprouted round, deathly pale berries the size of his head and even larger and from them emitted a stench like decay. No druid—no night elf—would have dared dine on such offerings even if starvation were the only other choice.

The horrific metamorphosis left nothing untouched. Teldrassil's bark had cracked in many places and through those cracks could be seen pulsating veins of black sap. The sap emerged first as a dribble, then steady streams. Tiny vermin sprang forth over the World Tree, millipedes and other creatures crawling in and out of the trunk in numbers that suggested even greater corruption within.

"No . . ." murmured Broll. "No . . ."

A darkness spread from Teldrassil, quickly expanding beyond the two druids. Although the night elf did not turn to watch its growth, he immediately knew that it had already stretched far beyond Teldrassil's physical reach all the way to the mainland, infecting the lands there with the giant's disease.

Then a sound erupted, like that of heavy rain. Tearing his gaze from the befouled trunk, Broll looked again to the crown.

What he had taken for rain proved instead an even more violent rustling of the leaves. The branches were swinging back and forth, shifting with such force as if seeking to free themselves of the sinister leaves.

And they were succeeding. Thousands of macabre leaves began to fall. It was indeed raining, though the drops were not made of water.

The falling leaves had also transformed. They became small, black and emerald creatures vaguely shaped like night elves, but with legs

like beasts and backs bent like tauren. They were but dread silhouettes, with no distinct features to their narrow heads but wicked,
curled horns. Emitting nerve-fraying hisses, they plummeted in endless streams toward the two druids—

"Broll Bearmantle, are you all right?"

Startled, the night elf staggered back. But when he regained his
composure and opened his eyes, he found that the World Tree had returned to its normal state. The branches were still and the leaves were
again attached and lush green.

Hamuul leaned close, the tauren's expression all concern. Broll belatedly nodded, and when a horn sounded, he was gratefully spared
from trying to either understand or explain what had just happened.

"We need to move on," Broll urged. "The convocation is about to
begin."

The tauren blinked and followed the night elf. A few moments later
the two came into sight of the area where Fandral had decided to call
the gathering.

There were more druids than Broll had seen at any other recent
convocation and still others continued to arrive from the opposite direction. Two in particular immediately caught his eye. A dour young
female stood speaking with a male who, though outwardly confident
and indeed radiating much power, constantly clenched his hands as if
anxious about something. Elerethe Renferal and Naralex were partners in regret, even if the reasons for each were different. Elerethe had
sought to save the flora and fauna of Alterac Valley during the last war
between the Alliance and the Horde, but had been unable to prevent
the carnage caused by not only two fighting armies, but an orc shaman. After the war, she had sworn to restore the valley. Several years
later she was still trying.

Naralex had been the victim of greater ambitions, seeking to bring
life back to a place long without it. Accompanied by a small group
of like-minded companions, he had walked into the desolate Barrens
and had, with cunning spellwork, managed to bring forth enough water from deep, deep below to the parched realm to create a handful of
small oases. But then something malevolent had seized control of not

only his work, but also an unsuspecting Naralex and many of his companions. The trapped had then become *corrupted* . . . twisted, evil versions of themselves with no desire other than to spread the darkness. Naralex himself had slipped into madness, then sanity, then madness, and on and on, finding rescue only through the unexpected aid of a party of adventurers.

Unfortunately, while his mind was again more or less whole, Naralex could recall no clue as to what had taken him and the others. As for the Barrens, although they were at present quiet, on the orders of Fandral neither he nor any other druid had as of yet returned there. The archdruid saw no point in risking lives and energies for a place that the Great Sundering at the end of the War of the Ancients had made into a desert. As Fandral saw it, even arid lands had their place in the purpose of Azeroth.

Their gazes and those of several others fixed upon the newcomers . . . and reminded Broll yet more of his shame. The further a druid became attuned to nature and his calling, the more chance that his eyes took on the golden glow of Azeroth's life. Great druids were marked so.

But Broll Bearmantle's eyes remained silver with only a slight blue glow to them that thus far appeared to mean very, very little.

Shaking off his frustration, Broll started toward the pair, but then a second horn blared. The assembled druids turned as one toward the direction of the sound. A single druid with a green band on his left forearm lowered a goat's horn, then faced Teldrassil.

The ridged bark upon which the trumpeter focused rippled. Broll shuddered, momentarily recalling his bizarre vision. Then the bark cleaved, opening up a gap large enough for a night elf to enter . . . or, in this case, from which to step forth.

The druids bowed their heads in respect as Fandral Staghelm strode out among them with the bearing of one fully in command of all about him. His eyes gleamed gold as he nodded to many of those gathered. Fandral was clad more simply than most of the night elf druids, his upper torso covered only at the shoulders by protective wooden armor shaped somewhat like the heads of beasts, even down to their glaring eyes. His hands were covered in protective, open-fingered, woven gloves that extended all the way to the elbow, where the wooden ends flared out.

Fandral walked barefooted, a choice of his to display his oneness with nature. At the waist was the only sign of extravagance on his part—an ornate belt with a great ruby-colored clasp and a decorative, segmented ring hanging below it. Wrapped around each side was a long, flowing collection of pieces of bark.

"The forest is the lifeblood of the world," Fandral intoned.

"The forest is the lifeblood of the world," Broll and the other druids repeated.

"Teldrassil is the lifeblood of the world . . ."

Broll and the rest again repeated his chant.

"I am glad so many of you have heeded the summons so quickly," the archdruid then uttered. "I must confirm to you the worst. Teldrassil is ill . . ."

The news caused the rest of the druids to look at one another in some anxiety. In truth, what Fandral said to them was no great surprise, but it was a shock to hear the archdruid starkly speak it. Although nearly all the druids had had a hand in its creation, Teldrassil's growth had originally been Fandral's suggestion and he above all others guarded its health.

Fandral Staghelm had been the first to suggest the second World Tree, but Malfurion had ever blocked such a suggestion from becoming anything more. But despite Malfurion's opposition, Fandral's loyalty remained intact—after the discovery of the great archdruid's terrible fate, Fandral had stepped in and, with little protest from others, taken up the mantle of leader. His first mission, so he had solemnly proclaimed, was to save their beloved shan'do.

Under his guidance, the senior druids of the Cenarion Circle had determined that Malfurion's limp form should remain in his barrow den, located in the revered Moonglade. There, surrounded by the world's natural energies and the magical ministering of the Sisters of Elune, the body, deemed perfectly healthy otherwise by the Sisters, did not starve or suffer from lack of water. With this came the hope that, as powerful as he was, Malfurion might yet be able to return on his own.

Fandral had not relied on that hope alone, though. The Circle *had* made attempts to not only restore the body, but also call Malfurion's spirit back to it. The attempts failed every time. They had even turned to the mistress of the Emerald Dream—the great green dragon Ysera—but even that had gone for nought. *She of the Dreaming,* as Ysera was also called by the druids, had had no success in contacting him, either.

Until recently, all of this had been kept secret from the night elf race as a whole and even most of the Sisterhood and the druids. However, increasing questions had at last forced a reluctant Fandral to alert his fellow druids—if not the rest of the race—of the direness of the situation, hence the overriding reason so many had come to this sudden convocation. Broll believed all of the druids here had guessed, as he had, that the gathering would be somehow related to Malfurion's rescue.

But Teldrassil was at least as important a reason—if not a greater one to the night elves as a whole. The original goal of using the new World Tree had been to regain their immortality and enhance their powers. But Fandral had pointed out that the magical tree might also be their only hope to locate their founder's dreamform and initiate his rescue.

If Teldrassil is truly so ill, though . . . Broll frowned and saw his apprehension reflected in the faces of Hamuul and the rest.

Fandral strode among the others. His sharp gaze briefly rested upon Broll. Although it was clearly not the archdruid's intention, the glance again reminded Broll of his terrible failure. But then, that memory was never far from his mind.

The senior archdruid smiled, as a father to his children. "But do not dwell in utter despair, my friends," he said. "I have not called you here merely to speak of doom—"

"There is some hope?" one of the other druids blurted.

"There is more than hope!" Fandral proclaimed. "I have summoned you to this place, here at the roots of Teldrassil, so that we may aid the World Tree in its healing!" He smiled encouragingly. "And with Teldrassil well again, we can then return to the focus of our search for Malfurion Stormrage—"

"But how can we aid Teldrassil?" someone else called.

"With this." The archdruid extended his hand. In it lay an object that all recognized . . . and brought forth from Broll's lips a gasp of dismay and surprise.

Fandral held the Idol of Remulos.

The title was perhaps misleading, as the idol did not look at all like the one for whom it was named. Rather, the figurine had been crafted to resemble a rearing green dragon by Remulos, the immortal son of Cenarius and who himself was an astonishing sight. The lower half of Remulos's body was that of a proud stag, but where the shoulders of the front legs should have met the neck, instead a powerful, humanoid chest rose above. His hooves were cloven and powerful. Like his father, Remulos was half forest animal, the upper half most resembling a night elf druid. But the similarity ended there. His hands ended in leafy, wooden talons, and his hair and beard were comprised of leaves and shrubbery and moss.

Remulos was also guardian of the Moonglade. Indeed, Broll had wondered if the immortal druid would appear here, though Remulos had not joined in the convocations for some time. Rumor had it that he had performed his own search for Malfurion . . .

But it was not for the artistic merit that Fandral had brought forth the idol. A powerful magical artifact, it was certainly capable of aiding the druids' spells . . . if it did not do more harm first.

Indeed, Broll could not restrain himself. He dared blurt, "Archdruid, with the greatest respect . . . should that be part of our efforts?"

Fandral turned and eyed Broll sternly. "Your worry is understandable, good Broll. Anessa's loss was no fault of yours. You did what you could to save many lives and beat back the demons."

Broll fought not to cringe as he listened to Fandral's words, even though they were meant to put him at peace. A human face stirred in Broll's memories, a determined, dark-haired man with eyes that spoke of more loss suffered than even the night elf who had befriended him. Varian Wrynn had stood beside Broll when the druid had gone to retrieve the accursed figurine from a mad furbolg, the two having forged a deep bond earlier as fellow slaves and gladiators. Varian had done so even though he had had no inkling of his own past, no recollection that an entire realm was bereft of the man who was its king . . .

Fandral turned from Broll again. He held up the figurine, then indicated the World Tree.

"Once, we fed it so that it could rise from a single nut to the wondrous leviathan it is now! The effort cost us dear, but the rewards have been manyfold . . . a new home, food and water in bounty, and protection from our enemies . . ."

The druids nodded. Broll noted that Fandral made no mention of the immortality that remained lost to their people, but then, as Teldrassil's growth had not yet restored it, he thought perhaps the archdruid was sensitive on the subject.

The archdruid thrust the idol toward one of the nearest of the gathered. The other night elf instinctively backed up a step. "But in giving back so much, Teldrassil left itself open to illness! It now needs us again! In return . . . it will then surely show us the path to finding our shan'do!"

Fandral's enthusiasm was contagious. The others rumbled their agreement.

"The Dream is quickly being devoured by the Nightmare . . ." he went on more solemnly, stating the dread knowledge all shared. "With no recent word from its mistress, I have forbidden entry by any others after the last foolhardy attempts . . ." Fandral stared down his audience, as if daring any to disobey. "For Malfurion would surely want no more lives lost for his sake . . ."

He put his hand to his chest, then drew the outline of a circle in which he then added two vertical, curving streaks. The streaks represented the antlers of Cenarius. The full symbol itself represented the Cenarion Circle.

The druids clasped their hands together in preparation for the beginning of their efforts. Broll cleared his mind of concerns and petty mortal thoughts and instead began to put himself into a meditative trance. Beside him, Hamuul did the same.

Turning to Teldrassil, Fandral touched the great trunk with his free hand. His fingers ran down the coarse bark.

Within the World Tree, something stirred, something that every druid could feel as if it were a part of them. Even in his meditative state, Broll sensed a tremendous presence joining the convocation . . . Teldrassil's essence touching those who had helped raise it up.

The World Tree was more than merely the home of the night elves. It was linked to the very health of Azeroth. Ill, it affected not merely its immediate surroundings, but those lands beyond the island. Even the very air or the rushing seas were not immune. At the very least, a Teldrassil that was not well could not maintain the balance between nature and decay.

The ground shook, but neither Broll nor any of the others felt any fear, not even when what first appeared to be tentacles burst underneath them.

But these were not tentacles. Rather, they were the very *roots* of Teldrassil. Toward each of the druids a root moved, snaking up to them as if about to strike. Yet none moved away. They knew that Teldrassil did not seek to harm them, but instead asked for their help . . .

One massive root already twined about Fandral. As it did, from the main root tiny extensions sprouted. They, in turn, wrapped around the archdruid like creeper vines, until he stood half-shrouded by them.

It was a variation—a tremendous one, naturally—of one of the ways in which the druids communed with the flora of Azeroth. What could not be seen was that the tendrils permeated their very beings, almost merging night elf and plant as one.

Fandral held forth the Idol of Remulos. It now glowed a faint green, the color of the dragon it not only represented but also that of the true beast bound to it. Not even Remulos knew to which of the green dragons his creation had been bound, for that choice had been made in secret by Ysera. Whatever dragon had been chosen, it had been a mighty one, indeed.

Broll felt some trepidation as the magic of the figurine touched both him and Teldrassil's root, but his trust in the archdruid overcame his memories of the artifact's foul deeds. The magic seeped into the druid's mind and soul . . .

He became *Teldrassil* and Teldrassil became *him*.

Broll could not keep back the euphoria that filled him. He felt as if all Azeroth lay open to him, so deep and so far did the World Tree's roots already spread. He saw beyond the island, beyond the surrounding waters . . .

But before his consciousness could stretch further, Broll felt a tug. A hint of weakness touched him. But Fandral's thoughts filled his mind, assuring him—and the rest—of the safety of what he planned.

The power of the druids flowed into Teldrassil, feeding it. Strengthening it. With so much will and desire behind their offering, Broll was certain that whatever ailed the Great Tree would be vanquished and that then, as the archdruid had indicated, it would then be able to assist them in rescuing Malfurion—

No sooner had he thought of his shan'do, than Broll experienced a jarring in his consciousness. A darkness spread through his thoughts and he felt the same uneasiness that had hit him when he had imagined Teldrassil monstrously corrupted. Broll tried to dismiss that uneasiness, but it grew—

Broll Bearmantle . . .

The calling of his name shattered the last of the druid's calm. Did he know that voice? Was it—

The binding between Teldrassil and him snapped. Broll let out a gasp and fell to one knee. Vaguely, he sensed others around him, including Hamuul. Was it Hamuul who had called out to him, as he had earlier? No, it almost didn't seem real; the sound of it had vanished from his thoughts without a trace.

It was hard to focus, as if, like a dream, his mind was already slipping away to his subconscious . . .

Hamuul put a hand on his shoulder. Broll looked up. A handful of druids had surrounded him, mostly friends.

"I'm well," he told them, breathless. "Forgive me for shattering the spell—"

"You had nothing to do with it," Naralex commented as he crouched beside Broll, sounding quite puzzled. "Hamuul called attention to your bent body and we who were nearest quickly came, but you did not cut off our efforts . . ."

Naralex and Hamuul aided the druid in standing. Broll was flush with embarrassment. "If not my lacking, then what?"

But even as he spoke, he sensed through the land around him that the druids were no longer alone. A presence was fast approaching.

Broll looked toward Fandral, who was standing with his back to Teldrassil and his gaze upon the path to their left. It was now clear to him that the archdruid had stopped the spellwork due to the approach of outsiders.

A group of newcomers marched into the convocation without hesitation, those behind spreading out in protection of their leader. Although they were night elves, they could never be mistaken for druids.

All female and clearly of a religious order, they wore empty sheaths at their sides and quivers on their backs; Broll figured they must have left behind their weapons in respect to those of the druidic calling. He could tell from their lithe forms and gracefulness that these females were proficient in not only a variety of weapons, but hand-to-hand combat as well.

There were eleven in this party, though the number of their order was greater than that by far. They were clad in shimmering moonlight-silver robes that stretched down to their ankles. Long, elegant teardrops of silver began from the middle of their bodices and descended roughly halfway down, each end encased in a blue orb. Near the waist, arched, linked belts clasped onto decorative crests. The robes were very free-flowing, allowing much room and maneuverability for those also trained in martial arts. Even without blades or bows, the eleven represented a ready fighting force.

Their leader quickly—almost impatiently—scanned over the druids. She spread her hands . . . and through the overcast sky there suddenly shone the larger of Azeroth's two moons, illuminating the area.

"Our presence is not troublesome here, is it?" Tyrande Whisperwind politely asked. "After all, this is not where the Circle generally convenes . . ."

"The Sisterhood of Elune is ever welcome," Fandral answered. "Although surely a convocation of druids is of little import to the high priestess of the moon goddess and ruler of all night elves . . ."

"It would not be important, even with its location unusual," she replied, her expression hardening in a manner that made Fandral frown and the other druids stir, "if Elune herself had not revealed to me the dread truth."

There were rumblings among the druids. Fandral waved for silence. Frowning, he asked, "What 'dread truth,' High Priestess?"

Tyrande swallowed, the only sign that the news touched her especially. "Malfurion is *dying* . . ."

"Impossible! We have kept his barrow den secure and your own priestesses minister to his body daily. There is no reason for such a dire circumstance—"

"Nevertheless, there is," she returned. "His situation has changed. Malfurion is dying and we must act with all possible haste."

Before Fandral could respond, Broll found himself uttering, "And what shall we do, High Priestess?"

Tyrande's voice was edged with steel. "First, we must journey to the Moonglade."

3

THE TREE

The pain tore through him again and again . . .

He felt his body continuing its slow, horrific twisting. His arms had long contorted about his head and his fingers splayed and stretched in various directions. Of his legs, there was nothing but a thick trunk, the two appendages having merged what seemed more than a lifetime ago.

How long *had* he been standing here, rigid and unmoving? How long since he had fallen prisoner to the Nightmare Lord? What was happening on the mortal plane?

What had happened to *Tyrande*?

As he had done so many times already, Malfurion Stormrage fought against the agony. He would have cried out from the terrible effort—if he still had a mouth. Only his eyes remained untouched by his monstrous captor, for the fiend desired him to see his own transformation, to see the hopelessness of his fate.

Gone was Malfurion the night elf. In his place was a macabre, skeletal tree, an ash. Leaves with sharp thorns already grew from what had once been the arms and fingers and were now branches. The trunk bent at awkward angles where once the torso had met the hips. The feet had splayed out into what were now crooked roots.

Trying to tear his mind from his agony, Malfurion pictured Tyrande's face, recalling that moment when the two of them had silently realized their love, when she had chosen him over his ambitious brother, Illidan. He had secretly thought she preferred his twin, for, though reckless, Illidan had made great leaps in his learning of sorcery. More than that, his efforts in the struggle against the Burning Legion had shown him to be something of a savior—at least in the hearts of many night elves, and sometimes in that of Malfurion himself. But Tyrande, by then an apprentice of Elune, had apparently seen something greater in the fledgling druid, something special. What it was, he still did not know.

Malfurion found himself drawing some strength from his vision, but tremendous guilt also accompanied thoughts of Tyrande. It had been by his decision that she had been left alone to guard Azeroth for so many centuries while he and the druids walked the Emerald Dream. It mattered not that his choice had been for the sake of their world and had proven the correct one to make. He had still abandoned her.

The archdruid suddenly wanted to howl. The thoughts and emotions were his own, but were they influenced by his captor? It would not be the first time. The insidious presence had infiltrated his mind many times already, playing havoc with the night elf's memories and thoughts. This, as opposed to the horrific transformation, was the more subtle part of his torture.

There should have been no pain. After all, this was the Emerald Dream and he had entered it in his dreamform, not his physical one. Pain such as this should have been impossible under those conditions.

As if to disprove that fact, his body wrenched further. Again, he could not release his agony by screaming.

Malfurion?

The voice cut through his pain. He seized onto its existence as if a lifeline. It was distant . . . barely a whisper . . . but it sounded like . . . sounded so very much like—

Malfurion? It . . . . Tyrande . . . you are . . .

Tyrande! If his call would have been audible, he felt certain that it would have been heard miles away. *Tyrande!*

Malfurion? The voice grew stronger. Malfurion felt his hopes leap. For ten thousand years and more he had known her and for ten thousand years and more he had loved her. She should have hated him for all the absences that he had taken in quest of his calling, but always she had been there in the end. Now . . . now once again, Tyrande had proven that *nothing* would stand between them.

Malfurion? Her call was more solid, more imminent. Almost as if she were actually near—

A shadowy form coalesced ahead of him. All sense of pain had now fled his dreamform. The archdruid felt as though he might weep as he peered at her approaching silhouette.

The glow around Tyrande marked her as different from he or any druid traveler, for it was a subtle yet powerful silver that marked the power of Elune. Malfurion would have smiled, had he had a mouth. How she had come here, he did not know . . . but she was *here.*

Tyrande spoke, but the words took a moment to reach his mind. *Malfurion? Is that . . . is that you?*

He started to reply, but Tyrande's next reaction left him stunned. She pulled back in clear revulsion.

How . . . disgusting! the archdruid heard.

Tyrande retreated farther. She shook her head.

Tyrande . . . Tyrande . . . But his calls to her went unheeded, as if she no longer could hear him. Instead, the high priestess put out a hand as if trying to ward him off.

No . . . she finally blurted. *I expected better of you . . .*

The archdruid was confused. However, before he could again attempt to speak to her, a second form materialized behind her.

I warned you, my love, the second, larger figure rumbled. *I warned you that he was not what you hoped . . .*

Malfurion was speechless. He knew that voice. Dreaded that voice. It reminded him of yet another great failure, perhaps the greatest.

Illidan came into focus, yet it was not Illidan as Malfurion's twin and brother, but rather as the monstrosity that he had become.

Illidan Stormrage was a demon. Atop his head were huge, curled horns like those of some gigantic ram and massive, leathery wings that sprouted from near his shoulder blades. Illidan's countenance was now a distortion of its former self, the jaw more pronounced and the mouth full of sharp teeth. The cheekbones were higher. A mass of wild, midnight blue hair draped the face.

A band covered where once Illidan's mortal eyes had been. Eyes that had been burned out by the Dark Titan Sargeras during the War of the Ancients—a mark of Illidan's loyalty to the master of the Burning Legion. In their place, a searing green glow that marked demon fire enabled Malfurion's brother to see not only the world around him, but all the mystical energies inherent in it.

Illidan, Tyrande murmured with affection. Her gaze still upon Malfurion—and no less revolted—she added, *Illidan, just look at him . . .*

The demon tromped forward on heavy hooves. He was much larger than he had been as a night elf. His chest was broad, indeed, broader than it should have been. Illidan's upper torso was naked save for arcane tattoos that also glowed green with power. His only garment was a pair of ragged pants, a remnant of his mortal past.

Calm yourself, my love, Illidan responded, his lips moving out of sync, too. To Malfurion's horror, his twin draped a muscular arm across Tyrande's shoulder, cupping it with a hand that tapered into twisted talons.

And to the archdruid's greater horror, Tyrande took comfort in Illidan's embrace.

I cannot stand to see him! He is not at all what I once thought!

Illidan grinned over her head at his altered brother. *The fault is not yours, Tyrande! He is the one to blame . . . he left you . . . he abandoned me . . . he demanded that all follow his dictates, even if that meant tragedy for them . . . he is only earning his just reward . . .*

A lie! Malfurion insisted, but neither paid him any attention. Instead, Tyrande turned her back upon Malfurion, returning Illidan's embrace with fervor.

So many centuries wasted on him! the high priestess bitterly remarked. *He was always content to let me wait . . . his own desires were always more important than me . . .*

The demon looked down at her and lifted her chin with a hooked claw. *I would never do that to you, my love . . . I would make you and me one . . .*

Tyrande met his horrific gaze. She smiled. *Then, do it!*

My love . . . He put both taloned hands upon her shoulders.

His eyes blazed. The fire shot forth. It enveloped Tyrande. Malfurion cried out, but for naught. The high priestess was engulfed.

And then . . . Tyrande *changed.*

Horns thrust out of her forehead, horns that rose high, then curled. From her back issued forth two small nubs that quickly swelled, then expanded. Webbed wings stretched. The nails of the slim hands that held Illidan grew and blackened.

No! Malfurion tried again to shout. *No!*

Tyrande turned her eyes back to the archdruid . . . but now they were fiery green orbs. She frowned at the helpless Malfurion.

You did this to me . . . she said. *You . . .*

The archdruid let out a silent plea—and woke.

He was still in his dreamform; still trapped and painfully twisted. But he discovered that the heart-wrenching pain he had just suffered was not real—at least, not yet.

But Malfurion took no relief from that. This was not the first time he had endured such a nightmare and it was becoming harder to tell when he slept and when he was awake. His tormentor played a wicked game with him, one that the archdruid knew he was slowly losing.

And even though it *had* only been a nightmare, it left him more exhausted, more susceptible.

Tyrande . . . Malfurion thought. *I am so sorry . . .*

Perhaps she no longer even thinks of you, came a new voice in his mind. *After so long, after being abandoned so often, after leaving the fate of so many to her while you hid from the world and your responsibility . . .*

Malfurion tried to shake his head, but he no longer had a head to shake.

The voice came again, seeming much like a poisonous adder slithering through Malfurion's soul. *Just as you abandoned the other so important to you, abandoned him to betrayal, to imprisonment, to damnation . . .*

Illidan. Malfurion had tried to save his twin, but in the end, Illidan's ambition had turned him into the very thing against which he had fought. A *demon.* Had Malfurion acted differently from the beginning, perhaps seeking to help his brother rather than imprison him . . . Illidan might have been saved. *No!* the captured archdruid managed to think. *I did try to help him! I came to his prison time and time again in the hopes of turning him from his fatal path . . .*

But you failed . . . you always fail . . . you failed yourself and because of that, you will fail your Azeroth . . .

In the Emerald Dream—the *Nightmare*—what had once been Malfurion Stormrage contorted yet more. He no longer glowed the bright green hue that dreamforms took on when they entered this magical realm. Instead, a darker, more sinister shade of green now swathed him.

An even greater darkness hovered around the imprisoned archdruid, the only visible evidence of the thing that called itself the Nightmare Lord. From that foul gloom, scores of tendrils fed into Malfurion, not only fueling the alteration of his form, but seeking to tear further into the night elf's mind as he slowly transformed ever more into a tree.

A tree of inconceivable, agonizing pain . . .

Malfurion's barrow den was as Tyrande Whisperwind had seen it in both her vision and previous excursions. Little there was that spoke of the person behind the legend. It consisted of a series of underground passages that never saw the light of the sun, but night elves were creatures of the darkness, and, in addition, had mystical powers at their command. Instead of oil lamps, the cool, soft illumination of the moon now kept the main chamber lit, compliments of the devoted prayers of the Sisterhood.

The archdruid lay as if sleeping, which, in a sense, he was. Only his open eyes gave any initial hint that there was more to the matter.

The priestesses on duty had moved aside. One by one, the party stepped before the unmoving body, the druids kneeling in homage to their founder while the newly arrived Sisters of Elune simply bowed. Broll thought the scene more one of a funeral or at least a family gathered around a loved one's deathbed, but kept such thoughts to himself, especially with Malfurion's beloved so near.

When it was the high priestess's turn, she leaned so close that at first it appeared she was going to kiss Malfurion. To most, that would have not been surprising. However, at the last moment, Tyrande pulled back and instead briefly stroked his forehead.

"Cold . . ." she muttered. "Colder than he should be . . ."

"We have kept constant with the prayers," Merende immediately responded, a hint of surprise in her tone. "Nothing should have changed . . ."

There was no anger in Tyrande's voice as she replied, "I know . . . but he is colder . . . Elune's vision is truth . . ." She stared. "And his eyes are losing their gold . . . as if he is losing his ties to Azeroth . . ."

She finally stepped back, making room for the lead archdruid. Fandral spent even more time over Malfurion than the high priestess had. He muttered under his breath and passed both hands over the body. Broll saw him send a pinch of powder over the chest and wondered what Fandral intended. The priestesses and druids had performed scores of spells to aid Malfurion not only in the preservation of his body, but also his potential return.

Wiping away a single tear, the senior archdruid stepped back. Broll prayed to the woodland spirits that whatever Fandral attempted would help. They needed Malfurion more than ever, especially if Teldrassil's illness proved something beyond their powers to cure.

"My Sisters shall increase their efforts," Tyrande said after a brief discussion with Merende and the other tending pair. "Elune will surely enable them to keep the body alive . . . at least for a while . . . but this must be solved soon."

"There is nothing more that we can do here," Fandral remarked with a respectful glance at Malfurion Stormrage's body. "Let us return to the outside . . ."

As the druids and others obeyed, Broll noticed Tyrande return to touch Malfurion on the cheek. Then her expression hardened and she strode after Fandral as if about to rush off to war.

The somberness of Malfurion's chamber gave way to the lush beauty of the land above—a hilly forest region dotted with countless mounds, beneath which lay the sanctums of other druids. Between the barrow dens, stone and wooden arches draped with lush, living greenery gave the Moonglade an exotic look.

Yet it was more than just its physical appearance that made the Moonglade what it was. As a druid, Broll in particular could sense the inherent peace of this place. There was little wonder that it had been chosen as a sacred location by those of his calling.

"So tranquil a place," the high priestess commented.

"The spirit of Cenarius is very much a part of it," Fandral replied, looking pleased by Tyrande's compliment, "and present also in its guardian, his son . . ."

"Would that I were my father," came a voice that brought with it a sense of springtime. "Would that I were . . ."

The druids had not heard the figure approach, as his footsteps produced no hint of a sound. They immediately knelt in respect and even the priestesses acknowledged Remulos's appearance with a formal bow. However, he looked not at all pleased with such a greeting.

"Rise up!" he demanded of the druids as the air around him filled with the scent of flowers and the grass grew more lush beneath his hooves. "I am in no need of honoring from any of you," Remulos added dourly, his leafy mane shaking. "I am an abject failure!"

Fandral stretched a hand forward in protest. "You, great one? Surely no such words could be used for the lord of the Moonglade!"

The almost–night elf visage peered down at the gathered figures, his nostrils flaring the way an angered stag's might. He focused briefly on Broll—who immediately looked down—then turned toward Fandral. "They are apt words, Fandral, for my efforts to seek aid for Malfurion have accomplished nil. He still sleeps . . . and now, worse, I presume. For what other reason could there be for such a contingent to come to the Moonglade?"

"He is . . . dying at last," Tyrande admitted.

Shock overtook Remulos's expression. The four, swift legs stepped back soundlessly, colorful wildflowers blossoming in his tracks.

"Dying . . ." The shock faded, replaced by something darker. "It makes sense . . . for the Nightmare is swelling faster than ever, its gibbering madness now audible throughout most of the Emerald Dream! Worse, it moves more swiftly, too, catching more of the Dream's defenders unaware . . . and corrupting them in both body and spirit . . ."

To hear even Remulos speak so only added more credence to the fears that Broll, Tyrande, and the others felt. Broll clenched his fist, for a brief moment wishing for the comparative simplicity of his years as a gladiator.

Despite how brief the clenching was, either it or some other noticeable sign of emotion made Remulos look again to him. Yet Remulos's words were not for Broll, but rather Fandral. "The idol is still in your care, Archdruid?"

"Yes, great one."

Remulos eyed Fandral. "Make no use of it. Hide it away. Let not its power touch Azeroth . . . at least for now . . ."

Several of the druids, Broll included, glanced at their leader. Fandral did not mention his recent choice, merely nodding to Remulos and responding, "It is safe within my dwelling. And so shall it remain."

"Bear in mind what I said. I can give no more reason at this time . . . for I am not certain myself on it . . ."

"I give you my oath," Fandral swore.

The towering deity acknowledged, then retreated more. As he did, his form somehow blended with his surroundings—both near and far. "This news, though dread, stirs me to new action. High Priestess, you have my sympathies . . ."

A brief lowering of her eyelids was Tyrande's response. By then, though, Remulos had already *become* his surroundings, vanishing as if an illusion created by the leaves, branches, and other flora of the mystical glade.

But his voice yet remained. "One last warning, my friends . . . there have been whispers . . . of sleepers appearing throughout the various kingdoms, sleepers of all races . . . they are said to be those who cannot awaken no matter how much their loved ones might try . . . listen for tales of those, just as I will . . . they may be of import . . ."

And then, he was gone.

"Sleepers . . . who cannot awaken . . ." Tyrande muttered. "What can he mean?"

"He may mean nothing at all," Fandral pointed out. "As Remulos said, these are but whispers. They are likely no more than that."

Hamuul grunted. "I have heard . . . from an orc whose word I trust . . . that there is a village where five strong warriors could not be stirred."

The lead archdruid did not look convinced in the least. "The word of an orc—"

The tauren shrugged. "There was no reason for him to lie."

"Malfurion is caught in the Emerald Dream . . ." Tyrande remarked thoughtfully. "Does not this sound as if tied to that somehow?"

Giving a low bow to her, Fandral shook his head. "High Priestess, you make a reasonable mistake. Though we call it the Emerald Dream—or Nightmare, as it is now—druidic projection and normal mortal sleep are two entirely different matters."

"Yes . . . I suppose you're right." A bitter cast returned to her face. "He should have never gone by himself. Not after warning others of your calling to beware the changes in the Emerald Dream."

Broll watched as Tyrande closed her eyes for but a moment, and her anger transformed into sadness.

"He knew druids had already been found as he is now," Tyrande continued, "poor souls who didn't have his strength and will to keep their bodies alive after their dreamforms were gone far too long . . ."

That the high priestess was so knowledgeable about their calling surprised no one. She had been there since the beginning, since their shan'do had first begun his training. As her lover, he would have surely shared his experiences with her.

"He did what he did, Tyrande Whisperwind, as we shall do what we must do," the lead archdruid responded. Fandral looked more at ease. "And the World Tree Teldrassil still remains our best hope of saving him."

The high priestess did not seem so confident in the archdruid's declaration, though she did nod agreement. She glanced at Broll, whom she knew better than most other druids. He gave her what he hoped was an expression of reassurance.

Fandral began to say something else to the high priestess, but a sound caught Broll's attention, turning it from the conversation.

The hair on the former slave's neck stiffened as he recognized the noise. His eyes darted to the trees and other greenery, where the leaves shook as if rattled by a violent wind.

As had occurred with Teldrassil earlier, the leaves of the trees and bushes all over the Moonglade burst into the air, rendering deathly nude the branches and stems. The leaves rose up into the sky . . . then poured down with deadly accuracy toward the party.

As they did, they once again began to change shape, to become the swelling silhouettes of creatures with hints of cloven feet and legs more animal than night elf.

But then there came a change to the previous vision. Between the night elves and the monstrous attackers there formed a figure that glowed with the light of the Emerald Dream. Broll instinctively thought of Malfurion, but this shape was smaller and not at all formed like one of his people. Rather, it more and more resembled—

"Broll!" a gruff voice whispered in his ear. "Broll Bearmantle!"

The night elf shook. The demons again became leaves and the leaves, yet once more in a replay of the vision of Teldrassil, returned to their proper places among the greenery.

Broll looked into Hamuul's concerned eyes. He realized that he and the tauren were alone. The rest could only be seen in the distance, already leaving the area.

"Broll Bearmantle, something ails you." Hamuul stepped around to face his friend. "The others did not notice, for when I saw you stiffen, I stood so that they would think we spoke. Even then, the false conversation I had with you did not even penetrate. You were—you were as our shan'do is."

Feeling his legs weaken, Broll seized Hamuul's arm for support. When he answered, it was with a rasping voice that startled him. "No . . . I was not like Malfurion. I had . . . I had a vision . . ."

"A vision? How can that be?"

The night elf considered. "No. Not quite a vision. It was as if . . . as if Azeroth . . . or something else . . . were trying to warn me . . ."

Realizing that he now needed to confide in *someone*, Broll quickly and quietly told the tauren what he had experienced. Hamuul's nostrils flared often as the tale was told. As was common when one of his kind was unsettled or excited, the tauren also snorted more than once.

"We should pass this on to the others," Hamuul suggested when Broll was finished.

Broll shook his head. "Fandral won't see it as anything more than anxiety . . . or maybe madness. To him, Teldrassil is the key . . . and he is probably right."

"But your visions—now twice seen, as you say—must be of significance, Broll Bearmantle."

"I'm not so sure . . . if there's truth to what I saw . . . whatever I saw . . . why am I the only one to see it?"

The tauren mulled this over for a moment, then replied, "Perhaps you were the one best suited . . ."

"The best suited for what?"

"Though I have been honored to rise to archdruid, Azeroth yet contains many mysteries the answers to which I do not know. The answer to your visions is something I suspect you will discover on your own as Azeroth desires it . . ."

The night elf frowned, then nodded. With nothing more to add to their secret discussion, they hurried on to catch the others. However, as they journeyed, Broll glanced surreptitiously at the tauren, a great wave of guilt washing over the night elf.

He had left out one thing from his visions . . . or from the *last* to be precise. Just before Hamuul had stirred him from the sinister tableau, Broll had finally come to recognize the figure that appeared almost as a guardian against the evil raining down on him . . .

It was the *Idol of Remulos*.

4

Shadows Stir

"The mangy curs must be holding out in the lowest shafts," Marshal Dughan growled to his men as he peered through the eye slits of his helmet into a deep passage of the Jasperlode Mine. A spray of dust caught in his throat, and he turned and spat on the ground. "I think it's safe to call a momentary halt."

The sounds of clanking armor echoed off the mine's walls as the marshal's fifteen men relaxed their guarded stances. But Zaldimar Wefhellt, a fair to middling mage from Goldshire who had accompanied the group on their quest, maintained his position with eyes fixed on the dark tunnel.

"I told you to stand down," Dughan snapped.

The gray-haired, bearded mage ambled toward the others. Although he was well respected in Goldshire, Zaldimar would not have made a name for himself in one of the capital cities. Still, though the group of men Dughan had scrounged together was strong enough to defeat the mongrels on their own, he was sure the mage's spells would help bring about a swift and merciless execution.

Located in the northern foothills of Elwynn Forest, Jasperlode Mine had been one of the crucial supply points for the raw metal ore needed for weapons and armor. But with so many pressures on Stormwind, the number of military forces guarding the forest's mines had dwindled to nil, and Jasperlode and the rest had become horribly infested.

Unchallenged, the kobolds—long-snouted, whiskered humanoids who were generally more annoying than dangerous—had moved back into the area. They were not skilled fighters, nor were they particularly bright, but they bred like rabbits and existed in large numbers . . . but not for long, if Marshal Dughan had his way. He had made major progress over the past few weeks; between Jasperlode and Fargodeep Mine further southwest, he could not begin to count how many he had already slain, so constant had the hunt become.

Dughan removed his helmet. Broad-faced with cropped hair, a thick mustache, and a goatee, he had done his share of fighting in his younger days. Elected as marshal after the mysterious death of his predecessor, Dughan had, over the past few seasons, brought and kept order and peace to Goldshire by clearing out not only the kobolds, but wild wolves and bears, bandits, the fishlike murlocs, and more.

But now, the kobolds had returned.

"Those vermin are going to fight tooth, nail, hammer, and ax when we come upon them," Dughan said, "but they'll also be cramped together in some narrow places . . . and that's where you come in, Zaldimar . . ."

The mage, his purple and blue robes immaculate despite the dust that caked the rest of the party, nodded gravely. "A series of arcane blasts would be the most effective course—"

Dughan cut him off with a wave. "Spare me explanations. Kill, wound, and panic as many as you can before we need to wade in. Can you do that?"

Zaldimar nodded. Dughan replaced his helmet, then signaled the group on. He chopped at several thick webs obscuring part of his path, remnants from the huge mine spiders that generally preyed on anything foolish enough to enter and, especially, on kobolds. Indeed, cutting one web sent an old kobold skull dropping to the floor, where its rattling echoed throughout the mine.

Dughan swore. The kobolds might already have suspected the men's presence, but now he'd given them confirmation.

Several of the men coughed from the dust, which seemed thicker than usual. And it did not take long to discover why. One of the side shafts—a passage that would have led to a secondary exit for the miners—had collapsed. Several tons of rock, earth, and shattered wooden braces met the marshal's intent gaze.

"An accident," Zaldimar proclaimed. "I warned them they were putting too much stress on that area when last we came down here to clean out kobolds."

"Never mind," Dughan said. "What matters is it makes our task simpler."

Zaldimar nodded. There were limited directions the kobolds could have gone. The only exits were now cut off. A confrontation was only moments away . . .

They came upon a corpse, but not one they expected. It was a mine spider, one the size of a large dog. With its poison and other weapons, it was more than capable of trapping a kobold . . . and possibly a human.

This one had been hacked to pieces. In the dim illumination, the marshal could see several sets of prints.

"The kobolds are getting smarter, it seems. They're ganging up on the spiders to wipe them out."

"Something to think about," Zaldimar commented.

Nodding gruffly, Dughan tightened his grip on the spiked mace. With his free hand, the marshal instinctively dusted off his tabard. The fierce gold-and-blue lion's head on his chest once more shone prominently. He gave the order to move forward again—

Far in the darkness ahead, a gravelly voice muttered and a second, anger-tinged voice followed.

A brief flame—like that from a candle—materialized further down . . . then was quickly doused.

"Zaldimar . . ." Dughan whispered.

The mage stepped to the forefront. He raised his hands and gestured.

A purple light flared, accompanied by a pulsating sound. The arcane blast darted down the tunnel toward where the brief flame had been.

A moment later it struck . . . then struck again . . . and again. The mine shook. Dust and small fragments of rock pelted the fighters and the marshal cursed the mage's carelessness.

The passage ahead was briefly filled with a purple aura so bright that Dughan had to shield his eyes. From the other end came a chorus of growls.

The marshal blinked as his eyes adjusted.

"By the king!" Dughan gasped.

The passage was packed wall to wall with kobolds. There were more rat-faced fiends than any of the reports had indicated—far more. Suddenly, Dughan's trained force appeared very lacking.

The kobolds in the front of the throng let out bestial cries and waved their weapons. Their tails whipped back and forth, signaling their growing agitation. Not one of them appeared wounded from Zaldimar's attack.

"Prepare for an orderly retreat," Dughan commanded. The fighters were ill prepared for this. Instead of clearing the mine, he and his men were now at risk of being slaughtered.

Ahead of him, Zaldimar stood silent, staring at the creatures as the illuminating effects of his arcane blast began to fade.

"Do something, mage! Fire another one!"

The spellcaster twisted around. Zaldimar's expression was of utter puzzlement.

"I—I must have another minute . . . these spells, they are draining on my body . . ."

Though he was no mage, the marshal knew that Zaldimar needed to muster everything he could—and quickly. He seized Zaldimar by the arm and dragged him back to the rest of the party. "You must try, Zaldimar! Our lives . . . very well may depend on it!"

Before the mage could respond, the kobolds poured forth. What had once seemed comical and only of threat to small children—kobolds were no more than four feet high at best—was now a frightening and deadly danger to all.

"Pull back! Pull back! You three! Keep your blades up front with my mace!" Dughan shoved Zaldimar behind him. Even if the mage wasn't of any use, the marshal was not going to leave him behind to be slain.

The first of the kobolds reached the defenders. Dughan swung at one, then dueled another, much larger creature.

"You no take candle!" it roared, the item in question set atop its head on a small holder. Kobolds could see well in the dark, but in the mine they still needed illumination in the deepest places.

"I—don't—want—your damned candle!" Dughan shouted back.

He swung again and again. One rat face after another came into view, only to be cut down by the marshal's skilled hand. Around him, his men proved their mettle—smashing, slicing, and stabbing the kobolds without mercy.

The tide had turned. The vast scores of kobold enemies became piles of corpses. A grin crossed Dughan's face.

In the end, Goldshire's force stood knee-deep in blood and bodies. The stench of dead kobolds proved a hundred times worse than their living odor, but the men were willing to suffer it, so complete had their victory been. Even the last of the kobolds' candles had been doused.

Marshal Dughan counted his troops. They were all present. Some had minor injuries—mostly scratches—but all were still accounted for and fit.

No . . . there was one who was not present. "Where is the mage?"

The others shook their heads. Dughan prodded the bodies where he had last seen Zaldimar. There was no sign of the spellcaster's presence or departure.

Dughan guessed that the powerless Zaldimar had likely fled before the battle. The coward would no doubt be found back in Goldshire. "Let's be moving on," the commander decided. "Make sure the other shafts are clear." He was doubtful that they would find more than a couple of kobolds after this, but even those had to be eradicated.

They started back, Dughan taking the lead. The marshal covered his nose; the smell of dead kobold was growing worse even though the men were leaving the corpses further and further behind. *Next time, we'll flush them outside, where the wind'll help . . .*

Suddenly, Jasperlode shook as if some explosion had taken place deeper down.

The braces ahead of the party creaked ominously.

Dughan thrust his sword ahead. "Move!"

But as the band surged on, one of the more distant braces cracked. The two halves swung down.

"Watch out!" the commander roared.

The roof of the mine collapsed at the weak point. Worse, it began a chain reaction. Other braces snapped.

Masses of earth and stone crashed to the ground.

The men fled back, but then the roof gave way. The dust and darkness blinded Dughan and his men, who shoved into one another as they sought escape.

Then the marshal heard a bloodcurdling scream.

He stumbled into an open area just as the collapse began to subside. Coughing, Marshal Dughan tried to focus and was able to make out the shadowy forms of at least three men.

When it became quiet enough for him to be heard, he called, "Sound off!"

Eleven voices responded, some of them pained. Eleven, not fifteen.

The devastation made it pointless to try to see if the other four were still alive. As it was, Dughan had to get the rest of his men to safety. There was only one choice, to head back to where they had fought the kobolds. Sometimes kobolds dug secret burrows in the mines, ways out. At least it was a hope.

"Follow me!"

The path proved darker and longer than he recalled. Only the powerful stench verified to Dughan that he was nearing the area. But as he led the group swiftly through the passage, he collided with a rocky wall.

"What is this?" The wall meant that they must have passed the spot where the kobolds had first been seen . . . but where were the bodies?

Dughan fumbled in his pouches for something to illuminate their surroundings, but found nothing.

A purple glow suddenly arose just to his side. The marshal whirled, his mace at the ready.

Zaldimar stared back at him from behind the glow. Dughan could see nothing else save that face. The mage had a drawn, intense expression.

"Does that help?" he rasped.

"Where the blazes have you been? Have you seen any sign of a way out? The area we came through is impassable!"

Zaldimar nodded. "I know. I made certain."

"You—what?"

The glow expanded. Dughan's eyes widened.

The mage's garments had changed. He now wore a black, armored outfit with skulls at the knee braces and on the chest. A cowl rose high behind his head. His eyes glowed a monstrous dark purple.

"And as for escape, a simple spell will enable me to leave here."

Marshal Dughan thrust the pointed tip of his mace under Zaldimar's chin. "You'll take us with you, then!"

Something moved at the edge of the light. It struck down the marshal's weapon. As Dughan fought to retain his grip, he caught a glimpse of a familiar snout.

"Kobold—" But the word died on his lips as Zaldimar further increased the insidious illumination.

It was not merely a kobold . . . but a dead one. The creature's gut was wide open and putrefying organs half-hung loose in the gap. The kobold clutched its weapon and stared with sightless eyes at the officer.

And as the light expanded, Marshal Dughan saw that there were many, many more . . . all the kobolds he and his men had vanquished and seemingly numbers beyond even that.

"What's happened?" he demanded.

"They serve me now . . . as I serve our rightful lord . . ." rasped Zaldimar, his grinning face like a skull. "And as you will, good marshal . . ."

The kobolds moved forward. Marshal Dughan and his men pressed together.

"It won't hurt long . . ."

Utterly silent, the kobolds surged forward. Dughan smashed through the throat of one, which had no effect. In desperation, he struck harder and lopped off the entire head.

But the body kept attacking.

"I must leave you for a little while," Zaldimar murmured. "I have to prepare for Goldshire next . . . a task with which you and your soldiers will assist once you've been . . . converted."

"Damn you—" But Marshal Dughan cut off as the necromancer vanished . . . and with him, the *light*.

The air grew thick, harsh. The fetid smell of dead kobold was everywhere. Without the magical illumination, he could not see the figures coming toward him.

A man shrieked. Sounds of fear arose from the others. Dughan could do nothing to help; he was desperately trying to fend off the horrific tide of attackers.

Another man cried out. A moment later, the monstrous sound of something moist being torn apart echoed in the shaft.

"Marshal?" the man next to him pleaded.

"Keep fighting!"

But then Dughan nearly fell to the side as the soldier was dragged past him. The hapless fighter called out again . . . then produced a sickening scream as the familiar soft sound of weapons thrusting into flesh echoed from the walls.

The clash of arms grew fainter . . . fainter . . .

Marshal Dughan knew he was the last standing. He felt the undead kobolds converging on him. For the first time, their eyes glowed, a deathly white aura that sent shivers up his spine.

And among them, he saw the illumination of the eyes of taller figures—torn and beaten figures, from what he could make out.

His own men, now part of the ungodly throng.

They surged forward. Marshal Dughan swung wildly. His mace met flesh again and again, but the kobolds and the mutilated soldiers with them pushed on unimpeded. They were everywhere now, seizing at him with their claws, biting, or striking him with their weapons. He cried out as the undead overwhelmed him—

• • •

Marshal Dughan lay in his bed even though daylight already shone upon the town of Goldshire. He shifted uneasily. His brow was furrowed and sweat drenched his body. His lips moved slightly, as if he sought to speak—or scream—and his hands clenched so tightly that the knuckles were bone white.

Without warning, Dughan rose to a sitting position and shrieked. Yet the marshal did not awaken, but rather slumped down upon the bed again, where he once more shifted and sweated and moved as if fighting off something in his dreams.

His shriek had been a loud one, loud enough to be heard through much of the town. Yet no one, not family nor servants, came to see what ailed the marshal. They could not. There was no one in all of Goldshire who could . . . for all were in their beds. All were asleep.

And all were suffering nightmares.

Although she was high priestess of the moon goddess, Tyrande always thought the sunrise a beautiful sight, if somewhat stinging to the eyes of a nocturnal being such as herself. When she had been young, so very young, she had not thought it so painful. In fact, she, Malfurion, and Illidan had often ridden out during the day, when most others had slept, exploring the world of light. Malfurion had even begun his lessons with Cenarius during daylight.

Perhaps I am growing old at last, she thought. Among night elves, Tyrande was one of the longest surviving. She had outlived so many friends, and all her loved ones save two.

The distance required to reach the Moonglade meant that the high priestess, her personal guard, Archdruid Fandral and his accompanying druids had to sleep there for a day before returning to Darnassus. While many of the druids were comfortable enough using the barrow dens, the underground chambers reminded Tyrande too much of other places in the past she wished to forget, such as the dungeons of Azshara's palace.

As queen, Azshara had chosen to sacrifice her people for her vanity and obsession, and had willingly opened the way to the Burning Legion. Her chief advisor, Xavius, had goaded her on, and the two contributed greatly to the countless deaths caused by the demons. Tyrande wished never to think of Azshara again, but many reminders were there that forced her to remember.

Thus, forsaking the barrow dens, she, her followers, and a few druids utilized tents created from vines and leaves nurtured by her hosts.

In her tent—set a respectful distance from where Fandral and his fellow druids rested—the ruler of the night elves practiced her fighting skills. The tent was ten feet by ten and woven from leaf strands taken from Teldrassil itself. Expert weavers had created patterns in the tent that bespoke of the Sisters of Elune, especially the moon symbol, which was repeated over and over. Blessed by the Mother Moon, the tent also had a faint silver glow about it.

There was little décor within, Tyrande caring only for the necessities. A small wooden table and stool were the only furniture, and those had been provided by the druids here. Her moonglaive she had left by the blankets—the latter also woven from Teldrassil's leaves— that served as her bed. The ancient, triple-bladed weapon was a favorite of her race and especially of the elite Sentinels. Aware of the many threats looming in the world, Tyrande practiced often with the glaive.

Now, however, she sought only to work on her hand-to-hand skills, in great part due to a need to stretch her muscles. Dealing with Fandral had caused her enough tension, but having had to sail with him to see Malfurion's body had dealt her far more damage than she had imagined it would.

Fandral . . . while she had respect for him and his position, his plans did not satisfy her. She had acquiesced for the moment, but more and more the long wait his work suggested went against her natural tendency to act quickly and decisively, act as a warrior . . .

Dueling with her own desires, Tyrande thrust herself harder into her efforts. The high priestess arched her arms and kicked out. She had come far since her days as a novice, in some ways further than Malfurion, who, during those past ten millennia, had all too often left Azeroth for the apparent perfection of the Emerald Dream. There had been times during his disappearances when she had grown to resent him for leaving her . . . but always their love had overcome those darker emotions.

Tyrande spun and struck out with her left hand, the straightened fingers forming a curved edge capable of crushing in a throat. She positioned herself on the toes of her right foot and extended her right hand upward—and suddenly sensed something behind her.

The high priestess spun fiercely on her toes and kicked out at her assailant. No one should have entered without warning. Where were her sentries? Still, Tyrande attacked merely to incapacitate, not slay. Any intruder would be needed alive in order to answer questions.

However, instead of striking anything solid, Tyrande watched her foot go *through* a murky black-and-emerald figure. The shadowy assassin scattered into a thousand patches of mist, then re-formed.

But the night elf had already moved on to take up the moonglaive. As she did, she glimpsed two more of the nightmarish figures. There was a blurriness to them that made it impossible to identify any true features, but Tyrande thought them to appear half animal in form. For some reason, that stirred up irrational fears in her.

In that short moment the other two demonic shadows lunged. Tyrande brought up the silver glaive just in time, the curved blades slicing through both.

But the glaive only caused the upper and lower halves to momentarily part. Immediately re-forming, the fiends slashed at her with long talons that suddenly sprouted from their hands.

"Unngh!" Tyrande stumbled back as best she could, trying to recover from the attack. There were no bloody slashes where the talons had cut, but the night elf felt as if daggers of ice still impaled her. A part of her wanted to drop her weapon and curl up on the ground.

But to do that surely meant death. The high priestess swung wildly with the glaive, more to force her attackers to keep re-forming than because she hoped it might hurt them.

A second, more terrible cry escaped her as she felt icy daggers plunge into her back. Distracted by the others, she had not sensed another attacker behind her.

The glaive slipped from her shaking grip. Tyrande wondered why, with both her cries, no one had come to investigate. Perhaps the demons had made it so that, to the outside, all was silent here. The assassins would slay her and no one would be wiser until someone came for other reasons.

No . . . that will not happen . . . Tyrande insisted to herself. *I am a priestess of the Mother Moon . . . the light of Elune is a part of me . . .*

And as this thought coursed through her, it melted both the ice within her and the fear seeking to dominate her will.

"I am the high priestess of the Mother Moon . . ." she declared to her shadowy adversaries. "Feel her light . . ."

The silvery glow filled her tent. The black-and-emerald figures cringed from its glory.

Despite this promising reaction, the night elf did not relax. She opened herself up to Elune. The soft comfort of the Mother Moon enveloped her. Elune would protect her daughter.

The silvery light intensified a thousand times stronger.

With low, hissing sounds, the monstrous assassins dissolved as if truly made of nothing but shadow.

Suddenly, all was black as pitch. Tyrande gasped. The light of Elune was gone, and she was somehow seated on the ground, in a meditative pose. The high priestess shot a glance toward the glaive—it was still by the blankets, where it had been before the intruders had burst in. Or had they? The icy pain in her back returned—or perhaps it was just a chill creeping down her spine. She swallowed, her mouth dry and her heart still racing.

As Tyrande stood up, a guard suddenly burst into the tent. Masking her emotions, Tyrande met the sentry's puzzled gaze. From the other priestess's expression, she knew nothing about the attempted slaying of her mistress.

"Forgive me," the guard murmured. "I heard a gasp and feared something had happened . . ."

"I merely overpracticed and was out of breath."

The other night elf frowned, then nodded. She bowed at the waist, beginning to depart at the same time.

Something came to Tyrande's mind. This strange, sinister vision had settled matters in her mind, but if she planned to move independently of Archdruid Fandral's intentions, then Tyrande first needed to make certain of one thing. "Wait."

"Mistress?"

"I have a task for you . . . concerning one of the druids . . ."

Having been a slave once, Broll Bearmantle found barrow dens too cramped; thus, he slept, as some others did, out in the open in a chosen part of the Moonglade. Hamuul slept a short distance away to his right. There existed a kinship between the pair, as both were somewhat unique in one way or another among those of their calling.

Indeed, other than Varian Wrynn and young Valeera Sanguinar—a *blood elf rogue,* of all things—Hamuul was perhaps the night elf's closest friend. It made for a strange—and to many, *disturbing*—collection of characters, but Broll no longer cared what others thought.

Several troublesome thoughts weighed on the night elf as he lay there—too many to allow him to fall asleep. As the tauren snored next to him, Broll's concerns focused for a time on Valeera, who had become almost like a daughter to him. As a blood elf, the youngling was addicted to the absorption of arcane magical energy, a path her kind had turned to after the destruction of the high elves' fount of power, the Sunwell. Broll had almost managed to help her overcome it . . . but then circumstance had forced Valeera to return to her kind's ways. They had parted company, at least for a time, shortly before his summons to the convocation. He hoped she was better, but feared that her addiction might have worsened again.

Grunting, Broll tried to calm his mind. At the moment, he could do nothing for Valeera, unless he had help . . . and that brought his thoughts back to his shan'do. For the first time something occurred to him—or rather, *tried* to occur to him. The main thrust of it remained just outside of his weary mind's reach. The druid tried over and over to concentrate enough, but instead, the truth seemed to slip further and further from him. He almost—

There came a sound from among the trees behind him, a hint of something like a gasp of breath.

Father . . .

The night elf stiffened. Had he heard . . . *her?*

Broll quietly pushed himself up to a sitting position.

Father . . .

There it was again. He knew that voice better than he knew his own. Broll trembled. It could *not* be her.

It could not be . . . could never be . . . *Anessa?*

He glanced at Hamuul, whose snoring remained steady. The sharp-eared tauren had noticed nothing. To Broll, that verified that he had only imagined that he had heard—

Father . . . I need you . . .

Anessa! Broll gasped. He *had* heard her!

The druid reacted instinctively, rising up and peering into the woods in search of his daughter. He did not call out, fearful that not only would that alert others to his situation, but also send his beloved daughter running.

But . . . a part of his mind reminded him . . . *Anessa is dead . . .* and I'm responsible . . .

Despite being well aware of that fact, Broll felt his heart beat fast. He took a tentative step in the direction from which he believed the call had come.

Father . . . help me . . .

Tears welled up in the otherwise stolid druid's eyes. He remembered her death and his part in it. The old agony stirred again. Memories of the battle arose anew.

Yes, Anessa was dead . . .

But she calls me! the most basic part of him insisted. *This time, I can save her!*

Something shadowy moved among the trees well ahead of him. Broll veered toward the half-seen form. Suddenly, the druid's world *rippled.* The trees twisted as if made of smoke. The indistinct figure grew more distant. The sky became the ground and the ground the sky. Broll felt as if his bones had turned to liquid. He tried to call out to his daughter.

Something moved toward him from the woods. As it neared, it swelled to horrific proportions. Even then, the druid could not make out any distinct features. It almost looked like—

Broll tried to scream . . . and then woke.

His focus began to return. Slowly, the night elf registered several things wrong with what he last recalled about his surroundings. He did not stand at the edge of the woods, but rather lay on the ground as if still sleeping. Squinting, Broll glanced up. By the position of the bright sun, several hours must have passed.

The songs of birds and the sigh of the wind greeted his ears, but another sound was missing. He looked over his right shoulder and saw Hamuul solemnly gazing back at him. The archdruid was down on one knee next to his shaking friend.

"You are awake, yes," the tauren remarked, reading Broll's remaining uncertainty. "Is there something amiss? You look—"

The night elf did not let him finish. "It was a dream. Or rather, a *nightmare . . .*"

"A dream . . . as you say . . ." Hamuul was silent for a moment, then said, "I awoke sooner than you know, for, this being day and I not a night elf, I but lightly napped. I heard you say something. You mumbled a name," the tauren went on with some slight hesitation. "A name close to you."

"Anessa . . ." Bits of the nightmare came back. Broll shivered. He had dreamed of his daughter before, but never in such a manner.

The tauren briefly bowed his head again at mention of Broll's lost child. "Anessa, yes . . ." He peered up at the night elf. "You are well now, though, Broll Bearmantle?"

"I am good now. Thank you . . ."

"This was not natural, Broll Bearmantle . . . no more than your earlier visions . . . though different from them in all other ways, I think."

"It was only a bad nightmare, Hamuul." Broll's tone told the other druid not to argue that point. "Neither it nor the other instances mean *anything.*"

The tauren blinked, then finally shrugged. "I will not press the point, my friend, as I would only worsen your pain . . . but we both know better . . ."

Before anything more could be said, there came a faint rustling sound from the woods. Broll immediately tensed and Hamuul's eyes widened.

From behind the trees, a figure emerged. However, it was not some shade of Anessa returned to the mortal plane. Rather, it proved to be one of the priestesses who had accompanied Tyrande to the Moonglade.

"My mistress wishes to speak with you, druid," the slim figure murmured to Broll. Her gaze shifted to the tauren. "She would have you come alone . . . with all due respect, Archdruid . . ."

The priestess did not wait for a reply from either, instead vanishing back into the barrow den woods. As a druid, Broll could have easily followed her, but her cautious stance and her short, somewhat mysterious message had made it clear that such a reaction would have been unwise. He was to come on his own, as if the decision were his.

"Will you go?" asked Hamuul.

"Yes," came the night elf's immediate reply. "I will."

"I will tell no one."

The tauren's promise meant much to Broll. Nodding his gratitude, the night elf followed the priestess's path. His thoughts were already on the possible reasons why the high priestess of Elune and the ruler of the night elves would desire a secret encounter with him. Tyrande Whisperwind had something in mind that she wished few others to know . . . including Archdruid Fandral Staghelm.

And, unsettling as it was, Broll had the terrible feeling that he knew just what she desired.

5

A Druid's Betrayal

"He has come," the guard murmured to Tyrande from the tent's entrance.

"Bid him enter and watch for anyone who might approach," the high priestess commanded.

With a nod, the guard retreated outside. A moment later Broll Bearmantle respectfully entered. The druid bowed deep, as a subject would to a ruler. In a low voice he said, "High Priestess, you summoned me . . ."

"Be not so formal with me here, Broll. We have known each other for some time."

The druid nodded, but said nothing.

"Please," the high priestess started, gesturing at a grass mat with intricate moon patterns fashioned into it. "Be seated."

Broll shook his head. "I prefer to stand, thank you . . . no disrespect meant."

She nodded. "Very well. I shall keep this short, anyway . . . and I say right now that you have every right to turn my request down."

His thick brow rose. Tyrande could, if she truly wanted to, complicate his life by *ordering* him to do whatever it was she desired.

But that was not her way. "Broll . . . you are the only one here I could ask of this. Malfurion trusted you very much, and so I place my faith in your hands—after all, you wear the mark of greatness, and your actions during the Third War have demonstrated its capabilities." She glanced up at his antlers.

"You flatter me, my lady . . ." The druid cast his eyes downward. "And exaggerate. My time away from my calling would hardly have left me high in his opinion . . ." His eyes shifted to the glaive, which now lay up on the table.

Tyrande watched him closely. She had placed it within view on the chance that the primitive weapon would remind Broll of his gladiatorial past. She had considered him for this task hoping that his recent outside exploits might stir his personal loyalty to Malfurion enough that he would step beyond the Cenarion Circle's current chosen course of action.

"I do not exaggerate. Before he vanished, Malfurion made himself very clear. He understood the grief and anger you suffered and knew that you had to work through it by yourself." Her eyes narrowed. "Let me be blunt, Broll. Malfurion's dreamform must return to his body. Elune's vision was clear; he is dying and dying quickly! He will not last through Fandral's plans! I am certain of that. I know he means well, but it is clear that Fandral is unwavering—not even I can change his mind. You and I must rescue Malfurion from whatever prison holds him."

He hesitated. "You're absolutely certain? There can be no mistake about your vision?"

"It was from the Mother Moon." She stated it with absolute confidence. Elune played no tricks on her faithful.

To her relief, the druid finally nodded. Broll's determined cast showed her that she had chosen correctly.

"I know you. I know Elune." Like most night elves, Broll had grown up worshipping the Mother Moon. The calling to the path of the druid had come later, but it had in no manner erased the respect he had for the deity. "And though there's much merit in Fandral's course, there's been that which leads me to believe more as you do. If you've a plan, my lady, I'm agreeable to it. Something must be done and, with all due respect to Archdruid Fandral, I fear that Teldrassil will be more of a distraction than a path. What do you have in mind?"

His decision to agree was an abrupt one, but not without substance behind it. Yes, Broll had at first been satisfied, even hopeful, with Fandral's plan; but hearing Tyrande's plea had stirred to the forefront thoughts of uncertainty that he realized had been growing since the last and most heinous of his visions. Something foul was at work—something that surely was the Nightmare. That these visions suddenly pressed him so, and that the last concerned his deceased daughter, had added weight to the high priestess's concerns. Something very terrible was imminent and that thing seemed most likely Malfurion's doom.

No . . . healing Teldrassil would indeed take too long, the druid thought. *But Fandral wouldn't understand that . . .*

There was still no answer to his question, so he repeated it.

She looked away. Much of what Tyrande intended was based on knowledge gleaned about the druids through Malfurion. There was a tremendous possibility that the high priestess had made some false assumptions and, if so, then her plan had failed before it had even begun.

"I want you to go to Bough Shadow . . ."

He rightly stiffened at mention of that name. It was immediately clear to him her intention.

"Bough Shadow," the sturdy male muttered. "I understand what you want. It makes the most sense . . . especially with time so precious as I now believe . . ."

Her hopes grew. "Do you think it might work?"

"My lady . . . it may be the only chance left to us . . . but it won't be easy . . . unless . . ."

She waited, but when Broll continued to look inward, finally had to ask, "Unless *what?*"

Shaking his head, the druid murmured, "Best you not know." Looking more determined, Broll added, "But I'll get there."

"There is still the question of the convocation and Fandral's plans," the high priestess went on. "You will have to wait until all that is settled—but I'm afraid we've no time to waste."

"There is only one thing with which I need to deal, High Priestess, and if Archdruid Fandral does not catch me at it, I will be gone immediately after." His brow furrowed. "It does require I first return with the rest to the Cenarion Enclave, though . . ."

Again Tyrande waited for more explanation and again Broll gave none. She finally nodded to the druid, trusting that whatever secret he held from her was for her own—and Malfurion's—good.

"I thank you," Tyrande murmured. Her expression tightened. "But there's one more thing. You won't go alone. I will be sending Shandris to meet you . . . you are familiar with Auberdine, I'd imagine?"

"I've been there. It's not a place conducive to druidic ways . . . and, like my brethren, I prefer another mode of travel. Is that where we're to meet?"

"Yes, then the two of you can proceed on to Ashenvale."

His expression did not hide his dislike for her decision to add a partner to his travels. "With all due respect to the general and her considerable skills, I'd much prefer to go alone."

She was adamant. "You will not. If I must order you to—"

Broll grunted. "You needn't. If you really think this best for Malfurion, then . . . I'll trust to you, high priestess."

Tyrande's mood softened. She reached out abruptly to touch his shoulder. As she did, a faint glow of moonlight briefly spread over the spot. The moonlight briefly engulfed Broll before fading *into* him. "You have the blessing of the Mother Moon . . . and my gratitude, too."

The male night elf bowed low. "I'm deeply honored by both, my lady."

"I am Tyrande to you."

The druid bowed, then began to retreat from her presence. "No . . . to Malfurion, you are . . . to me . . . you are my high priestess, the embodiment of our people's hopes . . ."

He slipped out of the tent. Tyrande pursed her lips, wondering if she had done the right thing.

Then her gaze returned to the glaive . . . and her determination hardened.

• • •

Broll said nothing to Hamuul when he returned and the stolid tauren did not ask. The night elf did not sleep much that day, and when the druids prepared to take their leave of the Moonglade, he only acknowledged the high priestess with a respectful bow no more intimate than that performed by any of his brethren.

The Sisters of Elune had their own method of travel—mighty hippogryphs—for the return to Darnassus, and so, after sharing a few words with Tyrande Whisperwind, Fandral Staghelm led the druids to a private clearing in the Moonglade.

"I have determined that the situation here merits immediate continuance of our efforts to heal the World Tree," the lead archdruid announced as they prepared to depart. "We will renew our efforts this very night—"

"This very night?" a druid blurted. "After so long a flight?"

"There will be a period of meditation first, naturally, and I will work to reconsider how best to utilize our power, since we'll not have the Idol of Remulos to add to it after all . . ." Fandral waved away further discourse. "It is settled! Now, for Malfurion's sake, let us be on our way quickly . . ."

Fandral raised his arms.

As one, the druids shrank. They bent forward and feathers burst from their violet skin. Their noses and mouths distended, becoming beaks.

The small flock of storm crows took to the air, nearly invisible against the night sky.

Fandral, a larger bird with silver streaks along each wing, led the druids at a swift pace, eager to reach Teldrassil. The sight was a rare one, for only the most skilled and powerful of druids were able to learn the mysteries of flight. Indeed, with the exception of Broll, all the rest were archdruids of reputation. It was another hint of the power he wielded, yet could not focus enough to truly attain his place among his brethren. That he was here at all was Fandral's doing, and that made Broll feel even more guilt for what he intended.

Broll flew further back in the flock than usual. Hamuul flew some distance ahead. The tauren was the only other concern Broll had other than Fandral, but Hamuul was focused on maintaining his pace. The tauren was mighty, but he was also fairly old for his kind and thus had to push harder than most of the night elves.

After several long hours, the World Tree materialized ahead. Fandral banked and the flock descended'. . . and Broll stealthily fell back, veering upward. Beating his wings as hard as he could, the transformed night elf surged higher and higher. The great trunk of Teldrassil was like an impossible barrier ever before him, yet the druid pressed on.

And then . . . the enormous crown welcomed him. Broll the bird darted in among its vast branches.

Part of what looked to be the foliage itself moved. Though he only glimpsed it for a mere second, the long, thrusting tusks, the massive, woodlike form, and the leafy coat were enough for the druid to recognize it as an ancient, one of the primal beings who not only protected the World Tree and the night elf realm, but also taught Darnassus's warriors the darker side of nature and how to use it in combat.

The ancient did not appear to notice Broll in turn, which was to the druid's preference. While not of any physical danger to him, he feared the being might inadvertently tell Fandral of Broll's presence. Though the reason for that would eventually become known to the archdruid, Broll desired that it be later rather than sooner. For by then, he would be long gone.

And, if things did not work as Broll intended, very likely dead.

The druid adjusted his path to avoid other, more cunning sentries hidden among the branches. The Sentinels, Darnassus's armed force, guarded Teldrassil's crown. They were led by the zealous Shandris Feathermoon, who was totally devoted to her ruler.

There were few more capable or experienced than Shandris, whom Tyrande had rescued on the battlefield during the initial conflict against the Burning Legion so long ago. Shandris had been an orphaned child, one of so many. Under the high priestess's tutelage, she had risen to become one of the race's most skilled warriors.

It made for perfect logic that Shandris would be Tyrande's chosen servant for this crucial mission. The high priestess would trust no other with such a desperate mission. Indeed, Broll was honored to be among her chosen servants.

Sensing that he was near his destination, Broll pushed aside all other thoughts. Barely a wing beat later, the storm crow burst through the foliage . . . and into the area of the capital known as the Cenarion Enclave.

As with so much of Darnassus, it was impossible to see that this sacred place was part of a city built atop a tree *itself.* Tall trees—oaks and ashes especially—lined the enclave. Each tree bore mystic runes shaped from the very bark. Within the circular grove created here, a handful of unique structures molded from both living trees and carefully shaped stones represented the usual gathering place for convocations. The largest of these served as the new residence of Fandral Staghelm.

The storm crow did not head directly for the archdruid's sanctum, instead alighting on a branch that allowed him to overlook the area. The Cenarion Enclave radiated a sense of tranquility—and it was indeed a restful place—but it was not without its own guardians, especially those set into place by Fandral himself.

Broll fluttered to another branch deep enough to avoid being detected from anything within the enclave and yet near enough to the archdruid's sanctum. He had to make his incursion swift, but cautious.

All looked calm, but as Broll studied the green and crimson edifice, he noted the fine strings of vines crisscrossing it. Cocking his head, he eyed the tiny buds running along the vines. They were a subtle indication of just what plant decorated the building . . . and the only hint of Fandral's cunning. Even most of the other druids would have proven hard-pressed to identify it.

Twisting his head, the storm crow plucked a feather from his body. Ignoring the slight twinge of pain, Broll took to flight, drifting high above the vines. He dropped the feather.

The feather drifted onto a bud, which opened immediately. From it burst a sappy substance that encased the feather, causing it to drop to the ground with a thud. The sap had quickly hardened.

There were hundreds, perhaps thousands, of such little buds. With such numbers, they could easily cover Broll with a similar prison, leaving him trapped until Fandral returned.

Broll surveyed the vines, watching. A few small bees darted past the buds unhindered.

The storm crow let out a small but triumphant sound, then fluttered down to the ground. He made certain to keep away from the archdruid's sanctum.

Once on the ground, Broll returned to his true form. He wasted no time, murmuring under his breath. The druid did not speak words, but sounds that all had a sharp, buzzing tone to them.

A moment later Broll heard more buzzing. Continuing his own sounds, he watched as bees began to gather before him. They flew around him, seeming more curious than anything else.

The druid changed the tempo of his spellwork, and the swarm immediately reacted. The bees flew en masse toward the vine-covered structure.

Broll transformed into a storm crow again and followed behind the bees, whose numbers continued to swell even as he joined them. They were all here in response to his call, which he had broached as an invitation. The bees congregated where the night elf now indicated, a thick part of the vines surrounding a window opening.

It would have been impossible for Broll to dart through the window, even if he had raced as fast as the wings would let him. However, the bees now clustered over the buds, seeking in vain the blossoms that they had been told were there. Broll regretted the subterfuge, but had not had any other choice.

The moment that it appeared all the buds were occupied, the druid dove for the window. As he reached it, he saw some of the buds move. However, the bees' presence prevented them from unleashing their imprisoning sap.

His avian bulk barely fit through, but fit it did. Broll alighted on the floor, then reverted to his normal self. He knew where Fandral kept what he sought, and knew that the archdruid would not think anyone audacious enough to commit the offense Broll now intended.

Paying no attention to the rest of his surroundings, Broll went straight to a chest woven from steelgrass. While outwardly appearing to be soft, when used in such a manner, steelgrass was as strong as metal. A normal night elf would have been unable to either cut through it or pry open the bound lid, but Broll was familiar with Fandral's methods, both of them having been taught closely by Malfurion. Indeed, Broll had learned a few things that he believed even Fandral did not know.

Placing his hands close together, the druid tested the weaving of the chest. He felt the binding spells Fandral had used and the manners by which the archdruid had had the steelgrass shape itself.

The strands sealing the lid unbound. Broll hesitated, then opened the chest.

The Idol of Remulos stared back at him, the dragon figurine seeming almost eager at his arrival.

The battle bloomed again in his thoughts. He saw the demons of the Burning Legion, and their commander, the pit lord Azgalor. Broll once more watched helplessly as the idol slipped from his grasp, then was cut by the demon's blade.

And again he saw those unleashed and corrupted forces envelop the only one still standing at his side. His daughter. Anessa's death had not been an easy one. She had been burned horribly, her flesh withering before his eyes—

Broll gritted his teeth as he forced the pain of his failure back. He dared not let his emotions take control of him. He had the statuette; that was what mattered most now . . . that and Malfurion's fate.

There had been a chance that Fandral might have disobeyed Remulos and summoned the statue back to him. But Fandral had indeed heeded the Moonglade's guardian and thus enabled Broll to achieve his goal here. The night elf gingerly removed the figurine, admiring not for the first time its surreal majesty. For a moment, he marveled that such an exquisite work could have also been the source of great evil. Of course, the idol had since been "cleansed"; perhaps that made the difference.

The night elf thought of Remulos's warning, but could see no choice, considering the course he intended. Broll needed the idol. He would just have to take special care.

His hesitation at an end, the druid quickly resealed the chest.

So now I add thief to the list of my accomplishments, Broll thought bitterly. *How Varian and Valeera would laugh . . .*

He secreted the statue in the confines of his cloak. As with the rest of his garments and personal effects, it would go in that magical place they did when he transformed.

But when the druid shifted once more to the semblance of a storm crow, he heard a heavy thud. Cocking his head, Broll found the idol lying at his talons.

Letting out a low, frustrated caw, Broll fluttered up, then gripped the statuette in his claws. When at last he wielded the idol, he was urged to greater swiftness. Others might not take too much notice of a storm crow in flight, but a storm crow carrying a statuette would surely raise more questions than he preferred.

Flapping, Broll turned himself toward the window. As he did, his gaze fell upon another statuette, this one set upon a branch that had been shaped to act as a table or shelf. There were runes etched into the statuette, but it was the subject matter that caught the druid for a moment. The figure was that of a younger night elf with some great semblance to Fandral. However, it was not Fandral himself.

Valstann . . . Broll dipped his head in acknowledgment of the night elf the statuette represented. Like Broll, Fandral had lost his only child, in this case his son. Although the circumstances had been highly different—the archdruid had not been responsible for Valstann's demise—the losses had always been one bond between the two older night elves.

A bond that Broll's act would forever sever.

He could sense the bees beginning to lose their interest. Pushing hard, Broll headed for the window. Outside, the druid could feel the first of the swarm taking off. He beat harder, then folded in his wings as he dove through the window.

Bees scattered out of his path. Too many. That meant that some of the buds were now unobstructed.

Something struck his left wing near the tip. Broll rocked to the side. The involuntary action was all that saved his head from being encased in the sticky substance.

He was struck again on the right leg before he finally flew out of range. Even then, Broll did not slow. He had done the unthinkable and his only hope was that his mad plan would make all the difference.

Malfurion was lost in the Emerald Dream. There was no contact with the Great Aspect Ysera, nor any of the other green dragons who guarded the magical plane. Tyrande's suggestion to go to Ashenvale made the most sense, but for there to be a true chance of success, they would need aid of a kind greater than a lone druid of questionable skill and some priestess of the moon goddess.

And through the Idol of Remulos, Broll hoped to contact just that aid . . . if the attempt did not kill him in the process.

Thura chopped her way through the thick vegetation, her straightforward orc mind seeing no reason why the magical ax could not be used for such a mundane task. After all, what was a weapon good for if one was unable to reach one's foe?

She felt that she was nearing her goal. The journey might still take days or it might be over tomorrow, but the key to finding the treacherous night elf was so very close.

The forest finally gave way to more open ground and the beginning of a chain of tall hills. The orc saw several cave openings of various sizes among them. Thura gripped the ax as a weapon again. Caves could mean danger, especially in the form of hungry animals or feral trolls.

As she entered the hills, Thura noted an odd silence draping over the region. Where were the birds? A few insects announced their presence, but nothing large called out or even flew in sight. That suggested that the hunting would not be good here . . . and that perhaps she might become the hunted.

However, barely minutes into the new terrain, rest finally demanded Thura's complete attention. She had no choice but to risk sleep. She glanced at the dark cave mouths around her, choosing at last one that looked too small to house some great predator, but large enough to suit her needs.

The cave extended only a few yards before ending at a curved wall. After assuring herself that there were no hidden openings that might obscure some threat, the female warrior settled down in a corner that gave her a view of the cave and the entrance.

She had little in the way of sustenance left and this Thura cautiously divided up. Three pieces of dried goat meat, some slowly rotting tubers, and half a sack of water. Thura ate one of the pieces of meat and one tuber, then permitted herself two small swallows of the brackish water. She ignored the protests of her stomach, which had been left insatiate for days. Both game and fresh water had grown extremely scarce since she had entered this region. Somewhere, she would find enough to keep her going until she had fulfilled her blood oath. Only then, if she survived that, would Thura concern herself with her mundane needs—

A hiss reverberated through the cave.

It took the orc a moment to realize that the sound had come from without. Fighting back her exhaustion, Thura rose and headed to the mouth. She clutched the ax tightly. The hiss had come from no ordinary serpent or lizard, but rather something much, much larger.

The lack of birds and animals in the area now made more sense.

Thura waited, but heard no repeat of the sound. She finally took a step out, ever ready to take on *any* foe.

A great wind suddenly rose up, so powerful that it almost shoved the sturdy orc back into the cave. The darkened region became darker yet, as if something sought to block out the stars and moons.

And, briefly, something did. A great patch of shadow darted over Thura's location. It raced past her, continuing on deeper into the region.

The orc stepped farther out, trying to see it better. In the distance, the massive form descended beyond the horizon.

After waiting to see if it would take to the sky again, Thura returned to the cave. She settled down, but kept the ax in her grip. A faint glimmer now shone in her eyes.

This was a sign. When last she had slept, there had been one difference in the ever-repeating dream. There had been a hint of something at the end—a briefly glimpsed, vague form she had only belatedly identified.

A form very much like the one that Thura had just now observed.

There had been a dragon.

6

DRAGONS AND DECEIT

Malfurion felt the shadow loom over him and knew what it meant. A new torture was imminent.

The dark emerald lines spread further over him, at first seeming to form jagged, bony fingers that turned out to seem instead the silhouette of a vast, macabre tree that dwarfed that which the archdruid had become. Yet even as limited as his field of vision had become, the night elf knew that though there was a shadow . . . there was no other tree.

Can you taste their dreams? the Nightmare Lord taunted. *Can you taste their fears? Even your dearest are not immune to it . . .*

Malfurion did not respond, though he knew that his captor could still sense his emotions. In that regard, the archdruid continually sought to focus inward. The more calm that he could bring to himself, the better his hopes for the others.

And the better that the Nightmare Lord did not know of his true efforts. His captor believed the spells surrounding the night elf prevented Malfurion from reaching out to his beloved Tyrande or anyone else and, for the most part, that was true. But the archdruid had not trained hard over ten thousand years to be utterly defeated. He could not, and *dared* not, reach out to Tyrande or certain others, but there were paths of communication, though they required delicacy and complicated paths. If the Nightmare Lord even suspected once . . . then Malfurion was surely lost and with him perhaps all else.

The shadow grew and twisted, almost as if the sinister tree slipped around to better view its prey. Malfurion himself suddenly twisted anew, the tree of pain that he had become taking on a new, more vile aspect. From his boughs, the leaves sprouted black flowers. Each flower's birth was as a needle thrust into the night elf's eyes. There were hundreds, soon covering most of his upper torso.

From each blossom there suddenly swelled an emerald egg. Malfurion wanted to scream, but, of course, could not.

Out of one of the eggs burst a thing with tentacles and wings. As it moved, it oozed pure terror.

A second fiend burst free, followed by a third, and more. They crawled over Malfurion, scraping and biting as they moved.

At last the horrific multitude left the archdruid. They flowed over the small patch of space that he could see, as if awaiting commands.

The shadow moved nearer, as if caressing them. *Wrought from your own fears, stirred by my desire . . . they are beautiful to behold, are they not?*

As if by some unheard signal, the swarm spread out in different directions. They quickly vanished in the deep, dank green fog that surrounded all but Malfurion's immediate vicinity.

There are more and more sleepers, my friend, more and more of those susceptible to these pets and those before them . . . their nightmares are feeding me through you and the others . . .

Malfurion did his best not to acknowledge this truth, that his own abilities were aiding in the spread of the Nightmare beyond the Emerald Dream, yet concern did creep in. Concern that, unfortunately, his captor could sense.

Yes, my friend, you have betrayed your people, your world, and your beloved . . . you know the truth of it . . .

The archdruid's form twisted more. Another silent scream echoed through the night elf's mind, but it was insufficient to stifle all the pain. Despite his training, despite his skills, Malfurion could not hold back the torture completely.

Go mad, Malfurion Stormrage . . . go mad . . . but know that even it is no refuge . . . I know . . . I will be there waiting for you . . . there is no place within where you may hide . . .

The shadow of the monstrous tree receded from Malfurion's sight, but the archdruid could still feel its nearby presence. Even as new, gnarled branches sprouted from what had once been his arms, Malfurion remained aware that the Nightmare Lord had only just begun to use him. The night elf was key to the creature's plot, for Malfurion was a powerful link to both this realm and Azeroth.

But he was not the only key. Malfurion knew that all too bitterly. The evil that was the Nightmare had snared others more powerful in their own way than him . . . and while the night elf had been granted a particularly horrific fate, those others served in a more accursed manner. They were now willing followers of the darkness, helping to spread it, eager to see it engulf the mortal plane.

The Nightmare Lord had *dragons* to do his bidding. *Green dragons* . . .

There is something unspeakable seeking dominion over the world, the cowled figure thought as he perused a series of floating globes before him. Seated upon a chair carved out of a stalagmite, the gaunt, *almost* elven figure studied the image within each globe. At his will, they reflected images of places all over Azeroth.

He wore the violet robes of the Kirin Tor, though his current course of action was his own. Indeed, there was much about his activities that they did not know—not even their leader, who had been his pupil and who understood the truth about him. The figure, who oft watched over the younger races, now had to focus on the various dragonflights, for after so many centuries of consistency, the great winged creatures were in flux. That was a concern that would have been important to many, but especially to Krasus.

After all, he was one of them.

In appearance, he was lanky, hawklike of features, and had three long, jagged scars running down his right cheek. His hair was mainly silver, with streaks of black and crimson. The silver did little to bespeak his true age though. To learn more of that, one had to peer into his glittering black eyes—eyes of no mortal creature. The eyes and the scars were the only hints of his true identity as the great dragon Korialstrasz.

He was also chief consort of the queen of the red dragonflight and the Aspect of Life, the glorious Alexstrasza, and, as such, was her principal agent when it came to protecting Azeroth.

And such was his role now, for a situation had arisen that touched upon *both* his great concerns: Azeroth and his own kind. There was an evil spreading not only through the mortal world, but one that greatly touched the Emerald Dream, too. He had tried contacting Ysera, but she was not to be found. Indeed, he could not contact any of the green dragons save one . . . and Krasus would have nothing to do with that particular figure.

He did not have to ask just who was truly responsible. For anyone else, the question would have had no definite answer, but Krasus knew. He knew with all his soul the evil behind it.

"I know you, Destroyer," he whispered as he viewed another globe. "I name you, *Deathwing* . . ."

It could only be the black dragon, the crazed Aspect once called Neltharion the Earth-Warder. Krasus rose. He would have to act immediately—

Familiar laughter echoed throughout his mountain sanctum, a hidden place situated not all that far from where once fantastic Dalaran, city of the magi, had once stood. However, now a gaping crater marked what even Krasus had been forced to admit was one of the most astounding—if potentially catastrophic—spells ever cast. Dalaran's absence meant that few had reason to come to this desolate place . . . unless they sought the dragon mage himself.

Krasus leapt to his feet. He instinctively waved his hand to dismiss the images from the globes—then saw with dread that they all bore one vision. It was an eye, the burning eye of the *Destroyer* . . .

"Deathwing—"

Even as he blurted out the black dragon's name, the globes exploded. Savage shards flew throughout the chamber, striking stone walls, limestone outcroppings, and, most of all, Krasus. The spell he cast to shield him from them proved useless and the force of the shards' attack sent Krasus flying back against the stone chair.

Though he appeared mortal, his body was still more resilient than that of any elf or human. The stone cracked and both Krasus and the chair went tumbling. However, Krasus paid the collision little mind, the agony caused by the many shards embedded in him far worse.

Yet still he struggled to his feet and prepared a counterattack. While not as powerful as an Aspect, Krasus was among the most versatile and cunning of his kind. Moreover, Deathwing had dared attack him in his sanctum, where a number of elements existed that would serve Alexstrasza's consort.

But the moment he summoned the energies needed for his spell, the shards glowed bright. Shock ran through his body.

Those pieces that had struck elsewhere around the sanctum tore loose of their places. Registering this, a pained Krasus hunched over. His body began to swell and his arms and legs twisted, becoming more reptilian. From his back burst two leathery, vestigial wings that immediately began to grow.

Deathwing's laughter filled the sanctum. Again the shards glowed. Krasus, midway through his transformation into Korialstrasz the red dragon, faltered.

The other shards reached him. However, instead of striking Krasus as the previous had, they began adhering to his body. Krasus sought to burn them off, even shake them off, but to no avail.

Then, those in his flesh pressed hard. The dragon mage could not move. To his horror, he found that the shards were *compressing* him. They crushed him into a smaller and smaller thing, as if he had no bones, no substance.

And as the shards utterly encased him, Krasus found himself trapped not in a globe, but a golden disk.

His eyes widened. "No . . ."

A monstrous face peered at him from outside. The scarred, burnt visage of Deathwing. "Korialstrasz . . ."

In response, the dragon mage attacked his prison with all his magical might. Yet instead of weakening the disk, his efforts only made it glow brighter.

"Yes," mocked Deathwing. "Feed my creation . . . it's only fair . . . you destroyed the last . . ."

Krasus shook his head. "This is not possible . . ."

"Oh, yes," the black behemoth returned, his grin growing toothier. "You will feed my creation forever . . . you will be the heart of my new *Demon Soul* . . ."

The dread disk flared. Krasus shrieked from pain—

And then, for a brief moment, he saw himself—or rather, his true self, Korialstrasz—asleep in the mountain sanctum. Overwhelmed by the pain, the vision was gone in an instant, yet Krasus had a revelation. He had wondered how he could have so poorly expected this confrontation. More to the point, he doubted that Deathwing would re-create the foul artifact in such a manner.

Krasus knew the truth.

He was dreaming.

His real self was the sleeping dragon. He was caught in a nightmare such as he had never experienced.

With that knowledge, Krasus fought against what was happening. His prison was not real. Deathwing was not real. It was all illusion.

But nothing happened.

Deathwing laughed, his face contorted through the side of the disk. "I will conquer your queen and make her my mate! My children will rule the skies and Azeroth will be scorched to a cinder, eradicating the short-lived vermin you love so much!"

This is only a dream, a nightmare! Krasus insisted. *A nightmare!*

Yet, though he knew that, though he began to understand the reason for it, Krasus could not wake . . .

The hippogryphs waited uneasily near the shore, the winged beasts unfamiliar with the terrain here. They were used to flying to Auberdine, but the severity of the situation had meant the party needed to land close to the Moonglade.

One of the males—a frayfeather with rich blue and turquoise plumage—reared up on his equine hind legs. Named after the highlands from where they came, frayfeathers were excellent flyers. A priestess next to the hippogryph quickly murmured soothing sounds. The male dropped back down, the talons at the end of his avian forelegs digging into the ground. The antlered head—akin to that of a huge bird of prey—bent down to be petted.

The Sisters of Elune were alone, the druids having flown on ahead using their miraculous shapeshifting abilities. Tyrande had not pushed for them to wait, and she knew that Fandral had been eager to depart. That suited her needs.

She studied the Moonglade for a moment, then said to her ever-faithful guards, "I wish to walk alone for a moment. Please wait here."

They clearly did not care for her suggestion, but they obeyed. Tyrande turned from them and headed back to the wooded area from which they had but recently emerged. She entered, savoring both the moonlit night and the calm of the forest.

Despite the serenity of her surroundings, the high priestess still found herself yearning for the peace of the temple. She had never felt comfortable as ruler of her people, especially in regard to decisions that could endanger others' lives. Each life was precious to her. Yet she recalled how the night elves' previous ruler had willingly let her people be slaughtered for her own glory. To Azshara, the people had simply existed to live or die at her whim.

"But I am *not* Azshara . . . I will never be Azshara . . ." the high priestess growled not for the first time to herself.

"You could never be her, mistress . . . you're a far more worthy ruler."

Tyrande turned, her frown growing. " 'More worthy?' Her most devoted followers probably gave her similar praise, Shandris."

The newcomer wore armor from the neck down, including a form-fitting breastplate, shoulder guards, and padded metal and leather leg guards running from her hips down to her matching boots. Most of her armor was of greenish hue, though trimmed with a violet that was akin to the skin color of most night elves.

"At least you earn that praise." Shandris Feathermoon removed her gauntlets. She came unarmed to the high priestess, as was custom back in Darnassus . . . a custom that the general of the night elves' army herself enforced with vigor. Her features were even sharper than those of most of her kind, and there was in her ever-narrowed eyes an almost zealous determination. Tyrande knew that zealous determination was all due to her, that Shandris Feathermoon in many ways felt she existed only to serve the high priestess.

Tyrande recalled the orphan whom she had saved during one of the Burning Legion's horrific advances during that terrible war some ten thousand years past. The innocent, fearful eyes were so different now. Shandris had become the daughter Tyrande had never had . . . and like none she would have expected.

Shandris stretched her neck, which was protected by a leather and metal collar. Below her eyes, the jagged tattoos that marked an earlier rite of passage now seemed to mock Tyrande, for they added to the younger elf's fearsome look. The high priestess had never wanted to turn the frightened young orphan into a war machine, but she had.

"We will not debate the issue, Shandris," the high priestess remarked dourly, referring to her general's lofty opinion of her.

"Good, because I'm right." Although she paid her savior every respect, Shandris was the one person who also spoke plainly and bluntly to Tyrande. Changing the subject, the general asked, "I came separate and in secret to this place, as you commanded before you departed the island. Now, perhaps you can tell me why. I assume from our proximity to the Moonglade that it has something to do with the druids." The younger night elf paced back and forth as she talked, in many ways her movements reminiscent of a nightsaber, one of the great toothed cats used as both ground transport and a heavy weapon by the Sentinels.

"Yes, it involves the druids . . . and Malfurion, in particular."

Shandris nodded, her expression unreadable.

"We must find a way to bring him back to us, Shandris. For many reasons. Whatever is going on in the Emerald Dream not only involves the druids, but I believe that it is touching Teldrassil . . . and perhaps other parts of Azeroth as well . . ."

The general's eyes narrowed to slits. "There were some vague reports . . . mostly scattered and uncertain at first . . . from the human and dwarven lands. They mentioned in part something about those who can't wake up. Something like Malfurion's situation, come to think of it . . ."

Tyrande glanced at the moon for reassurance. Then, putting a hand on the other's shoulder, she murmured, "Elune indicated to me that Malfurion is dying. I expect you know that already."

The general gazed into her eyes. "I do. And I'm sorry. So sorry."

Tyrande smiled sadly. "Thank you. But Elune also indicated that this is beyond my own personal concerns and that I must look to absolutely whatever must need to be done for the sake of Azeroth itself . . . and that is why I have summoned you."

Shandris Feathermoon immediately went down on one knee. "Give whatever command you must of me, mistress! I will do what you say, go where you say. My life is yours . . . always!"

The old guilt returned. "I have a tremendous favor to ask of you. A favor, not a command . . ."

"Ask it!"

"You know of Broll Bearmantle."

"More warrior than druid, that one, mistress," Shandris said as reply.

"Broll is heading to Ashenvale in the hopes of rescuing Malfurion. You understand how?"

In her desire to be the best commander possible, Shandris had created a network for gathering information that stretched far beyond Darnassus and the night elf lands. Thus, Ashenvale, a part of the latter, was easily within the province of her studies. Shandris's expression tightened, but there was also a hint of approval.

"It's daring. Dangerous. And the only hope at this point, I'd say."

"I do not intend for him to enter alone."

"I suspected you had something in mind, so I prepared in advance for a longer journey!" The other night elf's eyes glowed with anticipation. Shandris leapt to her feet, her fist pressed against her breast. "I can depart immediately from here! I know the danger and the necessity of this mission! It cannot be entrusted to just anyone—"

"Exactly." Tyrande straightened, determined that she speak now as ruler. "And that is why *I* shall be the one who will join him."

Her words struck like lightning. Shandris stumbled back a step. She gaped at the high priestess.

"You? But Darnassus needs you! I am the one who must go—"

"Elune has shown me that I, as her high priestess, am best suited. This task will require the full teachings of the Sisterhood and as its head I could ask no other to do this. In addition, no one knows Malfurion as I do . . . no one is bound to him as I am. If his dreamform can be found, I am the one who will be able to do it." Her gaze was strong. "And while saving Malfurion is of the utmost desire for me personally, he may also be *Azeroth's* only hope. As high priestess I *must* be the one who accompanies Broll . . ."

Shandris finally nodded. But though agreeing, the general still had questions.

"What does Fandral think of this?"

"I do not answer to Fandral."

"Sometimes he seems not to understand that." There was a brief moment of humor in Shandris's eyes. She was one of the handful aware that he and her mistress did not always see eye to eye on matters of how Tyrande governed, especially when her decisions affected the druids and his sphere of influence. Then, growing serious again, she continued, "And Darnassus?"

"Darnassus must be yours to guard, Shandris, as you have done when I have had to leave it for other matters of state."

"This is hardly the same . . ." Still, once more the warrior went down on one knee. "But I will protect the city and our realm as always until your *return.*"

Her pointed emphasis of the last word was almost a demand that Tyrande make certain that she *would* come back. The night elf ruler reached out and touched Shandris on the cheek.

"My daughter . . ."

At those words, the hardened warrior leapt forward and wrapped her arms around the high priestess. Shandris buried her face in Tyrande's neck.

"Mother . . ." she whispered in a voice that sounded exactly like that of the frightened orphan of so long ago.

Then, just as quickly, Shandris pulled back. Other than a tearstain down one cheek, she looked again like the seasoned commander of the Sentinels. She saluted Tyrande.

"I've just the mount for you," Shandris said. "As I said, he's ready for a long journey. Also, there is no finer. He's not far away. Just follow me."

Shandris turned crisply and led her deeper into the woods. Neither spoke, but both were deep in thought.

After almost five minutes Tyrande heard the shuffling of a large creature. As Shandris did not show any concern, the high priestess was content to follow.

A moment later they confronted a large male hippogryph tethered to a massive oak. His plumage was more striking than those animals ridden by the group, the feathers darker and more dramatic, with crimson lines across the ebony wings and slight turquoise markings on the upper edges. Crimson feathers also lined the otherwise blue-black head. The hippogryph also wore a protective helm over his head and some body armor. Although all hippogryphs were powerful, this one was of a species especially adept at war.

"He and I have flown into battle together often. You may trust him as you trust me," the general said quietly. "His name is Jai'alator."

" 'Noble blade of Elune,' " Tyrande translated. "A proud name that."

The hippogryph bowed his great head. The winged creatures were not simple beasts. They had an intelligence and were considered *allies*, not servants. They *allowed* themselves to be ridden.

"I am honored to fly with you," Tyrande told the hippogryph.

Shandris undid the reins and handed them to her mistress. "He answers to 'Jai.' If you fly just above the trees, the others won't see you depart. I'll join the party in a few minutes, then delay them some more."

Nodding, the high priestess took the reins. "Thank you, Shandris." Tyrande recalled one last thing. "Shandris . . . be on alert."

The general's eyes narrowed. "For what?"

How to explain what she had fought against? "For that which the light of Elune must melt away . . ."

Shandris frowned at the explanation, but said nothing. She saluted once more, then whirled around and marched off in the direction of the other priestesses.

The high priestess wiped moisture from her own eye, then turned her thoughts to her imminent journey . . . not the least problem of which would be convincing *Broll Bearmantle* to take her to Ashenvale.

To the Great Tree.

And to the portal into the Emerald Dream.

7

AUBERDINE

Broll landed just beyond sight of Auberdine, already impatient to be on his way from its vicinity. Although officially part of the night elf realm, the region in general—called Darkshore due to the odd mist that tended to blanket everything—was mostly shunned by his race. There had been attempts made to settle this land—some of them not by his kind—but all had fallen to failure. Ruins dotted the wilds, many of them now housing threats to travelers willing or forced to journey through the area.

Auberdine was the only stronghold, if it could be called that. It was a dismal place by not only night elf standards, but even those of humans or dwarves. There ever seemed a cover of storm clouds over the area and a chill wind that cut through to the soul. Auberdine existed more out of necessity than anything else, for Darnassus required some place on the immediate mainland where dealing with the outside world could take place.

Those of his people who populated the town were generally looked down on by the inhabitants of the capital, a failing that even Broll found himself suffering at times. Auberdine consisted of outcasts and misfits. True, there was a garrison of the Sentinels there and even some druids, but they remained as separate as possible from the townsfolk.

Broll returned to his true form, and cursed as he shook his foot. In his storm crow form, his arms became his wings and his feet his talons. Unfortunately, some of the buds had struck at the latter, leaving the druid with the idol sealed to that foot.

Broll drew some herbs from a pouch at his waist and scattered them over the sap. As if snow touched by the sun, the sap finally softened, then melted away. The Idol of Remulos dropped ignominiously to the ground.

Retrieving it, Broll peered ahead. The path was dark, and although that did not bother a night elf much, he wondered why there was not some illumination on the horizon even despite the mists. In fact, he could not recall any glow at all during his descent. Auberdine should have been lit enough to be seen from where he was, if only for the sake of the other races who frequented the settlement.

With a grunt, the druid moved on. He could have landed closer to the town but had not wanted to call any more attention to his presence than necessary.

Secreting the idol in a hidden place in his cloak, Broll picked up his pace. He hoped that Fandral would not notice his theft for some time. There was no reason for the archdruid to retrieve the figurine . . . but Broll never trusted his luck.

As he reached the top of a hill, the druid grew more wary. He still could not see any illumination from Auberdine, and this close the mist should have been no impediment whatsoever.

A sense of dread rising within him, Broll reconsidered his earlier choice not to fly directly to the town. He drew the idol out again, placing it down by his foot.

But as he raised his arms, he realized that he was not alone. The flapping of wings immediately stirred images of Fandral in pursuit of the errant druid, but what Broll located in the sky was no storm crow, but rather the hazy shape of a hippogryph.

The beast had a rider, too. Although he could not make her out, there was no doubt in his mind that it was Shandris Feathermoon.

The figure was maintaining a low height, flying just above the trees. Indeed, she vanished from his sight before he could signal her. Broll doubted that Shandris was going to land directly in Auberdine; like himself, she would find a place just beyond the town. They were both being overly cautious, but it was a trait that had served Broll well in the past and no doubt had done the same for the general . . . and it made more sense with the odd lack of light.

Broll quickly finished his transformation, then, clutching the figurine, rose up into the air. Like the hippogryph rider, he kept low over the trees. The druid traced the other's path as best he could, but Shandris was nowhere to be seen. That likely meant that she had already landed.

Auberdine was now not that far off. The low-slung, wooden buildings rose like shrouded tombs. At the very least, there should have been bridges and paths illuminated by lamps, but all Broll could make out were the arched outlines of what might have been a pair of the structures.

What's happened in Auberdine? None of the druids at the convocation had mentioned anything amiss and surely at least a few of them had passed through or over the region. If anything had taken place here, then it had done so in the last day or two.

The druid descended. Shifting back into his true form, he secreted the idol, then moved to the outskirts of town. A deathly silence was all that greeted Broll. Indeed, even the woods lacked the cries of nocturnal creatures, not even insects.

Broll touched an oak, hoping to learn something from it, but discovered something unsettling. The tree was asleep and not even the druid's prodding could wake it up. He went to a second tree, this one an ash, and found it the same way.

More disturbed, Broll finally decided to enter the mist-shrouded town. Curiously, the mist *thickened* as he entered. Even the sharp vision of the druid could pierce the veil only a few feet at a time.

The druid sniffed the air. To his relief, there was no hint of rotting flesh. He had feared that some disaster—plague or attack—had taken the population, but, for the moment, that did not seem the case. The wetness of Auberdine's air, due in great part to the nearby sea, should have been enough to cause swift decay of any dead body. Several hundred bodies would have made quite a stench.

The architecture of Auberdine bore the typical curves of night elven culture and in general these would have been some comfort to Broll, but in the mist, the arched buildings began to resemble macabre structures made not of wood, but rather *bone*. Broll even went so far as to touch one just to make certain that some dread metamorphosis had not actually taken place. Yet the wood was wood . . .

Something moved further in. The sound was a brief one and not repeated, but Broll had caught it. Reflexes trained by his calling and honed by his years of fighting immediately enabled the sturdy night elf to leap into hiding behind a building. He did not think that the other had heard him, which gave the druid the advantage.

A brief grunt escaped the mist. It was no sound uttered by a night elf nor any similar race. The sound had a bestial origin. Something very large prowled Auberdine's stone and earthen streets.

Reaching into a pouch, Broll brought out a powder that mildly stung his fingers. Ignoring the irritation, he leaned around the corner.

A huge shape converged on his location. Whatever the beast, it had finally smelled him.

Broll threw the powder directly at it.

The beast let out an angry squawk and leapt up. Broll ducked, hoping that the creature would not land atop him. However, not only did it not fall upon the night elf, but the beast did not even alight on the path behind him.

Instead, it continued skyward, leaping atop one of the nearby buildings. Once there, it perched and began sneezing and growling.

At the same time a silver light ate away the mist surrounding Broll. He whirled to his right.

The light emanated from above, and bathing in its glory was clearly a priestess of Elune. Broll started to tell her to douse the illumination, then saw exactly who it was who approached.

"My lady . . . Tyrande! What're you doing here?"

"Meeting you, though not as I originally planned." Her eyes darted from one shadowed corner to the next, as if she expected other, less desired, companions to join them.

The druid gaped. "You told me it was Shandris who was to meet me! I expected her to come—"

"So did she. This had to be my quest, though . . . and the more I see of this place, the more I know my decision was the right one. If I'd told you then that it would be me, you might have refused and I could not let that happen. My apologies for the subterfuge."

"High Priestess, you shouldn't be here! There's something terribly wrong going on in Auberdine . . ."

She nodded gravely. "Come with me and you will see just how wrong it is."

Above them, the beast—her hippogryph, as Broll had suspected even before he had accosted him—made a low, angry squawk.

Tyrande whispered something to her mount. The hippogryph reluctantly descended, landing near his rider. He kept one baleful eye on the druid.

"What did you do to Jai?" she quietly asked, one hand running over the creature's beaked countenance.

"An herb with stinging properties . . ."

The high priestess briefly smiled. "You were fortunate. I daresay if you had tried that anywhere else, Jai would not have flown *from* but rather *through* you. He knew, though, that I wanted a prisoner if possible. A live one."

As Tyrande continued to pass her hand over the beast's face, Broll commented, "The effects of the herb will pass in a few more moments."

"We do not even have time for that." A faint glow from above emanated over the hippogryph's eyes. Jai shook his head, then seemed much happier. Nodding her satisfaction, the high priestess looked again to the druid. Her expression remained dark. "Come with me. I have something to show you."

With the hippogryph trailing her, Tyrande led Broll to the nearest of the dwellings. She then shocked the druid by entering the domicile without any hesitation, a sign that things were even worse than he had imagined. He was filled with a sense of dread over what they would find inside.

The interior had some of the trappings of a night elven home, but the plant life within looked sick, weak. The mist that covered

Auberdine permeated even inside the dwelling, adding to the feeling of imminent disaster.

Jai, too large to fit through the entrance, peered uneasily inside. Broll watched as Tyrande glanced into the sleeping quarters. Withdrawing, she indicated that Broll should look as well.

With much wariness, the druid complied. His eyes widened at the scene within.

Two night elves—a male and a female—lay on woven mats. The female's arm was draped over the male's chest. They were utterly motionless, which told Broll the worst.

"It is the same in the other places I have looked," his companion solemnly remarked.

The druid wanted to approach the pair but held back out of respect. "Do you know how they perished?"

"They are not dead."

He looked back at her. When Tyrande added nothing more, the druid finally knelt by the two. His eyes widened.

Quiet but steady breathing escaped from both.

"They're . . . asleep?"

"Yes—and I could not awaken the ones I found earlier."

Despite what she said, Broll could not resist gently prodding the male's shoulder. When that failed to wake him, he did the same to the female. As a last attempt, Broll took hold of an arm from each and shook. Backing away, the druid growled, "We must find the source of the spell! There must be some mad mage at work here!"

"It would take a powerful one indeed to do all this," said the high priestess. She indicated the door. "Come with me. I want to show you one more thing."

They left the home, and with Jai in tow, Tyrande led Broll over a bridge that connected to the more commercial areas of Auberdine. The mist kept many of the details of the village hidden, but Broll spotted a sign written in both Darnassian and Common that read, LAST HAVEN TAVERN.

Broll knew that the tavern, of all places, should have been lit and alive. Along with the local inn, the tavern was one of the few public gathering places in the town.

Jai took up a position outside the entrance, the hippogryph peering into the mists in search of any potential foe. The high priestess strode inside without a word, her silence again warning Broll of what was to come.

The tavern was not like the home, which had been in order despite the bizarre scene inside. Chairs were scattered over the wooden floor, and some of the tables had been overturned. The bar at the end was stained not just from years of inebriated patrons, but also from several smashed bottles and barrels.

And all over the tavern lay sprawled the bodies of night elves, a handful of gnomes and humans, and a singular dwarf.

"I landed not far from this area and was disturbed when I saw no life or lights," the high priestess explained. "This was the most immediate public place, and so I entered."

"Are they also . . . asleep?"

Tyrande bent down by one human. He was slumped over a table, and looked as if he had fallen there from sheer exhaustion. His hair and beard were disheveled, but his garments, despite some dust, were clearly of a person of some means. Next to him lay a night elf, a local. Although the night elf lay on his side on the floor, his hands were still stretched forth toward the human. Like the human, the night elf looked oddly unkempt. They were the worst in appearance, though all of the sleepers in the tavern looked as if they had been through some struggle.

"A fight broke out here," Broll decided.

Tyrande stood. "A very polite fight, if that was truly the case. The only bruises I found were caused by their falls. I think these two collapsed." She gestured at the dwarf and a few of the other patrons. "See how these others are positioned?"

After a moment's study, Broll scowled. "They look like they're taking a rest. All of them!"

"They are all asleep now, even this first desperate pair. Look around. The tavern looks as if it was set up for defense."

"I should've seen that myself." Indeed, the druid noted now that the tables and chairs created a wall of sorts that faced both the entrance and the windows. "But a defense from what?"

Tyrande had no answer for him.

Broll squinted. In fact, he had been compelled to squint more often for the past few minutes despite the fact that, with the sun down, his vision should have been sharper. "The mist is getting thicker . . . and darker."

Outside, Jai let out a low warning squawk.

Tyrande and Broll hurried to the entrance. Outside, the hippogryph moved anxiously about. However, there was no sign of anything in the vicinity, as more and more the deepening mist limited the distance that could be seen.

A moan came from inside, and Broll brushed past the high priestess to investigate its source among the slouched figures near the back end of the tavern. Then another moan arose from a different direction. Broll identified it as coming from the night elf near the human. He bent down next to the figure.

Tyrande joined him. "What is it? Is he awake?"

"No . . ." Broll turned the sleeper's head slightly. "I think he's dreaming . . ."

A third moan joined the previous. Suddenly, all around them, the slumbering figures wailed. The hair on the back of Broll's neck stiffened as he detected the thing all the voices had in common: fear. "Not dreams," he corrected himself, rising and glancing back at the entrance. "They're having nightmares. All of them."

Jai again made a warning sound. Returning to the hippogryph, the pair saw nothing . . . but heard much.

There were moans arising from all over Auberdine.

"This is tied to Malfurion," Tyrande stated with utter confidence.

"But how?"

Jai stepped forward, the beast's head cocking to the side, listening.

A murky figure briefly passed into and out of sight. It was shorter than a night elf, more the height of a human. The hippogryph started after it, but Tyrande quietly called his name. The animal paused.

The high priestess took the lead again. Broll quickly moved to her side, ready to use his arts to aid her. Jai kept pace behind them.

"There!" she hissed, pointing to the left.

Broll scarcely had time to view the figure before it again vanished in the fog. "It looks as though it's stumbling. May be a survivor."

"The mist seems to thicken most around our quarry." Tyrande put her hands together. "Perhaps the Mother Moon can remedy that."

From the shrouded sky directly above the high priestess, a silver glow descended in the direction of the mysterious figure. It burned through the fog, revealing everything in its path. Broll's brow rose as he watched the glow veer like a living thing stretching out to find the stranger.

And there he suddenly stood: a male human. His clothing bespoke of better times but he had clearly been put through a long decline of station. He stared back at them with eyes hollow from what seemed to be a lack of sleep. The human was more haggard looking than any of the group they had found in the tavern. Somehow, though, he kept moving.

"By Nordrassil!" blurted Broll.

The human had not only kept moving, but before the eyes of both night elves, he had also just *vanished.*

"A mage," Tyrande snarled. "He is the cause, then, not a victim . . ."

"I don't know, my lady." Broll could explain no further, but there had been something in the manner of the man's disappearance that had felt . . . familiar.

The druid focused on what he had seen. The human had looked at them, then he had started to take a step . . :

"He walked *through* something . . . walked *into* something," Broll muttered to himself. And when it had happened, the druid had sensed . . . what?

"Vanished, walked into or through some portal—what does it matter?" argued Tyrande, her aspect even grimmer. She quickly stepped back to the hippogryph and seized from the side of the saddle her glaive. "He may be the key to Malfurion . . ."

Before Broll could stop her, the high priestess darted toward the spot where the human had stood. Broll could not deny that perhaps the stranger was the culprit, as Tyrande had said, but even he knew that more caution was needed, especially if their quarry was indeed a spellcaster.

Arriving at the human's last location, Tyrande held the glaive ready while murmuring a prayer. The light of Elune surrounded her, then spread for several yards in every direction.

But of the human, there was no sign.

Broll joined her. "Great lady, I—"

She grimaced at him. "I am not Queen Azshara. Please do not call me by such titles as 'great' and such—"

More moans—the fright in them so very distinct—pierced the thick mist as sharply as the light of Elune had.

"We must wake them somehow!" Broll growled. "There must be some way . . ."

Jai let out a warning. Suspecting that the human had reappeared, both night elves turned at the sound—

And there, obscured by the mysterious fog, several figures lurched toward them as the mist carried forth a haunting, collective moan.

Broll experienced a rising anxiety. He suddenly felt the need to run or cower. He wanted to roll into a ball and pray that the shadowy figures would not hurt him. A nervous sweat covered the druid.

What's happening to me? he managed to ask himself. Broll was not prone to fear, but the urge to surrender was powerful. He looked to Tyrande and saw that the hand in which she held the glaive was shaking, and not due to the weapon's weight. The high priestess's mouth was set tight. Even Jai revealed hints of stress, the powerful hippogryph's breathing growing more and more rapid.

Tyrande looked to the left. "They are over there, too!"

"And to our right," Broll added. "If we look behind us, I'll wager they'll be there as well."

"I will not be sent to my knees crying like some frightened child!" Tyrande abruptly declared to the half-seen shapes. Her hands shook harder despite her words and served to fuel Broll's own swelling anxiety.

From above the high priestess emanated a silver light that wrapped over both night elves and the hippogryph. It spread toward the shadows, illuminating the first staggering shape.

And in the moonlit glow, they beheld a thing that was rotted and decayed. It stared with blank, unseeing eyes and a face twisted in pain even in undeath—a face that Broll suddenly registered as identical to the night elf lying on the tavern floor.

But if the face was that of the sleeper, the form was not. Rather, it was the shadowy outline of a thing Broll hoped never to see again. The night elf wore in body the semblance of a demon of the Burning Legion.

As the mob closed in, a second being was revealed, bearing the tormented face of the human, but his form, too, was otherwise that of a demon.

"They've—" Broll muttered to himself. "They've returned . . ."

"No . . . it cannot be them!" Tyrande murmured. "No satyrs . . . please . . . no satyrs . . ."

The two night elves remained frozen. They wanted to defend themselves, but the monstrous figures converging on them had left the pair with minds in such turmoil that their bodies were paralyzed.

At that moment a new figure stepped out right in front of the druid and his companions—the ragged human they had been chasing. He stumbled toward them, his eyes looking past.

Broll blinked his eyes, trying to adjust them, but it seemed the mist had thickened—or had his eyes gone out of focus? The fiendish forms with the faces of Auberdine's unfortunate inhabitants were once again simply murky shapes. Suddenly, the druid had the sensation of being near to the ground . . . and, feeling around with his hands, discovered he was on his knees. He realized then that he had been dreaming; that the demons he had seen had existed only in his subconscious.

"By the Mother Moon!" he heard Tyrande growl, but only as a faint echo. "What—?"

The hollow-eyed human who had stepped out of nothing finally spoke through the unnatural darkness. "Don't fall asleep again . . . Don't sleep . . ." he whispered. Broll felt an arm drape over his shoulder and then he and Tyrande, kneeling alongside one another, were held together weakly by the haggard human who crouched behind them.

The world faded. It did not vanish. It *faded,* as if it were more memory than substance.

And, in addition, it took on a deep green hue.

There was no Auberdine. Merely a landscape barely seen. Broll tried to focus his thoughts enough to comprehend where they were, but then the landscape shifted as if they were racing along it at a pace impossible for any mortal creature.

Just as suddenly, their new surroundings lost their greenish hue. Distinct features popped up all around them. It was again night and though there was mist, it was not nearly so thick as in Auberdine.

Broll discovered he was moving. This revelation made him react by trying to control his movement when apparently he should not have done so. The druid fell forward.

The ground was hard but, fortunately, covered by some vegetation. Broll managed to land on one knee. Next to him, Tyrande had better fortune, continuing on for several steps until able to control her own actions.

It was the high priestess who first managed to speak. On legs that were clearly unsteady but able to hold her, she surveyed their surroundings. "Where—where are we? This is not Auberdine!"

It was not Auberdine and, at first glance, it was nowhere with which the druid was familiar. He shook his head, trying to better focus. Some things that had just happened were beginning to make sense . . . not the sense he desired, though.

"Not Auberdine . . ." rasped the cause of their confusion. The bedraggled human stumbled by Broll. He looked from the druid to the high priestess, his expression beseeching. "You woke me enough for that . . . I managed to walk . . ."

Rising, Broll took hold of the man by the arm. While the stranger in no physical manner reminded him of Varian Wrynn, his distress stirred the night elf's memories of his friend. Whatever this human suffered, it was at least as terrible as Varian's long loss of memory.

"What did you do?" Broll asked. "Did you really take us through—"

The stranger pressed against him, the eyes burning into Broll's. "I'm so tired! I can't stay awake! Please don't let me sleep—" He let out a guttural sound, then collapsed unconscious against the night elf.

Taken by surprise, Broll had to quickly adjust his hold. He gently lowered the human to the ground.

"We need to wake him up!" Tyrande declared. "You heard what he said! You saw Auberdine!"

Broll peered closely at their new companion. "We couldn't wake him now even with both our abilities combined. He's deep asleep."

"He is our only clue to Malfurion!" The high priestess reached down as if to shake the human, then hesitated. Her expression suddenly calmed. "Forgive me . . ."

"There's nothing to forgive." Broll looked over the man. "He wears an outfit that once saw courts, but other than that, there's nothing I can identify."

"He seems a most unlikely mage to me."

The druid nodded. "That I'll agree . . . and no mage could've done what he did." The former gladiator snorted. "No human or dwarf and not even many night elves, for that matter . . . unless I'm powerfully mistaken what just happened to us."

She frowned. "What else could it have been but magic? Odd magic, but certainly that! He took all of us—" Tyrande paused. "Not Jai . . ."

Broll had already considered the hippogryph. "He sleeps, my lady. Jai is part of Auberdine now."

The high priestess looked sad. "Poor creature . . . so many poor creatures . . ." Steeling herself, she asked, "And what of this one, then? If not a magic spell, then how did he take us out of Auberdine and deposit us here?"

"There's only one way." Broll's tone could not hide his own disbelief at what he was saying. "I think . . . I think that for perhaps a single moment . . . he took us into and out of the *Emerald Dream*."

8

LUCAN

Something different moved near Malfurion's enshrouded location, something both familiar . . . and not.

The archdruid wondered what new torture the Nightmare Lord intended now. The agony of his continual transformation still assailed him, but Malfurion had managed to keep that one part of his mind shielded off from it. He knew that his captor was aware of this and sought to break down that shield and so expected that this was to be the next effort.

Malfurion was not certain of his own ability to hold off anymore. To do what he had done and still suffer his torments had taken so very, very much out of him. The Nightmare Lord knew well how to torture him, striking through just who and what the archdruid loved or feared the most.

The shape was huge, though not so much as the shadow of a gigantic tree that was all Malfurion knew of his foe. The new shape moved with a confidence and sinuousness that disturbed the night elf. He wished that the thick, unsettling mist surrounding his tiny prison would just for a moment disperse so that he could see the thing better and understand what new evil it brought with it.

I am here . . . came a voice in his head. However, it was not the Nightmare Lord, but rather the new shape. Nor was it talking to Malfurion; he simply heard it as it reached out to another.

And that other came forth. The shadow of the tree bent over

Malfurion's own twisted form, the Nightmare Lord's branches reaching like tendrils toward the newcomer.

There was silence. Malfurion realized that his captor spoke to the shape, but unlike the latter, the Nightmare Lord kept his desires hidden from his prisoner. The night elf wondered why that was necessary.

The new shadow let out a mocking laugh. *Yes . . . it shall be done so . . . what a jest it will be . . .*

The archdruid would have frowned if he could. This was not a new torture for him—at least not directly. Rather, his tormentor had some task for this other shadow.

Understanding that brought resolve to Malfurion. He let his pain focus his powers. He was still in the Emerald Dream—or Nightmare now—and although his efforts thus far to pierce the mist and see how the realm had been changed by the evil that had swept over it had failed, perhaps . . . perhaps Malfurion could manage enough for something more focused.

The veil would not part. The shape continued to be nothing more than that. Still, the archdruid concentrated, using the same methods needed to peer into oneself for the meditation that preceded the dreamform leaving the body. Sensing all there was to this unsettling visitor became Malfurion's all. He had tried this with the Nightmare Lord and failed, but if they did not expect him to try again on the newcomer . . .

Too curious a vermin you are!

Malfurion's mind was struck by a mental force so great it momentarily stunned him. That had the curious effect of lessening his agony—if but for a second.

I go . . . the shape said to the night elf's unheard tormentor. The archdruid managed to refocus enough to see the shape dwindle in the thick mist.

The shadow tree that was the Nightmare Lord's presence here now twisted back to loom over Malfurion. *Too much spirit still, but not for long . . . so much effort costs, does it not? How fares your mortal cloak, my friend?*

The night elf understood immediately. He felt the weakness that originated not from his dreamform but his actual *body* increase. His attempt to learn more had cost him valuable power.

The shadow branches draped over his eyes, almost as if they desired to pluck them out. Yet Malfurion was aware that his eyes were perhaps the safest part of his dreamform. The evil that held him wanted him to see, even if there was nothing to see . . . or perhaps *because* there was nothing.

You wish to see? Why you only had to ask, my friend . . . it is the least I can do for one who gives so much to our desires . . .

The branches stretched forward, separating into two sets that in turn acted as monstrous hands that *pushed away* the mist . . . revealing for the first time what the emerald realm had become.

Malfurion would have screamed if he could, albeit not because of pain.

The branches receded. The mist closed about the trapped archdruid once more.

The mocking voice filled his head. The glee in it was like daggers that constantly thrust at the night elf's mind. *And we are indebted to you for so much of this, Malfurion Stormrage . . . so much . . .*

The shadow tree vanished. The voice stilled. For the moment Malfurion was being left to dwell on the horror that he had seen. It was but the latest torture designed to break that part of him that had not yet surrendered.

But what his captor did not know was that the night elf had also learned something that he desired to know. Two significant things, in fact. One was the identity of the Nightmare Lord's servant. The answer should have been obvious, but due to Malfurion's constant suffering, it had taken the creature's own abrupt anger to reveal him.

A green dragon indeed served the evil . . . but not just any green dragon . . . He prayed that Ysera knew, lest she be caught by surprise. If the mistress of the Emerald Dream was captured, then all was truly lost.

And the second thing, which had come with the unveiling of Malfurion's true surroundings, served to verify a choice that the archdruid had made long ago.

If there was a chance at all of him saving Ysera and the Emerald Dream, then Malfurion would have to die.

Despite what they had seen, despite what that potentially meant for them, Tyrande and Broll knew that they also had to sleep. The shocking struggle in Auberdine had taken more out of them than they had realized.

They had no idea as to where they were in conjunction to either Auberdine or Ashenvale, but the druid had told her that he thought that they were closer to their goal. Unfortunately, she was now without Jai, which meant that they could not fly. As powerful as Broll's storm crow form was, it could not carry her and their intriguing companion.

Tyrande continued to study the slumbering human. He appeared a harmless figure and she sensed no overwhelming magical presence around him, even though, as not only high priestess of Elune but one who had through the centuries studied the various magics, she should have noticed *something*. There *was* that about him that bespoke of some kind of magic, but it was very subtle, almost as if an inherent part of his most basic being and not enhanced by any study of the mystical arts.

She glanced at the heavens, which were going from gray to black. A day had passed, a precious one lost as they waited for the human to wake up. Though he muttered in his sleep, he did not act like the townsfolk. His nightmares might be vivid, but they had not come to life.

Recalling Auberdine again, the high priestess shuddered. She and Broll had come close to falling victim just as poor Jai had. Tyrande relived the nightmares she had suffered—hellish, grinning satyrs come to take her to their master—and gave thanks that the human had come when he had. Broll had told her of his own monsters, in his case ghastly demons of the Burning Legion. For both night elves, the creatures had worn horrific parodies of the sleeping inhabitants of Auberdine.

Not for the first time, Tyrande wanted to shake their new companion until he woke. Malfurion slipped closer and closer to oblivion—or worse—with each passing day. However, she and the druid had come to agree that there was no use in attempting such a futile act again. The human had remained unconscious even despite their initial harsh efforts; it seemed he would not wake until *he* chose to wake.

But I will not lose him again! Tyrande insisted, her expression tightening. *I will not lose him even if it is his own fault that he's come to these straits—*

A sense of shame washed over her even as she thought that. Malfurion had gone in search of a possible threat. He had had the best interests of not only the druids, but all Azeroth when he had gone . . . just like so many times before—

Tyrande shook her head, trying to clear it of her regrets. She gave thanks when she heard Broll stir.

He did not notice her expression shift, his attention first on the human. "Still sleeping, I see."

"I have my doubts that he will awaken."

"Me, too. He doesn't act like the others, but to sleep the day through after half the night before that . . ."

The high priestess toyed with her glaive. She was glad that she had taken it from Jai's saddle. If she had not, the weapon would have been left behind in Auberdine. While Tyrande carried within her the gifts of the Mother Moon, they did not make her invincible. The glaive was a sturdy and necessary weapon. "Do we leave him here? I dislike doing that, considering how he helped us."

"I'm of the same mind. Still, we need to reach Ashenvale and while I could carry him for a time, he'll slow us down even more."

She finally said to him what she had been considering for most of her time awake. "You should go on alone. You planned to do that when first I suggested Ashenvale."

Broll looked aghast. "I wouldn't abandon you here! Especially after Auberdine! We proceed to Ashenvale together"—he thrust a thick thumb at the human—"and hopefully with this one in tow . . ."

"Then what do we do?"

The druid looked guilty. "Something I planned to do beyond

Auberdine, anyway." From his cloak, he produced what he had taken from Fandral's dwelling. "It's time I tried to bring some worthiness to my theft, if that's possible."

She could not believe what she was seeing. "Is that—is that the Idol of Remulos?"

"Yes."

"I had heard that you passed that on to Archdruid Fandral's keeping—"

"And now I've borrowed it." His expression asked her not to pursue that matter further. When Tyrande nodded, Broll, appearing no more relieved, added, "It may be our best hope if we're to make successful use of the portal."

"How so?"

"Remulos said it was linked to a green dragon of great power. The Aspect Ysera would not tell him which when she added her influence in its crafting. He suspects the identity, as do I, having faced it briefly when seeking to cleanse the idol of its corruption. Though I didn't know the name, I felt its great power. It should be one of her consorts."

Which meant to the high priestess a dragon with knowledge and might comparable to few. Tyrande understood Broll's reasoning. "You think you can contact him through the figurine?"

"It was worth my honor to hope that, yes."

She did not like the sound of that. "What will Fandral do when he finds out you removed this from his sanctum?"

Broll shrugged. "I've no idea, but if I survive all this, I'll find out then."

Tyrande studied the figurine, praying that it would be worth the price for the druid . . . and for them. "What do you hope to do . . . and can I help in any way?"

"There's nothing you can help with. I've got to do this myself." Broll set the figurine down on the ground in front of him, then sat with legs crossed. The eyes of the dragon stared directly into the druid's. "I'm trying something different. Don't want to use the idol itself . . ." He suddenly choked up. "Never thought I'd have to see the damned thing again, for that matter . . ."

The high priestess said nothing, aware of the pain involved in Broll's previous encounter with the figurine. She knew the agony he had suffered when, weakened, he could not save his daughter from the idol's twisted forces. He was speaking more to himself than her.

Facing his palms toward the idol, Broll began muttering. The idol was still bound to the dragon, wherever he was. The druid hoped to tie into that link and touch the dragon's mind. Tyrande knew exactly why. The green dragon might be able to give them a clue to what was happening, but, more important, it was possible that he might be able to assist them in passing through into the Emerald Dream. Once, the idol itself had been able to do that—Broll had used it so, where there he had battled his own rage in the manifestation of his bear form. But that had been before the Nightmare had made even the untouched places difficult to reach. Certainly, having one of that realm's guardians at their side would increase their chances of not only survival, but success.

A faint hint of emerald light softly bathed the idol and as it did, a faded stream of energies rose from the figurine.

The magic linking the idol to the mysterious dragon.

Her attention was suddenly taken by Broll, around whom another faint glow of a more forest green now arose. Curiously, it did not emanate from him, but rather had arisen from the grassy soil upon which he sat. As a druid, Broll received much of his power through the flora and fauna of Azeroth and for the first time, Tyrande was seeing it so. There was also power within him—she was well aware of that from Malfurion—but this was an aspect of her beloved's calling that she had not really considered. In some ways it was akin to her calling upon the Mother Moon.

Perhaps Malfurion and I are not so different even there, the high priestess thought. *And perhaps that is why we have been pushed apart so much . . .*

It was a reminder of what she should have known so well, having experienced the teachings of Cenarius and having fought beside her beloved and other druids. Azeroth was so much a part of a druid; it touched them constantly. Malfurion, so attuned, surely felt everything much, much more than Broll.

He can no more turn from his calling than I can from mine . . . yet those callings intersect just as our lives do . . . if we survive this . . . we will learn how to make both intertwine . . . and learn how to finally be together . . .

If we survive . . .

The forest green then began to expand to the magical stream that reached through the plane of Azeroth to wherever the dragon currently lurked. Yet barely had it begun when it seemed to falter. There was resistance.

Broll muttered something.

The resistance lessened.

"No! You mustn't!"

The human was in their midst, as wild-eyed as ever. He was half on his knees, desperately reaching for the idol.

As he closed on it, Tyrande saw around him a landscape that was and was not where the trio was situated. Part of it seemed so simple.

The other part—

The high priestess kicked out. However, it was not the human who was her target, but rather the Idol of Remulos.

The dragon figurine went flying. It bounced against a rise, then landed atop a small rock.

Broll, his spell shattered, peered at the pair with a combination of frustration and confusion. "What by the World Tree are you doing?" he demanded of Tyrande. The druid leapt to his feet and seized the human by the scruff of the neck. "What mischief are you about? What sort of trick have you played on her?"

The man's mouth moved, but no sounds escaped it. The images Tyrande had seen around him had faded, and despite her best attempts to sear them in her memory, they vanished into oblivion . . . just as dreams both light and dark tended to do.

But she recalled one thing. Jumping to Broll's side, she kept him from further frightening the disheveled human. "Leave him be! He was trying to help us!"

"Help us? He tricked you into breaking the spell just when it was starting to work!" Yet clearly respecting her opinion, Broll still loosened his hold.

"Wasn't working, wasn't working," the man babbled, his eyes looking past them. "Only working for them, bringing them . . ."

"Who?" Tyrande asked, putting a calming hand on his shoulder.

Some focus finally came to his gaze. He glanced at her. "I . . . I don't know . . . *them* . . . the nightmares . . ." The man looked down. "I slept . . . I can't sleep . . . don't sleep . . ."

"Who are you?" Broll asked, his tone much kinder. "What name do you have?"

"Name?" For a moment the focus vanished. Blinking, their companion seemed to pull himself together a bit. "Lucan . . . Lucan Foxblood . . ." Some vestigial pride made him straighten. "Third assistant cartographer to His Majesty, King Varian! On a mapping mission to—to—" His expression became that of a lost child. "I don't remember that, anymore . . ."

"Do not concern yourself about that," Tyrande quietly urged. "Tell us. How did you know that what we did risked danger?"

"I—I just did. It—it has to do with that place in my dreams . . . I felt them . . . I felt something near . . ."

Broll retrieved the figurine. "Might've just been the one we were trying to reach."

Although this made sense, Tyrande still recalled how she had felt after viewing whatever it was she had seen behind Lucan Foxblood. "No . . . he has the right of it, Broll. There was something sinister approaching us. That's why I did what I had to. I trust his word in this . . ."

Lucan looked at her as if she had just saved his head from the ax. "Thank you, glorious lady! Thank you!"

"Calm yourself, Lucan. You are among friends . . . and do not thank me. Your instinctive reaction may have saved us."

"You really think so?" the druid asked, still eyeing the statuette. "Maybe so . . . maybe so . . ." He set the statuette down. "In that case, there's one thing left to do." Broll looked to Lucan. "Do you know where we are?"

"No . . . no . . . I just kept going . . . I just kept going . . ."

"As I thought." Broll stepped back. To Tyrande, he said, "Didn't tell you before, but while you slept I took a brief fly up. Didn't recognize where we were, but thought if I tried once more, we might have a better idea of what to do next."

Tyrande was not bothered by the revelation, aware that Broll would not have endangered her and Lucan. She nodded agreement to his new plan. "What of the idol?"

He shrugged. "What of it? We don't use the damned thing, it won't be dangerous. It can sit there until I return."

Spreading his arms, he took on his storm crow form. Lucan gasped and stumbled back to Tyrande, who felt some guilt. She and Broll were far more versed in magic than most humans.

"It's nothing," she told Lucan. "Nothing to worry about."

"My—my cousin took up the calling . . . wizardry, I mean," Lucan muttered, almost sounding pleased at remembering. Then his frown returned. "He's dead now."

As so many are, the high priestess thought, recalling the lives lost in the last struggle. *And now . . . what comes to wreak havoc on Azeroth this time?*

Broll took to the air, diverting her musings. She and Lucan watched with admiration as the huge bird soared up into the sky. Tyrande envied this particular skill of Malfurion's calling. To *fly* like that . . .

Yet hardly had the storm crow reached a respectable height than he immediately dove back toward his companions. Lucan simply stared, perhaps not understanding, but Tyrande knew that Broll would not have returned so quickly if not for news of import.

She grabbed the idol before Broll reached them, certain for some reason that they would need to move. The druid's countenance when he changed back was verification that her notion was at the very least close to the truth.

"Did you find out where we are?" Lucan innocently asked.

"What did you see?" Tyrande interjected. "Are we somewhere near the Horde's territory?"

"The Horde's the least of our troubles," Broll growled. "We need to find cover and quick . . ."

He seized Lucan by the arm and started to drag him toward one of the hillier areas. Tyrande kept pace at the druid's side, the idol tucked under her arm.

"What is it? More of those nightmarish creatures, like in Auberdine?"

Broll snorted. "No . . . just possibly a bigger nightmare." He jutted a finger toward the sky to the east. "We've got a dragon out there . . . and it's black."

Thura eyed the strangers from a hilltop further to their west. Two night elves and a human. Two males and a female. She discounted the human immediately, for despite seeming in the prime of his life, he hardly looked the warrior. The two night elves, on the other hand, appeared to be more worthy opponents. The male was likely a druid. Thura respected the power of those who drew from nature.

The female most intrigued the orc, for she had always had the desire to compare her skills to those of her gender from the other races. The night elf moved with impressive grace and the glaive she carried was one that required strength and long training. Thura naturally trusted to her ax but wondered how the fight would have gone otherwise.

But the reality of her situation quickly erased such idle curiosity. What mattered was that these three were here. Here when she was. They were tied somehow to her quest, the most obvious reason having to do with the two night elves. Her prey was one. These were likely comrades from battle. The female might even be his mate.

The orc's broad mouth split into a wide, grim smile. *They are why I am here*, she decided. *They will lead me to him . . . they will lead me to this Malfurion . . . this betrayer of comrades and destroyer of life . . .*

She had seen the druid perform great magic, becoming a bird that could fly high. Even more than the female, he would have to die quickly when it came to fighting them. He looked to be powerful, though clearly not as much as the murderous druid in her dreams. Still, he would be good practice for the duel with her true foe.

Then Thura saw why the druid had flown for so short a time. The great dark form rising into the sky was the one that she had seen only as shadow before. Now it was flying toward the area where the trio had been, and though they were fleet of foot, even the human, they were surely doomed. The orc cursed, realizing that the best clue to her prey's whereabouts was going to be eaten.

Then, an astounding thing happened.

The dragon's prey simply became *nothing*. One minute they were running and the next they were gone. Only a momentary hint of some greenish illumination gave her any sort of answer. She assumed that one of the night elves had cast some sort of spell taking the trio far away.

Yet what surprised her more was when she looked again to the dragon. The great leviathan immediately turned, then, wings beating hard, left the vicinity. There had been no hesitation; the dragon had departed with all haste.

And most curious to Thura was that, though the darkness had not given her a perfect view of the departing behemoth . . . she would have sworn that the dragon had fled in sudden *fear*.

9

To Pursue a Dragon

The druids were weary. They had given of themselves as much as any living being could, and though Fandral told them that their efforts were not in vain, still it was difficult for many to believe that. Teldrassil looked no different . . . and, indeed, to Hamuul Runetotem, there was something about the World Tree that now bothered him more.

Worse, his concern was compounded by Fandral's sudden curiosity as to Broll's absence. With so many gathered and so much urgency, the disappearance had managed to go unnoticed until after the casting. Now, though, the lead archdruid seemed to be making a particular point about it.

Hamuul had promised to look for Broll, but that had mainly been to assuage Fandral. Unfortunately, there was only so much Hamuul could do in regards to a promise that he knew—with much guilt— had no hope of being fulfilled.

He had tried to stay far from the convocation, but knew that his own absence would eventually be noticed as well. Hoping to avoid further questions, he kept to the edges of the group, moving here and there as if still seeking.

Hamuul edged his way to Naralex. Although as exhausted as the rest, the night elf stood observing a single seed in his hand. As the tauren neared, Naralex gently waved his other hand over the seed, at the same time murmuring as if to an infant.

The seed burst open. A tiny tendril rose out of it. When it grew to more than four inches, Naralex shifted his free hand to the left. The shoot arched in that direction.

The night elf made a curving motion to the right. Retaining the arch to the left, the new plant now grew to the indicated direction.

"This is what we're meant to be," Naralex solemnly stated to Hamuul. "Nurturers of life. Gardeners of paradise . . ."

"If Azeroth were perfect, yes," agreed the tauren, "but it is not."

"No . . . it isn't." Bending, Naralex set the seed on the ground. He drew a circle around the seed.

The ground within the circle churned. The seed sank down until only the shoot remained.

Naralex tidied the area around the plant, then turned his attention to Hamuul. "And have you found our brother Broll?"

The tauren fought to keep his nostrils from flaring. "I am still searching for him."

The night elf's eyes narrowed. "We both know that he never returned with us, brother Hamuul."

Hamuul neither confirmed nor denied it. "I promised Archdruid Fandral Staghelm that I would look for Broll. I must continue."

In what under some circumstance might have proven a dangerous act, Naralex thrust a hand out to stop the departing tauren. "Archdruid Fandral's moved on to other things. He's not even here at the moment, brother Hamuul."

"Not here?" Again, the tauren sought to hide any wariness.

"While you were . . . elsewhere . . . he suggested that we all do what we can to cleanse our thoughts so that when he returned, we could begin anew with another spell for Teldrassil."

"And where has he gone in the meantime?"

Naralex gazed up . . . and up. "The enclave, naturally. He said he's seeking guidance in the seclusion of his sanctum there."

Hamuul snorted before he could stop himself. He had his suspicions as to where Broll Bearmantle had flown, though exactly what the night elf had intended then was a matter of conjecture. The tauren could imagine one thing in particular, but Broll would not have been so audacious . . . would he?

Naralex lowered his arm. "I thought you'd like to know. Do you think that perhaps our brother Broll might have had a similar thought . . . seeking guidance in the enclave, I mean?"

Fully recovered, Hamuul replied, "I doubt that Broll Bearmantle will be found up there."

The night elf nodded ever so slightly. "I thought as much, also. I'm glad we're in agreement."

Leaving Naralex, Hamuul pondered matters. Naralex had been trying to give him a warning, in case there was some reason that Broll would be up in the enclave. The night elf had likely wondered why Broll would not have returned for the convocation and came up with what he believed the most likely answer.

And that meant that Fandral had probably done the same.

Frowning, the tauren bent back to look up in the direction of unseen Darnassus. He hoped he was correct in one thing, that Broll Bearmantle was *not* up in the enclave. In truth, the only reason he would have gone there would have been to seek something in Archdruid Fandral's sanctum. Hamuul feared that it would turn out to be the Idol of Remulos. The tauren knew of no other thing that Broll would have thought of to use. After all, it was tied to the Emerald Dream, where Archdruid Malfurion Stormrage's dreamform had gone missing.

And it was also bound to the one method that someone as impetuous as Broll might use to find their missing shan'do.

He would not . . . Broll would not risk that . . .

Hamuul blinked. Yes. Broll would.

A shadow passed over him. Turning, he saw a huge storm crow descending. It could only be Fandral returning, the lead archdruid this time choosing the swiftness of the avian form to the more artful entrance he had utilized at the beginning of the convocation.

As the storm crow alighted, it transformed. Wings became arms, legs grew. Talons became feet. Feathers flew away or became hair and garments. The beak receded, turning into a mouth and nose . . .

Fandral once more himself, straightened. Among all the druids assembled, his eyes fixed upon distant Hamuul.

Grave disappointment filled the night elf's gaze. It was all Hamuul needed to see to understand that Fandral knew *everything* Broll had done.

The tauren prayed that his friend knew what he was doing.

They had shifted again. Broll knew it, even though once more he had been unable to focus long on the place through which they had moved. He was certain that it had been the Emerald Dream . . . but then why were his memories of those moments as hazy as the mist enshrouding Auberdine?

And, more important, how was a human—a *human!*—able to physically cross into the mystic realm almost without realizing it?

There was, however, no time at present to seek such answers from Lucan Foxblood. The three were still on the move, for Lucan's sudden action had taken them not farther from the dragon . . . but rather nearly *underneath* it.

"Get down!" Tyrande whispered.

The shadow swooped past them as if racing the wind itself. The gust it in turn created nearly accomplished the high priestess's suggestion. The trio were buffeted to their knees.

Yet . . . the dragon did not turn. It did not bank and drop upon them. Instead, it dove deep into the hills just beyond their position . . . and did not rise up again.

Broll was the first to voice what the others also surely thought. "At that speed, it should have either come up or crashed . . ."

"What is a black dragon doing here?" Tyrande asked. "Wherever here might be . . ."

"It wasn't black."

The night elves looked to Lucan. Still very wild-eyed, he repeated himself. "It . . . it wasn't black . . . it was green . . ."

"A color-blind human," Broll grunted.

"If he were color-blind, he would not be seeing green instead of black," the high priestess pointed out. Her tone reassuring, she said to Lucan, "Tell us why you say the dragon was green."

He shrugged. "It was near enough to see."

The druid shook his head. "Well, that's an answer. Not the right one, since we were just as close to see it and it was *black*."

Tyrande studied the human. Finally, "Yet an answer I sense with some grain of potential truth, Broll . . . at least as Lucan knows it." She checked her glaive. "I think we should investigate this dragon who might be black, might be green. There could be a reason we ended up so near it."

"And if it turns out to be a black dragon?"

She started in the last direction that they had seen the beast fly. Tyrande readied the glaive for tossing. "Then, we kill it."

Lucan looked to Broll as if hoping he would tell the man that she did not mean what she said. Instead, the druid gripped the cartographer by the arm and led him after, saying, "You're better with us than not . . ."

Lucan did not look at all convinced.

They wended their way over the hills, moving as quickly as Lucan's presence permitted. He was not slow, but he was neither in optimal health nor a night elf. Still, he kept pace better than Broll would have expected, considering all the human had been through.

They paused only once, when Broll felt an itch on his neck. He looked behind them.

"What is it?" Tyrande quietly asked.

"Thought someone was following us . . . but I'm wrong."

A short while later the high priestess called a halt. Lucan took the moment to catch his breath while the night elves conferred.

"If the dragon landed . . . it must be very near here," Tyrande remarked.

"Agreed. We've seen a few caves, but nothing large enough for such a huge creature . . . and this one's bigger than many, no matter what its color might be."

"Yet we never saw it in the air and the landscape, while hilly, would also force the dragon out in the open if it tried to crawl along."

Broll considered. "Maybe there's something to what Lucan said after all. If the dragon's—"

Tyrande stared after him. "Where *is* Lucan?"

The druid spun around. The human was no longer where he had just left him.

For a moment the night elves looked at one another as if thinking the same . . . that Lucan had once more drifted off into what Broll suspected was part of the Emerald Dream. Then, a brief clatter of rocks beyond them told the pair of a simpler truth. Lucan had merely stepped away.

Or rather . . . he was climbing up the side of the hill at a pace impressive considering his exhaustion.

"Lucan!" the druid called as cautiously as he could. "Lucan!"

But the cartographer ignored him. Broll finally went in pursuit, Tyrande only a step behind. This near a possible dragon's lair, they could ill afford being given away.

Lucan pushed himself to the top of the hill. Broll managed to grab him by the ankle just before the human would have started down the other side. The druid pulled himself up next to the other.

"Have you gone mad—?" Broll thought for a moment that he already had his answer, for Lucan stared at him as if what remained of his sense had abandoned him once more.

"It's down there," Lucan finally murmured. He pointed at one of a handful of caves marking the area below. "That one with the sharp point to the entrance. That's where the dragon is."

"And how do you know this?"

In answer, Lucan could only shrug.

Tyrande joined the two males. "Did I hear him correctly? The dragon is down there?"

"He's sure about that, if nothing else." A sound caught Broll's attention. He eyed the path from which they had come. "There *is* something or someone behind us . . ."

"Never mind! Lucan is moving again!"

Broll turned to see that with the druid no longer holding him and both night elves distracted, the man was indeed heading down the other side of the hill. Aware that they left some pursuer on their trail, Broll nevertheless leapt down after Lucan.

He managed to catch up with the cartographer near the base. Spinning Lucan to face him, Broll was confronted by the same almost blank look.

"Do you wish to die?" he asked the human.

"No . . ." Lucan seemed to finally register where he was. His face grew even paler. "I just . . . I just went where I had to."

Giving up the hope of making sense of his companion, Broll started to tug Lucan back to Tyrande, who was just behind them.

A low, mournful reptilian hiss escaped the cave.

The three stood frozen. The high priestess took a step toward the cave.

"There must be another entrance!" she muttered. "That's far too small for a dragon."

Broll grimaced at what he was thinking. "Then . . . it's a good entrance for us!"

Tyrande nodded. Lucan swallowed and said nothing.

Concerned for the human, who was certainly no experienced fighter like Varian Wrynn, Broll said, "There are some large rocks over there. You can hide among them. If we don't return in roughly an hour's time, keep heading on the path we're taking. I think I do know vaguely where we are and it's closer to Ashenvale than I thought."

To both night elves' surprise, Lucan steeled himself and replied, "No. I come with you. You helped me . . . and I brought you here."

There was no time to discuss it. Broll nodded. Tyrande pulled a dagger from her belt and handed it to Lucan. He took it, though he clearly understood its uselessness against a dragon. Still, the weapon gave some comfort . . . and it was probable that the human knew that he could also use it on himself if it came down to it.

Broll sought to take the lead, but Tyrande had already moved ahead. She looked almost eager to confront the dragon, as if that would somehow bring Malfurion back to her.

Or bring her to him if they both die? the druid wondered with some sudden worry.

Tyrande held the glaive ready to throw as she entered the mouth. The cave was dark, but while that might have bothered Lucan, it did not concern either night elf. Still, the high priestess cast a tiny glow, perhaps for the human's sake or perhaps to attract the dragon's attention.

"Stay close," Broll reminded the cartographer. He did not doubt that Lucan intended to, but with the man's habit of wandering, it was good to remind him.

The cave twisted from one side to the next and grew narrower as they entered. It was now barely large enough for two of them to walk side by side. That a dragon lurked somewhere ahead meant that there *had* to be another entrance. That was something to remember, if this one became blocked to them.

Of course, that other entrance would also enable the dragon to give chase.

The cave grew cooler. Black dragons tended to prefer more warm abodes, which added merit to Lucan's suggestion that Broll had been mistaken. Yet the druid and the high priestess had both seen an ebony creature. If not a black dragon, then why would one of any other color masquerade as such?

Broll abruptly recalled something that their current dire circumstances had pushed to the back of his memory. Once, in the past, he had faced the dire daughter of the great black dragon Deathwing. Onyxia had been a monster herself, but what Broll now remembered was that she had been able to transform to other forms . . . including much *smaller* ones.

He touched Tyrande on the shoulder. The high priestess silently turned.

"Beware," Broll whispered. "These tunnels may be large enough for the dragon after all."

Her eyes narrowed. Tyrande Whisperwind, too, was aware of this particular draconic ability, even more so than Broll, who did not know of her ties to the red dragon Korialstrasz. "Yes," she muttered. "We must be very wary . . ."

There came a sound, a slight movement, from deeper within. The three immediately tensed. Broll kept Lucan behind Tyrande and him. The high priestess pushed forward before Broll could keep her back.

Only a few yards farther they came to a larger chamber riddled with gaps large enough to mean passages. The chamber was perhaps ten times the druid's height, and the rough edges revealed paths—some of them precarious—that could be used to reach many of the possible passages.

But more important . . . among the stalagmites that dotted the chamber floor, Broll saw prints. He knelt down to investigate them.

"They look to be from one of our own," the druid commented to Tyrande, "or maybe one of Lucan's. They're on top of one another, too. Whoever they belong to has tread this area often."

"I feel a draft," she commented. She lowered the glaive. "There's at least one other entrance nearby."

"Do we search for it?"

"Which way do the footprints most head?"

He studied them closer, finally pointing to his right. "That way . . ."

As Broll rose, Lucan blinked, then started to speak to Tyrande. Sensing this, the high priestess slipped her free hand to his wrist and gently squeezed.

"The direction of the air current matches up with what you say," the high priestess remarked, releasing the human's wrist. "We can either follow them or—"

Tyrande cut off, her expression suddenly focused.

The light of Elune bathed the chamber.

And in its light was revealed a figure invisible to them until now, but whom Lucan had evidently sensed with that peculiar talent of his. Tyrande had realized what he was about to say and silenced him in order to surprise the watcher.

He was clad in a long, hooded garment that resembled a combination of a mage's outfit and that of some human priests. The figure stood a few inches taller than Broll, who was not short himself at seven feet, but was more lithe of form. His hands were akin to those of the night elves, but though his face also had some similarity to theirs, it was of a much paler cast, like no elven offshoot either knew.

That was as much of a view as any of the three were permitted, for the hooded figure immediately stretched forth a hand toward the most obvious threat, the high priestess.

It was a mistake of which Broll eagerly took advantage.

The druid flung himself at the mysterious caster, but not as a night elf. Gone was Broll, replaced by a hulking, furred figure more than twice his girth. The druid's mouth and nose elongated, growing together at the same time to create a savage maw. Huge, clawed paws seized the caster. Broll was now a ferocious bear.

His foe staggered back under the bulk and momentum. For a moment the hooded figure looked ready to fall back.

Suddenly, a green aura surrounded Broll's adversary. The druid went flying to the side, finally colliding with two hard stalagmites, shattering one. The bear slumped, momentarily stunned.

Tyrande held her glaive ready, but did not attack. The high priestess met the caster's gaze.

And only then, seeing those eyes, did the high priestess feel she should know who it was she faced. His guise was somewhat changed, of that Tyrande was certain, else his identity would have immediately been known to her. She tried to recall his name . . .

Then, to the shock of all three, he let out an anguished cry, flung an arm over his face . . . and began to transform.

"Wait!" Tyrande shouted. "Wait! Unless you are of the black dragonflight, we seek your help, not battle!"

The transformation, so barely begun that his true form had not even been in the least noticeable, ceased. Letting his arm drop, the caster stared at her with what seemed *pity*.

"You would be best served facing one of Deathwing's ilk, little night elf! One of them would be less of a monster for you to face than me!"

"A monster, are you?" Broll rumbled, reverting to his true form. He peered around him, seeking what in his guise as a bear he could not carry with him.

It lay at the feet of his foe, who now plucked it from the chamber floor. "Ah! This damned thing! I felt its presence! Would that she had never asked of me to lend my power to it!"

The druid rose. "Then you *are* the green dragon bound to the Idol of Remulos!"

" 'Bound' is the proper word!" The figurine went flying in Broll's direction. As the night elf caught it with one hand, the dragon hissed, "Tied to it with all my essence . . . though admittedly even my Ysera could not have foreseen the terrible things that would come from that. When it was first done, it was to allow us to be of immediate aid to Remulos or those he thought worthy to wield it." He glared at the druid. "And speaking of wielding . . . I know you by the signature of your magic, if not your name! You employed that thing some time past and with dread results . . ."

Broll grimaced. "Aye, very dread ones . . . and then, when I thought it lost, it turned out instead to have become tainted."

The hooded form laughed harshly. "That taint was nothing to the true danger, druid . . . you are fortunate that I am a wreck of a creature rather than the foulness that might have touched your heart a short while back . . ."

The druid stood ready to attack again, though he was wise enough to hold off for the moment. There was more to learn . . . and perhaps a chance to avoid blood. "What do you mean by that?"

His adversary looked incredulous. "Are you blind to the Nightmare? Have you not felt it?"

"Aye, I've felt it, as have most others of my calling! Dragons we may not be, but we, too, have fought for the Emerald Dream—"

"Utter babble!" The lanky "elf" swelled in size as he shouted, his words ending in a roar. "You know nothing! You understand nothing! *I* did not understand, I who stood at her side! I betrayed her, betrayed the Dream, and helped the Nightmare Lord begin his encroachment on not only that realm . . . but this mortal plane as well!"

Now Broll at least understood what faced them. Even as the dragon became less "elf" in shape and more true to his nature, the druid shifted toward Tyrande. They would need all their power to hope to even escape from this dragon.

"I know you now," he calmly said to the half-altered leviathan. "You're one of the *corrupted*! You're one of those turned by the Nightmare against Ysera—"

Great leathery wings spread across the length of the chamber. Long, sharp horns thrust back from the head. The dragon's girth filled more than two-thirds of the space. Green dragons were sleeker than most, more ethereal, but this one was a behemoth who had to arc his lengthy neck in order to stand. The eyes—Broll realized that the dragon had been peering at them all the time, when, in general, the eyes of a green dragon were shut, for the beasts lived half in the Dream at all times—stared with a wildness that more than matched Lucan at his worst.

" 'One of the corrupted'. . . what a simplistic turn of phrase, little night elf . . . you hardly understand what that means! You hardly understand what it is to have your mind, heart, and soul—'soul' as we dragons understand it—stripped away, eaten by darkness, and forced back into your screaming shell!" Again the harsh laughter erupted, shaking the cave so much that some of the stalactites broke loose. The trio was able to avoid those nearest and the dragon was not in the least distracted by the tons of limestone and rock that crashed against his scaled hide.

" 'One of the corrupted,' " the green leviathan repeated with self-mockery. "Would that I would have been merely 'one'!" The great reptilian head dove down, coming within a few yards of the night elves and the human. Broll and Tyrande stood their ground and even Lucan brandished his tiny dagger. "I was more than that, little creatures! I was the one most trusted of her, most dear . . . and because of that, my betrayal was far worse and far more terrible in ultimate consequence! Have you seen the sleepers? Have you seen their shadows? All of that began with my help . . ."

Tyrande dared speak up, her voice even and comforting. "I know you now, though you wear another unfamiliar form. But clearly you are free of the corruption now. Clearly you overcame it . . ."

"Through others . . . and what I did not know then was that it would call to me again . . . every moment . . . it calls to me! It desires me more than most, for I am . . . was . . . *her* most favored . . . her *consort* . . ."

" 'Consort'?" Broll gritted his teeth. "You are—"

The dragon roared, silencing him. The eyes—the cold, emerald eyes—fixed on the druid and Tyrande. "Yes . . . I am Eranikus, first consort of Ysera . . ." His jaws opened wide. "And, knowing that, knowing I exist here . . . all of you must die . . ."

10

ONE BY ONE

Stormwind was the strongest of the remaining bastions of the human race, a kingdom that had survived the destruction of much of the continent and even rebuilt itself after the First War. Varian Wrynn now ruled Stormwind—or ruled it again, since he had been king, then vanished for a time, only to recently return. From Stormwind Keep, in the capital city also named for the kingdom, the brown-haired, fiery leader sought to keep both his land and the Alliance intact. Varian was a driven man, made more so by the death, nearly thirteen years earlier, of his beloved wife, Tiffin, during a riot. His only solace was his son, Anduin—only an infant in his mother's arms at the time of her tragic death—who had suffered as king during Varian's long absence.

And so it was not surprising that with so much tragedy and struggle already behind him that King Varian had trouble with dreams. Of late, he preferred to sleep only with the use of numbing potions that kept those dreams away, but only as a last resort. Until weariness demanded that, it was more likely that Varian would be found walking the battlements.

A tall man in midlife with a rough-hewn handsomeness and brown hair that refused to be tamed, Varian was to his people the epitome of a champion. But now there came a threat that Varian could not understand how to handle.

His people were not waking up.

More to the point, each day found the numbers growing. It had started with one or two, then five, ten, and more. With each newly discovered slumberer, the populace grew more pensive. Some thought it a disease, but the scholars with whom the king conferred were certain it was far more. Some force was specifically attacking Stormwind through a curious form of attrition . . . and Varian knew exactly who it was.

The Horde.

There was no proof, but it made perfect sense to Varian. There were far too many elements among the Horde that could not be trusted to keep the peace. The orcs aside—and they were also among those of whom Varian was suspicious—the king could not see any reason to believe in the honor of blood elves—high elves who had turned to absorbing demonic magic after the loss of their vaunted power source, the Sunwell, and had subsequently become addicted to the fel energies. Nor did he have any faith in the undead Forsaken, who claimed to be free of the Lich King's mastery. Of all the Horde, the tauren were the only ones who did not immediately make Stormwind's ruler want to reach for his weapon, but since they sided with the orcs, that made them, too, untrustworthy.

Varian decided to compose a missive to send to Lady Jaina Proudmoore, archmage and ruler of Theramore Isle off of the southeastern side of the continent of Kalimdor, which itself lay west across the Great Sea. He had debated composing one for the past several days, but, ever reliant on himself, had put it off over and over. Now, though, the king suspected that he should have done so the very first time he had thought of it.

A helmed and armored sentry on the wall, the proud Stormwind lion on her breastplate, saluted sharply. She was the first guard that Varian had come across for some time. Even the keep's personal contingent was down by more than a third its normal strength.

"All clear?" he asked.

"Yes, my lord!" The sentry hesitated, then added, "All clear save for that damned mist building up yonder . . ."

Varian glanced over the battlements. It *was* thicker than the night before . . . and the night before that. The sentries had initially noted its slow buildup about a week ago . . . just before the morning when the first sleepers had been discovered.

He recalled the last time Stormwind had been draped in such a mist. That had been to cover the advance of the undead Scourge. The ghouls had used it to sweep toward the capital. But while there was that distinct similarity, there was something more ethereal and even more sinister. This fog seemed alive . . . and touched the mind as well as the body. Indeed, it seemed as much out of a dark dream as it did real.

The king blinked. For a moment he could have sworn that he saw something *moving* in the mist. Varian leaned forward but could not make anything out. Still, he was not a man prone to imagining things.

"Keep alert," he warned the sentry. "Pass that on to the others."

"Yes, Your Majesty."

As he left, Varian could not stifle a yawn. He would have to rest at some point soon, but not until he took some of the potion the alchemists had created for him. Then at least there would be no dreams—

Varian frowned. The potion seemed to help him sleep. Did it also help keep him from whatever touched those who could not wake? He had not considered that. The king knew he was not by any means versed in alchemy, but he seemed more rested than anyone else. Was there a connection between the nightmares the sleepers all seemed to be suffering and the fact that he did not have any dreams at all?

The notion made enough sense to Varian that he picked up his pace. It should still be possible to convene the alchemists and others who might better understand and press his argument. If they believed him, then perhaps it might be possible to let others use the sleeping potions and avoid more victims—

He almost ran into an out-of-breath guard just stepping up to the battlements. Varian, assuming that the man was late for duty but having no time to reprimand him, shifted around the soldier.

"My lord! I've—I've been sent to find you!" the man gasped. "Dire news, my lord!"

Varian instinctively thought of the movement that he believed he had noticed in the mist. "Out there—"

The helmet hid most of the man's features, but his tone revealed his great confusion. "Nay, my lord! We—we found him sprawled in a chair in the great room! He—he was not outside!"

Intense fear gripped the king. Seizing the soldier by the shoulders, Varian roared, "Who? Who?"

"The—the prince! Prince Anduin—"

Varian felt the blood drain from his face. "Anduin—my son—is dead?"

He all but tossed the man aside as he charged down the steps into the keep. All was a blur to Varian. He had only just regained his memory and his son! What vicious assassin had claimed Anduin?

Speeding to the great room, where once confirming the guest list for the balls that took place there had been the most important task concerning the wide, high-ceilinged chamber, Varian came across an anxious group of guards, servants, and other staff.

"Aside!" the king cried out. "Make way!"

The wall of people separated. Varian saw his son.

The youth was a fine mix of his father and mother, with hair a bit lighter than Varian's and a face softer not only due to Tiffin's traits but less worn by the ravages of life. Still, for someone not quite thirteen years of age, Anduin seemed much older.

He also appeared at that moment, at least to Varian's eyes, *unbloodied.*

Anduin still lay half in the chair. The captain of the guard, a gruff veteran with a cropped brown beard, looked as if he wanted to adjust the prince to a more comfortable position but was afraid to touch the royal heir.

Varian saw only his son, and so with nothing else on his mind but that, he barged past the captain and reached down to Anduin.

He saw the youth's chest rise and fall. The king's hopes rose . . . until he heard Anduin let out a whimper.

His son had joined the sleepers.

"No . . ." the lord of Stormwind whispered. He shook Anduin, but the boy would not wake. "No . . ."

Finally rising, Varian growled, "Carry him to bed. Gently. I'll be there before long."

Two of the guards did as he commanded. To the captain, the king added, "Summon the alchemists! I want to see them all immediately—"

A horn sounded. As one, those assembled looked up. Varian knew by the signal from where the call originated: the battlements from which he had just departed.

"Take care of Anduin!" he reminded the guards. "And summon the alchemists, Captain!"

Not bothering to wait for any response, the king raced back to where he had just been walking. On the battlements, a handful of soldiers stared off into the direction of the mist. When one happened to look back and see the king, he immediately warned the rest. The sentries stood at attention.

"Never mind that!" Varian stepped past them to look beyond Stormwind City's edge. "What do you—"

He froze. Now there *were* definitely distinct figures moving within the mist. Hundreds of them . . . no . . . there had to be thousands . . .

"Get every available fighter to the—" Again Varian stopped, but this time for another reason. Even though the mist and those within were still far away, for some reason the king was certain that he recognized *all* of them. In one way, that was not so astounding, for they were the same two people over and over and over.

They were Anduin . . . and his mother.

But this was not the beloved Tiffin of Varian's memory. Each of the doppelgängers staggered toward the city on legs that were half-bone, half-greenish, rotting flesh. Tiffin's once-beautiful face was ravaged by worms and other carrion insects. Spiders crawled in her ragged hair and the gown in which she had been buried was soiled by dirt and torn. The monstrous scene repeated on and on.

And as for Anduin, while whole, he stayed close to his mother, allowing one skeletal hand to wrap around his neck in what looked more possessive than loving. To Varian, it was as if the horrific apparition was telling the king that their son was now *hers*.

"No . . ." Varian wanted this to be a nightmare. He wanted to find out that he was among the sleepers. There was little that could shake him, but this was a dark tableau of which he could have never imagined. It had to be a nightmare . . . it had to be . . .

But Varian realized that, unlike his son, he was living something *real,* even if it, too, was in its way a nightmare. The king had been taking the potions before the first of the sleepers; he was certain that they had somehow protected him by granting him no dreams. Unfortunately, Varian had not made the connection in time to prevent his own son from falling prey.

And now, whatever lurked behind the sleepers, behind their troubled dreams, was encroaching on the capital wielding his own worst fears.

That gave Varian some strength. He turned to the nearest guard—the female with whom he had earlier spoken—and asked, "Do you see anything in the mist?"

Her shaking voice was enough to tell him how terrible the sight was to her. "I see . . . my father . . . dead in battle . . . Tomas . . . a comrade in arms . . . I see—"

King Varian looked to the assembled guards. "You see nothing but your imagination! Nothing but your fears! It or they know your fears and are feeding on them! These are nightmares, which mean that they are not what you think . . ."

They clearly took some heart from the strength of his voice. Varian hid deep his own anxiety at the thought of Anduin and Tiffin. If even while aware that they were false visions he was still affected by them, how were the rest of those in the city faring?

From outside the capital's walls and near the edge of the mist, another horn sounded. One of the patrols on evening duty. Varian had for the moment forgotten about them. They were one of about half a dozen out this night . . .

"Give the recall!" he ordered the nearest trumpeter. "Give it now! I want them all in!"

The soldier blew the signal. Varian waited.

One patrol to the west responded. Another further south did. From the northwest came another.

The fourth signal came from those near the mist. Varian breathed a sigh of relief as the horn blared—

And then the sound cut off too soon.

Worse . . . there was no reply at all from the other two.

"Again!"

The trumpeter blew. The king and the soldiers waited.

Silence.

Varian eyed the moving figures in the mist. Again, it was as if his view magnified to give him a much closer look. He knew that it was not by chance, but rather some work of whatever encroached upon his city. It sought to let him see what was happening, see and fear . . .

And what the monarch of Stormwind saw did make him shudder, for it answered more questions. The many Anduins and Tiffins were no longer alone. Their ranks had been joined by shambling figures clad in armor marked by the proud lion on the breastplate. Yet Varian could also see the prone bodies of those same men on the ground, even their steeds collapsed with them. Indeed, many of the gaunt-faced soldiers rode mounts that had eyes without pupils and bodies that were twisted.

"It is the Scourge come to claim us again!" someone shouted.

Without looking at who had been speaking, the king commanded, "Silence! This is magical trickery, nothing more! Nothing!"

Then . . . the mist and its army paused just before the walls. The Anduins and the Tiffins looked up, their soulless eyes upon those of Varian. Behind them, the other figures also stared up at the battlements.

Without warning, the Anduins and Tiffins looked over their shoulders at the unholy throng. Varian could not help but follow their gazes.

At first he saw only the soldiers mixed with them. Then other half-seen figures became apparent. Though their forms were indistinct . . . dreamlike . . . their faces were horrific parodies of normal folk.

And then . . . among them he saw a more distinct figure. A woman fair of face and with long, blond hair. If she had not been dressed as a mage, Varian might have ignored her as one more shadow.

It was Lady Jaina Proudmoore.

Her expression was as dire as the rest, a thing caught between horror and death. Varian stepped back, understanding that the situation was even more terrible than he had imagined. As if to verify this, to Jaina's right another figure formed from the very mist. The face was unknown to the king, but that did not matter. He spotted another take shape and another.

"Why do they not attack?" asked the guard with whom he had originally spoken. "Why?"

He did not answer, though he knew the reason. They *were* attacking. Piece by piece. The attrition of which he had earlier thought had a second purpose to it. The enemy was not merely reducing the ranks of the defenders; it was adding to its own. With each new sleeper—especially those like Anduin, caught unexpected by exhaustion—their numbers grew.

King Varian understood that all they had to do for the moment was wait . . . and victory would be theirs.

Tyrande prayed . . . and Elune responded to her servant.

As if a full, silvery moon itself suddenly filled the chamber, the light of the goddess magnified a thousand times, bathing all in its glory. Yet for the high priestess, Broll, and Lucan, the illumination comforted. It did not hurt their eyes, but soothed them.

Not so for Eranikus. The green leviathan reared back, his sleek yet massive form colliding with the wall and ceiling behind him. The chamber shook and huge chunks of stone broke from the cave walls. However, the Mother Moon's light kept any of it from the trio.

The dragon let out a furious hiss. Yet rather than lunge again, Eranikus backed further. As he did, he began to shrink and transform.

"Consider yourselves fortunate!" he roared. "More fortunate than I could ever be . . ."

Already the dragon had all but reverted to the false elven shape. Only traces here and there marked him as what he truly was.

Broll was already in action, but this time his attack was not physical. Instead, he cast a spell.

Eranikus let out a tremendous exhalation. The false elf blinked. He looked upon the high priestess.

"A powerful attempt," he complimented, "and almost successful . . . but I can never truly be soothed, even by the calm, loving light of Elune . . . too much tortures my heart . . ."

Still, the hooded figure neither renewed his attack nor fled. Instead, he fell against the wall and shut his eyes. A shudder ran through Eranikus.

"I failed her so much. I failed her and all else . . ."

Tyrande prayed to Elune to lessen the moonlight, leaving it at a level that still served to allow Lucan to see all.

Eranikus slumped, finally ending up sitting on a part of the wall that thrust out like a chair.

"Great one," she murmured. "If corrupted you once were, now that is clearly not so. Whatever failures you think you have committed, you now have the chance to right them."

For her suggestion, Tyrande received another bitter laugh.

"Such naïveté! You have lived how long, night elf? A thousand, five thousand years?"

She stood proud. "I fought the Burning Legion when it first came to Azeroth! I faced Azshara! I was there when the Well of Eternity was destroyed!"

"More than ten thousand years, then," Eranikus responded, his tone sounding not at all impressed. "A mere speck of time and experience compared to that of one of my kind and certainly one of my age in particular. Still, you have some meager way by which to measure my misery. Can you think of your most terrible failures?"

"I am well aware of them, yes . . ."

"Then multiply them by a magnitude as great as the World Tree is high and you will quite possibly barely understand . . ." Eranikus glowered, but his mood was steered toward himself. "I have done terrible things . . . and the worst of it is, I might do them again!"

Broll and Tyrande looked to one another. The high priestess finally said, "But you're free of the corruption . . . I was there . . . it was the light of Elune, in fact, through myself and several priestesses that finally cleansed you! I would've recognized you immediately, if not for your changed form!"

"So I believed also . . . but as the Nightmare grew stronger, I discovered the truth! The shadow of it will always be within me so long as it exists . . . and because of me, it exists throughout my queen's realm . . ." He snarled. "And that is why I do not wear the night elven form you know, and why I disguised myself as a dragon of black when forced to fly out for sustenance! I wanted no one to know it was me! I wanted no one to come in search of me!"

"But Ysera and the Emerald Dream—" the high priestess began.

"Call it as it should be! Call it as it will be! Call it the Emerald *Nightmare*! *Our* Nightmare!" As he shouted, Eranikus leapt to his feet. His form shifted, becoming again something part elf, part dragon. There was also more of an ethereal look to him, as if he were part dream himself.

Then the hooded figure solidified. Eranikus stared off into space, his expression horrified. "No . . . I almost . . . I should not have nearly done that . . . the line between the two realms is fading . . . but it should not be this bad yet . . ."

Behind Tyrande, Lucan shifted into the shadows. Broll noticed the movement and Eranikus noticed Broll observing it.

"Humannn . . ." the green dragon, still a bizarre mixture of his two selves, stalked toward Lucan. The elven face now bore a blunt muzzle and teeth too sharp for the mortal form. Small wings flapped back and forth in agitation, and what should have been hands were savage paws with long nails. "It comes from the humannn . . ."

The high priestess took up a defensive position in front of the cartographer. "With all respect, this one is under the protection of Elune."

Broll moved toward her. "And under the protection of this particular druid, too."

Eranikus waved a hand.

The two night elves found themselves thrust in opposite directions, leaving Lucan to face the green dragon.

Steeling himself, the man stepped forward. "Slay me and get it over with, if you want! I've been through far too much to be worried about being eaten by a monster."

"I prefer simpler fare," Eranikus answered bluntly. His countenance reverted to something more elven as he studied the haggard mortal. "I only wish to see you deeper . . ."

Tyrande was on her feet, the glaive ready to throw. However, Broll, also rising, gestured for her to hold back. He could sense that the dragon did indeed mean no harm . . . at least for the moment.

And should that change, Broll already had an attack in mind.

Eranikus towered over Lucan, who was not that short a human. The cartographer bravely looked up at the half-transformed dragon, who reached a taloned finger toward his chest.

"You humans are always the most fascinating of the dreamers," Eranikus murmured, sounding more calm. "Such a diversity of imagination, of desire. Your dreams can create beauty and horror in the same moment . . ."

"I don't like to dream," the man stated.

This brought an unexpected chuckle from the dragon. "Nor do I these days . . . nor do I."

The taloned finger came within a hair's breadth of Lucan . . . and suddenly *both* figures took on an emerald glow.

Broll shook his head. "That can't be possible! He's a human! There are no human druids!"

"What do you mean?" Tyrande asked the dragon.

"The other realm touches him, is part of him, can be open to him," Eranikus replied, marveling. The finger withdrew. "I know you, if not by name! I have seen you, though you were barely out of the shell then . . ."

Lucan Foxblood swallowed, but otherwise remained steadfast. "I'm merely a cartographer."

"A maker of maps, a student of landscapes . . . the closest your human mind could come to recalling and accepting a part of you that was not of your doing . . ." Eranikus hissed. "Nor hers, either."

" 'Hers'?" the human repeated.

"She who bore you, little one! Your mother, brought to the Dream most foully by a fey creature who seduced a young female whose man had abandoned her just as she was about to give birth! I came upon the thing as it waited for the infant in order to claim it for whatever dark purpose it had. The creature fled at my coming, leaving a mother dying from her great exertions and a lone, weak, male child . . ."

Lucan looked to Broll and Tyrande as if hoping this made more sense to them. It did not.

"You were not a dream and so did not belong. My queen did pass you on to one who knew humans better, though he was of our kind, a red dragon called Korialstrasz—"

"I know that name!" blurted the high priestess.

"Well you should! He is chief consort to the Queen of Life, Alexstrasza"—Eranikus's brow furrowed angrily—"and a more competent, trustworthy mate than I was to my beloved . . ."

Tyrande began to comprehend some things. "You carried him out of the Emerald Dream?"

"After using a spell to heal his weakness! At my queen's request—though it was a strange one, I thought—I gave some minute part of myself so that he would live . . ."

"Which would explain why he saw you as your true self, when we saw you as the black dragon you desired others to believe hunted here."

Eranikus hissed. "Hunger forced me out farther and farther. It seemed the best disguise . . . against all but him." He eyed Lucan dubiously. "Never did I think I had created some link between us with that act so early on . . ."

"And so this is why he runs in and out of the Dream almost without realizing it?" Broll asked.

To the surprise of the two night elves, his question had the effect of filling the powerful dragon with renewed dread. "Does he? He does?"

Eranikus bared his teeth at Lucan, causing the man and the night elves to prepare for the worst. "He passes into the Nightmare?"

"So we believe," Broll replied, his spell ready. "And comes out of it uncorrupted, if not untouched."

"It should not be . . . but the birth was there, and so the calling is from there . . . yet Azeroth calls him, too . . ." Eranikus stepped back, his gaze never leaving Lucan. "And how long have you suffered this, little mortal?"

"My name is Lucan Foxblood." Having found he could stand up to a dragon, the cartographer had also found he did not like being called "little mortal."

"The right of correction is yours in this instance," Eranikus returned in a tone that said not much *else* was the human's right. However reasonably a dragon might converse with a creature not of his kind, most still did so with the innate sense that their kind were the first and foremost children of Azeroth. "Tell me now! When did you first suffer so? Do you remember?"

"I've always dreamed of an idyllic land, free of the interference of time and people . . ." Lucan remarked, looking almost nostalgic. His expression then darkened, though. "But the first nightmares . . . the first bad dreams . . ." He paused to think, then told them.

Eranikus frowned. "A few scant years. A blink for dragons, but much time for mortals, I know . . ."

"Too long a time," the cartographer returned.

"And too coincidental a time!" snarled Broll, causing the rest to look to him. He peered grimly at Tyrande. "From what I've gleaned, Lucan's nightmares began *just* before you found Malfurion's body . . ."

For all their size, orcs could be extremely stealthy. Thura was one of those stealthy orcs. She had successfully tracked the trio without being seen and had even followed them near enough to hear their voices. Not all the words had made sense and some had been unintelligible, but one word in particular spurred her on.

The evil one's name. The base night elf. *Malfurion.*

Thura missed the word that followed his name, or she might have wondered if her prey was already dead. Thus, she only knew—or believed—one thing. Soon she would confront Brox's slayer and he who would also ravage Azeroth . . .

The orc slipped back, still amazed. The dragon was not there now, but rather some wizard, it seemed. She had not heard enough to know the truth there, either. To Thura, wizards did not rate highly; they were cowards who fought from the back of the battle using methods no honorable warrior would accept. That she felt differently about shaman and even druids was merely a prejudice based on her people's choices. In her eyes, it only meant one more obstacle that she would face in order to avenge her blood kin.

The orc crept along the landscape seeking a spot from which to watch the hill as a whole. No matter from which exit they left, she would see them. Then, as she had always done, Thura would follow the trail she was given, whether it be by dreams or tracking Malfurion's companions.

A sound from above sent her flattening against a nearby hillside. Gazing up, Thura grunted. Now she could account for all her enemies. The last had revealed itself, though the orc still did not know how it had slipped out without her seeing it.

The shrouded form of a dragon glided over the region. Thura watched as it hovered above the hills where she had thought it nested. In the night sky, the dragon was a great, black silhouette. Indeed, it was hard to separate the dragon from the darkness. It was fortunate that Thura had seen the beast under better conditions, or else at this moment she would have questioned her eyes. The dragon looked much, much larger than before, *huge* in comparison. In fact, it was so huge that there was no possibility of it being the one she had seen earlier. This was truly a giant among giants.

Thura gripped the ax, ready to use it if need be, but the dragon ceased its hovering and went on the move again. Beating its wings hard, it flew away.

And if Thura had known the land better, she would have realized that the dragon was heading in the direction of Ashenvale.

11

TO BOUGH SHADOW

Little light filtered in from outside. Most of the illumination in the cave was still due to Tyrande's work. Still, the faint light from without appeared to put the dragon further on edge.

"This is not natural," he muttered at one point. "The sky should be brighter than this." Eranikus shut his eyes for a moment. His expression hardening, he opened them again and informed them, "You should not have stayed! I have seen the outside. There is less cloud blocking the sun than a mist that should have burned away by now. It is not natural . . . I feel . . . I feel the Nightmare closer than ever . . ."

The green dragon rarely called the realm by the name by which it had been known since time immemorial. For him there existed only the horror that it had become.

He made no mention either of the fate of its mistress, Ysera, which boded ill to Broll. Yet despite also clearly being concerned about his queen and mate, Eranikus refused to accompany them to Ashenvale—the central subject of what had become an argument raging all night.

Eranikus remained in his false elven shape, as if even being himself for a short time risked being corrupted again. The dragon had bade them leave more than once, but neither the druid nor the high priestess would, not even when threatened. It was obvious to both that with matters so grave in the dream realm, they would need the aid of someone who knew the realm even better than Broll. Fortunately, it had become quite obvious that for reasons of his own, Eranikus had no intention of causing them harm.

"I have been very patient," the dragon growled, turning from them. "Leave before I cast you out of this place."

"You could've done that more than once," Broll pointed out. "And you haven't."

"Mistake not my misery for weakness!" Eranikus retorted, turning on the night elf. "Nor my regret! I have done great evil and know that, but there are limits to my patience . . ."

Lucan listened to all of this with a sense of impending doom. The points of the discussion were well above his head, but he did understand that matters were growing worse and that, despite his desire otherwise, he was somehow linked to them.

A desire to have at least a little quiet had been gradually building up inside him. The cartographer finally gave in to it. With the night elves still arguing—*arguing*—with the dragon, Lucan decided to step away from them. Not far. Just enough to give him some peace.

Eranikus blocked the path by which the trio had entered, so Lucan headed in the opposite direction. He chose a passage at random, only caring that it be lengthy enough to escape the voices. More and more, he just wanted to be away.

Although he was hardly as stealthy as either the druid or the high priestess, the human escaped the chamber without notice. Already breathing easier, Lucan stumbled down the jagged, narrow passage.

The voices drifted after him. Dissatisfied, Lucan moved further on. The argument faded to mere sounds, but that was still not enough.

Lucan had left the field of illumination, but a dim finger of light from ahead gave him at least some visibility. He instinctively strode toward it.

An exit to the outside world finally greeted him. It was barely brighter outside than where he was and tendrils of mist crept into the passage, but despite his wariness, Lucan felt the urge to continue. There could be no harm in taking a single step outside. If it looked even the least treacherous, all he had to do was enter again.

Convinced by such logic, the human left the passage. He was greeted by a vague landscape that at first put him in mind of the pristine, emerald one of which he had always dreamed and which, though he apparently stepped into it, now feared.

Still, being outside after a night in the cave gave Lucan some relief. *I'll only stay out here a moment,* he promised. *Perhaps . . . perhaps then they'll know what to do . . .*

The one thing of which he was certain was that not in the least did he desire to travel to this Ashenvale. He had already realized that in some manner the place was tied to the dream realm. Lucan had not told the night elves that the more he was near things bound to what the dragon rightly called the Nightmare, the more the feeling of constantly slipping between Azeroth and it increased. Everything related to the dream realm called to him.

That, Lucan finally understood, was why he had ended up here in the first place. He had been heading toward the dragon from the start, for Eranikus was not only a part of his astounding and terrible past— a past with which Lucan was still coming to grips—but the dragon had, at least in the past, been an integral part of the Nightmare. Whatever had stirred up this part of Lucan seemed determined to set him on a path into the other realm . . . something he desperately wanted to avoid.

The cartographer paced back and forth. Throughout the night, while the others had struggled to come to some agreement, he had tried to comprehend why this should be forced upon him. An orphan raised by good folk in Stormwind, he had expected his life to begin and end as it did for most people. Magic and monsters were not for him. His thirst for travel focused only on how better he could make the maps on which his master would sign his own name. Lucan had no desires above that.

He was not a coward, not in the least, but neither was he an adventurer beyond his dreams.

The last thought made him grimace. *'Tis my dreams that are the problem!*

A clattering of stone made him look around. Only then did Lucan see that he had walked farther away than he had intended. The passage was now a faint shape some distance behind him.

Turning, he headed with all haste for it.

A powerful figure seized him from behind. He smelled a body more unwashed than his. Lucan caught sight of the hands gripping the ax handle that squeezed the air from his chest—thereby also keeping him from shouting for help—and noted foremost that they were thick and green.

"Orc—" he gasped, the word barely even a whisper. Lucan tried again, but this time did not have any air. He began to grow dizzy and his vision grew cloudy.

It also grew . . . green.

As that happened, the pressure on his chest vanished. However, a powerful force shoved him to the ground. Lucan fell on his face, the ground feeling much softer, more pleasant, than he knew it should have.

"Yes . . ." rumbled a voice that, though deep, was also female. "I am close . . . the place of emerald shadows . . ."

"Em—emerald?" Lucan managed. He looked up, and to his horror saw that the voice had spoken the truth. He was in the other realm . . . only this time he had not merely passed through.

Before the cartographer could register more, he was dragged up to a standing position, then spun halfway around.

It *was* an orc and it *was female,* although with a face that Lucan hoped for her sake was attractive to her kind. The mouth was very broad and the nose short and squat. The eyes so balefully fixed on him were the only features he could call attractive. In fact, they would have been striking on a human female.

The head of an ax jutted up under his chin. The orc growled, "Take me to him!"

"To—to who?"

"The honorless one! The base slayer! The evil threatening all! The night elf who calls himself Malfurion Stormrage!"

Lucan tried to pull his chin up, but the ax followed. Through clenched teeth, he answered, "I don't know—know where to find him!"

This did not sit at all well with his captor. Lucan wondered why he did not slip back into Azeroth as he always had in the past. He concentrated . . . but nothing happened except that the orc pressed the ax head deeper into his chin.

"You know! The vision told me only last night! I saw you there, when he slew great and loyal Brox—"

"I've no—no idea what you're—" He stopped when a stinging sensation under his chin informed him that the ax head had drawn blood.

"It was different again! Each time it tells me what to do! I am close, human! I will avenge my blood kin . . . and you will help, or you will share the night elf's fate!"

Lucan knew that she meant it. He carefully murmured, "Yes . . . I'll lead you there."

The ax head lowered. The orc leaned close, her breath almost as strong as the scent of her body. She looked through him, her mind elsewhere. "My vengeance is destined . . . I dreamed that you would come out and where that place would be and it happened! Malfurion *will* die . . ."

She spun him back around again so that he could lead her. Only then did Lucan for the first time see the place through which he had previously only stumbled half-dead or rushed through.

The landscape nearest them was of an idyllic nature, an untouched place of natural beauty. Long, flowing grass spread over fields dotted with sloping hills and lush trees. It was clearly a place untouched by civilization. There were signs of wildlife, especially birds in the distance. It was truly like something out of a dream, he thought.

Then the cartographer noticed that there were no birds in the immediate area. *All* of them were far away. Seeing nothing in the direction he faced, he peered over his shoulder.

Lucan gaped. Even though the sight was still some great distance from their location, it so shook the human that he instantly tried desperately to return to the mortal plane to escape what he saw . . . but to no avail.

As if she did not see what no living creature could miss—and what no living creature should desire to face—the orc used the ax handle to brusquely shove Lucan forward . . . toward the Nightmare.

Eranikus shivered. "The way was opened!" He peered around. "Where is the human?"

All argument was forgotten as the trio sought Lucan. Broll picked up the trail first. "He went this way!"

Tyrande followed the druid, but Eranikus whirled the opposite direction. Neither night elf had time to concern themselves with the dragon, who seemed steadfast in his refusal to help them.

Broll broke out into the open moments later. The mist was thicker and much too reminiscent of Auberdine.

"Do you see him?" the high priestess asked.

"No, but in this muck, he might be only a few yards away."

Tyrande held one palm before her and began praying under her breath. The mist began to move back, as if pushed by some unseen hand.

But in the area revealed, there was no immediate sign of the cartographer. The druid again studied the ground, quickly finding Lucan's barely visible tracks.

"He went along this way, but it looks like he was pacing a lot. He—" Broll paused, then all but pressed his face against the hard ground as he took in other details. "There's another set of prints . . . and by their shape, I'd guess an *orc*."

"An orc? Here?"

A heavy flapping of wings caused both night elves to look up and behind themselves. Overhead, the immense form of the green dragon appeared in all his terrible majesty. He was huge in comparison to most dragons either had seen, other than the Great Aspects. Yet Eranikus was also sleeker, longer, than many. He hovered, his huge, webbed wings spreading far to each side. Two long horns darted back from the top of his head. His narrow jaws opened, revealing an unnerving array of sharp teeth as long as Broll's arm. Under his chin, a slight tuft of hair gave Ysera's consort a more scholarly look.

More astounding, Eranikus *shimmered* slightly, as if not completely attuned to the mortal plane. It added an ethereal quality to the leviathan and marked the ties he still had with the Emerald Dream despite his previous troubles.

Eranikus surveyed the region.

"There is no sign of the little human, anywhere, though admittedly I am near blind, using my eyes like some mortal creature!" the dragon finally hissed. Unsaid by him was the fact that, under the circumstances, he dared not view the world through dreamsight. That risked too much contact with the Emerald Dream . . . and so, the Nightmare. "And the way has closed again!"

"He was taken," Broll explained, "by an orc, it seems."

The behemoth bared his sharp teeth. "He must have tried to escape using his unique circumstances."

"If he did . . . then he took the orc with him," Tyrande pointed out.

Still hovering, Eranikus cocked his head. "I have smelled orc here, but it was a small scent, meaning perhaps one, and no orc would be foolish enough to seek me . . ." He hissed again. "Unlike night elves!"

Broll did not like the sound of the first part. "Why would an orc stay here for days? What could they want from this place?"

"It could be coincidence," replied the high priestess, "but I rather think someone wanted the orc here from the start. The orc's presence, coupled with Lucan's own and his past association with Eranikus, make it too difficult to believe that any of it is due to chance . . ."

A sinister rumbling escaped the green dragon. He glared at the night elves. "I will join with you long enough to bring you to Ashenvale and make certain that your path is clear! No more than that!"

While both were grateful, Broll had to ask, "But why change your mind? Why draw so near to what you dread so much?"

Eranikus stared into empty air as he contemplated something. Finally, "Because I do not like the notion that perhaps something has been *working* all this time . . . just so this orc can reach the Nightmare!"

The druid was incredulous. "But for what reason?"

The great dragon looked troubled, so troubled that the night elves' unease grew by volumes. "Well we might ask, little druid . . . well we might ask . . ."

He descended to the ground and with a tip of his head indicated that the two should climb atop near his neck. Tyrande had ridden dragons before and so obeyed without hesitation. Broll frowned, but followed immediately. His avian form could not possibly keep up with a dragon's pace.

The moment they were ready, Eranikus took to the sky. He circled once, then headed in the direction that the druid had assumed Ashenvale lay.

"How long before we reach it?" Tyrande shouted. "How long before we reach Ashenvale?"

"Not so long, but perhaps too long!" the dragon roared back. "Press yourselves against my neck and hold tight!"

They raced through the heavens at a speed that nearly took the night elves' breath away. The gusting wind might have been harder to take, but Eranikus arched his neck to give them some protection.

Broll dared lean to his right just enough to see something of the ground. What he noticed left him with more concern. There was mist everywhere. It was not one thick blanket, but neither was there any separate patch. Indeed, the pattern reminded him of something.

As a druid, it finally came to him. *Branches . . . the tendrils of mist look like branches from some evil tree . . .*

The resemblance was enhanced by areas that brought to mind leaves with jagged edges. That brought back memories of the visions Broll had earlier suffered, and he pondered their connection to all this.

On and on they flew. The hills became wooded lands. The air cooled some. The woods thickened into lush, green forest that Broll knew from past journeys.

"I see it . . ." Eranikus informed them. "Bough Shadow lies just ahead . . ."

"Just ahead" to the dragon still meant to his passengers that it was out of sight for several minutes more. Then . . .

"I see it!" cried Tyrande.

Broll tapped her shoulder in acknowledgment. He, too, could at last make out the Great Tree.

It was dwarfed by its mightier siblings, but it still rose high over the region, a monarch in its own right. From a distance, the tree seemed in good order, even if its base was covered by mist. Its vast branches spread nearly a mile across, and within its boughs could be found a multitude of creatures, including many of those who served as its guardians. It was one of a handful of such trees, the others located in the astounding Crystalsong Forest—a mystic place in chill Northrend where, in addition to normal fascinating trees, formations of crystal grew—the Hinterlands—east of Aerie Peak, home of the gryphon-riding Wildhammer dwarves—murky and dangerous Duskwood, and the deep, dank jungle of Feralas.

There were portals located in all these places, but for the druids and Broll in particular, Ashenvale was the most secure, the most safe. Thus far.

However, as they neared, the dragon said, "The area is empty. I see no one, night elf or otherwise . . ."

"That can't be," Broll returned. "The druids were summoned away, but there were others who would be here!"

"We shall see." Eranikus circled once, then descended.

As the dragon alighted, the night elves got their first glance at the tree's huge base . . . and the portal that represented their best hopes.

Vine-wrapped, fluted columns with wide capitals marked their ultimate destination. A path composed of pieces of stone passed between them, leading to the tree.

The portal itself was round. Its surrounding border was shaped from the tree's living roots. They wrapped around one another, forming an arch. With the arch was a second border violet in color and radiating energy.

But it was the core that most demanded attention. Within the portal, a swirling mass of emerald energy constantly shifted. At times, streaks that resembled miniature bolts of green lightning flared.

The key to their hopes of reaching Malfurion, the reason for seeking this place, was this portal. The physical path to the Emerald

Dream and the Nightmare—the only path that might still be at all trustworthy—lay open to them.

And that in itself now presented another concern.

"It is as you said," Tyrande remarked to the dragon. "There is no one, though there should be many guardians."

"Could they be to the east?" Broll suggested. "The Horde's been getting very cocky about trying to harvest that part of the forest. It was something Malfurion was concerned about years ago already."

"That is a point," conceded the dragon, "but those who serve here serve most my queen . . . they would not depart without her com—"

Eranikus let out a fearsome roar of pain as a huge boulder crashed down upon his back. Caught unaware and having just carried the two night elves, he had not raised defenses against such a primitive but powerful assault.

As the dragon sought to recover, a second missile collided with him. Eranikus tumbled toward the portal, bowling over several columns.

The night elves turned to face the enemy, Broll transforming into the ferocious bear and Tyrande wielding the glaive.

Out of the forest burst a gigantic figure who seemed spawned by the very trees. His body was covered in thick bark and he had a long beard of leaves. Two tusks thrust from his mouth and his eyes were filled with a golden rage focused not on the night elves, but the dragon.

"Corrupted . . ." he grated, his voice akin to the scraping of wood against wood. "You will not pass . . ."

"An ancient of war!" the high priestess called.

As quickly as he had transformed, Broll reverted to his true shape. He ran toward the lumbering figure, unafraid of the fearsome paws that resembled huge, sharp splinters capable of skewering a mere druid.

"Gnarl!" Broll shouted at the top of his lungs. "Gnarl, ancient of war, protector of Ashenvale and Forest Song! You know me! You know me!"

The ancient hesitated. The mighty creature wore only a few bits of armor that looked more ornamental than protective. Fearsome faces and mystic patterns decorated them. In truth, the ancient needed little protecting. There was not much that could injure one of them. The ancients were among the first creatures of Azeroth, the first guardians of its life.

Gnarl cocked his head as he studied the druid. There was a hint of resemblance to a hound in the jagged face, but the eyes bespoke of an intelligence much greater. Indeed, ancients of war helped teach night elf warriors much of their skills.

"I know you, yes, night elf! You are the wanderer and friend called Broll Bearmantle . . ." Gnarl briefly bent his head. "My sorrow still for the death of your youngster . . ."

The comment made Broll clench a fist, though he hid that from the ancient. With lives that made those of night elves look so very short, ancients often saw years like seconds. To Gnarl, Anessa's death was an incident that had only just happened and so was very well recalled. Gnarl did not mean to remind Broll . . . not that the druid ever forgot, anyway.

But Gnarl then returned his attention to Eranikus, who had finally righted himself. The dragon spread his wings and hissed at the ancient, yet though Gnarl was smaller, the guardian did not look afraid to directly face Eranikus.

"Corrupt one! You were warned . . ."

"I come here only to bring these two to help my queen and their friend—your friend, also! Malfurion Stormrage!"

"Stormrage . . ." Gnarl looked uncertain. "We have felt his absence strong . . . yet also his presence . . ." The eyes glared at Eranikus. "As we have sensed your nearing presence for the past day . . . and the corruption you bring with you . . ."

The dragon started to shrink back. It was clear by his reaction that what the ancient had said struck a chord.

"He's freed of his corruption!" Broll corrected, coming to Eranikus's defense. "He is an ally and a friend to us again! You should know that!"

"No!" Gnarl raised a mighty hand. "I saw him return to his evil! He—" The huge figure blinked. "No . . . that was a nightmare . . . one of many of late. He does not seem corrupted . . . yet . . ."

Taking advantage of the ancient's hesitance, Broll asked a question that had been bothering him. "Gnarl . . . where are the other guardians?"

The forest dweller's expression turned grimmer. "Some to the east, some to the north, some to the south. The others . . . those who remained behind with me . . . the others sleep and do not wake . . ." He shook his head. "I hid them safe . . . but I have grown so tired myself . . . I may soon be joining them."

"What happened?"

Gnarl told them how the guardians—including ancients, night elves, green drakes, dryads, and especially those of the green dragonflight—had been without commands by Ysera for far too long. They had grown concerned. That concern had turned worse when a dryad named Shael'dryn had come to them after fleeing her moonwell. The wells—bound to the magic of nature and the light of Elune—were places of healing for both the land around them and those who drank of their waters. Magi and other spellcasters could even refresh their mana, a gift of the Mother Moon to Azeroth's other defenders. Shael'dryn had been the one watching over the northernmost.

"I know her," Broll said with a slight, wry smile. "A jester of words, a lover of puns . . ."

Gnarl shook his craggy head. "No humor was there in her when she came. She warned of—of attackers in the dark, seeking the wells. The dryad only called them shadows, though she said that they reminded her of something else."

No one heard the intake of breath from Tyrande, who then asked, "Where is she? It might be wise to speak with her."

"That is impossible," the ancient answered. "She has slept for two days now."

He went on to tell them how, after hearing from the dryad, the ancients and other guardians had then divided up to head to the moonwells and other strategic locations. They had left Gnarl and the others in charge of the portal's protection.

"There were more than a dozen . . . all strong, especially the dragons and drakes . . . and at the time, we did not know yet about the unwaking sleep. That happened only after we divided up and said our farewells . . ."

"You were played like pieces in a chess game," Eranikus pointed out, not without some satisfaction at someone else's mistakes. "Hmmph!"

Although Gnarl obviously did not care for the dragon's comments, he did not defend himself and his comrades. Instead, the ancient gestured at the portal. "I will not stand in your way . . . go, if you think it some good . . ."

"I am not foolish enough to enter there! That is for these two!"

Now Gnarl did show his contempt, though Eranikus ignored him. Forgetting the dragon, the woodland guardian said to Broll, "Forest brother, I would go with . . . but there must be someone here . . . other than him . . ."

"That's understood. I'll go alone—"

"We go together," Tyrande curtly interjected.

As ever, there was no arguing with the high priestess. Broll shrugged. "Then let's get on with it."

Eranikus moved to the side. The night elves strode toward the glittering energies.

Tyrande exhaled. "It looks so . . . beautiful."

"Once, it was."

"How do we enter?"

"Just walk in," the druid replied, "and then be prepared for anything."

"I always am."

"Fare you well," Gnarl grated, the ancient raising one heavy hand. "There is still the sense of corruption near . . ."

"The Nightmare covers much of the Dream," Eranikus impatiently pointed out. He acted more anxious now that the two were about to enter. "I sense its malevolence more than ever. Once you are through, I shall depart!"

Broll, in the lead, paused to look one last time to the dragon. "We thank you for your aid, though."

"Thank me not for helping you to possible disaster, little night elf!"

Tyrande, peering at the portal, interrupted. "Broll, there is something—"

The portal flared. The emerald energies darkened, then *swelled*, expanding to encompass the pair.

As the night elves tried to come to grips with what was happening, mocking laughter rang in their ears and a fearsome head that seemed as much mist as real lunged toward them. Like the energies of the portal, the creature was of a dire green shade.

"We've been waiting for you . . ." the dragon said.

12

NIGHTMARE'S SERVANTS

The green dragon was not so great in size as Eranikus, but he was large indeed and eager to take the night elves. Broll cast the calming spell that had worked at least in part on Ysera's consort, hoping to slow the attacking beast.

But for his efforts he received only more of the malevolent laughter. The dragon would have fallen upon him if not for Tyrande, who shoved the druid aside and threw her glaive.

Glowing with Elune's majesty, the triple-bladed weapon whirled unerringly at its target. The tip cut across the dragon's snout just above the red region that almost resembled a beard, and though the monster seemed half-insubstantial, a wicked flash of dark emerald energy escaped the cut. The horned dragon arched his neck, more furious than wounded. His wings spread wide, revealing red membrane that contrasted sharply to his overall verdant appearance. Lethon's fiendish orbs were wide with rage and it was clear that, unlike Eranikus or others of the green dragonflight—who generally kept their eyes shut and observed all through the half-waking, half-sleeping state—the corrupted behemoth saw quite well.

"You must be taught your places . . ." the beast hissed as the glaive returned to Tyrande.

"Away from the portal!" Broll ordered. "Retreat from it!"

The pair backed up, trying to return to Ashenvale, but the energies of the portal spread to follow them. No matter how hard they pushed, they could not reach the mortal plane.

Then a mighty figure reached for them. Gnarl, half-submerged in the portal energies, grabbed Tyrande with one huge hand and Broll with the other even as the sinister dragon surged forward.

"You cannot escape . . . the Nightmare is all around and all within you!"

As he said that, from the very air surrounding the night elves there formed shadow creatures that made Tyrande gasp. Although only silhouettes, they bore the semblances of satyrs, their muscular legs akin to those of furred goats and ending in heavy, cloven hooves and their heads bearing sharp horns that curved back. There were hints of other satyr features, the long tails and beards, the torsos and heads bearing resemblance to night elves. The outlines of their savage claws were quite clear. That they were shadows added some new dimension of horror to those who had faced the true fiends in the past.

Their numbers increased in rapid order, threatening to overwhelm the trio. Gnarl thrust the night elves behind him, then confronted the shadow satyrs. They leapt upon the ancient with eager abandon. They scratched and tore and bit with ebony fangs and claws. They tore through the hard bark skin. A deep brown sap dribbled from wounds all over the ancient, but Gnarl seemed unimpressed by the injuries he received.

The ancient seized one shadow and squeezed. The silhouette scattered into a thousand pieces of shadow. Gnarl plucked another off of him, then did the same.

But the pieces from the first then gathered again in different places. From the one destroyed shadow was born half a dozen more. The same happened to the fragments of the second.

Yet the ancient had bought his two companions time to plot their own counterattacks. The high priestess threw her glaive. The weapon became whirling death, severing shadow after shadow. The moonlight surrounding the blades then burned away the cut silhouettes.

As for Broll, he transformed, again taking on an ursine shape. The huge, dark bear fell upon the shadow satyrs. Claws ripped and tore at the silhouettes, claws aglow with wild, purple flames. The shadows fell by the scores as Broll let his animalistic instincts all but take over.

The dragon's foul laugh drowned out all other sounds. He swept toward Broll. *"Your little flames won't hurt me!"*

The leviathan opened wide and exhaled. A great cloud of utter darkness shot forth.

It enveloped the druid. Broll could neither see nor sense anything. Growling, he slashed and bit, but found no substance.

Father! Father!

The massive bear snarled in distrust and anxiety. Broll knew his daughter's voice.

No, Father, no!

He knew that this was not real, that this was a nightmare of the dragon's doing . . . but the cry felt so real.

Just for a moment, Broll caught sight of a female night elf. That strengthened his yearning for Anessa. The druid reverted to his true form—

The shadows pressed him . . . but out of them also came the figure he had glimpsed. She gripped him tight and pulled him with her.

"Broll! Wake up!"

He blinked, not certain when his eyes had closed. "A-Anessa?"

"No! Tyrande!"

"Tyrande . . ." The druid's senses returned. He stood next to the high priestess, who had one hand wrapped around his waist while with the other hand she manipulated the huge, gleaming glaive. Elune's light still embraced the weapon, giving it power against the shadow satyrs.

"He comes again!" she warned.

Broll did not have to ask who, for the monstrous dragon already loomed over them. Of Gnarl there was no sight, and the druid also wondered what had happened to Eranikus. Had he led them to this point so that this other dragon could deal with them? *No . . . that makes no sense! If he had, he'd be here, too, making certain of our deaths!*

But what mattered most at the moment was surviving. The dragon dove down. His mouth opened wide and Broll feared another exhalation of dark nightmares.

Then, with a guttural roar, Gnarl reentered the scene. Bits of his bark skin hung from the ancient's body and the sap dripped everywhere, yet Gnarl showed no slowing as he seized the reptilian monster.

"They will not be yours, Lethon!" he grated.

"*You will all be ours . . .*" the corrupted dragon mocked. "*Azeroth and the Dream have been inexorably intertwined since the world's creation . . . and thus you are linked to the Dream and what it is . . . You cannot hide from that within all of you . . .*"

Lethon . . . Broll knew that name. "He was slain!" the druid told Tyrande as they battled to escape the energies of the twisted portal. "Lethon should be dead!"

"Then how does he exist here?"

The druid suddenly understood. It explained why the energies had reached out to the pair. "Only his dreamform still thrives! He's a green dragon, one of those most bound to the Dream! Whatever corrupted him must've been able to keep that part of him 'alive,' but only so long as he stays from the mortal plane."

"What happens if he does not?"

"We should try to find out," Broll muttered. "Eranikus be cursed! If he knew about this . . . if this is why he left us to face the Nightmare alone . . ."

There was no time to say more, for the dark green shapes were converging on them again and, worse, Gnarl was finally losing ground to Lethon. Although the guardian was gigantic himself and embodied the power and sturdiness of the huge tree he resembled, Lethon was too strong. The dragon battled the wounded ancient down, then raised a paw that ended in massive claws.

The night elves had no hope of aiding him. Indeed, they were not only driven back by the ancient, but were then separated from one another by the fiendish silhouettes.

"Away from me!" Tyrande roared, trying to fight her way back. With the whirling glaive and the light of Elune, she cut a swath through the infernal ranks. The shadow satyrs before her melted away as if dew touched by the morning sun.

Broll returned to his bear form, using the magical purple fire to enhance his powerful blows. Yet the nightmares seemed without end.

Lethon, meanwhile, had returned his attention to Gnarl. The ancient had managed to rise up on one knee but could still not fend off his gargantuan adversary.

"*I have you now!*" Lethon cried with a savage grin revealing many, many teeth.

"I have lived long . . . I do not fear death . . ."

This caused the corrupted dragon to laugh more harshly. "*Dead, you serve us no purpose . . .*"

With one mighty paw, he swatted Gnarl toward the deep mist.

The ancient managed to bring himself to a halt at the very edge. Clearly staggered, he nevertheless defiantly rose to resume battle.

From out of the mist came a dark, grasping hand. It was small, but it seized Gnarl's leg with a ferocity that caused the ancient to look down. As he did, a second, identical hand seized one arm.

Other hands shot from the mist. They clustered together, as if all part of the same host. Gnarl growled and tried to pull away, but too many now had hold of him.

Broll roared a warning to Tyrande. The two night elves tried to fight their way to their rescuer.

Despite his titanic struggles, the ancient could not free himself of even one grip. More and more hands seized him. They grasped him as something starving might a morsel. Slowly they began to drag Gnarl back to the mist.

Lethon came between the giant and the druid. He swirled before Broll, the dragon's chuckle sending involuntary chills down the great bear's spine. Broll roared at the dragon as he tried to find some way past. Farther back, Tyrande struggled as the shadows renewed their attack on her position.

"*You waste your breath . . . no one can escape . . . no one can flee . . . you will belong to us . . .*"

Gnarl was half into the mist. Even still, more and more hands clutched at his arms, grappled with his legs, and clawed at his torso. Others pulled back the brave guardian's head and even sought to smother his voice.

But Gnarl managed one shout. "Escape through the portal! Escape through the—"

The hands—shaped like those of night elves, humans, orcs, tauren, and other creatures of Azeroth—now all but covered the ancient. There were so many that Gnarl himself could barely move. One foot was dragged into the mist. A shoulder joined it, then the entire arm. Gnarl's head vanished into the impenetrable fog.

The ancient shuddered. He seemed to go limp.

The hands pulled the rest of him within.

Tyrande had been seeking a path on the other side of Lethon, but not until Gnarl had vanished did it suddenly open. So desperate to reach their ally, the high priestess took a few steps forward before realizing that not only was it too late for Gnarl, but that Lethon had let her commit herself in order to make her the next victim.

The first hands reached out, as hungry as ever. Forced to save herself from Gnarl's fate, the high priestess turned from Lethon to battle the hands with both Elune's light and the glaive.

A titanic bellow shook the three combatants. A glistening form appeared among them. Eranikus.

The emerald dragon's closed eyes fixed on Lethon.

The corrupted leviathan suddenly roared. He twisted and cried out, *"The trees . . . they close in on me!"*

As he said this, Broll and the others saw what appeared to be soft, misty trees truly gathering around the corrupted dragon. To the druid, they seemed harmless, healing . . . but to Lethon it appeared as if their mere touch was poison.

But then Lethon shook his head. The trees of mist dissipated.

Lethon's expression toward Eranikus was murderous. *"I am beyond such petty dream attacks! Indeed, you dream too much, dear Eranikus . . . you dream too much and understand too little of what I have become through the growing power of the Nightmare . . ."* The seared areas healed. Lethon leaned forward and though he did not stand as great as Eranikus, he was fearsome. *"But you will understand again, when you are one of us once more . . ."*

Lethon's eyes widened . . . and as they did, they changed, revealing that what the party had seen earlier had been illusion. Now came the dread reality.

They were pits, pits so dark that they seemed to want to swallow those upon which they were focused. There was in them the same hunger, the same horror, that the hands had exhibited. Yet in the dragon, it became a different evil, a personal one.

"I am only corruption now, Eranikus! It has consumed me and I savor that consumption . . ."

"Then . . . there is no reason for you to continue to be . . ."

Ysera's mate glared at Lethon.

Broll noticed that the corrupted dragon did not cringe or fight. Instead, Lethon waited . . . with *anticipation*.

"Eranikus!" the druid shouted. "Beware! There is another!"

Lethon's head turned and the hollow eyes sought to tear out Broll's very soul. The druid let out a gasp but fought the dread feeling.

The mist nearest Eranikus coalesced into a horrific form that was the Nightmare embodied. It was one of Eranikus's kind, but only just. The great majesty that was a green dragon had been replaced by a thing so diseased that its flesh rotted. It was female, but only barely recognizable as so now. There were tatters in the violet membranes of the wings, and a stench of decay washed over the night elves.

Tyrande shuddered, reliving the initial war against the Burning Legion, when the land was covered in the innocent dead. Broll let out a rumble of pain as he watched Anessa perish again, along with so many others in the far more recent battle against the demons at Mt. Hyjal.

The new terror had sinister black orbs whose centers were a chilling bone white. She seized upon a startled Eranikus, sinking skeletal claws into his forelegs.

"Have you forgotten dear Emeriss?" the macabre dragon asked in a voice that literally chilled. *"We yearn to have you back with us, Eranikus . . ."*

"No! I will not let the Nightmare take me again!" He turned his stare upon her.

She spat. A putrid green substance covered Eranikus's eyes.

He roared and tried to wipe the foul stuff away, but she held him tight. Worse, Lethon now joined her in the attack.

"*We have missed you so much . . .*" Emeriss cooed. "*Do not fight our embrace . . . accept the inevitable . . .*"

"No! Never! I cannot! I will not!" Yet, despite his protestations, Eranikus could not prevent the pair from beginning to drag him toward the mists. There, the hands reappeared, grasping at the air in anticipation of the struggling leviathan.

Neither Broll nor Tyrande could do anything; they were barely able to hold their own as the shadow satyrs renewed their eager assault.

Crimson fire from behind Ysera's consort bathed Emeriss and Lethon. Startled and enraged, they released their hold and retreated to the mists. Eranikus immediately fled the portal, in his anxiety utterly forgetting his two companions.

But other aid came to them. Two great hands made of soft, red energy swept away the dark throngs, then gently lifted the druid and the high priestess as if they were toys. The hands withdrew, pulling them to safety beyond the portal.

The dark emerald forces immediately after returned to their normal state.

Eranikus lay sprawled far to the side, Ysera's mate panting. His gaze was turned from where the night elves and their savior stood.

Their savior . . . yet another dragon.

A red dragon.

A very, very large red dragon, one who dwarfed even Eranikus.

Two massive horns thrust back from a proud, reptilian head. Most of the behemoth's body was of a stunning crimson, but the chest had a great patch of silver to it, as did the paws. Small webbed patches extended from each side of the head.

Yet what set the dragon apart from any of the others—aside from the immense size—were the eyes. They were not the glittering orbs of Eranikus's flight, but rather a smoldering golden light that, despite the night elves' previous predicament, brought calm and hope.

When the dragon spoke, her voice was commanding but soothing. "They have fled. They did not expect me. Sad to say, I did not expect them, either, or else I would have been ready to aid you from the beginning."

"You . . . are an Aspect . . ." Tyrande solemnly declared. "You are—"

The gargantuan dragon bowed her head. "I am . . . Alexstrasza. And I know you, Tyrande Whisperwind, from both that long-ago struggle now called the War of the Ancients and the blessing of Nordrassil soon after it."

"Alexstrasza . . ." The high priestess stirred at the thought of another name related to the Aspect, that of a second valued ally. "Krasus! Is he here also? Does he still live? He would have some answers for us—"

The dragon shook her head. Her gaze grew troubled. "There are many sleepers, Tyrande Whisperwind . . . and he is among them."

The female night elf frowned. "I am sorry for you."

The Aspect cocked her head, startled. "You are sorry for me?" Alexstrasza glanced at Broll, who hid his curiosity as best he could. Like most druids, he knew of the two magi Krasus and Rhonin, very active in these times, who were said to have played a part in Malfurion's growth as a druid some ten thousand years before. How that could be, his shan'do had never made clear. "And is he, also?"

"He does not know. I know because of Malfurion."

"As is just, considering your part in so much, Tyrande Whisperwind." To Broll Alexstrasza said, "And it is just that you also know. My consort Korialstrasz and the mage Krasus are one and the same."

"One and the same?" It explained so much, yet Broll knew that he would have never made such a connection himself.

The great dragon rose up on her hind legs and folded in her wings. As she did, she began to shrink. Her wings shriveled, quickly turning into nubs, then nothing. Alexstrasza's forepaws became arms and her legs twisted outward, resembling more those of a night elf.

Now barely twice the height of Broll and only a fraction of her former girth, the Aspect continued her remarkable transformation. Her maw receded into her face, becoming a separate nose and mouth. The horns dwindled and lush hair sprouted. In another blink of an eye the change was nearly complete, and a figure who was and was not any sort of elven offshoot stood before the druid and his companion.

Lush tresses of fiery hair—and, indeed, there were licks of flame constantly escaping the wild mane—cascaded down her slim shoulders. Alexstrasza was clad as a warrior maiden, with long, armored boots rising to her thighs and a breastplate that accented the curve of her feminine body. Her hands were shielded by intricate gauntlets reaching almost to the crooks of her arms and a crimson cloak that resembled a membraned wing in form fluttered behind her. What had been her horns were to Broll's amazed gaze either an intricate headpiece well-placed atop her head . . . or still smaller horns.

Crimson, violet, and touches of blue-black—all framed with gold edging—were her garments' colors, and her skin was a soft brownish red. Her face was rounder than that of Tyrande or any night elf, almost as if mixed with human traits. Her nose was smaller and her mouth perfectly curved. Her hair formed a widow's peak and then framed her face on both sides.

Only the Aspect's eyes had not changed, save to have adjusted for her size. Broll and Tyrande both instinctively went down on one knee and bent their heads in homage. Although they served other patrons, all honored the Life-Binder.

"Rise up," she commanded. "I do not seek subjects, but allies . . ."

Rising, Tyrande solemnly said, "If Elune grants it, what power I wield both with my glaive and through my prayers to her will I offer! I stood with yours against the demons ten thousand years ago and if, as I think, our concerns coincide, I will do so again!"

"They do." The glorious figure looked to Broll. "And you, druid? What say you?"

"Our lives are owed to you already, mistress, and you're sister to She of the Dreaming. I can think of no other reason for you to be here save our own, and so there's no argument as to whom I lend my hand . . ."

She nodded gratefully. "My Korialstrasz, my treasured mate, lies in a troubled slumber from which he cannot wake, though I sense he tries. He is far from the only one, my children, as you likely already suspect. Not only are others of my kind affected—though fewer since dragons do not need to sleep as much as most races—but this dread slumber has touched every other race. Worse, it finds particular interest in those of prominence and power: magi, kings, generals, philosophers, and the like."

"Shandris!" Tyrande breathed.

"If she is one of yours, my child, then her chance is better. The night elves have not suffered to the degree of many races. I find this intriguing. I think that we have another ally, though I am amazed if my guess is correct . . ."

Before she could say more, a moan arose from the side. Broll glared at Eranikus, who still lay where he had fallen after escaping his corrupted kind. "A better ally than *that* sorry sight, I hope! Fleeing for his life after letting others take the lead to a place he better knows—"

The green dragon raised his head. His reptilian features were twisted in a pathetic look. "You do not understand even now, little druid! Did you not see them? Did you not understand what Lethon and Emeriss have become? Did you not also want to flee?"

"Not without any of my friends."

With another moan, the dragon turned away. "You do not understand . . ."

Alexstrasza turned to the gigantic beast. Although her expression held no anger, her tone was not one of forgiveness. "Nor do I, Eranikus . . . and that in itself says much concerning your actions." As the green dragon began to protest, the Aspect cut him off. "And, yes, I know what it is like to be a slave to the dark will of something else, a slave responsible for abominable acts."

Eranikus eyed her, then finally nodded. "So you do."

"And I also know more about what is happening here than even you do." She stepped just in front of his immense jaws and, though in her present form was so much tinier than him, stood as the greater over the lesser. "I know that Ysera was aware of your redemption and survival . . . and aware of your choice at the last moment not to return to her side after all for fear that the Nightmare might yet cause you to someday betray her again."

His powerful gaze was as nothing to her. Broll, watching, had at first wondered why he did not shut his lids and see her through the ways of his kind. Only now did it occur to the druid that to resume doing so meant Eranikus opening himself up to the Nightmare, the last thing he desired.

"She—knew?" the behemoth finally asked Alexstrasza. "She knew that as I flew to her in the Dream, I sensed the Nightmare calling to me despite the cleansing of my corruption, calling to me with such strength that I understood my renewed confidence was but a false hope?"

"She knew immediately. Yet she loves you so much that she accepted your choice in the hopes that eventually you *would* still return to her."

"And now . . . and now it is too late . . . she is taken also . . ."

The Aspect's own amazing eyes narrowed. "No . . . not yet."

Eranikus looked with desperate hope to her. "She is safe?"

"Hardly that." Alexstrasza extended a hand to include the two night elves. "There is more known to me about the Nightmare than any of you three have thus far learned. It is a danger that Ysera has fought for some time . . ."

Ysera, the red dragon informed them, had noticed her dreams grow dark, even despite her absolute control of them. At first she had blamed her own concerns but then had discovered the truth too late. The nightmares she experienced touched Azeroth, took lives of their own, and reached into the minds of the mortals there.

It was then that Ysera had made a terrible error of her own. The mistress of the Emerald Dream had looked into the slumbering minds, seeking the source of what had even infiltrated her own subconscious.

She did so unaware that the source of the threat desired just that of her.

"Lethon came upon her while her mind was deep in her search beyond," Alexstrasza told them. "He was accompanied by shadows, the satyrs that these night elves just fought. They fell upon her dreaming form while he took that which was most desired . . . the *Eye*."

Eranikus jumped to his feet. His gaze became all but impossible for Broll and Tyrande to behold. "The Eye of Ysera taken? I had feared as much! How can you say then that my beloved queen is not prisoner?"

"The Eye is where Ysera and her flight most often congregate in the Dream," Broll quietly informed Tyrande. "It's said to be the most idyllic place there. Malfurion's seen it and I know Fandral, also, but few others even among us druids. I'm told it's a valley nestled among great, encircling hills. The land is lush and filled with grass and flowers, but the name comes from the magnificent golden dome in the center, where Ysera herself dwells . . . dwelled . . ."

The green dragon snorted. "A pale though acceptable description of it, little druid! There is no more perfect place in all creation!" He suddenly moaned. "The Eye taken! Where then is my queen if not captured?!?"

Now Alexstrasza shook her head sadly at his continued rage. "No. Ysera avoided capture. She is fighting. She, her remaining consorts, and a handful of others fight not only to save themselves, but to seek the truth at the Nightmare's dark core. She has no intention of letting either her domain or Azeroth fall to this monstrous thing!"

"She is mad! If she falls prey to it, all is ended! The Nightmare felt so powerful, I believed her already taken, but if she seeks its truths and its power, it will make of her something worse than Lethon or Emeriss and, through her, alter both planes into a horror far worse than anything we have thus far experienced!"

"She does what she must do," Alexstrasza calmly replied. "And I seek to help her as I can. I add my strength to hers from afar, watch over all tentative advances by the Nightmare into this world, seek those who can help . . . and watch for the corrupted, the unwaking."

The male dragon finally looked down. In a tone of self-loathing, he muttered, "You do all that for her while she risks herself so and I . . . I sit in a cave, hiding from the doom of the world! Hiding from the defense of my love and my queen! I know your Korialstrasz of old just as I know you, Life-Binder! I am not worthy to be in your presence or that of my Ysera . . ." Alexstrasza almost spoke, but Eranikus shook his head. "But if there is hope of becoming worthy of her, there is but one path for me!"

The great green dragon spun to face the portal. Its energies pulsated softly, innocently.

Eranikus moved toward it. "I no longer sense the Nightmare near. The accursed corruption has shifted again. It is safe for the moment to enter . . . but beyond that . . ." He looked to the night elves. "Your part ends here."

"No, we go with you," Tyrande countered. "I do not think our coming together was all chance. Someone seeks to bring together those who best can serve Azeroth and its survival. Nothing happens without reason . . ."

"Of course, someone does!" Ysera's consort abruptly responded, expression shifting to desperate hope. "It must be my queen! Even with so much no doubt assailing her, she works and plots for our salvation! I should have seen it—"

"Not Ysera. Not my sister," Alexstrasza sagely interjected. She eyed Tyrande and Broll. "I think another seeks to guide you . . . and I think it is *Malfurion Stormrage* himself."

It comes together, Malfurion dared hope, the archdruid doing all he could to shield those thoughts from his captor. *They may suspect . . . but that is good so long as he doesn't . . .*

The dread shadows suddenly stretched over the tree of pain that was the night elf. The insidious presence of the Nightmare Lord surrounded Malfurion and filled his mind and soul.

Have you come to love the agony? Is it so much a part of you that you cannot tell it from yourself?

Malfurion did not respond. There was no point in responding. Doing so only served his captor.

Keeping counsel with your own thoughts, Malfurion Stormrage? The skeletal tendrils of the shadow tree wrapped around the imprisoned archdruid. *Shall we discuss those thoughts . . . those dreams . . . those hopes?*

Despite himself, the night elf could not help but be jarred by the last. Did the foul thing know?

Let us share some considerations . . . let us share some ambitions . . .

The archdruid buried his thoughts as deep as possible. His plan was near to fruition. There was a chance . . .

The Nightmare Lord laughed in his head. *And, most of all, Malfurion Stormrage, let us talk of foolish dreams of rescue . . .*

13

AT THE EDGE OF NIGHTMARE

The druids were exhausted. They had spent themselves so much that several would not likely be of help for any further casting for days. Their combined might had fed and fed Teldrassil, but with no visible success . . . at least so far as Hamuul could tell.

As for the tauren himself, he had become a pariah to most of the others, although officially there had been no censure, no condemnation by Archdruid Fandral concerning whatever Broll had done. Fandral had not even informed Hamuul just what the missing druid had done. He had merely eyed the tauren disapprovingly, doing so long enough that the others understood that Hamuul had lost favor.

Naralex and a few others defied the shunning, but Hamuul did his best to steer clear of them out of concern that they, too, would suffer. The aged tauren was willing to shoulder his responsibility in enabling Broll to go unnoticed long enough. He trusted his friend. Fandral had a right to be angered, though.

The lead archdruid had insisted on keeping them at Teldrassil's base, far from Darnassus. Only he had thus far returned to the city. Each time he returned, Fandral pressed the druids in some new fashion. He assured them that they were making progress, that the World Tree was healing.

Hamuul had to assume that he was not an adept-enough archdruid to sense what Fandral did.

The tauren sat cross-legged a bit distant from the rest. The druids were meditating, trying to regain their strength for Fandral's next spell. Hamuul had never felt so drained in all his life, not even during the weeklong hunt that had been part of his rite of passage from child to adult. That had required fasting during the entire trial.

I am getting old . . . was his first thought. Yet none of the night elves appeared any stronger than him. Thus far it seemed that the lead archdruid's plans had done little more than bring every member to the brink of ruin.

Thinking again of Fandral, Hamuul looked for him. However, the other was nowhere to be found. The tauren could only suppose that Fandral had perhaps again returned to the Cenarion Enclave to consult some ancient text. Hamuul hoped that it would provide them with more tangible results than they had achieved thus far.

Finding himself unable to meditate, the tauren rose. Seeing that none of the others paid him any mind, he strode toward the World Tree.

Even though Hamuul had not been one of those in favor of a second such giant, he could not only appreciate the majesty of it, but also Teldrassil's effect on the world. As a tauren, Hamuul very much believed in the balance between nature and the lives of the various races of Azeroth. That had been why he had sought out Malfurion Stormrage in the first place and asked to be instructed in the druidic arts. And even though Hamuul had only been a druid for a few years, he believed that he had proven himself well. Otherwise, he would not have risen to become one of the few archdruids and the only one of his kind.

The tauren wished there was more *he* could do beyond what he had done for Broll. He still felt that Broll's choice was somehow the right one, despite how it crossed Fandral's good purposes. Standing just before Teldrassil, he looked up into the clouds where Darnassus lay. If the portal had been very near, Hamuul might have been tempted to just walk through it. As it was, his only other choice was to fly . . .

With a grunt, he leaned with one hand against Teldrassil. There was more he needed to do. If Broll—

Someone was whispering.

Hamuul stepped from the tree and looked for the speaker. However, the whispering immediately ceased.

His thick brow wrinkling in thought, the archdruid neared the trunk once more.

The whispering started up again. Hamuul stared at Teldrassil . . . then looked down at his foot. There, the side of his right foot touched one of the World Tree's roots.

He placed his hand on the trunk.

The whispering filled his head. Hamuul could not understand it. It was not any of the tongues spoken by the intelligent races of Azeroth. Rather, it reminded him of something else, something the tauren should know well—

"Shakuun, guide my spear . . ." he murmured, blurting a tauren oath. Shakuun had been his father's father, and tauren called upon their venerated ancestors, who watched over them. The oath as he spoke it was not to be taken literally; Hamuul was asking his grandsire to help him come to grips with what he had discovered.

The archdruid was listening to the voice of Teldrassil.

All druids knew the language of the trees, although some understood it better than others. This was not the first time that Hamuul had touched and listened to the World Tree, but this was the first time he had heard these whispers. The voice of the World Tree was usually heard more in the rustle of its branches and leaves and through the coursing of the sap that flowed as blood up and down the vast trunk. It could be heard as a whisper, but one with understanding.

But Hamuul could make no sense out of what he heard now. The whispers were without proper rhythm, without form. As the archdruid continued to listen, they went on and on as if—

"What is it you do, Hamuul Runetotem?" Fandral's voice suddenly said.

Smothering his startlement, the tauren turned to the lead archdruid.

He had not sensed the night elf approach, which said something for Hamuul's present state of mind. As a tauren, he prided himself on his belief that his people were the only ones who could truly sneak up on one of Fandral's race.

Hamuul chose to be honest. This was something Fandral of all druids should know.

But how to explain it best? "I fear . . . Archdruid Fandral, will you listen to Teldrassil for a moment? I fear that things are worse than we thought! When I touched my hand to the trunk just now—"

The night elf did not wait for him to finish. Fandral placed his palm flat against Teldrassil. He shut his eyes and concentrated.

A few breaths later, the lead archdruid looked at the tauren. "I sense nothing different than before. Teldrassil is not yet well, but there is improvement."

" 'Improvement'?" Hamuul could not prevent himself from gaping. "Archdruid, I sensed—"

Fandral, his expression sympathetic, interjected, "You are weary, Hamuul, and I have been remiss in my treatment of you. You have a loyalty to a friend who must answer for his recklessness, I fear. It was beneath me, though, to show such disappointment with you when he is to blame."

"I—"

Fandral raised a hand. "Hear me out, good Hamuul. I have just returned with some knowledge of interest. It will make for a new and stronger attempt to cure what still ails Teldrassil. You, with your strong spirit, would be of tremendous value in that effort, but you need to recoup your strength more. If you fear that there is something more amiss with the World Tree, then this is surely good news to you."

Bowing his head, the tauren replied, "As you say, Archdruid Fandral."

"Excellent! Now, come with me. I would tell you more about our next effort. It shall be very exerting. It may take more than a day's meditation to recover from it . . ."

Fandral started off. Hamuul could do nothing but follow. Yet even

as he listened to the night elf begin to explain, he also looked back at
the area he had touched. He *had* heard the incoherent whispering and
he knew that it was the voice of the World Tree. Had not the lead archdruid also investigated, the tauren would have been even more anxious than he was. Still, enough of a concern remained that Hamuul
continued to wonder . . . and worry.

To Hamuul Runetotem, the whispering meant one and one thing
only.

Teldrassil was going *mad.*

They did not enter the portal immediately, although that had been
their intention. Eranikus and Alexstrasza cautiously probed ahead,
their powers reaching deep within to see if there still lurked some trap
by the corrupted Lethon and Emeriss. Only when they were satisfied
that there was not did the dragons agree it was safe for Eranikus and
the night elves to proceed.

"About damned time," Broll muttered. Tyrande nodded, mirroring his opinion. They were both filled with an urgency to find Malfurion. One particular thing that disturbed both was the missing Lucan
Foxblood and this mysterious orc. The orc was likely an accidental
intruder, and yet . . .

"You do not yet comprehend the full threat of the Nightmare," the
green dragon responded with some bitterness. "Be not so desiring of
entering it without all preparations made."

"Time is of the essence."

Alexstrasza dipped her head in agreement. "So it is, Broll Bearmantle, but if I am correct and Malfurion Stormrage has somehow
been trying to help guide you, then he would want matters thought
through first." The dragon smiled grimly. "And we have done
that now."

"I am ready," Eranikus declared.

"Are you certain?" asked the Aspect.

The bitterness grew more evident. "I am. I owe it to my Ysera."

The Life-Binder bowed her head. A warm, comforting glow

radiated from Alexstrasza. It touched the trio. The night elves smiled and even Eranikus looked thankful.

"May my blessing keep you safe and guide your hunt to success," the Aspect declared.

"We are honored and thank you," Tyrande replied.

Eranikus took a breath, then stretched his wings. "I will go ahead . . . to guard the way."

The energies within the portal swelled up as he approached. To his credit, the green dragon did not hesitate. He stepped into the portal.

And then he was gone.

Broll and Tyrande strode up to the portal.

"You should stay here," he said to her.

"I have remained apart from Malfurion much too long already," she retorted.

Before he could say anything else, she had leapt through.

Broll let out an exasperated sound, then followed.

The sensation of physically entering the other realm was akin to the feeling that one got just before falling asleep. Broll had not had time to think about that when Lethon had attacked them, but now he recognized it. It was far different from sending his dreamform here. When he did that, it was as if he had cast off a heavy weight and was finally free of all his worldly problems.

Not so now. More than ever, he was aware of what the Nightmare could hold, even if at present he could only see the thick mist ahead. The Nightmare had not entirely departed after all.

"We cannot travel like this," Eranikus proclaimed. The dragon fluttered just above the night elves, his wings beating in slow motion. He looked as if seen through the ripples of a rushing river, something else that Broll had not had time to notice during the desperate struggle. The same could be said for Tyrande and even the druid himself.

The dragon arched his back, then breathed upon the mist. A soft spray of what appeared to be speckles of emerald light touched everywhere ahead.

"Elune, protect us!" the high priestess gasped as the way cleared.

At that moment Broll would have gratefully accepted the aid of any deity or demigod. Even the company of a dragon did not at the moment seem enough.

Before, the Emerald Dream had been a place that was the world of Azeroth as seen as if no races such as the night elves had ever existed. Its hills and mountains had been perfectly shaped, for erosion did not exist here. High grasses and beautiful trees had spread across a rolling landscape. The fauna had been unafraid, peaceful. To druids, it had seemed a paradise.

But now no name was more apt, at least for the area before them, than that by which Eranikus called it . . . *Nightmare.*

The land was draped in a wet, festering substance that bubbled. The beautiful emerald shading had become the putrid color of rot. What trees there were had become deformed parodies of themselves. Their leaves were black, sharp, and filled with poisonous stickers. Small dark vermin crawled over the scabby bark, often pausing to dine on the thick, odorous sap dripping from cracks in the trunks.

"Cenarius, preserve us . . ." the druid rasped. Still eyeing it all in disbelief, Broll took a step forward. A crunching sound beneath his feet made the druid look down.

The ground was *covered* in small green-black scorpions, sinewy millipedes, finger-sized cockroaches, spiders with bodies as large as fists, and more. A thick, sticky tar now coated the underside of Broll's sandal, the results of crushing several of the creatures with his step.

"They are everywhere," Tyrande breathed. "They cover the ground for as far as the eye can see . . ."

"Not for long," the green dragon responded with much determination. He breathed over the ground. It was as if Eranikus had exhaled flames. The crackle of thousands of tiny bodies burning to a crisp filled their ears, and even the dragon shuddered at the sound.

The land Eranikus had razed was now charred black. He nodded at his handiwork.

But from the crusted forms there came movement. Out of one burnt roach carapace burst a number of segmented legs. A new cockroach as horrific as the last emerged from its predecessor.

And to the dismay of the three, the act was repeated from every ruined corpse. Whatever Eranikus had destroyed was replaced . . .

Tendrils of mist played around the macabre scenery, as if seeking to regain the air Ysera's consort had cleared. The green dragon let out another burst, which pushed the mist away again . . . for the moment.

"It is monstrous . . ." the high priestess said, trying without success to carefully pick her steps. Each footfall was followed by more crunching and the sound of the thick tar oozing from the shattered bodies. Worse, the moment that she stepped away, the hideous rebirth of her victims began.

"This is only part of it . . ." Eranikus muttered, the gleam of his eyes muted in this place. "I sense that the Nightmare has strengthened, worsened more than I could ever have believed . . ."

And as he spoke, they all became aware of movement at the edge of the mist. Shapes that were almost seen . . . but not quite.

"The shadow satyrs have returned," Tyrande decided.

Eranikus said nothing. Instead, he exhaled again, bathing the closest of the vaguely seen forms. As with the fiendish creatures beneath their feet, there immediately came the sound of burning.

But then, frantic and pleading shrieks all but deafened the trio. Stunned, the green dragon quickly cut off his attack. Broll and Tyrande clutched their ears at the terrifying sound. These were not the cries of monsters vanquished.

"May Ysera forgive me!" Eranikus managed as the mist burned away and his victims lay revealed.

They were—or *had* been—night elves, humans, orcs, dwarves . . . members of all the mortal races. What remained after Eranikus's merciless attack were charred bodies that continued to quiver, that sought to reach out for help or at least an end to their suffering.

Ignoring the vermin, Broll raced to the nearest, Tyrande at his side. Eranikus remained where he was, the green dragon clearly shaken by the harm he had done.

"The sleepers . . ." Broll realized. "These are the sleepers . . ."

"I may have slain all of them in Azeroth as if I had stood over the bed of each and scorched them with fire!" Ysera's consort growled.

"Unable to escape their dreaming, they would have suffered as they have here!"

"You don't know that," argued the druid. "You don't—"

The brittle bones of the night elf over which he had been kneeling shifted.

A blackened, fleshless hand gripped his wrist and a skull with two ruined eyes bent up toward him.

The ruined corpse shrieked its agony again. It reached with more ravaged fingers.

Broll tugged as hard as he could. "I can't free myself!"

Tyrande readied the glaive, then hesitated. Instead, she prayed.

The shrieking subsided. The skeleton faded away.

But other victims renewed their mournful cries. Tyrande continued her prayer, using one hand to spread the power of her patron across the visible landscape.

The ravaged bodies disappeared. Only when the last had gone did the high priestess cease her efforts. By then, she was shaking.

Broll and Eranikus were not much better. "They were suffering!" the druid spat. "They were really suffering!"

"I did not know!" the dragon retorted defensively. "I would do no harm to the innocent! It is the Nightmare," Eranikus reminded them. "It knows what hurts you the most, what you fear the most . . . and it feeds off that . . ."

Tyrande took some hope from that. "Then, is this all illusion that we face?"

"No . . . the greatest nightmare that the Nightmare offers is its growing reality."

That settled it for Broll. "We must find Malfurion and quickly . . ." He looked into the mist, for the first time realizing the enormity of what he suggested. "But . . . which direction?"

"I will find where he is," the high priestess declared with utter conviction. She looked haunted. "No one, not even you as a fellow druid, know him as I do, Broll."

He did not deny that fact. "But I have a thought as to how to search, also. I—"

The landscape abruptly shifted. The night elves were tossed to the infested ground. Eranikus chose to rise up over the trouble. However, even there he was buffeted.

At last things calmed. Tyrande pushed herself up, quickly wiping off those millipedes and other carrion creatures that still stuck to her. Broll murmured a spell, but the vermin would not listen to him. They were not like the fauna of Azeroth. Like the high priestess, he resigned himself to brushing them away.

Eranikus alighted. The high priestess eyed him reprovingly. Surprisingly, the green dragon looked away in guilt.

"What happened now?" Broll asked Eranikus. They were now in a hillier region, with ominous, shadowed paths that disappeared into the infernal mists.

"This is the Nightmare; ask me not the reason for anything that occurs here save that it is not something we should want!"

Tyrande peered ahead. "There is a castle or some structure ahead. On that third hill."

Both the green dragon and Broll shook their heads, the druid saying, "There're no buildings anywhere save the Eye."

"Then whatever I see must be part of the Nightmare." Before she could add more, there was yet again movement in the mist. The high priestess did not waste time, illuminating the vicinity with the Mother Moon's light.

But what she revealed was not what any of them expected.

It was Lucan Foxblood.

"You!" Broll rumbled. He seized the human before anything could separate them. Lucan stared at him with eyes as wide and as hollow as death, but was clearly no phantasm.

"You're real . . ." he whispered. A faint, somewhat mad grin flickered across his drawn face. "It's you . . ." He looked to Tyrande and his grin grew a little calmer. "And you . . ." Then he saw what loomed behind the night elves and his growing relief vanished.

"We are all your friends," Tyrande reassured him.

Lucan settled down. "Real . . . all of you . . ." His eyes darted to the side. "I tried to leave, but something held me here . . . I tried to leave, but something wanted her to keep on . . ."

The druid seized hold of the last part. " 'Her'? The orc, you mean? A female?"

"Yes . . . yes . . ."

"You know as well as I do that there is little difference between a female and a male orc when it comes to battle," Tyrande pointed out to Broll. "One should never underestimate either."

"I wasn't thinking that. Just wondering who she might be and why she happened to be here."

"Her name is Thura," Lucan offered almost tonelessly. "She came to kill him. She came to kill your Malfurion Stormrage."

The pronouncement made even the dragon gape. Tyrande seized Lucan by the throat, but Broll managed to calm her.

"Hear him out, my lady! He's not to blame!"

"He said that she wants to slay Malfurion! He brought her here to do it—" But Tyrande finally caught herself. "Against his will, though . . . I know that . . . Lucan . . . I am sorry . . ."

Lucan gave her a nervous smile. It was clear that he liked the high priestess.

Broll brought him back to the subject. "The orc! She came to kill Malfurion . . . why? How would she know how to find him? Did she say?"

"The visions . . . she babbled something about visions . . . she said that . . . that they led her to me . . . that they showed her the path to him piece by piece . . . the visions were helping her avenge her kin and save Azeroth, too, she said . . ."

"An orc blood oath," Tyrande muttered. "I know them well. She will not stop until she either is slain or succeeds." The high priestess shook her head. "The second part . . . it must be madness . . ."

"Whatever the case, something wants her to succeed," the druid added. To Lucan, he asked, "But the first thing . . . she thinks Malfurion slew one of hers? What of it? Orcs understand death in battle."

The human concentrated. "She said—she said that he was a 'base murderer.' That he betrayed his friend and killed him when his back was turned in trust . . . I think."

It was more than Tyrande could stand. She brandished the glaive, which made Lucan step back in concern. "Lies! All of it! A threat to Azeroth? Ha! Truly madness as I said! And even the declaration of betrayal—Malfurion would never do such a thing! As proof of that, he has rarely even had the opportunity, for the number of orcs he could claim as comrade could be counted on one hand!"

"It was only one time she mentioned! She said a name! Bruxigan . . . Broxigan—"

"*Broxigar?*" The high priestess staggered back. She dropped the glaive. Tears welled up in her eyes. "Brox!" Tyrande shouted to the others. "An orc who lived before his time! As a novice, I befriended him when he was captured by my people! He fought the Burning Legion and Azshara's servants alongside us"—she swallowed—"and he died holding the way, so Krasus has affirmed, against the demons' dread lord himself, Sargeras!"

The druid's gaze sharpened. "It must be him who she speaks about."

"But he was Malfurion's *friend!*" the distraught high priestess went on. "They never fought with one another, and Malfurion honored him with me when it was all over! You must remember, Broll! Our people raised up a statue to him, the only orc ever to be given homage by us!"

"I recall it . . . now." Broll frowned. "Then if it's him she speaks about, she's been tricked . . . and the Nightmare sounds like the cause . . ."

"For what reason, though?"

"Isn't it obvious, my lady? Because he's a threat to the power behind it even now. It gives us some hope at least, then. It means he must have some ability to fight for himself."

Tyrande seized on that hope. Eyes drying, she said, "Then we must hurry to him! Lucan, when you escaped, did you pay attention to which direction she went? I know the mist is everywhere, but there is that . . . castle . . ." The high priestess pointed at the distant shape. "Do you know in relation to that?"

He straightened, looking a bit more confident. "Yes, yes, my lady! It . . . it's my calling to know locations and directions!" The cartographer pointed to his left. "That way . . ."

"We would fly," offered Eranikus, "but I fear he would not be able to direct us from above. The mist would be too thick to see . . ."

Tyrande had already taken Lucan by the arm. "Then we move now." To the human, she commanded, "Lead us!"

Nodding, Lucan walked a step ahead. Tyrande kept her glaive ready. Broll took the man's other side and the dragon rose just above the trio.

"This orc still bothers me," the druid said. "I fail to see what danger she holds for my shan'do."

The green dragon sneered down at him. "And you are correct! An orc is hardly a menace in a place like this! Even if the Nightmare guides her, your Malfurion Stormrage is first among you druids! His deeds are honored among my own kind! No earthly weapon would be a danger to him . . ."

Lucan swallowed. "She has an ax."

Tyrande looked at him, her expression wary. "The orc carries an ax?" She spun him to face her. "Describe it to me!"

"It was an ax with two edges. A battle ax."

"And how made? Was the head of iron or steel? Quickly! Tell me!"

Broll moved to calm the high priestess, but she waved him back. Tyrande waited breathlessly for Lucan to answer.

"Not iron or steel," he finally answered, his face screwed together in concentration. "I think . . . it looked as if it was all made of *wood* . . ." The human nodded. "Yes, wood! I've never seen an ax head made of wood before! Doesn't sound very practical unless it's really sharp, and even then it's likely to break—"

" 'Made of wood,' " the female night elf whispered in clear dismay. She looked to the other night elf. "You don't know! You weren't there when Cenarius himself made it for Brox!"

"I remember hearing *something* about that," Broll replied. His expression mirrored hers now. "Forged from wood, blessed by the demigod . . . and so powerful it is said to even have cut Sargeras . . ."

"And she hunts Malfurion with it," Tyrande added. The high priestess stared into the mists, especially at the half-seen structure—the only structure. "Lucan, did you really escape her?"

"No . . . she said she didn't need me anymore. She was near."

"Near . . ." Eyes widening, Tyrande gripped her glaive . . . and suddenly rushed into the mist.

14

THE NIGHTMARES WITHIN

No! Malfurion could not help thinking. *No . . .*

He had known that as matters came together, that his secret hopes would be at greater risk. The Nightmare Lord had taunted him about rescue, even tortured him with suggestions and images of Tyrande lost and dying in the mists.

Or worse . . . becoming a part of what the archdruid knew was gathering more and more near the nexus of the Nightmare and just beyond the mists surrounding him.

I must . . . do something more . . .

He could not sense his captor near, which by no means meant that he was not being observed. Thus, Malfurion had to act in the most subtle of manners.

With effort, he made the branches that had been his arms move. The night elf had done so more than once, generally in search of some relief of his agony. That agony remained, but the tiny part of his mind shielded from it had something different in mind. A possible distraction.

The true act was below the surface, below where his roots anchored him to the ground. For the most part, they served the Nightmare Lord's purpose, keeping him in one place and feeding into him the horror that dwelled even below. However, with the night elf so trapped, it was not a surprise that his captor might be confident and in confidence might miss the fact that a single, tiny root had become of the greatest importance to Malfurion.

Through concentration and will, the archdruid had managed mastery over it. The smallest of a multitude, it was ignored by the Nightmare Lord. Thus, Malfurion used his every moment to strengthen his power over that one part, make it do what he needed.

And now he needed it to feed deeper into the ground, feed beyond the other roots. Malfurion called upon all his teachings in this, the binding of druid to nature. He coaxed the root to growth, pushed it down, down, past the vermin that burrowed in the dirt, that worked to more undermine what had once been the Emerald Dream.

Then, when he was deep enough, he had it turn. Always wary for the presence of the Nightmare's master, the archdruid focused his will on driving the root beyond his vicinity and into the mist.

Closer and closer it came to its goal. He had no choice but to press on, even if it alerted the shadow tree. Time was a nebulous term in this place, but for Malfurion, at least, it was running out. Either freedom was to be his . . . or damnation would take him and he would find himself willingly serving the horror.

Inch by inch the night elf pressed. The lone root was nearly there.

Malfurion sensed the shadow tree stretching forward.

The skeletal branches traced the earth before him. The Nightmare Lord did not speak, which boded ill. The shadows spread toward the direction that Malfurion had sent the root.

Low, insidious laughter touched his thoughts, but Malfurion fought back fear of discovery.

The fools still press uselessly . . . the Nightmare Lord mocked. *Even with their numbers dwindling* . . . *and their losses drawn to the Nightmare* . . .

They will persevere! the archdruid responded, hoping to draw any attention away from his own efforts. *The Nightmare will be vanquished! You will be vanquished!*

They do not even know what it means to persevere . . . the shadow tree retorted. *They do not even know what it means to plan and wait* . . . *and wait . . .* There came more of the horrific laughter. *And we shall be rewarded for our waiting . . . we shall engulf Azeroth . . .*

The shadow retreated from sight. Malfurion did not for an instant take heart in that. Not only would the Nightmare Lord be observing him, but the dark fiend was constantly manipulating countless matters. The archdruid knew better than most what was happening. If his plan did not work . . .

The root reached where he desired.

All Malfurion could do now was wait . . . and pray.

Unable to stop Tyrande, Broll had no choice but to race after the high priestess. He did so not as himself, however, but as a great cat. Pouncing into the thick fog, the druid used his heightened senses of smell and hearing to make up for the limited visibility.

He picked up her trail immediately. In fact, it turned out to be easier to follow her than Broll had even imagined. Although she had put her love for Malfurion above her own safety, Tyrande was not foolish enough to forget the dangers they faced here. Broll was certain that they had not yet confronted the worst of the Nightmare. The high priestess of Elune left a path of moonlit steps that cleared away the horrific flow of ghoulish parasites. Broll was not so delicate with his own effort; his claws ripped away at the creatures as he raced on.

He caught a glimpse of a figure ahead, but it did not exactly follow the route taken by Tyrande. Letting out a low growl, the druid veered to avoid it. Broll had no time for confrontations—

The ground before him swelled up. Black bugs poured away from the eruption.

Father! Father!

Anessa was there before Broll, her arms outstretched in desperation, her face beseeching. She had been slighter of build than Tyrande and a hand shorter. Her eyes were full of innocence and incomprehension.

Broll buried his claws in the ground and came to a halt. *You're not real!* he thought at the apparition. *You're not real!* In his mind, he saw her again engulfed as the merged power of the idol and the demon taint swept over her. This was how she had perished, due to Azgalor's strike and his failure. Anessa was *dead . . .* dead.

Father! Please save me! the vision of Anessa cried.

And yet, despite the sure knowledge that this was not his beloved daughter, the druid felt his nerve begin to slip. A part of him so much wanted to try to save her—

Emerald tendrils seized Anessa. She squealed and tried to flee them, but they held her tight.

The cat reared back, reverting to the night elf. *This isn't how she died—*

The emerald tendrils curled tighter and tighter. Anessa's body crackled. Her head was caught in a terrible grip.

The skull cracked, yet Anessa still cried for his help. However, now out of her mouth—and out of every broken part of her body—there spilled the millipedes, roaches, and other carrion eaters. With them poured a deep, inky substance that bore the green tint of rot.

Before Broll's horrified eyes, the last recognizable traces of his daughter vanished within the tendrils. All that remained were the grotesque things that had poured forth from her. They spilled to the ground, spreading among the filth already there.

"You—*are*—real . . ." managed a voice that a stunned Broll needed a moment to recognize was not his own. "Unlike she, who was a semblance created to draw you into the Nightmare . . ."

A huge figure emerged from the mist ahead. Broll shifted to bear form and threatened the shape with his claws.

"No, druid . . . I mean you no harm . . ." It was an ancient.

Broll reverted. "Gnarl?!?"

But almost as soon as he blurted that, the druid realized that he was wrong. The figure resembled Gnarl to a point, but was built more bent at the shoulder and his tusks were longer. His barklike skin was of a more greenish hue, even taking into account the current surroundings.

Moreover, this ancient, like Gnarl, was known to Broll. "I remember you," the night elf managed. "Arei . . ."

The ancient of war bowed his thick head. Many of the leaves that should have been part of his beard and mane were withered. The ancient looked very weary. "I am that one . . ." His gaze surveyed the druid. "And you are Broll Bearmantle." Arei squinted. "As I have, through a portal you came . . . Ashenvale, I would guess . . ."

"Yes."

The giant being frowned. "And from your words, Gnarl no longer keeps it safe?"

Swallowing, the night elf replied, "Gnarl was taken . . . by the Nightmare . . ."

Arei let out a sound akin to a massive tree slowly cracking in half. It sent chills through Broll, for it was such a primal cry. He could sense Arei's great loss at this news.

"Another fallen . . ." the towering guardian murmured. "Our numbers dwindle as the Nightmare's multiplies . . . we fight a battle we cannot win . . ."

"Who is 'we'? What do you do here?"

"What we can." The ancient looked away. "Come . . . he will need to know you are here . . ."

"Who do you speak of?" Broll asked, but the ancient had already stepped deep into the mists. The druid stood where he was for a moment, torn between following Tyrande and obeying the ancient. However, the answer was made for him, for the high priestess's trail was now gone and even in the form of the cat Broll doubted that he would be able to pick it up.

There remained one hope . . . that Arei or this other of whom he spoke would know the whereabouts of Malfurion Stormrage. That would at the same time put the druid back on Tyrande's trail. With that desperate hope in mind, Broll resigned himself to chase after the ancient . . . and pray that he was not falling into another terrible trap by the Nightmare.

• • •

Tyrande was very aware that she had been unduly reckless in rushing into the mist, but an overriding fear for Malfurion had taken her. Throughout the many millennia that their hearts had been intertwined, she had faced the terrible prospect of his dying several times. Yet not since their first struggle against the demons of the Burning Legion had the high priestess felt the horrible dread that she did now.

Brox's ax had brought it home to her. She knew its power, knew its monumental strength and its powerful magic. In Brox's grip, it had done great things, mighty things . . .

And now that strength and magic had been turned upon Malfurion. She could only assume that this was the Nightmare's last horrible jest for both she and her love.

No! You will not die! Tyrande almost angrily thought at Malfurion. *I will not let you do this!*

Her anger was misplaced, of course, but it drove her on. Tyrande had only the vague shape of a keep that evidently should not exist here to guide her path. Even through the thickest of the mist, it remained just visible enough. Again, she was aware that it could be a trap, but it was her only clue.

Tyrande remained aware that there was something else lurking in the mist, something that ached to reach her. She knew that it was tied to the sleepers that Eranikus had feared he had harmed through attacking their dream shapes, but sensed that it went deeper and darker than even those.

And whatever it was pressed closer and closer as she progressed.

The murky keep appeared no nearer than previous, which also concerned her. In the Emerald Dream, distance and time were without finite meaning. Malfurion had taught her that much. For him, his captivity might have seemed like centuries, not years. He could be very nearby, yet she might have to run the equivalent of days to reach his location.

"No!" she murmured. "I will reach him and soon!"

No . . . no . . . no . . . the mist suddenly whispered in a thousand voices. *No . . . no . . . no . . .*

The high priestess glared at the dank, nearly unseen landscape, seeking the whisperers. She prayed to Elune and the glaive glowed. Tyrande brought the weapon's illumination to the left, but the wedge it cut revealed only more scattering carrion bugs.

But just beyond the light—

Tyrande moved toward it, but whatever it was retreated with the mist. It was there, just vaguely seen.

And waiting for her to make a fatal misstep.

Mother Moon, guide me now . . . steel my will . . . the night elf prayed.

Will . . . will . . . came the whispers.

She could not help but shiver. They did not only echo her words, but her very thoughts. Was there nothing safe?

Nothing safe . . . nothing safe . . . nothing safe . . .

Tyrande had her answer. Nevertheless, she did not even consider retreating. Her desire, her mission, was a clear one. She had never thought that she might sneak up unnoticed to Malfurion. The high priestess expected to fight and fight hard. Therefore, if the Nightmare did know she was there and what she intended, it hardly made a difference.

"I will face anything you throw at me," she muttered to the mist. "And I will vanquish it!"

There was no mocking whisper. Whether that was for good or ill, Tyrande could not say.

She pressed on. Although the vermin fled from her, she could hear them quickly returning in her wake. In addition, the ground itself grew more and more slick as a black-green substance that reminded her of the bugs' insides covered everything. She had to pull her feet free, an act most often accompanied by a sickening, sticky sound. Her progress slowed.

"It will take more than this," she told the mist.

A feminine chuckle wafted through the mist.

The chuckle chilled Tyrande more than anything else thus far. She knew that laugh, still dreamed of that laugh.

It was Azshara's laugh.

But the queen of the night elves was at the bottom of the sea that marked where her city and the Well of Eternity had once been situated . . . at least, as far as Tyrande knew. It was that tiny bit of doubt, though, that knowledge that she had never actually *witnessed* Azshara's death, that had caused the nightmares she had suffered on and off over the centuries. Even though the mad queen—enthralled by the power of Sargeras and thinking herself the titan's future consort—had surely had no opportunity to flee Zin-Azshari, perhaps she still *had* managed somehow.

So, this is your plan now! she thought defiantly at the mist. *A bold choice, but overreaching!*

To emphasize her defiance, she spread her hands wide as if welcoming this new attack. However, nothing happened. There was no sudden materialization of the dread queen nor even a further chuckle.

"Play your games, then," the high priestess said out loud. "I have more serious matters with which to deal."

Once more she trod on, scattering the vermin and fighting for footing. At last the night elf seemed to edge closer to the shrouded keep. Tyrande felt in part that her utter determination now aided her in making progress; the Nightmare was bending—at least somewhat— to her will. Nevertheless, she took the added precaution of making a silent prayer to Elune that the keep would neither abruptly disappear nor recede at the last moment.

The smell of decay, already present, grew more powerful. The ground became more slick. At times Tyrande could almost swear that it *pulsated,* as if some great thing slowly breathing. The high priestess told herself that this was merely the Nightmare seeking to break her resolve, but she moved more warily nonetheless.

Then her foot slipped. Tyrande could do nothing to keep herself from falling face-first into the nauseating muck. A foul slime covered her lips and burned her tongue. She quickly spat it out, not certain if it was poisoned.

Her glaive lay some distance away, the point of one blade obscured in the fog. Tyrande pushed herself to a kneeling position, the effort taking more than she expected. The ground was so slick here that her hands could barely find a hold.

A scraping sound turned her attention back to the weapon.

Something was pulling it into the mist. The glaive slid along the ground, more and more of it disappearing.

The night elf lunged for it, only to fall flat again. Now only the tip of one blade remained visible.

Calming herself, she summoned forth the light of Elune, directing it toward the glaive—

Something slithered behind Tyrande. The night elf immediately looked in that direction, but saw nothing. Quickly, she returned her attention to the glaive.

It was gone.

Azshara's chuckle once more touched Tyrande's ears.

Trying to whirl to the source of the sinister laugh, Tyrande only succeeded in miring herself even more. She finally resorted to Elune's light again, hoping that it could make the ground harder.

But as she attempted this, once more she heard slithering. Tyrande refused to give up her effort but could not help also trying to see what was coming toward her—

Something muscular but moist curled around her throat with the harshness of a whip. Tyrande abandoned her spell to struggle with what was now choking off her air.

It lifted the high priestess more than two feet from the ground. At the same time, the slithering grew louder.

And again came the too familiar laughter.

"Such a darling, beautiful creature you are! I had forgotten!"

Tyrande, still struggling to breathe, was turned to her right.

A monstrous, blue-green face leered at her. It was elven, yet almost akin to some monstrous fish. Finlike projections extended not only from the head, but coursed down the scaled back. Indeed, scales covered the face and curved chest as well.

The hands were webbed and clawed, more like those of some ocean predator. They, though, were still more akin to a night elf's form than the lower part of the thing's body. Rather than legs, it moved upon what appeared some combination of a snake's and an eel's slippery torso.

It was, in fact, the lengthy, spiny *tail* of that torso which sought with growing chance of success to strangle Tyrande.

"So pretty," it cooed in Azshara's voice.

Despite her losing battle for air, Tyrande stared wide-eyed at the creature. It was and was not the queen. There was just enough of Azshara's features in the scaled face, though the eyes were fiery red orbs that sought to burn into the high priestess's mind.

And all around them, other slithering forms converged. Those that were female bore some resemblance to night elves, but the males were more primitive and savage. Their faces had become like those of carnivorous fish, and it was clear from their eager red orbs that they would not have been averse to tasting her flesh.

If this was Azshara, then Tyrande knew that these could only be the Highborne, the caste of loyal servants who had joined her in her madness. Nothing had existed for them but to serve her glory, even if thousands of other elves perished.

Now . . . they still served her. Now, they, like Azshara, had become a horror of which Tyrande was familiar. The serpent form was unmistakable.

They were *naga*. The foul underdwellers of the seas.

"Once I offered you a place in my court," the queen murmured cheerfully as with her tail she pulled Tyrande so near that only inches separated their faces. A thick stench emanated from Azshara . . . a stench associated with a corpse left rotting for days in the waters. "Such a fine lady-in-waiting you would have made . . ."

Tyrande struggled to call upon Elune. Yet the light she already wielded only faded more. As it decreased, the naga pressed closer, more eagerly. They crowded her . . .

"And serve me you still shall . . ." the queen said with a fanged smile.

The night elf's legs began to meld together. Azshara was turning her into a naga.

Tyrande pulled tighter at the coil around her throat. She could hardly keep conscious, much less think.

Yet in that last haze of consciousness, Malfurion's face filled her thoughts. He said nothing, only gave her a look of encouragement.

It stirred the high priestess to one more effort to call upon her patron. Although Tyrande could not speak, she mouthed Elune's name.

The silver glow of the Mother Moon filled her.

She lost consciousness.

Azshara—all the naga—were nowhere to be seen. Tyrande lay motionless on the slick ground, the carrion bugs slowly encroaching on her body. The mists tightened around the high priestess.

But Tyrande still did not move. She lay there, with her hands at her throat . . . *around* her throat.

As if she had been strangling herself.

15

DEFENDING THE DREAM

T he stout walls of Orgrimmar lacked the "cultured" touch of Stormwind City's, but their savage glory could not be ignored. Tall and with massive watchtowers overseeing the surrounding lands, they offered warning to any foolish enough to attack that a high price in blood would be paid. Stern orc guards patrolled the walkways inside, and it was not uncommon to see among their number the Darkspear trolls, tauren, and even the undead Forsaken.

And though the interior might have seemed to humans as a barbaric place, with its populace divided into small valleys rather than quarters and its village-like construction more in tune with the nomadic past of the orcs, it was clear that Orgrimmar was as important a center of community to those who dwelled there as the capital of Stormwind. Thousands lived here, trading, learning, preparing for war . . .

Lying at the base of the mountain nearest the valley of Durotar, Orgrimmar was a symbol of the struggle the great liberator Thrall had faced to finally give his followers a true home. As Thrall had done in naming the valley after his murdered father, so had he named the city for the warchief who had taken the then-escaped slave and gladiator into his protection and who had later chosen Thrall as his successor.

Thrall himself ruled from Grommash Hold, set in the Valley of Wisdom, a central part of the capital. Grommash Hold displayed every bit the barbaric beauty of the orc warchief's domain, with great, rounded buildings topped with sharp spikes, huge rounded entrance-ways leading inside, and displays on many of the gray stone walls that marked past victories of both the warchief and the Horde in general. Among those displays were the fearsome, mummified heads of the creatures used by the Burning Legion, weapons and armor from the demons themselves, and, further on, armor and banners of another foe—the Alliance. That the last was now an ally did not matter to the orcs—these had been victories and so were honored as such.

But glorious victory was not on the minds of the orc guards and the shaman who clustered in the warchief's sanctum. The warriors watched anxiously as the shaman drew circles over a prone figure ly-ing in the rough-hewn oak bed and covered by the wide animal skins used as blankets. Each time the shaman withdrew his hand, the war-riors would lean forward in anticipation . . . and then pull back in de-feat.

The figure in the bed suddenly thrashed, then muttered something. His hands clutched in vain at the open air. Then one hand swung as if wielding an ax.

The violent actions did not encourage the onlookers; they had wit-nessed them many, many times. Thrall was no closer to stirring than he had been after the shaman's previous attempts.

"He continues to the terrible dreaming," the grizzled shaman mut-tered. "It plays itself over and over and *nothing* I do penetrates it . . ." The aged orc, his remaining strands of hair silver-white, peered through deep-set eyes at a sinewy dagger set on a round, wooden table nearby. With care, it had been used to prick the slumbering warchief in the hopes that a sudden, sharp pain might break the nightmare.

That, too, had failed.

"Do we put him with the others?" asked one guard tentatively. He was immediately struck hard on the side of the head by another orc. The first glared at the second and, if not for the wizened shaman thrusting himself between the pair, a fight would have broken out.

"Shameful, both of you! The great Thrall lies spelled and you turn against one another! Is this what he would want?"

The two chastened warriors shook their heads. For all that they were twice the girth of the bearskin-clad shaman, they feared his power. He was not the most skilled of his calling in Orgrimmar—in fact, that title rested with Thrall himself—but of those shaman still *awake*, he was the best hope.

That hope, though, was fading.

From the other side of the chamber, there came a mournful howl. As one, the orcs turned to eye a huge, white wolf baying at the window. The animal was so great in size that any one of the warriors could have ridden on it as if it were a horse. Indeed, the warchief used his most loyal companion just for that purpose. The two were legendary partners in battle. The wolf had the run of the building, and no guard ever complained over that situation.

The massive beast let out another howl. The sound shook the warriors and the shaman more than anything else had since the discovery of Thrall's condition.

"Hush, Snowsong," murmured the shaman. "Your hunt-brother will be freed yet . . ."

But the wolf then began trying to crawl up and out of the window. However, the gap, though large, was not suitable for the giant hunter. With a frustrated growl, Snowsong turned and lunged for the closed door.

The shaman's eyes widened. "Open it for her! Quick!"

One of the guards rushed to obey. He barely had the door swung back before Snowsong barreled into him. Like a loose leaf caught by a fierce gale, the burly orc flew back, finally crashing against a wall. The wolf continued on unimpeded.

"Follow her!" the elderly shaman ordered. "She senses something . . ."

Pursued by the orcs, the white wolf charged through the hold. She paused at two more windows that were of insufficient size, then finally scurried toward the huge doors at the front entrance.

The guards on duty there stiffened at the astounding sight racing their direction. Before the shaman could call to them, one had the sense to shove a door open. If the wolf sought the outdoors with such urgency, the guard had likely assumed that there was some danger lurking there.

Snowsong bounded outside. The wolf paused only to regain her bearings, then ran toward the nearest part of Orgrimmar's surrounding wall.

Although he was far older than his companions, the shaman surprised them by proving the faster. With lithe movements more akin to the wolf's, he almost kept pace with Snowsong. There were other methods by which he could have moved even faster, but some innate caution stayed the elder orc's hand.

Trolls and orcs who had been going about their duties tumbled out of Snowsong's way. As they recovered, most drew their weapons. Orgrimmar had been on high alert for days and the wolf's urgency appeared to those who saw her to mark that the time of battle had come.

The shaman peered around as he followed. For all their numbers, there were less defenders of Orgrimmar present than there should have been. Worse, as they neared the wall, he saw that the mist had breached further into the capital. It was almost impossible to see the guards above.

Not for the first time, the elder orc wished that those greater in their knowledge and use of the old ways had not, with Thrall, been among the first of the unwaking.

Snowsong did not run all the way to the steps leading up to the watchtowers. Instead, the white wolf found purchase on a ladder leading to one of the lower levels of the wall. There, the cunning animal located one path after another until she finally reached the top of the wall.

The frosty fur of the wolf stood out even in the thick, emerald mist. The shaman climbed to the top a few steps behind the animal. As he did, he noted the nearest sentry standing as if frozen.

"What ails you?" the elder orc demanded. When the sentry did not respond, the shaman touched his arm.

Only then did the other orc's head tip to the side.

The shaman thought at first that the warrior was dead, but a hand to the chest enabled him to feel the rise and fall of breathing. He looked into the face and saw that the eyes were shut.

Though he stood, the sentry was *asleep*.

The shaman looked to the next . . . and saw the same.

Some of the guards following him reached the top. They stared with astonishment at their comrades.

"Send word!" the elder orc commanded. "Find more to protect the—"

Snowsong howled mournfully again. The wolf stood on her hind legs, her forepaws draped over the edge so that she could see beyond Orgrimmar.

The orcs looked to the area at which Snowsong gazed.

There were figures in the mist. Hundreds or more.

One of the guards seized a horn dangling from a wooden peg on the inside of the wall. However, before the orc could bring it to his mouth, he, the shaman, and the rest stood frozen.

The figures had stepped up to the edge of the mist.

They were orcs.

"Grago," one warrior grunted in surprise. "My brother sleeps . . . but I see him out there . . ."

"Hidra . . . my mate, Hidra, marches with them!" gasped another.

"A trick!" someone else insisted. "Mage tricks! The Alliance—"

"It is not the Alliance," the shaman baldly stated. He leaned forward. "It is all the ones who sleep . . . *all* the ones . . ."

And as he said that, his own greatest fear revealed itself in the forefront. Thrall suddenly stood there, but a Thrall that was a grotesque mockery of the warchief. His skin hung as if decaying and some bone showed through. He also had eyes that blazed red . . . the red of the demon-tainted.

All the shadowy orcs had such eyes.

"A trick!" the same warrior rumbled anxiously. "They think us fools! Illusions! I still say the Alliance!"

The shaman said nothing, studying the figure of Thrall as closely as he dared. He tried not to meet the murky form's gaze . . . but at last could not help it.

A vast, dark emptiness with an unsettling green tint seemed to open up before him. Only with effort did the shaman manage to tear his eyes away.

Yet, in that brief moment, his worst fears had been verified.

This *was* Thrall . . . or at least some essence of him.

And, worse, the elder orc had learned something else in that brief, terrible moment of contact. These nightmarish versions of the sleepers were awaiting some signal. When that signal came, the malevolent power that these shades represented would sweep down over Orgrimmar. Not in any true physical battle, of course. The vast legions that wore the faces and forms of the defenders' blood kin were there more to unsettle those still standing watch. When the darkness struck . . . it would strike each warrior in the most indefensible part of him or her.

His soul.

That the attack had not yet come did not give the shaman much hope, though. The signal—whatever it might be—was imminent. Very imminent.

"We must alert all . . ." the shaman muttered as he stepped back from the wall. "We must have everyone, young and old, prepare . . ."

However, what he did not add as he departed was that against such a foe, who likely could not be touched by ax, there was very little the defenders of Orgrimmar could do but *fall*.

Broll thought that he had lost Arei, but then the ancient returned to him.

"Stay near. We are very close. He knows you are coming."

" 'He'?"

Before the ancient could reply, a sudden, even thicker emerald-tinted darkness swept over them.

Gibbering voices filled Broll's mind. A chill seized his heart. He felt as if his skin were peeling away from his flesh and, worse, amongst the voices the cries of his daughter regaled him. The druid was being dragged into an abyss, where desperate hands clutching at him pulled him deeper . . . deeper . . .

Away with you! commanded a new and vibrant voice that gave the night elf a tether upon which to mentally grasp. The gibbering receded. The hands slipped away. The chill over his heart melted . . .

The darkness returned to the still-ominous mist. Broll discovered that he was on his knees, gasping. One hand clutched his chest.

A soft light spreading from in front bathed the druid. Broll lifted his gaze.

"Remulos?" he blurted.

But although the gleaming figure resembled the guardian of the Moonglade, Broll quickly saw that it was not him. Indeed, the druid realized that what he was seeing was not, as he and the ancient were, a being of solid form.

And when the night elf finally recognized who it was who stood— nay, *floated*—before him, he swallowed hard.

The reason for the resemblance to Remulos was obvious; this was his brother . . . Zaetar.

But Zaetar was dead.

Broll leapt to his feet. Zaetar had fallen in love with Theradras, an earth elemental. With her, it was said that he had sired as their progeny the first of the centaur. But Zaetar's violent children had rewarded him for their existence by slaying the woodland keeper. Legend said that a grief-stricken Theradras, unable to let go, had hidden away his remains.

Stay your hand! the antlered giant said. His mouth did not move, but Broll heard the words clearly. *Your concern is understandable, but the truth has changed . . .*

Even taking in account their surroundings and the fact that he was not flesh but spirit, Zaetar was of a greener tint than his living, younger brother. Otherwise, the two titanic figures were very much the sons of Cenarius. However, Zaetar's face was faintly longer and bore in it a constant sadness, the latter perhaps logical considering his state of life.

The druid looked to Arei, who nodded. The ancient of war appeared more haggard than just before the attack on Broll, which made the night elf wonder if Arei had also suffered.

You were both touched by the Nightmare, though Arei was better prepared for it, Zaetar said, an indication that he had read Broll's thoughts. That raised further wariness in the druid.

We are allies, Broll Bearmantle, the spirit insisted, spreading his open palms toward the night elf. As he "spoke," Zaetar's form wavered, as if he were part of the mist.

"He has led us throughout this trial," Arei added. "And is one reason we still stand . . ."

Though it is doubtful that we can stand more than the few weeks we have . . .

" 'Weeks'?" Broll blurted. "You've been fighting this for weeks?"

The spirit's expression darkened. He looked away.

"When I and mine entered, Zaetar and those he gathered had thought that they had been here for more than a year even though it had been but a few scant weeks," the ancient of war answered. The craggy face twisted into a frown. "What day was it when you entered, Broll Bearmantle?"

The night elf told him.

Arei's shock was clear. "Only eleven days? I was certain that we had been here ourselves for nearly a season . . ."

The Nightmare twists time even as it is known in this place, Zaetar commented angrily. *All is meaningless here save the struggle . . .*

"You spoke of others in here who also fight against the Nightmare," Broll said, thinking that perhaps one of them had found Tyrande. "I'm hoping that they can find she who was with me! Where are they?"

Now the spirit wore a grim aspect. He gestured at the dark mist. *Druid, they are all around us . . .*

As Zaetar said this, his hand seemed to sweep back the foul fog from all around. The air did not exactly clear, but Broll could now see for some distance.

And what he saw was the most shocking yet.

They stood alone or in small groups. They were scattered for as far as the mist allowed him to see, and he had no doubt that there were others farther on. They were druids, ancients of war, dryads, and others with ties to Azeroth's nature and the Emerald Dream. Some wore solid forms; others were in dreamform. A few were like Zaetar.

Among those in dreamform were some whom Broll did recognize and in that recognition was overwhelmed with horror. They were druids long lost on Azeroth, their bodies unable to cope anymore without food and water. Some had been dead for months, but their dreamforms appeared unaware that for them there was no returning.

Or perhaps they did know, for many of them remained at the forefront, doing what they could to halt the Nightmare.

And the Nightmare itself came in the form of the same dire darkness that had briefly overwhelmed Broll. It most resembled an insidious cloud or perhaps a massive swarm of black ants. It moved and weaved, and wherever one of those fighting it faltered, it poured forth with obvious eagerness. Lengthy tendrils darted well beyond Zaetar's companions, proof that their efforts were not sufficient.

The defenders struck at the Nightmare with a vast array of spells, the only real defense against such a foe. As most were druids, they fought using their calling. Hulking bears battled beside swift, darting cats, each bite or slash of claw accompanied by flashes of power. Yet although this seemed to hold the darkness in check, Broll could not help feeling that the defenders did not truly *injure* what they fought.

Above, a dreamform storm crow soared over the edge of the Nightmare. It showed some desperation that even in dreamform the druids had to turn to their other guises to add weight to their fight. The Emerald Dream had been a place where their calling had known no bounds, yet now all that had changed.

Other druids retained their original forms. These sought to

manipulate the Dream against the Nightmare. Under the guidance of some of Broll's brethren, lush grass grew taller than trees, then, as if swaying in some tremendous wind, *sliced* the encroaching shadows to ribbons that dissipated.

There came an avian cry. Caught up in its attack, the dreamform storm crow had not paid sufficient attention to some of the tendrils that it had severed from the Nightmare. Now some of those loose bits of evil had snared its wings.

As it plummeted toward the sinister mass, the spirit of Zaetar moved to help it. His power reached out to the stricken druid—

But before Zaetar could finish his effort . . . a murky shape that resembled a great dragon's head thrust out of the Nightmare and swallowed the storm crow whole. The horrified onlookers watched as the avian descended through the misty fiend's "gullet." In desperation, the druid reverted to his normal shape, but though he was in dreamform, he could not penetrate his monstrous prison.

The head descended back into the Nightmare.

The defenders returned to their overall efforts, but Broll sensed his comrades' morale drop. This could not have been the first such loss and would certainly not be the last.

Twice this number and more were there of us once, the spirit sadly verified to him. Zaetar clenched his fists. *But one way or another, they were taken . . . and now, as corrupted, they serve it . . .*

"Lethon . . ." the night elf muttered. The shadow had reminded him of the foul green leviathan.

There are worse things than dragons even, but Lethon and Emeriss have served the Nightmare well . . .

Broll had seen enough . . . or too much. "I've got to find Tyrande . . . she went in search of Malfurion! There's an orc loose here and she carries a weapon capable of slaying him . . ."

I have already reached out to all to see if there has been a sign of this, the flickering Zaetar responded, confirming that he saw within Broll's thoughts. *None have responded in the affirmative . . .*

"She headed toward what she thought a keep—"

There is no such structure . . .

"I saw the outline myself! I was following after—" Broll looked to Arei, but the ancient shook his massive head. "We saw it—"

The mist began to surround them again. One by one, the distant defenders faded from the worried night elf's view. Somewhere out there was his shan'do and the high priestess.

And a murderous orc.

Zaetar looked disturbed. *I know what you plan . . . it is foolishness! You will only give yourself to the Nightmare—*

"If it's to happen, it'll happen one way or the other!" Broll said with a snarl. He thought hard. "Where's the Nightmare worst?"

With resignation, the spirit pointed far to his left. The mist thinned enough to show the undulating emerald-black darkness. *That is only a shadow itself of what is within . . . stay and fight with us, Broll Bearmantle . . .*

In response, the druid transformed into his cat shape and bounded toward the spot. Arei started after, but Zaetar shook his head. *Let him continue on his quest . . . it may be that he will succeed and they will free Malfurion Stormrage . . .*

"Is this possible?" the ancient asked.

The spirit turned back toward the battle against the evil tide. Though he stood far from the visual edge of the struggle, his powers already assaulted the ever-growing evil. *No . . . but just as we are doomed to failure and still fight . . . so, too, will Broll Bearmantle and others such as Malfurion's love—the high priestess Tyrande Whisperwind— continue to seek him . . . even though in the end the Nightmare will consume them all . . .*

She was almost there. Thura could smell her prey . . . or at least thought that she did. He hid somewhere in the shadowy keep.

The orc did not know this foggy land, but what discomfort she felt while traversing it was minor compared to her eagerness at finally closing in on the cowardly murderer. Soon, so very soon, she would avenge her kin.

Something moved in the mist. Thura had been aware for some

time that there were others around her. They were more than beast, though they also seemed not quite like any foe she knew. In her mind, they likely served Malfurion Stormrage. Of course he would have others defend him.

She hefted the ax. Since entering the Emerald Dream, it had taken on a golden hue. Thura had accepted that as another of the weapon's mystic properties.

Something just at the left edge of her vision moved toward her.

The orc swung. The ax met no resistance, but she heard a hiss, followed by a wail. Thura caught a glimpse of something that stood on two hooved legs melt away as if it were truly only made of shadow.

But even as the ax cleaved through that figure, another came from the opposite side. The orc spun around. The ax felt so right in her hands as it sliced through another shadowed form.

Again, there came the hiss and the wail.

There were no traces of her fallen enemy nor any of the one preceding it. The other shadows in the mist had withdrawn to greater distances, a sign that they rightly feared her and the ax.

Sneering at their weakness, Thura turned back to her chosen path.

The keep was no longer there.

Thura uttered an epithet, then looked again. The keep was no longer there, but something else was.

It was a tree.

Orcs had learned to carve out lives in harsh, unforgiving lands and so the twisted, almost painful bend of the nearly obscured tree only slightly bothered her. However, Thura decided that such a tree was suitable for this dank place.

But it was not that for which she was searching. The keep had been her guide. Frustrated, the orc started to turn away. The keep had to be somewhere—

Just before the tree would have vanished from her peripheral vision, the orc noticed a change. She immediately focused on it again.

Only . . . the tree was now the distant and murky silhouette of a tall, cloaked figure.

Almost as quickly as Thura spotted the figure, the mist wrapped around it. What remained of the silhouette once more resembled the tortured tree.

But it was enough to the fixated orc to thrust her toward it. The silhouette had been telling. She recognized that outline, so often had she seen it in her dreams. A tall figure with the shape and stance of a night elf and adorned at the head with antlers. It could be no one else.

Gripping Brox's ax tighter yet, the orc grinned without humor. At long last, Thura had found Malfurion Stormrage.

16

THE SHADOW REACHES

Tyrande felt the gentle touch of a hand on her cheek. She stirred to find someone kneeling next to her.

It was a smiling Malfurion. He was exactly as she last remembered him. Tall, broad-shouldered for a night elf though not built like a seasoned warrior as Broll Bearmantle was. His face and eyes bore the centuries of toil he had performed in service to his calling and Azeroth. His antlers were long and proud, a symbol of his closeness to nature, to the world that he loved.

Heart leaping, the high priestess pushed herself up enough to tightly embrace the archdruid.

"Mal . . ." Tyrande whispered, sounding for the moment many millennia younger than she was. "Oh, Mal . . . I found you at last! Praise Elune!"

"I have missed you so much," he returned, holding her just as tight. His tone suddenly lost its pleasure. "But you shouldn't be here. You should go. I wasn't expecting you to be the one to find me first . . ."

" 'Go'?" The high priestess stood. Her expression showed her tremendous disbelief. "I won't leave you now!"

The archdruid looked around as if wary of something. Tyrande followed his gaze, but saw only the pristine, sweeping landscape of the Emerald Dream. It was as beautiful, as untouched, as Malfurion had ever described it—

Tyrande's head pounded. "This isn't right . . . there's something wrong about us . . ."

"This is only an image in your mind," the archdruid answered, his wariness growing. "I wanted you to see me, to know it was me!"

"Malfurion . . ."

"Listen to me! It's all about to fall into place. I need you to turn back! You can only be here because *he* suspected! I should have known that he would plan for this! I should not even be speaking with you, for fear he senses us and gleans the full truth!"

"Who? Who is 'he'?"

Malfurion grimaced. "You have to listen! If the Nightmare Lord has something in mind for you, then you need to leave as quickly as possible! He's why you managed to get this far—"

"I've nearly died more than once to reach you!" the stricken high priestess returned somewhat angrily. "No one has led me by the nose—"

"He likes to play his games, torture even those he needs! He roots into your dreams—" Malfurion broke off, laughing bitterly. " 'Roots'! He's not the only one who can root! He—" The archdruid suddenly spun from her. Peering at something Tyrande could not see, he growled, "Go back, Tyrande! Everything will be just as needed if you can do that! If you're not there, his trick will fail and mine will succeed!"

"What trick? What—"

Turning back to her, Malfurion muttered, "I can feel him! He knows, but not enough! I dare not say anything more, even to you, for your thoughts are more open to him! Now leave! It's your only hope!"

And, with that, he broke contact. Tyrande strained to maintain the link, but to no avail.

Yet she still felt as if he were near. It was a feeling she could not shake. Tyrande looked around. The foul mist was inches from her. At its edge crowded the black vermin, who seemed eager to return to the area where she stood.

The high priestess almost dismissed her notion . . . then for some reason she could not comprehend, glanced down next to her.

Less than an inch from her foot was a small, upturned root. It was like a thousand other roots nearby . . . and yet not. There was something, something not visible, that drew her to it. She felt an urge to touch it.

But as she started to, Tyrande felt Elune fill her. The high priestess stiffened as the Mother Moon made her understand.

The root . . . was somehow bound to Malfurion.

His words came back to her, his pleading for her to leave him be. Yet, despite the earnestness with which he had spoken to Tyrande, the high priestess was not at all prepared to retreat. If Malfurion had one fault, it was that he felt certain that only he should bear the burdens of the world and only he should risk himself. Tyrande suspected that it had something to do with all the lives he had watched be lost so cruelly during the War of the Ancients, lives that he likely felt he should have somehow been able to save.

She no longer had the glaive, but that did not matter. The night elf started on. There was no sign of the keep, only the cloying mist and the half-seen shapes ever lurking just beyond the edge.

That briefly made her ponder Malfurion's warning. *Am I being guided? Is he right?*

But even if that were true, the fact that she had been made aware of it gave her some advantage. Malfurion had gone out of his way to be very cautious when warning her. He had worked so that his captor—this Nightmare Lord—would not know.

Tyrande finally shrugged off her concerns. All that mattered was that she reach Malfurion.

The landscape did not change. The illumination she cast kept the vermin scurrying for the cover of the mist, and whatever else watched her from it also kept back. Satisfied that they were kept at bay, the high priestess continued to search for some sign of her beloved. He was near. The root proved that.

She allowed herself a very brief smile at his cunning. Even with his dreamform captive, he had managed to raise and manipulate some plant—some *tree*—for his purposes.

The root! Tyrande studied the angle of it. She made an estimation of direction. Certain that she had calculated correctly, the high priestess peered into the mist.

And in the dire fog, she suddenly caught a glimpse of one. Though it could have been any of ten thousand trees, Tyrande knew that it was the one she sought. The one that would lead her to Malfurion.

It was scarcely more than another shadow, but what a shadow it was. It rose and rose above her even though it was still some distance away. There were no leaves that she could make out, merely a number of wicked, skeletal limbs that at times resembled several giant hands.

The shadow wavered. Tyrande could not make out the actual tree itself, but it had to be somewhere near. Despite its clearly awful appearance, the night elf was encouraged by its very existence. She took a step toward it—

Something converged upon her from her right.

Tyrande whirled to meet it.

A powerful force struck her hard, a muscular body that crashed into the night elf with such force that Tyrande was thrown far. She landed on her back among the carrion creatures, crushing several. The rest scattered as the light of the Mother Moon spread over the area.

The high priestess started to rise—only to have the deadly edge of an ax pressed against her throat.

An ax she recognized even after more than ten thousand years.

"Night elf," rumbled the female orc wielding Brox's gift from Cenarius. "You're his mate . . ."

It was not a question. That the orc had not immediately attacked her again for being Malfurion's supposed partner both encouraged and concerned Tyrande. There was a chance that she might be able to talk sense into the other female . . . but there was also the question as to just *why* the night elf still had her head.

"My name is Tyrande—"

The ax pressed closer. "Name doesn't matter! You know him! He knows you! He'll come to you . . ."

"Malfurion is not your enemy—"

"He is enemy to all of us! He would destroy Azeroth!" The orc's eyes radiated hatred for the archdruid. "And, yes, the blood of my kin is also on his hands! Broxigar will be avenged! I, Thura, will take the coward's head—and maybe yours, too!"

Despite the threat to her, the high priestess could not let the accusation pass. "Malfurion is no threat to Azeroth! He is one of its protectors!" Tyrande's expression steeled. "And Brox was our friend! He perished saving us! We honor his memory!"

Her captor growled furiously. Yet she suddenly pulled the ax back.

Tyrande read the confusion in the orc's expression. Thura had obviously not slept much and that had taken its toll. It was also possible, the high priestess considered, that Thura also realized that she was being tricked into hunting Malfurion.

But the orc swung the ax toward Tyrande again. "Up!"

The night elf obeyed. On her feet, she had more of a chance against Thura, yet not only did Tyrande respect the warrior's skills, she also saw the orc as an innocent caught up in the machinations of the Nightmare Lord.

"Thought I had him," Thura muttered, half-speaking to herself. "Saw him and got close to where he was supposed to be . . . but wasn't there . . ." She glared at Tyrande. "Druid's tricks! Your mate's tricks!" The brawny female brandished the ax. "You'll take me to him!"

Tyrande stood steadfast. "To kill Malfurion? No."

"Then I'll cut you in two!"

"Is that what Brox would have done?" the high priestess countered. "Would he have slain someone for refusing, someone who will not battle him?"

Thura glared, then repeated her demand. "Lead me to him! Now!"

"I will not—"

She stopped as the orc suddenly glanced to the side. Tyrande heard nothing, but trusted to the skilled warrior's instinct.

The orc snarled again. Thura peered around, then grinned at something she saw. "The tree! The tree beckons again!"

Following the orc's gaze, Tyrande saw that the huge shadow had returned. She could still not see the tree that cast it, but knew it had to be close.

"He will be there!" Thura muttered gleefully to herself. "The vision said so . . ."

The high priestess could take no more chances. With Thura's attention diverted, she attacked. Tyrande could not trust to Elune's magic, the illumination too much of a warning against such a foe. It had to be her own martial skills.

Her outthrust fingers shot toward the orc's vulnerable neck.

Thura spun back. The blunt bottom of the ax handle swung against the side of the high priestess's head at a speed even greater than that with which the night elf moved. Tyrande had only a moment to realize that she had been outmaneuvered before the bottom hit her on the temple.

But the night elf's reflexes, honed by centuries of practice and battle, kept the blow a glancing one. As Thura shifted the ax around for a strike, Tyrande dove under, then kicked.

Her expert strike just below the orc's knee sent Thura falling to the side as her leg slipped. The orc's grip on the ax loosened. The high priestess reached for the weapon—

Tyrande . . . a voice called in her head.

"Malfurion?" She could not be certain, but it seemed to be him. "Malfurion—"

Distracted, she did not sense Thura's renewed attack. The orc's heavy fist caught her in the throat.

With a gasp, she tumbled to her knees. Desperately seeking air, Tyrande thought about the fact that Thura would next slay her . . . and all because of the voice. The high priestess fought to regain her breath in time to save herself.

And yet, the killing blow did not land. Finally able to breathe again, Tyrande managed to look up.

Thura was gone.

Tyrande struggled to her feet. She saw the great shadow and knew where the orc had gone. Still astounded that Thura had not attempted to slay her, the night elf gave pursuit.

But where the mist had in the past so readily given way to the Mother Moon's illumination, now it pressed against the night elf as if seeking to smother her. Tyrande focused her mind, seeking to calm herself. As she did, the silver light grew stronger and the mist receded some.

Knowing that she would have to be satisfied with that, the high priestess pushed forward. She concentrated on the vast shadow. It ever loomed nearer, yet still she could not make out the tree that cast it.

But she did make out something else. Another, smaller tree. Tyrande's step faltered at the sight of it. Its monstrously twisted form shook her to the core. She felt both repulsed by it and saddened for the obvious torture it must be going through.

Of Thura, there was no sign, and Tyrande feared that she had followed the wrong path. Yet as she started to turn to her left, something drew her gaze back to the horrific tree. Even as it was, it did not disturb her as the shadow looming over it, the shadow that still refused to reveal its source.

Something whispered. Tyrande spun around to face from where the sound had come, only to hear another in the opposite direction. A third caught her ear even before the night elf could turn to the second.

The mists were suddenly filled with whispers, but not just any whispers. Although Tyrande could not make out what they said, their sense was that of *pleading*. They needed help. They *begged* for help.

And despite the sinister aspects of the mist, the high priestess knew that the pleading was true.

Drawn to them by her innate compassion, Tyrande again turned from the tortured tree. She stretched a hand toward one of the murky shapes she saw there. For the first time it moved toward her rather than fled.

But something suddenly snagged her foot. Thinking she had walked into a trap, the high priestess immediately prayed to Elune, then shaped a spear of pure illumination from her light. Such an effort was costly to Tyrande, but she no longer felt as if she had any choice.

The spear came down on what held her foot. The light pierced as if made of true steel.

What she took at first for a tentacle immediately released its grip. Pinned by her gleaming spear, it writhed in obvious agony.

Only then did Tyrande realize that it was not a tentacle, but a root.

And realizing that, the enormity of what she had done struck her hard. The high priestess immediately dismissed the spear of light. As it vanished, Tyrande knelt to heal the root. She was not a druid, but she felt that surely Elune would take pity on the damage accidentally done to an innocent by her follower.

As she touched the root, once more Tyrande felt Malfurion's presence. It was so strong that she could almost believe that he was actually there as opposed to entering her dreams.

Her eyes widened.

She looked at the tortured tree. Her faced paled.

"Malfurion . . ."

The whispers sought to drive him mad, so Broll thought as he raced along the dank landscape in cat form. It was unfortunate that in this huge, feline shape his hearing was more acute. That only served the whispers.

But his nose served him. He had Tyrande's scent and it was no trick. He was near.

His paws were caked with the sickening ooze that was the vermin's insides, but even the acidic burn it caused was not enough to slow the druid. Each step crushed more of the foul creatures to mush and Broll's only regret was that behind him he knew that new ones formed from the shattered remnants of the old.

The mists continually threatened to engulf him, but with an occasional slash of his paw that was accompanied by magical purple fire, the cat kept both the mist and the lurkers within at just a safe enough distance.

Then, a huge rumbling shook both Broll and his surroundings. Despite his keen reflexes, the great cat was tossed around. Broll managed to roll back on his feet, then buried his claws in the ground as he regained his senses.

A huge shape swooped overhead. It was followed by another and another and another.

And even through the thick mist, the druid could see that they were dragons. Dragons of an emerald hue. Ysera's subjects were still defending the Dream. The druid counted at least ten and prayed that there were far more.

Just as they were about to leave him behind, one suddenly broke from the group. It dove down toward the druid, who saw that it was female.

"What do you do here alone, night elf . . . and in your mortal form?"

He did not recognize the dragon, but that was not necessarily a surprise. Transforming, Broll quickly told her.

She gasped in surprise. "Eranikus flies the Dream again! This—" She looked up in the direction the other leviathans had gone, as if hearing something. Her eyes widened.

The dragon growled, then said to the druid, "Night elf, climb atop! I will take you with me!"

"My friends—"

"Climb atop me! I will explain when we are aloft!"

She did not add anything about it being safer up above and Broll knew better than to believe it so. With corrupted such as Lethon lurking about and the abilities of the Nightmare still very much a mystery, it was possible that "above" was even less safe than the ground.

Of course, with a dragon as his mount, the night elf felt a *little* safer.

Yet, as they rose into the sky, Broll saw that the foulness of the Nightmare now extended far beyond where it had previously. He could no longer make out anything but mist-enshrouded hills.

No, he could make something else out. In what seemed every direction—even farther up—brief but brilliant flashes of magical energy erupted like lightning during a fantastic storm. Again, there came the intense rumbling, so powerful that it even caused the green dragon to waver a moment.

"What's happening?" he shouted.

The dragon twisted her head around so as to stare him square in the eye, though hers were closed, of course. "Did you not hear his call? You who are of his kind and seek him even now? Listen!"

"His—" But even as he started to speak, the druid *did* hear the call. It was the summons of the last one he would have expected to hear from, but the one from whom Broll had most hoped to hear.

Malfurion's call.

It was not in the form of words, and yet it summoned those fighting against the Nightmare to be vigilant. Something was about to happen, something significant.

It was clearly also warning them. Malfurion did not want anyone hurt or perishing because of him. Yet the archdruid—wherever he was—also obviously knew that this went beyond his imprisonment. This threatened *everything*.

"But how can this be?" the night elf asked. "And what do we do, then?"

"Can you not see it yet?" the green dragon called back, beating her wings harder. "Can you not feel its wrongness? Look ahead . . . and look within!"

Broll obeyed . . . and in the mist ahead, just barely discernible, formed a shadow. A shadow of a tree.

A tree so foul that nature could never have produced it.

"My shan'do is down there," the night elf growled.

"And with him the cause of the Nightmare," his mount solemnly added.

From where he was, the Nightmare was a vast gray-green mass that pulsated as if alive. Shapes moved through it, unsettling shapes that could not be identified and yet almost looked like things that Broll should have recognized. He wondered why they remained so hidden and wondered what would happen if and when they were revealed. The druid shuddered.

The Nightmare was also filled with powerful flashes of magic that came not only in emerald, but a brackish green, a bloody crimson and more. The druid could sense that the emerald ones were from the defenders . . . the others he could only assume had more vile purpose. Broll could sense astounding forces at work and knew that what he saw was only a hint of the monumental spells at play. However, for all that, the emerald-black that was the Nightmare had not retreated and, in fact, seemed darker yet near where he and the dragon were heading.

So dark . . . and yet the shadow cast looks more distinct than ever . . . the night elf thought. But where *was* the tree that made it?

"A question of great import, I think," the dragon responded, as if Broll had spoken out loud. In a tone more concerned, she added, "And one we hope to discover the answer to soon!"

The druid jerked as something else abruptly became obvious. There was now whispering even up where they flew. It had a frantic, hungry feel to it.

"There's something wrong! We'd better—"

But the dragon had also sensed the danger. She banked sharply in an attempt to avoid whatever was about to happen.

What had been whispers now became screams. There were so many of them that even as loud as they were—loud enough to force Broll to cover his ears—what they were saying could still not be understood. The druid found himself shivering uncontrollably and even the dragon strained as she flew.

A great black gap opened in front of the pair.

The druid blinked. Not a gap.

A deep and terrible maw.

And from its depths erupted the screams with even more force. Although he could not make out their words, he sensed their *fear.* Yet that fear was also a weapon being used against Broll and the dragon by the Nightmare Lord.

The druid noticed that the green dragon was no longer trying to fly forward. Her wings now beat hard in retreat. Yet they were still heading toward the evil gullet.

"It—is the power of their fear—the fear of the screaming voices—that pulls us! It is chaos and evil stripping their sanity to the core that fuels the Nightmare!" his mount roared. "Such force! It is as if I fight against thousands! It is all I can do to—to keep us this far from it!"

"A spell—"

"If I attempt to concentrate—on that—we will be in it before I can—can finish!"

But Broll had not been talking about a spell cast by the dragon. He could see that, despite her tremendous abilities, she needed her entire focus on fighting the pull. The attack had been crafted just that way, the druid saw.

Yet an idea had occurred in that regard, an idea that came so suddenly that Broll wondered at it. He did not know if it would work, but he would try.

And so, as his companion fought the physical fury of the shrieking gullet, the druid began channeling an unusual spell. It was meant to be a healing one, a spell of tranquility.

He concentrated, trying to recall what his shan'do had taught him. Indeed, as he focused, Broll could almost imagine Malfurion's voice guiding him along.

The secret of the tranquility spell is to call upon that most peaceful, most caring part of Azeroth's nature . . . of the Emerald Dream's nature . . .

They were nearly upon the dark maw. Broll sensed when he was just close enough to hope for success and so close that he dared not wait any longer. The druid reached out to that of the Dream that remained pure.

He cast.

The spell was a small thing in comparison to the evil and fear it confronted. Broll did not in the least hope to destroy the sinister gullet.

He only wanted to give the female dragon the chance she needed.

"Be ready!" the druid warned.

It all hinged on what Broll believed the screams were. All he had seen thus far indicated that the Nightmare drew much of its strength from the growing legions of innocents falling prey to it when exhaustion finally made them sleep. The Nightmare used their darkest emotions to stir up their fearful visions. And that fear was what attacked now.

The spell touched the nearest vague shapes, the tortured slaves of the Nightmare.

Just for a moment—the briefest of moments—some little bit of the Nightmare's hold of fear on the screaming voices lessened.

The female dragon let out a roar as she thrust herself far back from the abyss. Broll grabbed hold of her thick neck as he struggled to remain with her. The emerald leviathan beat and beat her wings until the dark maw was only a small speck.

But as quickly as the spell acted, it shattered. The screaming rose higher and more frantic again. The horrific abyss swelled, drawing them closer once more.

Then a huge emerald form materialized between the pair and the Nightmare. It spread its magnificent wings wide and from it radiated a wondrous glow that reminded the druid of what this realm had been before the corruption.

Away with you! it called to the Nightmare's attack. *Away!*

Behind the massive newcomer, other green dragons appeared. As mighty as their own efforts were, even combined those paled before the tremendous power of the gigantic dragon.

The abyss receded some distance. Though they were not vanquished, the screams faded to something now much more tolerable.

Ysera, mistress of the Emerald Dream, had come in response to Malfurion's call.

17

THE NIGHTMARE UNVEILED

Lucan was alone in the mist with a volatile green dragon. Worse, he was astride the neck of this dragon, something that Eranikus evidently liked less than even him.

"We shouldn't have split up!" the leviathan rumbled. "Not here! Not now!"

The cartographer said nothing. He was feeling worthless. Thus far, he had fled from one place to the next as he sought to escape his growing nightmares, been seized by one powerful figure after another, and looked down upon by most as at best a child.

And now he was surely in a place where what little skill he had even as an assistant mapmaker was fairly useless.

The green dragon peered at the murky realm, his ire continuing to rise. Much of it was bitterness directed at himself. "I should have been there for her, but *no*, I failed! Now she's out there facing the Nightmare without me!"

Lucan knew better than to make any comment. What point would there have been? He was nothing . . . no, less than nothing.

Eranikus let out another growl, but this one directed at the Nightmare. "What *is* it that keeps just at the periphery of our vision? What insidious force is the Nightmare still holding in reserve . . . and why?"

The human opened his mouth to make a suggestion, then quickly shut it. His ideas were hardly worth merit.

And yet . . . there suddenly came to his mind a glimmer of a notion, one that suddenly excited Lucan so much that it was all he could do to keep from shouting it out to Eranikus. What held him back was knowing that the dragon would never permit him to attempt such a thing, if it were even possible . . . and if it was wise to try at all.

But Lucan could not restrain himself. He had been rescued more than once by the others. It was time he repaid them for once by using his unsettling abilities to their benefit. At the very worst, he would rid them of his sorry self.

Lucan concentrated. At first, images of Stormwind surged up. He saw his lanky master, Lord Edrias Ulnur, chief cartographer to His Majesty King Varian, peering down with disapproval of Lucan's work . . . the same work later transcribed without change to Edrias's name. He saw the fine courtiers admiring the maps that bore Lucan's hand, but for which his superior earned the accolades. And he saw the fine ladies, especially two, who had stepped into and out of his life without knowing it.

It was only Eranikus speaking that stirred Lucan from these moments of past failure and regret. He paid no mind to what the dragon now cursed. Eranikus was far more bitter than even Lucan.

Lucan tried to concentrate again. This time the cartographer focused on the person he was seeking. The image came to mind immediately and with such definition that he knew he was on the right track.

Eranikus was now shouting with great gusto, but whatever it was the winged behemoth sought to tell Lucan was lost.

The cartographer had already vanished.

She is near . . . very near . . . Malfurion thought anxiously. *But does he know and know why?*

Despite his grisly imprisonment, Malfurion had done his best to secretly discern what little he could of those battling the Nightmare. He had dared not contact them, but had waited until that moment when his plans would come to fruition. Only the mistress of the realm had any inkling of what he planned, and that in itself had been through a single moment's thought he had relayed to her:

And now Ysera had launched her dragonflight into action. They, the druids, and other protectors of Azeroth had launched a full-scale assault that would still utterly fail unless he had calculated things just perfectly.

But until *she* reached him, Malfurion would not know if he had.

He sensed the Nightmare Lord looming near, but the sinister shadow appeared focused on the dragons and the others. Malfurion did his best to subtly mask her approach. It was imperative that she reach him and act without the shadow knowing.

Something moved through the thickening mist, something that the archdruid prayed only he could sense. As cunningly as he could, Malfurion not only kept her from seeing what truly lurked around her, but also kept them from noticing her.

She stepped into the small clearing surrounding him.

The orc grinned as her deep-set eyes fixed on the tree. She did not see it; rather, to her, Malfurion Stormrage the archdruid, the heinous murderer and corrupter, stood staring back at her, a defiant smile on his face. It was an illusion for her and her alone, one that Malfurion had carefully crafted, just as he had carefully crafted each successive vision driving her to this point.

Malfurion felt no triumph at bringing the orc Thura to this place. He risked both her soul and her life. Yet in his desperate search for that which could best serve to free him of this prison, he had sensed Brox's magical ax. Malfurion knew how it had ended up back with the orcs, though that tale had been one he had learned thousands of years later. The red dragon Korialstrasz—also known to a select few as Krasus the mage—had given it to the warchief Thrall while in the guise of an elderly orc shaman. That had been to honor Brox for his tremendous sacrifice in seeking to keep the titan Sargeras at bay long enough.

But the ax was even more powerful than the orcs knew, and no one understood that better than Malfurion. His own shan'do had imbued it with forces bound to the world, forces that made it as much of Azeroth as the very seas and land, the very air.

And it was with that ax that Malfurion hoped to vanquish the Nightmare and free himself.

Thura approached him. She did not question what she saw; the druid had influenced her dreams far too long. Thura took for granted whatever he desired. That filled him with even more regret; he had abused her mind, no matter what the reason.

"Night elf," she growled low. "You threaten my people, my world! And for me, there is the blood of my kin staining your dishonorable hands! I have come to put an end to your evil!"

Strike! he silently commanded her. *Strike!* Malfurion even suggested where she aim. It was vital that she hit him just so.

Eyeing what to her was the archdruid's stomach and what was in truth the center of the tree trunk, Thura added, "I give you one chance! I will let you make amends—"

The archdruid was taken aback. Despite what she surely thought of him, she was still willing to give him a chance to save his life!

Strike! he repeated again, radiating an image of contempt.

Thura glared at him.

"That's your answer," the orc snarled. She pulled back with the ax. "I gave you a chance for life . . . now I give you the certainty of death—"

A great silver sphere surrounded the orc.

No! No! No! the archdruid pleaded. *Not now! You do not know what you are doing!*

But his beloved Tyrande did not hear him even though Malfurion tried with all his will to make her. The lithe high priestess strode toward the orc, who completed her swing—or attempted to do so.

If not for Elune's light, the ax would have done its work well. As it was, although the ax did not reach the tree, the magic of the weapon weakened the sphere.

Letting out a grunt of surprise at the ax's power, Tyrande immediately kicked at Thura. Her foot struck the orc in the side as Thura sought to spin toward her. The orc stumbled back.

The high priestess pursued her attack, kicking twice more. The first landed hard on her opponent's chest, but the second the half-gasping warrior stopped with her forearm.

Thura then thrust with the ax, forcing Tyrande back. In response, the night elf summoned forth Elune's light, but before she could cast whatever spell she had in mind, Thura made a slash with Brox's weapon. Tyrande was forced to retreat.

All of this went on before an increasingly apprehensive Malfurion. The longer the pair fought, the less the chance that any of them would survive. He tried to steer his thoughts toward the pair but could not reach either.

How had Tyrande even located him at just this moment? Malfurion had been very well aware just how far away she had been. He had also done his best to secretly divert her, yet that had failed—

Another figure entered the fray, an unexpected one. He was a ragged-looking human who at first seemed of interest only due to the impossibility of his being here. However, Malfurion knew exactly who it was and now had his explanation as to how Tyrande had reached here at this critical juncture.

In their one secretive contact, Ysera had promised that her servants would lead to Thura the means by which the orc, as part of Malfurion's plan, could reach this realm without the Nightmare Lord knowing. Malfurion had assumed it to be a druid or one of Ysera's very dragonflight. But instead, she had somehow found a very unique *human*.

The ragged figure had crept up behind Thura. It was doubtful that he could have done so against a seasoned warrior if not for the current circumstances.

To Malfurion's further surprise, the man's sole attack appeared to be to grab Thura around the waist. What purpose that served became clear a moment later as both she and her assailant began to *fade* away.

And with her would go the ax . . . and Malfurion's last hope.

At the last moment, though, Thura twisted away from him. She fell to her knees.

As she did, Malfurion felt the Nightmare Lord's attention at last turn to what was happening around his precious captive.

It was too late, then, for the archdruid, but he tried his best to give warning to Tyrande and the others. His branches shook and the sharp leaves shivered as he threw all his will into alerting them of the danger.

Far too late . . . mocked the Nightmare Lord. *Far too late . . .*

Shadows draped over Malfurion, skeletal shadows of the unseen tree's reaching limbs.

But it was not for the archdruid that those limbs stretched. Instead, they aimed for the others.

Malfurion again sought to warn them, but only the human appeared to notice him. The man eyed Malfurion's macabre form and then gaped. He started to say something to the two combatants, raising the archdruid's hopes . . .

A tremendous emerald force swept over the area.

The shadow tree recoiled but held its position. However, the foremost regions of mist burned away and the horror that Malfurion alone knew still awaited within it likewise vanished, seeking the safety of those areas still covered by the foulness.

Tyrande and Thura paused in their battle to follow with their gazes the human's outthrust finger. And though Malfurion could not quite see the object of their interest, with his other senses he perhaps understood the enormity of it even better than they did.

The sky was filled with dragons, Ysera's dragons. All those that remained uncorrupted had come at this desperate point to attack the Nightmare and its sinister master.

More to the point, they had come to rescue *him*.

This was not how Malfurion had wanted it. The dragons risked themselves. Yet he could not help but take heart in how the Nightmare melted away before them. What had started out as a distraction in order for the archdruid's plan to succeed had now become part of the actual rescue. The Great Aspect had clearly understood that she could no longer trust for the orc to act as intended. Tyrande's intervention inadvertently threatened catastrophe.

The mists retreated as if burned. Wherever Ysera's servants stretched forth their power, the sinister tendrils of fog pulled back and the Dream was restored. The carrion bugs melted under the great emerald glow of the dragons' power, fading to nothing. The grasses and trees were restored.

And at that moment Thura used the battle to fulfill her quest. She abandoned a distracted Tyrande and shoved past the desperate grab by the human.

Malfurion urged her on. He watched as she raised the ax.

Tyrande saw her. The high priestess glowed in preparation of stopping the orc.

The shadow tree moved. Malfurion realized that Tyrande still did not believe that she could be manipulated. With nothing to lose, Malfurion began to maneuver another root that he had been working with since extending the other beyond his prison. That one had originally been set to aid Thura, not Tyrande. This one would now have to *distract* the other night elf, if only for a critical second.

But someone else suddenly came to Malfurion's aid. Even transformed, his identity was known to the trapped archdruid. Broll Bearmantle, racing along in his giant cat form, snarled for Tyrande's attention. That he did so meant that he knew what was intended, not a surprise to Malfurion as he had obviously arrived with the coming of the green dragons.

His appearance did as intended. Startled, Tyrande lost her chance.

Thura swung. The shadow tree that was the Nightmare Lord reacted too slowly.

The ax cut just as Malfurion hoped. Pain coursed through him, but after the continual agonies he had suffered at the whim of his captor, it was pain easily smothered. What was important was that in cutting into the tree, the ax—forged by Cenarius and with the life force of Azeroth fueling it—also severed the spells that had caught Malfurion by surprise and trapped him so.

With a cry that was of relief, not anguish, Malfurion shed his foul trappings. The black, thorned leaves melted away. The branches that had been his arms and hands shrank and untwisted. The roots withdrew, then became feet, which, in turn, became part of two separate legs again.

And the dark, diseased green that had been his coloring burned away to the brilliant emerald of his dreamform.

No . . . came the Nightmare Lord's voice. *It is not so simple as that* . . .

The shadows of several branches crossed Malfurion's chest. Despite neither they nor him having any solidity—or perhaps *because* of that fact—the night elf felt as if his chest were being crushed. The euphoria of his escape vanished as he felt his foe once more slipping into his thoughts and his very soul.

"Mal!" Tyrande shouted. She and Broll both surged toward the stricken archdruid. To his credit, the human followed.

Thura stood dumbstruck, the results of her attack hardly what she had expected. Her expression was that of someone just realizing that they had been tricked.

More shadow branches descended, brushing aside with ease Malfurion's would-be rescuers. Thura, realizing what was the greater threat, swung at one of the shadows draping her former target's chest.

There was a hiss as the magical wood touched the shadows. One of the shadow branches flew off as if made of substance. It landed some distance away, where it faded to nothing.

The Nightmare Lord howled, almost causing Malfurion to black out.

The ground erupted at Thura's feet. Shadow roots seized her legs and as they did, the orc suddenly let out a cry. One hand let go of the ax to claw at the air. The other's grip weakened dangerously.

The Nightmare means for her to lose Brox's ax! Malfurion struggled to help her, but the shadows squeezed tighter against his chest.

Come . . . he heard his captor murmur. *Come* . . .

But the archdruid had no intention of surrendering to the darkness. He strained and at the very least seemed to keep from being crushed.

All around them, the green dragons cleansed the area of the Nightmare. The only tendril still extending so far was around Malfurion and the shadow tree. Yet even despite the obvious threat of defeat, the Nightmare's master would not release him.

Malfurion understood why. The Nightmare needed him. He was key to the Nightmare's growth in both the Dream and Azeroth.

But others understood that as well. The shadow tree was abruptly bathed with the pure energies of both nature and dreams. The tree shivered while at the same time the night elf experienced a sense of euphoria.

Only one being could wield the power so in his mind and struggling to look up, he saw that she now hovered over them.

"No taint of shadow shall be left in my domain!" Ysera called. Her eyes were shut, but Malfurion knew that she saw with more accuracy than anyone where her foe was most vulnerable. "No child of mine left to Nightmare . . ."

Ysera opened her eyes. The Aspect's gaze sparkled and though it did not seem at all threatening to Malfurion, he sensed the dismay and fear that it brought out of his captor. The shadow branches fled the druid.

One of the other green dragons dove down to just above the group. Ysera's servant used magic to pluck up everyone, including Thura. It did not matter even that Malfurion was in dreamform; the dragon's magic lifted him as if he were flesh.

But as they were carried up into the sky, the archdruid heard the cry of a dragon ring out from near another region of the mists. From where he floated, Malfurion caught a glimpse of a large male of Ysera's dragonflight.

Eranikus.

Malfurion was well aware of the consort's troubled past and had sensed his presence on recent occasion. He had not expected Eranikus to be here, but was also not entirely surprised. Perhaps having sought to further redeem himself, the once-corrupted male had evidently moved with too much confidence toward the Nightmare.

And now it had him. Hundreds of horrific hands of mist clutched him tight. Within moments, all that was visible was his head, one forepaw, and a wing. He looked to Ysera in fear.

The Aspect reacted. She turned to rescue her mate, only for a moment turning her attention from the Nightmare—

And that was when the shadow tree swelled to a terrible size and *seized* her.

The ghoulish branches engulfed Ysera. Before even she could react, they thrust back, tossing her into the mists.

As that happened, Eranikus let out a savage laugh. His form shifted . . . revealing the insidious Lethon. Lethon's foul visage mocked the stunned defenders for a moment before the corrupted dragon, completely shed of the powerful illusion, vanished after the Nightmare's true prize . . . Ysera.

The other dragons immediately moved to rescue their mistress, but the Nightmare surged forward again with a ferocity that none, not even Malfurion, would have expected from it. Like a thousand krakens, tendrils of mist stretched out to seize the unwary. Two more of the green dragonflight were taken before the remaining green dragons reluctantly retreated.

As for Malfurion, he screamed in denial of what had happened. If not for Ysera seeking to save him, she would not have been lost.

The Nightmare expanded, rushing toward its adversaries with the pace of a raging river. The tendrils whipped about. There was no choice but for all of them to flee.

Yet, even knowing that, the archdruid fought to free himself from the safety of the green dragon's magic. He could not—would not—leave Ysera as prisoner of the awful power within.

Then, though the mist continued to surge on, it also dissipated some. Some of those among the green dragons took this as a sign of weakness, that perhaps having seized the mistress of the Dream that the Nightmare had overextended itself.

It was too late for Malfurion to warn the foremost of those impetuous behemoths. The first dragon who so eagerly dove toward the mist only made it that much more simple for the tendrils to seize her. Like those before, she was swallowed whole.

The rest were driven back. Indeed, Malfurion sensed those defending against the evil elsewhere were also pushed into abrupt retreat. It was as if they faced an entirely new and far more formidable adversary. Dragons, ancients, druids . . . they all fell back if they did not wish to join those already lost.

Yet, in the wake of their escape, the mist continued to fade. Slowly, the distorted landscape that had once been the Emerald Dream became more distinct. Once proud hills were now covered in blackened pockmarks and vermin crawled over them as if atop great nests. What trees there were had been stripped of most of their leaves and were now covered in small reddish suckers that moved like mouths and bore teeth. The branches twisted and turned as if constantly seeking anything unwary enough to step within their reach.

The ground was saturated not only with the bugs and other crawlers, but more of the sickening pus that oozed from jagged crevices now opening up everywhere. The stench of decay filled the air worse than ever.

And then the Nightmare at last revealed to the others what Malfurion already knew, at last revealed what it had *most* kept hidden. He had hoped that with his escape, its evil would be at least reduced, but that was not so. Indeed, it had become even more horrifying than what his captor had previously shown him.

Wherever the mist existed, so, too, did they cluster. Their ranks spread on as far as the eye could see and he knew farther than that. Worse, they were multiplying by the second, each face akin only in its anguish and hunger.

They were the sleepers taken unaware, but they were far more. Malfurion had fought demons and he had fought the undead Scourge. The horrific parodies that these sleepers had become made the former gentle-seeming in comparison. The sleepers were creatures drained of soul and so their forms reflected it. When they moved, it was both fluid and with evident wracking pain that made Malfurion's own past torture nothing.

Their shriveled flesh draped stretched skulls. Their mouths opened in continual shrieks and stretched wider than physically possible. Their eyes were sunk into their skulls and stared with a loathing at what did *not* share their suffering.

And still more of them came, more than there could possibly be on a hundred Azeroths. They were *every* horrible dream each sleeper suffered, and so their numbers were potentially endless. They grasped with clawlike hands as they moved, reaching . . . reaching . . .

Malfurion knew for what they reached and what they hungered. His captor had been only too pleased to not only show their suffering, but let him sense just what the Nightmare Lord had let them think was their salvation. To them, the only respite, even for a moment, was to steal and experience what those who had not yet fallen victim to the Nightmare still had . . . the ability to dream without pain, without fear.

But that was a false desire, something that they could never actually seize. It was merely a ploy to drive them on, to make them so desperate as to seize upon their friends and loved ones, all for the sake of the Nightmare.

And Malfurion knew that, despite how good most of these people were . . . their nightmare selves would not hesitate in the least to bring about Azeroth's destruction.

Their numbers continued to swell, continued to spread. The remaining members of Ysera's dragonflight were as nothing to them. The dragons attacked and attacked, but they might as well have been a few grains of sand seeking to stem a flood.

Malfurion knew why. He also knew that he had been manipulated all along by the Nightmare Lord. In the archdruid's cleverness, he had simply given the foul shadow what it truly desired. The night elf had served his captor as well as if he had been one of the corrupted . . .

"We must retreat from this place!" one of the elder green dragons roared to the rest. "We must regroup!"

Regroup? Why? Malfurion silently asked, still horrified at the role that he had played. *Of what hope is there?*

The Nightmare had never actually wanted him. Oh, its master *had,* but that had been a personal desire greatly outweighed by the ultimate need.

Malfurion had been the bait. His powers, his bond to Azeroth and the Emerald Dream had been strong enough to instigate the Nightmare's intentions, but never to truly fulfill them. For that, the shadow had needed the one being most tied to the magical realm.

The Nightmare had wanted the mistress of the Emerald Dream all along.

18

LOST DREAMS

I n Stormwind City, in Ironforge, Dalaran, Orgrimmar, Thunder Bluff, and all other cities, towns, and villages, the mist began to move. Even in the Undercity, where the undead should not dream, the mist seized the hidden nightmares of its inhabitants. The Forsaken were cursed with suffering their lost lives over again in dreams that offered them escape, but did not deliver that promise.

The Undercity was well-named for many reasons, the least of which was that it was buried under the ruins of what had once been one of the most grand of cities . . . Lordaeron's famed Capital City. However, in the Third War, Prince Arthas—corrupted by the Lich King—seized his father's capital and slaughtered King Terenas in his own throne room.

But the dread destiny of the Lich King had drawn Arthas to cold Northrend and during that time, the Forsaken—those undead who had broken from the Lich King's mastery—seized the ruins. Seeing the defensive advantages, they had carved out what would become their capital, stretching its catacombs to new depths and building what to many of the living would have very much seemed a terrible mockery of the undead's lost existences.

A sinister crest consisting of three crossed arrows—one of them broken—covered by a white, cracked mask could be seen throughout the city. It was the mark of the Forsaken and, especially, their queen. The Undercity was a place of dark, somber colors, stone walkways and steps. However, the undead did not sleep and so neither did the city. The Undercity had inns, forges, and businesses that catered not only to the undead, but visitors from the Horde, with whom the Forsaken had allied itself. There was *some* illumination in the form of dim lamps and muted torches. They were not merely there to serve the living, though the undead had no true need of light, but no one wished to admit that it perhaps gave its chief inhabitants a facade of some other existence.

But now . . . something new and unsettling even to those who had built the Undercity had swept into the Forsaken's capital. Something that resembled *sleep* . . .

The Forsaken's leader—the fearsome Banshee Queen, Sylvanas Windrunner—had studied the strange state of those of her followers who now seemed truly dead . . . and yet not. It was the merest of movements that proved the latter, if nothing else.

The Banshee Queen was beautiful even in undeath. She had been not only a high elf, but also ranger-general of lost Silvermoon. And even in her current role, Sylvanas was unique, for she was not ghostlike as banshees generally were, but had a solid form. Lithe, elegant, and with skin of pale ivory, she strode among the supine bodies gathered for her by her servants. All were the same. All gave her no answer, and that only served to increase her frustration.

Clad in form-fitting leather armor designed for easy movement and adorned also with a shroudlike hooded cloak bearing deep crimson hints, Sylvanas looked very much the harbinger of doom. Even the four undead high elf guards in attendance, with their rotted faces, their protruding rib cages, and their hollow eyes could not raise such fear as the banshee did.

"Well, Varimathras?" she demanded of a shadowed presence in the corner of the dank, cobwebbed chamber underneath her citadel. Her voice was seductive in the way that darkness was to some, yet also was akin to a chill wind. "Have you nothing to tell me yet?"

The shadow separated from the wall, to reveal a gargantuan figure, a *demon*. He wore leather and metal armor of the darkest ebony. Sylvanas's tone hinted of a tremendous mistrust between them. The demon joined her, striding on two huge, cloven hooves. His skin was of a bloody purple tone, even to the two vast, webbed wings sprouting from near his shoulders. His head was long and tapered, with a dark mane flowing from the base of an otherwise bald head. Two wicked black horns thrust up from the temples. Green gemstones marked his armor at the forearms and waist, their color and glow matching his inhuman orbs. Those eyes now met glowing, silver-white ones.

"I have cast spell after spell, burrowed deep into each of these fools . . . and they all reveal the same thing, Your Majesty . . ." he replied coolly. The demon cocked his head to the side and with analytical interest watched his mistress's expression contort.

"We—do—not—dream!" Sylvanas retorted, her voice so shrill now that the demon had to cover his long, pointed ears. Even then, his body was wracked by sharp pain. The cry of a banshee was a terrifying power and Sylvanas was the deadliest, most unique, of banshees.

"That—distraction—is beyond us," the queen of the undead added in a more calm manner. "They're not dreaming, Varimathras . . ."

"Not even—Sharlindra?"

Sylvanas could not help but glance to one still form. As opposed to the rest, it had been carefully set upon a stone dais. The body seemed more mirage than solid, more of an illusion fading away. It radiated a white aura with bluish hints. In life, she had been a beloved elven female and her grace was still evident even in undeath. Sylvanas had found the other banshee to be wise and, in contrast to the demon, *trusted* counsel.

But Sharlindra had been the first to fall. More unsettling, when Sylvanas, upon being brought to the body, had leaned close, she had realized that Sharlindra was murmuring something.

She still was. They all were. All evidence suggested that they were, as the demon had early on suggested, *dreaming*.

"This is a trick!" Yet Sylvanas knew from her own bitter experience that such was not possible. "This is a trick, just like the mists hovering above the Undercity . . ." She turned from Sharlindra, turned from Varimathras. Her eyes blazed as she considered just who it was who would use such tactics.

Only one name came to mind and as she spoke it—even in a whisper—Sylvanas's anger fueled her power and caused the very stone to shake. "*Arthas . . .* I would say this is the Lich King's doing . . . but that is no longer poss—"

With a gasp, Sharlindra suddenly opened her eyes. She stared up, seeing something that Sylvanas could not.

The stricken banshee smiled. She reached up a slim, ethereal hand. "*Life . . . I live again . . .*"

Her eyes closed. Her hand dropped. Again she murmured, though the words were not intelligible.

Sylvanas's eyes burned with more rage. She leaned over the still form. "What twisted jest is this? She has impossible dreams of the even more impossible! She dreams of *living*? Madness!"

"Not so mad," Varimathras remarked from behind her. "A simple spell, really."

Sylvanas swung around, gaping at the demon's unbelievable statement. Varimathras knew better than to mock her. He had learned quickly that his kind were not the only experts of torture. "You tread a dangerous line . . ."

But the winged fiend only shrugged. "I only speak the truth. Resurrection is a fairly easy casting for any dreadlord."

"It's impossible, you mean! I warned you—" Sylvanas's rage surged. She focused on Varimathras.

Still unperturbed, he gestured. "Let me show you."

An invisible force akin to all of the Undercity collapsing upon her sent Sylvanas to the floor. She instinctively went from solid to incorporeal, but nothing seemed to happen, for she still felt the harsh collision. Sylvanas briefly lost focus, but the cool, moist stone against her cheek stirred her back to full consciousness.

And then she realized that she should not have been able to feel those sensations to such depth. In fact, she had not felt this way since—

The incessant smell of rot and decay filled her nostrils as it never had since the city's founding. It was so intense that she coughed, an act that forced her to take a deep breath to calm herself.

Only . . . she did not need to breathe, either. She was dead.

Wasn't she?

Sylvanas eyed her hand. The whiteness had given way to a very pale pink.

"No—" She gasped at the sound of her own voice . . . of her voice before her transformation into a banshee.

Varimathras loomed over her. The demon presented her with a large looking glass with gold scrollwork on the frame and handle. "You see? I didn't lie . . . this time."

Sylvanas stared at herself, at her former, living, breathing self. She touched her cheeks, her chin, her nose . . .

"I'm alive . . ."

"Yes, you are." Varimathras snapped his taloned fingers.

The four undead high elves moved in and seized Sylvanas. Their stench was terrible. Small black creatures crawled into and out of areas where the flesh had given way to bone. Sylvanas wanted to throw up and the very fact that she wanted to stunned her more.

She fought to pull herself together. She had been a commander of the high elves and she was now queen of the Forsaken. Glaring at the guards, Sylvanas ordered, "Release me!"

But they only clutched her tighter. Sylvanas peered into the monstrous eye sockets of one—and saw such hatred of her that she stood speechless.

"They might be a bit jealous," Varimathras remarked, growing more shadowy again. "Really, they shouldn't be. You won't stay that way long."

The high elf was caught between fear and regret. "It doesn't last?"

"It would last, if we gave you the chance."

The speaker was not the demon, but rather someone who had entered without Sylvanas's knowledge. Yet though she could not see him from her angle, Sylvanas knew the voice so well . . . and shuddered because of it.

Varimathras had the guards turn her to face the newcomer.

To face a figure clad in black, icy armor.

To face the Lich King.

She fought to free herself, but the guards held her with the prover-
bial death grips. Worse, they dragged her toward the Lich King.

But this is impossible, Sylvanas remembered. *He is defeated! He is—*

Arthas cupped her chin. His human traits could just be seen
through the openings of the helmet. Frosty breath escaped him as he
spoke.

"So becoming as a high elf . . . and so more becoming as a
banshee . . ."

She was placed on a stone platform, then chained. Varimathras
joined the Lich King, who again cupped the captive's chin.

"This time . . . I'll make you right," Arthas promised. His cold
breath coursed over Sylvanas's face, but it was not the breath that
chilled her so.

Arthas planned to make her a banshee again . . .

Sylvanas still recalled the horrible agonies her last lingering life
force had suffered before her dread transformation. She knew that she
would go through a terror a thousand times greater now.

"No!" she cried out, trying to use her powers. Unfortunately, those
powers would not belong to her until the monstrous spell was completed.

Arthas raised his long, sleek sword, Frostmourne. Its evil was
as great as his. He held the point over her and as he did, he and the
weapon filled her frightened view.

"Yes, this time you'll be a properly obedient servant, my dear
Sylvanas . . . even if we have to raise you again and again and again
to get it right . . ."

Sylvanas shrieked . . .

"She will not wake," Sharlindra murmured, feeling in her a level of
fear not experienced since just before her death. She eyed the other
Forsaken around her and saw that they, too, were going through
the same thing. "She mentions the traitor Varimathras, slain by her,
and the Lich King, finally defeated! What sort of dream does she go
through—and *why* does she dream?"

Nearly half of Sylvanas's subjects were in a state like that of their queen. All but a few of the representatives of the other Horde races staying in the Undercity were likewise, though in their case that made more sense.

And worse, so much worse . . . the Forsaken were under attack.

Under attack by shadows of their own former loved ones, who had become something even more hideous than that which the once-living denizens of the Undercity now were. The Forsaken knew that they were not real, yet neither were they figments. What stalked the undead, what unnerved them as only their original demises had, were creatures somewhere in between. They ravaged the Undercity in a manner that served to bring home to the stunned Forsaken what it must have been like when the undead, as part of the Scourge, had overcome the once vibrant realm.

A shriek shook Sharlindra anew. This time it had not come from Sylvanas. This time it had come from directly above. She knew it for the cry of one of the other banshees, but it was no warning nor any weapon of battle.

It was a cry of fear . . . the fear of the unliving.

Sharlindra looked at those gathered with her. Frightening as they were to outsiders, the Forsaken now had a pathos about them that had nothing to do with their existence. Rather, those undead she studied looked uncertain, off balance.

More shrieks erupted from the upper recesses of the Undercity. The banshee looked to her queen, but there was no hope of guidance from Sylvanas.

"The mist . . ." warned a rasping voice. The speaker barely wore any remnants of flesh and only the magical properties of his undead state enabled him to speak, for his jaw hung loose on one side. "This mist . . ." he repeated.

Sharlindra looked to the steps leading down to their location. The dark green mist was seeping down the stone steps, as if a living creature slowly approaching its prey.

The Forsaken pressed away from it. As they did, though, in the mist there began to form figures.

The banshee stepped back. She knew some of them. By their reactions, others, too, recognized their kin and friends—the living who were more tortured than they.

The banshee let out a shriek that began as a desperate attack and ended in despair . . .

The Nightmare enveloped the Undercity.

In Stormwind City, King Varian watched as the mist and its ghoulish force surged toward the keep. From various parts of the rest of the capital, he heard screams.

We're being assaulted . . . and we can't fight them . . . Arrows had been tried. Arrows with oil-soaked, fiery tips. They had been no more effective than the swords, lances, and other weapons. What magi and other spellcasters were still conscious in the city were doing their best, but their effectiveness was limited.

The brave defenders of the keep awaited their monarch's orders.

Varian saw his son and dead wife, both still multiplied a hundred times over, cross through the gate as if it were air. Nothing impeded these living nightmares.

And knowing that, Varian found himself with no orders that he *could* give . . . even as his citadel, his kingdom, began to fall before him.

Throughout nearly all the known lands of Azeroth, the Nightmare surged forth. As it did, the mists faded enough for the waking to see what had become of its victims . . . and what would be their own fate. Despite that, though, despite whether it was the orcs in Orgrimmar, the dwarves in Ironforge, or any other race in any other realm, those left to defend against its terror did not for the most part surrender. They knew that they had no choice but to keep fighting . . . no matter how little hope they had left.

· · ·

But there *was* one realm oddly free of the mists. That was Teldrassil and, thus, Darnassus, too. That did not mean that Shandris Feathermoon did not know much of what happened on the mainland and beyond. The general was well-informed through her network.

A network, though, that was quickly collapsing.

Shandris lowered the last missive received from an agent near Orgrimmar. It echoed those from Stormwind City, tauren Thunder Bluff, and other locations where Shandris had spread her web.

The mysterious mist was moving. Worse to her, though, was the fact that she also had no information as to her mistress's location. Tyrande had been heading toward Ashenvale . . . and then had seemingly disappeared.

She is not dead! the younger night elf insisted to herself.

Discarding the parchment, Shandris abandoned her quarters. She could have taken up residence in the high priestess's abode, as Tyrande insisted whenever departing for matters of state, but Shandris preferred her spartan quarters. There were no decorations honoring nature, only weapons and trophies of war. Defending her mistress and her people had become Shandris's entire existence. Indeed, she had tried more than once during her mistress's absence to locate some trace of Tyrande through the visions of other priestesses.

That had failed. Instead, Elune had granted each of those priestesses another vision, one that confused the general.

It was a vision of Teldrassil being eaten from within. A horrid, festering decay would spread not from the roots but rather the crown. It would quickly devour the World Tree inside out. The vision had always been short, only three or four breaths in span. Shandris had gone over it thoroughly with each priestess and still did not understand it.

The vision had so troubled her today that Shandris could no longer sit still. Hoping to clear her thoughts, she had personally begun patrolling the length and breadth of the capital, wending her way from the fortified bastion of the Warrior's Terrace down into the commercial sections of the Tradesmen's Terrace, on through the mystic Temple of the Moon and across the lush, sculptured islets of the garden. There she had made a detour to the industrious Craftsmen's Terrace before returning to her quarters in the Warrior's.

That left only the Cenarion Enclave. Shandris did not fear stepping into the druids' stronghold. Nor did she respect Fandral so much that she would have stayed clear because of him; her first loyalty was to Tyrande. Even now, the general would have normally bypassed the enclave, but Shandris had learned long ago that to find answers it was often better to not seek the obvious source. The dread vision still in mind, she suddenly realized that there was one among the druids who might be of use to her. Someone who might be able to explain the vision without turning to Fandral.

Never one to ask of her Sentinels what she herself would not do, Shandris quietly departed the Warrior's Terrace. As she passed the more dour wooden structures, the constant sound of military training sang in her ears. To Shandris, such was more sweet than the music of her people. Not since her parents had been lost in the War of the Ancients had the general truly ever enjoyed music anymore . . . save for the songs and chants used by the priestesses during battle when calling upon Elune's power. Those had purpose, after all.

She started to turn . . . only to see a furtive figure crossing from the Temple Gardens to the north. The cloak marked him as a druid, but otherwise she could not individually identify him.

Shandris started on . . . then turned. She could not say why, but she decided to follow the druid.

The figure quickly vanished into the thick grove that was part of the enclave. Shandris easily followed. The Sentinel commander moved like a shadow among the tall trees. Many reminded her of miniature versions of Teldrassil, which in turn brought back thoughts of the priestesses' vision.

The druid came into sight again. There was something odd about his—she assumed the figure a male—gait and the fact that he kept the obscuring cloak around him. It was almost as if he did not like being in the enclave.

Then the druid came to a halt. The hooded form looked left and right, as if deciding where to go.

The figure made his choice. Shandris smiled, having guessed.

She followed—

Or rather, she *tried* to follow. Her foot caught on a root that the night elf was certain she had avoided. As Shandris moved aside, the root seemed to stretch from the ground, again catching her foot.

The Sentinel lithely twisted to avoid the root—and a branch caught her face. The force of it caused Shandris to fall back against the nearest tree.

The tree's roots bound her ankles. Shandris reached for the dagger she always carried, intending to quickly cut her way loose and move on.

Another branch struck her hard on the head. Stunned, Shandris momentarily went limp.

In that moment, the craggy bark *opened*. Even through her daze, Shandris sensed herself being drawn *into* the tree trunk.

She struggled to regain her concentration, but again she was battered on the side of the head. The interior of the vast oak surrounded her. Through blurred vision, the general watched the bark seal itself again.

A darkness even her vision could not penetrate surrounded her. Worse, a pressure was building in her chest. Shandris vaguely realized that the space she was in was too tight. She could not breathe—

The night elf passed out, aware in the last moment that death was coming.

Then the bark gave way again. The pressure eased. Fresh air stirred Shandris, though not enough to keep her from falling forward.

She landed in the arms of a powerful figure. Shandris struggled to recover, certain that her captor had come for her.

A musky scent assailed the night elf, shaking her into consciousness. She peered up at who held her.

It was a tauren.

Hamuul Runetotem gazed down at her with narrowed eyes. "So . . . it is you . . ."

19

AWAKE TO THE NIGHTMARE

There was no hope. In all his long existence, Malfurion had known such distress only once. That had been during the War of the Ancients.

The green dragon sent earlier by Ysera still carried him, Tyrande, Broll, Lucan, and even Thura from the catastrophe. Not only were the green dragons in retreat, but the defenders below, aware of what had happened, were also in complete disarray. Their morale was as low as Malfurion's, perhaps even lower. They knew that they had slowly been losing, but now they saw that their efforts had actually been nothing but lies. The Nightmare had teased them, waiting for its opportunity.

With Ysera . . . it can do anything! Why did she risk herself for me? True, Ysera's actual capture had been due to Lethon's trickery, but she would not have been at risk in the first place if not for her inexplicable interest in making certain of Malfurion's escape.

"It is gaining on us!" Tyrande called.

She spoke the dread truth. In his mind, Malfurion saw the gleaming shape of another druid in dreamform grasped not by the tendrils of the shadow tree, but by the previous victims of the Nightmare. The clawing hands rent the dreamform as if the night elf were made of flimsy cloth. He screamed as his very being was torn into a thousand pieces—

Barely a moment later, Malfurion saw the druid now at the forefront of the Nightmare's monstrous throng. His dreamform was now darker and gaunt. Now corrupted, he stretched his twisted fingers toward the nearest remaining defenders seeking to make them join him.

Yet however terrible his failure, however impossible the odds, the archdruid knew that he could not surrender to the inevitable. He could not let another fall to the Nightmare while he fled.

But as he again struggled to free himself, the green dragon shouted at him, "This is not the time! She did not give herself so that you would be lost again! My queen emphasized to us just before the attack that you are more valuable to Azeroth than even she and though we had trouble believing such, we must trust in her word now!"

" 'More valuable'?" Malfurion was incredulous. "Staving off the Nightmare for as long as she already had surely affected her mind!" He fought harder and finally felt her hold on his dreamform loosening.

Tyrande sensed what he was doing. She reached for the archdruid. "Malfurion! Don't!"

Her hand slipped through his dreamform. Malfurion struggled to pay no attention to her. A part of him wanted nothing more than to stay with Tyrande, but his duty was elsewhere.

However, to his dismay, his surroundings began to fade away. Too late, the archdruid realized that in seeking to free himself of the green dragon's spellwork, he had begun something else.

"No!" Malfurion tried to stop the inevitable—

"No!"

The archdruid sat up with a start. Pain immediately wracked his body. He clutched his chest and rolled over.

He was back in his barrow den, the accidental result of his attempt. It should have come as no surprise, the bond between his body and his dreamform naturally strong.

But something was wrong. Clenching his teeth, Malfurion struggled against agony. Was this the result of being gone so long?

The archdruid let out a guttural sound as he fought. In the back of his mind he became aware that he could not have possibly survived this long without the aid of others.

His body in general was in fair shape. That he could also sense. He felt the touch of Elune, a force the night elf knew well through Tyrande. Malfurion had no doubt that his love had been the one to organize efforts to save him.

Yet, though he groaned loud, no priestess now came to his aid.

Slowly, he won the struggle. As that happened, Malfurion suddenly sensed something only his experienced, highly attuned druidic skills could have uncovered.

The source of his suffering—and what still sought to *slay* him—was a small, very small touch of powder. He readily identified the magically-enhanced herb used in its making. *Morrowgrain*. Morrowgrain was rumored to be used in certain primitive curses. But while the herb itself was potent, someone had not been satisfied with its innate power. The subtle spell around it should have been enough addition to guarantee Malfurion's slow but certain death.

But whoever had done it had underestimated the healing light of the Mother Moon. The work of the priestesses had been enough to keep Malfurion's unoccupied body functioning, although eventually the poison would have done its work.

Malfurion fixed on the powder, gathering it back together from where in his body it had spread. He created of it a festering ball—

At that point the archdruid vomited.

He did not see the tiny sphere as it exited, but he felt its dire influence fade. Malfurion gasped for air as he slowly pushed himself up again.

Only then did he see the two priestesses. Both were sprawled on the ground of his barrow den. They were alive, but not conscious. Worse, they twitched and occasionally murmured fearfully.

The barrow den was also filled with tendrils of a sinister and too-familiar mist.

Malfurion had intended to meditate again in order to return to his dreamform, but now he cautiously headed into the mist toward the entrance. There was nothing that he could do for the priestesses, at least not for the moment. The archdruid needed to know the extent of the threat to the Moonglade.

But the tableau that greeted him as he stepped outside proved how wrong he could be. The Moonglade was entirely cloaked by the mist, giving it more the appearance of a graveyard. More disturbing was that there was not a sound to be heard, not even so much as a cricket.

Striding cautiously through the vegetation, the night elf came upon another barrow den. He slipped inside.

A still form in the familiar robes met his gaze. The hood obscured the sleeper's face. Kneeling next to the other druid, Malfurion touched the other night elf's wrist.

It was cold to the touch.

Malfurion quickly moved aside the hood.

The gaping mouth of the corpse sent shivers through the archdruid. The barrow den's dweller had obviously sent his dreamform forth but had not been able to return in time. Malfurion wondered if the unfortunate had been one of those combating the Nightmare or if he had perished before that.

Unable at the moment to do anything for the dead druid's remains, Malfurion retreated from the barrow den. He wondered how many of the other earthen dwellings had such bodies.

Knowing that he had more of a chance to help the living than the dead, Malfurion considered his best options. He no longer thought of meditation; the Moonglade had been tainted. To return to his dreamform here would be too risky. He had to go elsewhere, find the other defenders.

Most of all, he needed to find out what had happened to Tyrande and those with her. They had physically entered the Emerald Dream. To Malfurion, that meant a portal and the nearest to the Dream and the Nightmare was located in Ashenvale.

Yet barely had he determined to go there, barely had he begun to transform himself to storm crow form, than Malfurion realized that his efforts needed to be focused in a direction almost opposite to that in which he had originally planned to head. Although he had been long trapped, Malfurion knew that his people had been planning a new settlement to the west, an island off the coast. Even through the Nightmare, Malfurion had sensed the other druids' powerful efforts to do—something. Unfortunately, in trying to keep his efforts hidden from his captor, he had not been able to discover the results of those efforts. He had hints and suspicions . . .

The night elf gazed around the barely seen glade. There was no hint even of Remulos. Surely the Moonglade's guardian would have appeared upon sensing Malfurion's waking presence. Malfurion reached out with his thoughts but could still not find Cenarius's son. Had Remulos also joined the other druids?

The irony that he was as alone on Azeroth as he had been when a captive of the Nightmare Lord was not lost upon the archdruid. He started to ponder this—and then wondered why he was wasting more of his time instead of acting immediately, as he should.

Malfurion concentrated. Immediately, his surroundings wavered . . . and only then did he discover the true danger.

He had been *daydreaming*. It had not been his doing. The Nightmare was so powerful that it saturated the Moonglade. Caught up in his concerns for the others, the archdruid had not noticed when he had begun to slip into this half-slumbering state. It had likely been what had taken the priestesses guarding his body.

But the Nightmare had not been satisfied with that. Malfurion stirred to find himself under assault from the very glade itself.

The grass twisted around his legs, torso, and arms. The trees bent to smother him. They were all touched by the familiar dark corruption he had seen in the Emerald Dream . . . only this was the waking world. The Nightmare Lord had seized upon Ysera's great power to break the final barrier between dream and reality.

For just a brief moment Malfurion considered giving in to his doom. He was responsible for the Aspect's fall and for Azeroth's danger. Yet that thought quickly faded as Tyrande's trusting face formed in his thoughts.

The archdruid concentrated. *This is not your nature,* he reminded the grass, the trees. *This is a perversion of what you are a part of . . .*

He felt the grass begin to loosen. The trees, however, did not yet respond. They began to shake at their roots, as if seeking to free themselves while still striving to reach Malfurion. At the same time the bark shifted, forming a mockery of the night elf's own bearded visage.

"This is not your nature," Malfurion now said out loud, at the same time focusing his millennia of training on the flora. "This is a place of peace, of tranquility . . . this place touches the heart of Azeroth and is in turn touched by it . . ."

The grass released him. The trees suddenly stiffened. The images of his face vanished from the bark.

The Moonglade was calm again, if still mist-enshrouded.

Malfurion took a deep breath. What he had done was no small miracle, not against the might he had sensed at work against him. The Nightmare Lord had focused especially upon him. Fortunately, the evil had underestimated the archdruid in this of all places.

That settled one matter for Malfurion. He had to return to the Emerald Dream—what was left of it—before it was too late. The green dragon assigned to carry him off had said something about Ysera feeling him more important to the situation, important enough to risk herself.

Malfurion let out a growl of frustration at himself. He was *hardly* more important than the mistress of the Emerald Dream! Still, he owed *her* for her sacrifice and owed Azeroth for what his capture had permitted the Nightmare Lord to do.

He wondered why the Nightmare had not already engulfed the world. Its master had Ysera; why then wait? Was there something preventing his captor from ultimate victory?

If there is, I will not discover it standing here! he angrily reminded himself. *Any answers lie elsewhere . . .*

Without further hesitation, the archdruid transformed into a storm crow. Taking to the air, Malfurion soared from the Moonglade. Malfurion's wings beat hard as he rose higher and higher—

But then, at a place among the clouds, he suddenly hovered. Sharp eyes drank in a sight below that made the storm crow cry out. Perhaps he had been wrong, after all. Perhaps his hope that there was still some chance to salvage victory had merely been one last nightmare thrust upon him by a mocking foe.

The mist did not merely cover the Moonglade. It covered the land beyond it and beyond that.

In fact . . . it covered all of Azeroth that Malfurion could see.

"Malfurion!" Tyrande shouted. She looked to Broll. "What happened to him?"

"He must've cast himself back into his body! He should be all—"

The green dragon carrying them suddenly had to bank, for, without warning, the mists of the Nightmare erupted around them.

A horrific winged form materialized.

"The Nightmare desires these mortals . . . especially the female night elf . . ." the foul dragon Emeriss cooed. Her diseased and decaying body filled the air before them. *"Come accept the inevitable . . . Azeroth and the Nightmare are now one . . ."*

"You shall not have them!" the other dragon countered. She exhaled.

It resembled fire, but fire that was more ghost than real. Yet when it struck Emeriss, the corrupted dragon howled in agony and her body glittered as if suddenly covered in a million fireflies.

Ysera's servant did not wait. She dove around her struggling foe.

But an angry roar indicated that Emeriss had already shaken off her pain. A moment later the corrupted leviathan soared toward them.

"She flies too swiftly and I fight against forces that I cannot see but that slow me!" the dragon informed her charges. "There is but one thing I can do!"

The magic surrounding the mortals flared so bright that the night elves in particular were forced to shield their eyes.

"Find your Malfurion Stormrage!" their rescuer shouted to them. "My mistress would not lie!"

And with that, she cast them ahead.

Surrounded by her spell, they were protected from harm. Broll saw what she intended before the rest did.

"The portal! She's sent us toward—"

Before he could finish, they flew through.

The magic dissipated the moment that they were back in Azeroth.

Yet the green dragon had not intended for them to be injured in their landing. They emerged from the portal mere inches from the ground and when the spell vanished, the four simply came to a rest.

All but Lucan immediately leapt to their feet. However, as Broll approached the portal, the energies within . . . *froze.*

"Not possible . . ." he muttered. The druid jumped up to the portal and thrust a hand toward the magical gap.

It was like striking an iron door. Broll grimaced at the brief pain caused by his impetuousness.

The high priestess joined him. "Can we not get through?"

"No . . . either she sealed it after us . . . or something sealed it so that she couldn't follow . . ."

Tyrande shook her head. "She sent us to safety at her own expense . . . and all for Malfurion!"

The druid looked over his shoulder. "It's even a question whether she sent us to safety at all . . ."

They turned to face Thura. The orc had Brox's ax ready in her hands. She eyed the other three with wariness.

"Where is he? Where is Malfurion Stormrage?" she demanded.

Her question caused Tyrande to stride toward the husky, green-tinted warrior. As she neared, the high priestess glowed with the light of Elune. "He is beyond your petty reach, assassin!"

Thura met her glare . . . and then, to everyone's surprise, the orc lowered the weapon. She looked extremely weary.

"He is the one who made me chase him . . . he tricked me. Why did he wish to die?"

The night elves looked at one another. "He wasn't seeking death, not truly, anyway." Tyrande told her. "Your ax was needed to break the spell, I think . . ."

The orc slumped. "So . . . my purpose is false . . . I am nothing."

"Excuse me," Lucan interrupted, causing heads to turn to him. "Was he supposed to come through with us?"

The others looked to where he pointed. It was Broll who recognized the towering figure first.

"Gnarl!" he roared with joy. "You—"

"Get away from him!" Tyrande shouted, dragging Broll back.

The ancient of war let out a nerve-ripping laugh. As he stepped near, the fungus covering his body became evident. His leaves were filled with rot and his eyes glowed black.

"He wishes you to return . . ." the towering figure rasped.

His eyes were on Tyrande.

"Keep back!" The high priestess started to pray.

Gnarl's great arm swept toward them. Broll shoved the others back, taking a glancing blow that was still mighty enough to send him to his knees.

The ancient reached for the fallen night elf. Tyrande cut in front of Broll, her expression grimly set. "I'm sorry, Gnarl . . ."

The light of Elune struck the corrupted ancient dead-on. Gnarl stumbled back . . . and then righted.

"He is too strong for you this time," Gnarl mocked. "Azeroth is his . . . finally . . ."

As he spoke, the mists thickened. In them formed shapes that quickly defined themselves. Too familiar now were the grasping hands, the ever-shrieking mouths, and the desperate, hungry eyes.

The Nightmare's slaves surrounded them. The four pressed close together. Gnarl let out a harsh laugh.

Broll blinked. He was in the midst of a different battle and in his hand was a familiar object. The Idol of Remulos. The druid shook his head. *This is another dream! This is another trick!*

But his surroundings remained constant. Worse, he heard a voice nearby him calling for his help. Against his better judgment, the former gladiator looked—

Tyrande knelt beside a stone cairn. She was weeping, but it took her a moment to realize why.

Malfurion was buried here.

He was dead, though the cause of his death the high priestess could not recall. She only knew that she ached for him, ached for the life together that they had never been allowed to have.

"No!" Tyrande shouted angrily, rising at the same time. "I will not be cheated! We will not be cheated!"

She looked to the sky, where the moon shone full and bright. The high priestess raised her hands to the moon, to Elune.

"Grant me this wish! Fill me with your light as you never have before . . ."

Tyrande knew that what she hoped to do was wrong—indeed, something about the entire situation struck her as wrong—but a dread determination filled her. She *would* have Malfurion back! She would!

The light of the Mother Moon radiated from her. She gestured at the cairn. The silver glow bathed it.

The stones shook. A few at the top fell away.

A skeletal hand thrust out.

Tyrande tried to stop her spell, but it kept feeding Elune's light into the cairn. The hand shoved more stones away. Despite the silver nature of the Mother Moon's gift, the cadaverous fingers shone a sinister green.

Then, with a great rumble, the cairn burst apart. Stone rained down on Tyrande.

From the ruined burial mound, a monstrous Malfurion rose—

Thura stood surrounded by the elders of Orgrimmar. She felt ashamed enough to stand before them, but at their head stood the great Thrall himself. He looked terribly disappointed in her, disappointed and angry.

"You've shamed your kin," Thrall declared. "You were given a great weapon and took a blood oath to avenge Broxigar!"

She knelt. "I failed. I know. But the night elf—"

"Lives to laugh at you while the life fluids of Broxigar still drip from his foul hands!"

Thura had no reply.

The orc leader reached out. "You're not fitting to wield the glorious ax. Give it over."

Head bent low, Thura offered up the weapon to Thrall. A sense of guilt coursed through her as the ax left her hands.

Thrall hefted the weapon, admiring its balance and workmanship. Gripping it tight, he glared at the female orc.

"And now, you will make amends for your failure . . ."

He raised the ax high, preparing for a killing stroke—

Lucan stared at his companions. They stood as statues and with their eyes half-lidded. Their gazes seemed to have no focus.

They were caught up in the Nightmare.

Why he was not as they were was a question to which he had no answer. Likely because he was the least of the threat to the Nightmare. Even now, all the cartographer wanted most was to hide.

And in his desperation, that seemed the wisest choice to Lucan.

The human grabbed his three companions as best he could, hoping that his touch alone might be sufficient. They did not move even then, but Lucan had no time to concern himself with their conditions.

He tried to do what in the past seemed to work only when he was *not* trying. Yet there had been one or two recent moments when his conscious desire had enabled his unique ability to work for him.

The slaves of the Nightmare fell upon the helpless group—

Lucan and the party vanished.

They materialized in the Emerald Dream, the last place to which Lucan wanted to return. He felt certain that the Nightmare would be upon them there as well.

The others began coming out of their personal nightmares. They looked tired and momentarily disoriented.

Lucan was the only one to note the shadow suddenly covering them. He looked up.

"What do you want of me *now?*" Eranikus growled.

20

THE ENCLAVE

Hamuul Runetotem was not alone. Naralex, with whom Shandris was familiar, stood with the tauren.

His presence was enough to confirm the general's suspicions that they were the ones responsible for her imprisonment. She slipped out of Hamuul's grip and drew a dagger.

But Hamuul moved swiftly and surely against her attack. He thrust a hand out and deflected the dagger's path, but not without some injury to his extremity.

Ignoring the blood, the tauren barreled into her. As he did, he said under his breath, "You must stop this or he will certainly notice us, Shandris Feathermoon!"

"Who?" she quietly demanded.

"A traitor in our midst! A traitor who threatens all Darnassus and beyond!"

He stopped. Hamuul and Naralex peered at one another in grave concern.

"He knows . . ." the night elf druid muttered.

"Quickly! Stand between us!" Hamuul ordered Shandris. As some inner sense warned her to obey, the two druids began to transform into birds.

From the ground erupted long vines that sought to ensnare the trio. Shandris severed two with her dagger, then fended off more.

Hamuul had sought to fly up, but the tauren was caught by two other vines. As they snared his wing, what at first appeared as flower buds sprouted from the tips.

The buds opened . . . revealing wicked thorns that acted like teeth.

The tauren would have been bitten, but Naralex used his beak to bite through the vines. The tops dropped, yet the respite was only momentary, for, as with those that Shandris had cut, these two grew new roots.

Hamuul squawked something to Naralex. The transformed night elf immediately seized Shandris by her shoulders and carried her aloft.

But as they rose, something else fell upon them from the branches above. They were shadowy forms that seemed to sprout from the leaves themselves. Naralex, intent on bringing his charge to safety, flew right into their midst.

One of the shadow creatures thrust an ethereal hand into Shandris. She shrieked as a chill touched her very soul. The Sentinel commander lost her grip on the dagger. Her body shook.

Whatever her suffering, though, Naralex's was far greater. The shadow creatures swarmed all over him, tearing at the storm crow with wild relish.

Naralex's flight faltered. He tried to shake off his attackers, but when that failed, the druid veered toward the ground closest to the path out of the enclave.

He released Shandris from his talons the moment that he was close enough to avoid her being harmed by the drop. Still reeling from the horrific chill, she dropped to her knees.

A roar echoed in her ears. Hamuul, once again in his true shape, had seized several vines and with his great strength now tore them loose. However, rather than toss them aside, he threw them up into the air.

An emerald sheen surrounded them. Each snapping tendril shrank rapidly.

A moment later the seeds to which they had reverted dropped harmlessly around the tauren.

Unfortunately, as this happened, the shadow creatures also converged upon Hamuul. The tauren thrust a hand into one pouch and then flung the contents at the nearest.

Although his attackers seemed without substance, the brown pow-der the archdruid used landed on them as if the fiends were solid. Moreover, it had a devastating effect. The shadow figures twisted and contorted. They began to shrink and change shape. Their doom was accompanied by a chorus of monstrous hisses.

Hamuul's eyes widened. The shadows had been reduced to leaves. This had not been the intention of his spell. The tauren could only fathom that the leaves represented the true nature of their attackers.

"No . . ." he rumbled. "It cannot have gone that far . . ."

But his distraction cost the tauren. Another of the shadows thrust its hand through his back. As the horrific cold encased his soul, an-other shadow struck through his chest.

The tauren fell to his knees. His eyes glazed over.

Shandris saw him fall, but could do nothing. She started to throw her glaive—

Branches reached down and seized her. Some tore her weapon from her. The rest bound her tight.

Another, heavier branch struck the Sentinel hard on the back of the head, knocking her out.

Naralex let out a mournful squawk as he collided with the ground. At first glance, it appeared that he was being physically shredded to pieces, but each bit that the shadows tore away faded as they flung it aside.

The night elf resumed his normal shape. Gasping, he collapsed and lay still.

From the trees calmly emerged another druid. He stared at the fro-zen tauren, then at the stunned Sentinel.

"I'm sorry," Fandral Staghelm honestly told them, though they were not conscious enough to hear him. "You must believe me that I am."

The lead archdruid walked among the shadows, who moved respectfully out of his way. Fandral went to Naralex, who lay un-moving.

Leaning down, Fandral touched the other night elf's neck.

"Still alive . . ."

Rising, Fandral eyed the party with disappointment.

"Something will have to be done with you." He considered, a smile coming to his face. "Valstann will know just what! My son will have the answer . . ."

He started back to his sanctum without another glance at Shandris, the tauren, or Naralex. The shadow creatures surrounded the trio but did not touch them. Instead, the branches that held the priestess drew her up among the dark, leafy crowns. Others seized Hamuul and Naralex and carried them after her.

When that was done, the shadow creatures straightened. As one, they dissipated, their essence also rising up among the trees, where they reverted to their dormant form . . . the very leaves of Teldrassil.

The mists extended out even far into the sea. Malfurion could not believe its thickness. He beat his wings harder as the wind began to pick up. A gale was brewing, a gale that the archdruid was certain was taking shape only due to his presence.

Malfurion did not know what he planned—not completely—but some sense drove him toward the island where his people had chosen to make their new home. There was an urgency building within him that there was at least one key to the catastrophe engulfing *two* worlds.

A full-fledged hurricane struck.

Despite his awareness that it was brewing, its full intensity startled even Malfurion. He was thrust back as if he were nothing. Lightning raged, some of it striking perilously near. The archdruid found himself hurtling *away* from the still-shrouded island.

More bolts nearly struck him. It was not by luck that they did not. Whatever power had forged this fury desired to hit Malfurion; only the night elf's instincts kept that from happening.

His anxiety swelled with the tempest's strength. Each passing moment led Azeroth and all those he loved, especially Tyrande, toward doom. Yet, try as he might, Malfurion could barely save even himself. Again the archdruid wondered at Ysera's seemingly foolish sacrifice. She thought him more valuable to both realms than her—

Although Malfurion did not believe as Ysera had, at that moment he did recognize one thing. Once again, he had played into the Nightmare's hand. His uncertainties had fed into his own dark dreams again.

That was not to say that the storm was not real—the Nightmare's master now had that terrible power—but its intensity was magnified by the night elf's mind.

The fury lessened. Fueled by that fact, Malfurion focused on his destination. He beat his wings faster and faster.

The storm did not break; it simply ceased. Malfurion soared through the mists, aware that he had won a small battle. Overconfidence was as dangerous as fear.

Something loomed ahead, something so huge that even at the height he flew, Malfurion could not see its top. He knew what it was, even though he had been a prisoner since before its creation. Fandral had so often spoken of the need to create it, to bring back the immortality and glory of their race.

The second World Tree greeted his wary gaze. It was impressive. It was imposing.

And as he studied it more, Malfurion knew that it was also tainted by the Nightmare as nothing else on Azeroth had been.

The archdruid banked, his eyes ever on the gargantuan tree. Outwardly, what he could see appeared normal; yet his senses told him it was infested with the evil that had spread from the other realm.

How could they not see that? Malfurion wondered about the other druids. *What were they thinking? How could Fandral let this come to pass?*

As he drew near the island, he detected great activity below. Many druids were down there and they were all casting some coordinated spell. His hopes rose at first; the others had come to realize the World Tree's taint and were fighting it.

But no . . . a mere breath later, Malfurion realized it was just the opposite. The spell was a powerful one, but instead of cleansing the tree, it was inadvertently *feeding* the taint. He could feel it and was astounded that the others could not.

Without hesitation, Malfurion dove. At the same time, he sought to reach out to the other druids and warn them of the terrible thing they were doing.

Yet something blocked his attempt to contact the casters. It came as no shock to Malfurion, but it meant that he had to reach them with all due haste. The World Tree's taint, combined with Ysera's capture, all but promised the Nightmare triumph.

A mind suddenly touched his. At first he thought it one of those below, but then he determined that it instead came from *above*. More important, its way of thought was so very distinct, even despite the fragmented attempt to communicate, that he knew exactly who it was.

Hamuul Runetotem? In response to Malfurion's question, there was a fragmented response. It was as if the tauren were not entirely conscious. However, Malfurion did sense an urgency from the tauren, an urgency and a warning.

It was a warning so intense that the archdruid veered skyward again. He soared up, finally sighting the crown.

All looked as it should, but Malfurion could sense that the taint was as widespread up here as in the trunk. The archdruid approached the first branches with trepidation but necessary swiftness.

He passed the first boughs without any sign of threat. Indeed, deeper within, he even saw signs of fauna in the form of birds and squirrels. Was he wrong about the taint?

Higher and higher the storm crow rose. In one respect, Malfurion knew what he would find. Even before his disappearance, the discussions concerning the building of the new capital had been going on. Its location had not been decided then, but Malfurion had no doubt that he would find Darnassus atop the World Tree.

Which meant thousands of lives unaware that their very home had become something sinister.

Malfurion decided that he had no other choice but to plunge into the crown and enter Darnassus from underneath. It was the most direct path to where he sensed he would find the tauren . . . and possibly the secret of the World Tree's foulness.

Despite the size of his storm crow form, Malfurion darted with ease through the huge crown. He eyed the World Tree with some sadness, not only due to the taint, but also because of memories of Nordrassil and what it had once been. *If only they had waited! Nordrassil could be restored . . . with time . . .*

The foliage grew thicker and thicker, at last forcing Malfurion to slow. He could feel that he was nearly at his destination—

His path was suddenly a thick jumble of branches and leaves. Malfurion veered.

They shifted, again barring his way.

The archdruid tried to avoid them, but it was too late. He collided.

The foliage enveloped him. It sought to constrict his wings, to bind his beak, and twist his body until his bones would break.

Malfurion felt the familiar and dread presence of the Nightmare Lord. It was not direct, but rather as if the evil force had left a part of itself here.

Gibbering laughter filled Malfurion's mind. The leaves seemed to take on faces, shadowed faces that almost but not quite coalesced into awful creatures.

Transforming to his own shape only momentarily caught the smothering foliage off guard. The leaves immediately began shifting, becoming more and more hooved shadows eager to reclaim the night elf.

Regaining his breath, Malfurion concentrated. A powerful wind erupted in his vicinity. The huge branches were whipped back as if blades of grass, and the changing shadow creatures were blown away like the leaves from which they had arisen.

The night elf scrambled upward, then changed again. As the storm raged, he flew with all his might. More leaves followed up in his wake, seeking to catch him, but they were too slow.

Malfurion entered Darnassus.

There were two things that he instantly noted. One was the city itself. It spread proudly over the huge branches. His brethren and those others who had helped shape the new night elf capital had truly created a masterpiece.

But the second thing that Malfurion noted was that the city

appeared utterly ignorant of all that was not only affecting Teldrassil, but the rest of Azeroth. He saw movement in buildings and even heard music from one direction.

How could they not know? How could they remain so ignorant?

The answer was simple. Someone *wanted* them that way.

Still, it was odd that the Sentinels were not at least informed to a point. Malfurion knew Shandris Feathermoon very well; in some remote fashion, he was almost like a second father to her. She would not have left the city quite this unsuspecting.

But he had no time to find out what the Sentinels did or did not know; Hamuul's desperate contact had come from another direction.

Malfurion made his way toward that direction, avoiding all contact with other night elves, even druids. For their own safety, he did not want anyone knowing of his presence. For whatever reason, the Nightmare Lord had no desire to attack Darnassus just yet. It was a precarious situation and Malfurion did not like his choices, but so it would have to be.

He knew even before he reached it that he had arrived at the new Cenarion Enclave. This place of meditation and gathering in the proposed city had been long discussed. Malfurion himself had suggested many of the details that he now saw standing in bloom before him. But his heart was sickened when he sensed that the taint was strong here as well.

Malfurion alighted, his form shifting in the process. The area was silent, much too silent for a place where birds and other fauna should be in evidence day or night.

There was little choice but to avoid the trees lining the enclave. The archdruid knew that they were like the branches against which he had fought.

A suspicion that had long been growing in him stirred. The attack had all but verified it, although Malfurion still wanted to deny the possibility—

The thought was interrupted by a brief contact by Hamuul. It was stark in its need for haste. Malfurion tried to reach the other archdruid, but to no avail.

But he knew from where Hamuul had contacted him. Malfurion headed toward the structure that was center to the enclave's design.

It was also where he who had come to lead the druids since Malfurion's absence had chosen to make his new sanctum.

Malfurion neared the building—and stopped short in horror.

There were three figures bound in the vines that covered the sanctum. Their limbs were stretched tight and pulled to the side as much as possible. One was Hamuul Runetotem. The second was Naralex. The third was none other than Shandris Feathermoon. They all appeared to be unconscious . . . or worse.

Which meant that Malfurion had been tricked into coming here.

"So the legendary shan'do returns to grace us with his undeserved glory," the voice of Fandral Staghelm declared from all around Malfurion. "Always the only one who can save the world, because he deems himself the only one. I sensed you coming long ago and prepared a proper welcome . . ."

Malfurion did not turn to seek Fandral, aware that this was what the other desired. Instead, he spoke toward the building. "What's happening here, Fandral? Why are you doing this?"

"Is it not obvious?" the voice replied. "These three are a danger to our people! To all Azeroth!"

"These three?" Malfurion subtly sought Fandral's true location. In his mind, the Nightmare Lord had clearly played tricks on the other archdruid's mind. If Malfurion could confront Fandral, then he might be able to snap his brother druid out of the spell. "Shandris is a staunch defender of our race and Hamuul is an honest, worthy member of our calling as is Naralex—"

"Lies, lies, lies!" The words reverberated through Malfurion's head. "They seek to bring down everything! They seek to tear us apart! He has told me so!"

"Who, Fandral? Who?"

A section of the vines not being used to hold the pair in place suddenly curled around. They formed a thicker and thicker mass as tall as Malfurion.

The vines suddenly gave way.

Fandral Staghelm stared at his former shan'do. "You would want to know that, would you not? It is clear to me that you are a traitor, too!" His expression was one of honest grief—tinged with madness. "But you are too dangerous! The female, Naralex, and the beast—they're misguided. But now they sleep and dream. They will awaken refreshed, as everyone else will!"

Malfurion took a step toward Fandral. "No one will wake! The Nightmare extends beyond the Emerald Dream now! Everywhere save here is under siege by its evil and that evil fills this World Tree!"

"You still dismiss the need for my Teldrassil!" the other archdruid snarled, a sudden ferocity overcoming him. "But I have done so much with it! It has helped reshape not only our race, but all of Azeroth as well!"

"Teldrassil is tainted, Fandral! The Nightmare Lord infests it! Can't you feel that? Look into yourself and touch Teldrassil's heart!"

Fandral stared down his nose. "I know Teldrassil's heart better than you or anyone! I have given it my heart in turn and for that sacrifice, it gave him back to me . . ."

Only then did Malfurion note a shadow hovering behind the other night elf's left shoulder. It was one of the foul creatures that had attacked him on his way here.

But even though Fandral looked at the shadow, he did not seem bothered by its obviously sinister presence. Instead, Fandral smiled with familial affection at the fiend.

"Teldrassil has given me back my son, Malfurion. My son! Is not Valstann as proud and handsome as ever?"

He is consumed by his madness, Malfurion sadly realized. *He is beyond reach . . .*

And that meant that Malfurion had only one recourse. He concentrated—

Fandral frowned, his expression as sad toward his former shan'do as Malfurion's had been toward him. "I had hoped otherwise. That was your last chance, my teacher . . ."

The shadow that pretended to be Valstann laughed darkly, though only Malfurion appeared to hear it.

There was a terrible rumble. Malfurion was thrown to the ground. Only the spot where Fandral stood appeared stable.

The ground erupted and the trees bent down as if seeking to uproot themselves. A dark dread filled Malfurion as he sensed the taint swell within Teldrassil.

"I advised him that we should wait!" Fandral shouted. "But it seems Valstann spoke the truth! You, Darnassus . . . all of it . . . must be cleansed! Valstann and I will show our people the way and they will be the better for it! Teldrassil will be the instrument of a new, glorious Azeroth!"

He continued to babble on, heedless of the awful truth around him. Malfurion fought to regain some balance, but the ground burned like fire. Before his eyes, it blackened. Monstrous leaves as dark as night and with savage thorns sprouted everywhere.

The trees shook with more violence, some of them finally ripping free. They bore a rot that had not been evident before. From their shaking crowns fell hundreds of smaller thorned leaves.

The leaves began changing into the shadow creatures.

For the first time, Malfurion also heard shouts and screams from without the enclave. Darnassus had finally joined the rest of Azeroth. The terror of the Nightmare had arisen, if in a different and in some ways more frightening form.

The night elves' very home—Teldrassil—was their enemy.

21

STORM OVER STORMWIND

Broll stirred to consciousness, still aware that he could not recall just when he had fallen prey to the Nightmare. He found
himself standing with Tyrande, Lucan, and the orc . . . and
facing a very aggrieved Eranikus.

Worse, they were back in the Emerald Dream, or what remained
of it. The group was situated in a deep valley that still retained the
fading glory of the once-fabled realm. Tall hills surrounded them, but
although they looked like strong, stern sentries, the druid was well
aware how little protection they truly were.

The green dragon eyed Lucan as if he were a pest best disposed
of by devouring. To his credit, the cartographer faced the behemoth
without shaking.

"For the first and last time, take yourself and these others away
from me! Whatever foolish link ties us two together, you would best
be served removing it, human!"

"I only hoped to take us away from where we were," Lucan responded with more than a bit of exasperation. "I didn't know that
we'd also return to you!"

The dragon hissed. "If I had known that you would be so much
trouble to me, I would have left you as an infant in the Emerald
Dream! That a human would come to possess such dangerous and
haphazard abilities merely by being born here! Yes, better I had left
you to the whims of fate, then . . ."

Despite his protests, Eranikus's tone indicated to Broll at least that his anger was not truly focused on Lucan. The behemoth's fury was actually meant for himself.

But that was a matter with which Eranikus had to deal. Broll was more concerned with another situation, one which Tyrande voiced for him.

"Can you take us to Malfurion?" she asked the dragon. "We have got to find him! I have to find him!"

"For what purpose?" Eranikus mocked. "All is coming to a dire end! The Nightmare has taken my queen, my mate! There is no more hope! I have failed her again . . ."

This earned him a look of contempt from the high priestess. "And so you dwell in that failure! Well, we will not!"

Eranikus stretched his wings wide. He glanced around, almost as if afraid that the Nightmare would now sense him. Then, his anger momentarily overcoming his fear, he hissed, "You may go wherever you wish and do what foolishness you desire, just so long as I must never be reminded of what happened again!"

One wing swept toward the tiny figures. Broll pushed Tyrande toward Lucan and saw that to her credit, Thura also recognized his intention.

As for Lucan, he did as Eranikus obviously intended. Confronted by what seemed a threat . . . the human involuntarily shifted out of the Emerald Dream.

With him went the others. One moment, the green dragon loomed over them; the next, they stood on the walls of a great keep.

And in the midst of frantic, pitched battle.

On the one side, the horrific dreamforms of the Nightmare's victims flowed over defenses and converged on the keep. Their twisted, agonized forms, their shrieking mouths . . . everything about them stirred the most basic fears within even the hardiest of the group. Hollow eyes sought out anyone with whom they could share their torture.

On the other side, a dwindling band of defenders clad in familiar armor tried to stem what could not be stemmed. Tremendous their courage was, for none fled even though they were far out-numbered. As the cadaverous fiends neared, the fighters stood their ground.

To Broll's shock, he knew this place. "This is Stormwind City—and the royal keep!"

A soldier spotted them. He took a moment to register their odd arrival, then called to a couple of companions. The trio anxiously charged toward the newcomers, brandishing both swords and torches as they neared.

The orc moved to meet them in battle, but Tyrande blocked her path. "They think us a part of the Nightmare!" the high priestess shouted to Broll. "We must convince them otherwise!"

Before the others could prevent him, Lucan stepped to the fore-front. Hands forward with palms open to the oncoming soldiers, he shouted, "Wait! We're friends! I'm Lucan Foxblood, third assistant cartographer to the king! We must see him!"

The soldiers hesitated, more than one eyeing the orc among the party with great suspicion. Broll guessed what they were thinking. What sort of nightmare took such an odd form?

Signaling his companions to hold back, the lead soldier moved within weapon's reach of Lucan. He stretched the sword toward the cartographer, who did not move.

The tip touched solid flesh. The soldier looked even more relieved than Lucan. However, he then stared at Thura again.

The high priestess joined Lucan, cutting off view of the orc. "I am Tyrande Whisperwind, leader of the night elves and with me is Broll Bearmantle, comrade to King Varian! The orc is with us. She means no harm . . ."

"Broll Bearmantle . . ." that name at least registered with the sol-dier. He nodded his head in respect to both night elves. "My lady . . . we are honored—"

"The king . . ." Lucan reminded him. "We need to see King Varian immediately!"

"Best come with me, then," returned the fighter. "We've got to re-treat from here anyway!"

No sooner had he spoken than a scream broke out nearby. They turned to see another defender a few yards behind them struggling in the mist. Hands formed from the mist clutched at him and the macabre faces of the slaves of the Nightmare eagerly covered the hapless soldier as if seeking to devour him.

Before anyone could help him, the man disappeared. His own scream echoed after, becoming more horrific, more a part of the Nightmare.

"Quickly!" ordered the fighter who had first confronted Broll and the others.

They were led with great haste down a long set of stone steps and then across a yard to another part of the wall. As they reached this, Broll called to their guide, "The city! How's it standing?"

"In pieces scattered around! The Trade District, the harbor, the Valley of Heroes . . . all dark!" the man shouted back. "Some noise from the Old Town, Cathedral Square, and the Dwarven District . . . and the Mage Quarter is still bright!" He gestured to his right, where the druid saw a constantly shifting array of colors that marked spells going off. There were a few other areas where lesser displays of light also appeared.

" 'Twas much brighter yet an hour ago," the soldier continued. "We're not holding. No one's holding . . ."

"It is amazing any part is holding!" Tyrande interjected. "What do you say, Broll?"

The druid nodded. "As brave and as powerful as Stormwind's defenders—warrior or mage—are, they should've been engulfed by now . . ." He considered the matter further and came up with a slim hope. "It might be Malfurion's doing, but I think thus far it's She of the Dreaming's!"

"But Ysera is taken!"

Broll took a little pride in what he said next. "She is an Aspect, one of the great dragons! More to the point, she is the protector of the Emerald Dream! Even as the Nightmare's captive, I think she struggles, preventing them from using her against the Dream and us . . ."

Thura considered the grim tableau inexorably pressing toward them. "She struggles, but this city . . . and maybe Orgrimmar, too, will fall."

They began to ascend another set of stone steps. More than once their journey was accented by cries of terror and dismay.

"Ysera sacrificed herself in order to obtain Malfurion's escape!" the druid added. "She must think my shan'do can do something yet!"

"And what of us?" Tyrande asked.

Broll had no answer for that. He could not tell her what constantly ate at him. The last nightmare involving his daughter had brought his great failure back to him full-blown. He was not Malfurion Storm-rage. He was not even an archdruid.

He was only a rebellious former gladiator and slave.

But that was also what kept Broll moving on. The soldier finally brought them toward a familiar figure. Even with the armor obscuring everything, the stance was that of but one person.

"Lo'Gosh!" Broll roared.

The armored figure whirled. Through the helmet slits, Varian's wide eyes took in the sight before him.

Unfortunately, his initial focus proved to be on Thura. "An orc in Stormwind!"

The king immediately charged forward, his legendary sword, Sha-lamayne, already raised to strike. Shalamayne's great blade, with its unique narrow edge at the point and the thicker, angled edge further down, looked capable of cutting the orc in two. The gem in the lower part of the blade glowed like a furious sun.

Thura moved to defend herself. Varian saw this only as confirmation of his suspicions. He gripped tight the long, slender hilt, the backward arch at the bottom of the blade framing his taut fingers. "Let your blood be the first from a thousand orcs who'll die this night for what's happening! I'll—"

Broll took to the forefront. "Your sight's getting bad, Lo'Gosh! Not good for a king, much less a poor excuse for a gladiator!"

"Broll Bearmantle!" Despite registering his friend's presence, the king did not lower his sword. "Away from that damned green monster! I'll strike her down—"

"She is with us! She is not to blame for what's happening, nor is Thrall!"

Varian's disbelief was clear, but it was also clear that to reach Thura—who was quite willing to do battle—the lord of Stormwind would have to go through his old comrade.

"I don't even know if this is real," Varian growled. "Tell me that you're real, Broll . . ."

The druid reached out a hand. After a cautious pause, the lord of Stormwind took it. His gaze softened slightly as he pressed in return.

"It *is* you! Truly you—I think!"

"If you can feel those bones you're cracking, you know I'm real!" Broll and the king released one another. Their joy at their reunion was tempered by the dire moment. "Valeera! She isn't here by any chance, is she?"

"Haven't seen that blood elf rogue of yours in several weeks. You know how independent she can be!" Varian grimaced. "Believe me, we could surely use her fighting skills now, Broll. I hope she's not gotten caught stealing again. Hate to see her fighting for someone like Rehgar Earthfury or worse," Varian concluded, referring to the orc shaman for whom they had battled as gladiators and slaves of the Crimson Ring. All fights in the Crimson Ring were to the death and even Valeera had slain her share.

The druid did not hide his disappointment. He could only hope that, wherever she was, the blood elf was safe.

But just exactly where *would* a safe place soon be?

"I know you," Varian said, gazing past the night elf to Lucan. "Foxblood. We thought you lost."

The cartographer nodded. "I have been."

Tyrande received a short but very polite nod. Varian had met her in the past, just before regaining his throne. "Your Majesty . . ." He then turned his attention back to Thura. The sword rose again and fixed with deadly purpose on the orc. "But why bring this filth into Stormwind City, Broll? What were you thinking? Her warchief used a fog to skulk up to our walls in the past, like some honorless assassin! Rather than face us directly, he used plague to soften us, a foul weapon no true warrior would wield—"

"Thrall is no assassin skulking in the fog nor is he an honorless warrior!" she retorted. "You can't speak of him—"

Before it could get worse, Broll interjected, "Lo'Gosh! There's no time for this eternal arguing! She is with us! I vouch for her with my life! My life!"

"You place little value on your existence, then, Broll—"

"Stop it! There are more important matters! Tell me truthfully; how long do you think the capital has left?"

"I'd have said we were lost already, but though their progress is undeniable, they move slowly. Still, our weapons are for the most part useless against them and all but a few areas have grown silent. By tomorrow—assuming that there is even a tomorrow—there may be nothing holding out but part of the keep. If you've anything in mind at all that might save us, I'll lend what help I can. You know that."

"I'm grateful to hear that. I hope you'll still feel so after I've told you what we hope to do." The druid quickly explained his notions. Varian's brow wrinkled deeply as he tried to comprehend everything.

"I'll take your word for it, Broll," the monarch finally said. "The question remains, what to do about it?"

"My shan'do is the key . . . somehow. I believe he's the key." Broll indicated Lucan. "Your man's got a distinctive talent . . . but it has a tendency to send us on a different path. We need to reach Darnassus fast . . . faster than even I can travel on my own . . ."

"There are still some flying mounts left to us here in the keep," Varian suggested. "A couple that might be useful—"

Tyrande suddenly stepped up. "King Varian. If you can answer a question, it occurs to me suddenly that there might be another manner by which *one* of us could reach Darnassus much more quickly. Even more quickly than the swiftest mount you have."

"If I can answer in any way that aids our plight, by all means ask . . ."

"Do you know where our ambassador is now?"

Varian scowled. "Caught in her sleep like so many others . . . in her chambers, if I recall the report."

"We need someone to take us to her," the high priestess insisted.

"I can't leave command." The king looked from Tyrande to Broll. Finally, "Major Mattingly!"

A gray-haired veteran soldier in bright gold-and-red armor with a royal blue surcoat bearing the proud Stormwind lion head rushed up. His face was lined by long experience and he wore a short beard. In his right hand he wielded a longsword.

"The druid!" the major rasped when he saw Broll. "I know you . . ."

"And I you," Broll returned. "You serve under General Marcus Jonathan—" The night elf broke off, recalling what the soldier who had brought them here had said. The Valley of Heroes, where the general and Mattingly would have been stationed, had already fallen.

The major's eyes verified Broll's concern. "The general sent for reinforcements when first the mists began to take our men. He sent me to procure them. Before I could return, the mist covered the valley . . ."

"Damned fool here almost rode into it even then," Varian added without any anger. "But Mattingly knew we needed every man and ordered his just-gathered force back here . . ." To the major, the lord of Stormwind said, "You know where the night elf ambassador lived— lives. I need someone trusting but wary enough to get them there . . . though I've not been told exactly why."

Tyrande did not hesitate. "She has a hearthstone."

Varian's eyes were not the only ones to widen. Broll also knew of what the high priestess spoke, though even he himself had only twice seen one of the artifacts. A hearthstone was a palm-sized crystal, oval in shape, that was bound by arcane magic to not only its bearer, but a particular place. Most often, they were tied to great locations such as, apparently in this case, Darnassus. Distance did not matter.

"I'd thought them only legend," Varian remarked warily. "Things heard only in stories concerning magi . . . or elves."

"Or elves," the high priestess repeated with a brief, dour smile. "Interesting that your ambassador should have one."

"But good for us now, perhaps." Tyrande calmly responded.

Nodding, the king said no more. He looked to the major, who saluted. Mattingly signaled the others to follow him.

Varian made no attempt to stop the orc from following the night elves and neither Broll nor Tyrande dared leave her with the humans. Thura likewise appeared to have no inclination to stay.

But one member of their party proved a surprise. Rather than remaining with his king and countrymen, Lucan Foxblood also followed.

"You're home," Broll muttered. "Stay here!"

"I might be needed," Lucan argued, his eyes filled with a determination that would not be denied. "My abilities may be unpredictable and dangerous, but they may be of some use . . . in case of a need to escape . . ."

The druid said nothing more. They were already at the keep gates.

A shouted command from the major opened the way, though the sentries were quick to shut the entrance right behind them. As they exited the keep, Tyrande remarked on what all of them immediately noticed.

"The mist is thick here, but those poor souls are nowhere to be seen . . ."

"Why should they be here?" Broll grimly returned. "This part of Stormwind's already under their master's reign!"

Indeed, there came not a sound from anywhere nearby, though in the distance they could hear the shouts, screams, and explosions that marked the dwindling defense. The eerie silence was a stark reminder of what much of Azeroth was like at this point.

"She must hold on," the druid rumbled, referring to Ysera. "She must . . ."

"And we must pray that Malfurion is all right and can help us," Tyrande added. She did not say what was clear in her tone, that she was also simply fearful for him for his own sake and for the love she bore for him.

"Your ambassador keeps a dwelling in the Trade District," the major informed them, "though I've never understood why she would prefer that to the Park, where your people tend to congregate." When the high priestess did not explain, Mattingly tugged on his beard and changed the subject. "Best we avoid Cathedral Square. They're still defending it and we might get caught up in a spell. Also, we've got to avoid the canals . . . the mists are particularly strong in them . . . they caught a lot of people unaware down there when they first flowed into the city."

Lucan grimaced. "But that means we'll have to pass through the Old Town district."

This brought a harsh laugh from Mattingly. "At this point that won't make too much of a difference to most of the rest of the capital, Foxblood!"

They ran along a stone street upon whose northern side was marked an entrance to the Dwarven District. From there flowed more sounds of desperate struggle. The dwarves, at least, were still fighting.

With continued vigilance, the major led them across a walkway and into the Old Town. There, despite their guide's comment, the others could see that Lucan had been rightly concerned about entering. The Old Town district was a part of Stormwind City that had not been so hard hit by the orcs and thus had never needed true rebuilding. However, that also meant that less attention had been paid to its upkeep since then, and so while preserved, it was not nearly as pristine as the rest of the capital. True, the Hall of Champions could be found here, as well as the army's barracks, but so could beggars, thieves, and the poor. The streets were far dirtier than what the party had traveled thus far and there was an odor of decay that had nothing to do with the Nightmare save that it enhanced it yet more.

"Bodies . . ." Mattingly warned.

Three ragged humans lay sprawled to the side. The first had one hand curled into a fist. His mouth gaped. The other two looked as if they had been trying to help one another walk, for each had an arm around the other. The major left the others long enough to prod them.

"The first one's dead—of fright, it looks like to me—but the other two are sleeping like the rest," he reported. "We move on."

It was soon evident that, if not for their guide, there would have been a good chance that Broll and the others would have become lost. Even Lucan, a mapmaker, did not seem to know this part of Stormwind City well. In addition to the mists, the streets had a way of meandering to them that fueled the party's already great anxiety.

They came across more bodies, but Major Mattingly this time did not pause to examine them. It was clear that all were victims, whether still alive or dead being pointless.

With much relief, Broll saw that they were approaching the canal entrance to the Trade District. The mists were as thick there as in the Old Town, but there was no sign of the attack going on around the keep or the cathedral. Still, no one assumed that they would remain untouched by the Nightmare.

"We make a left once we get out of the passage," the officer informed them.

Leaning close to Tyrande, Broll murmured, "Why *is* the ambassador living in this part of the capital rather than the Park?"

In a barely audible whisper, the high priestess replied, "Because there are those I need her to meet in secret who would be too obvious in the Park." As Broll's gaze narrowed, Tyrande added, "There is no threat to Varian or Stormwind; the ambassador's duties are steered toward just the opposite, Broll. Now ask me no more."

He did as she bade, aware that, as leader of her people, Tyrande was forced into political actions of which perhaps even her trusted Shandris was unaware. It would not be simply for the sake of the night elf race, though that was paramount, but for the overall benefit of all the Alliance.

The Trade District bore the semblance of a much better kept, even more eclectic quarter. Broll would have been happy to walk its cobblestone streets had it been as it normally was. The bustling activity, the various races and callings . . . they reminded him of the richness that had been Azeroth.

But now the Trade District was too much a twin to the Old Town. The mist hung over the shops, inns, and other buildings as if over a vast and intricate necropolis. Worse, bodies lay sprawled in greater numbers, as if many of the inhabitants had simply collapsed in midstep.

"They dead or sleeping?" Thura suddenly asked. The orc had kept silent throughout the journey. Her tone indicated an uncertainty she had likely been trying to hide. These were not dangers for which a warrior trained.

"No time to check or to care," Mattingly replied. He pointed to a shadowed structure to the right. "That's the building there."

They reached the building—an inn—without any menace arising. Broll and Tyrande exchanged concerned glances; their fortune had thus far been too good.

"Best if some of us guard the way down here," the major suggested, eyeing the still street. The sounds of struggle were muted, as if Stormwind City's last defenses were failing.

"I will find the room," Tyrande decided.

"And I'll come with you," Broll insisted. "My shan'do would never forgive me for letting you go alone . . . and neither would I."

Thura grunted. "I stay here, where an ax has room to cleave."

"I'll stay, too." Lucan eyed the major and the orc and took up a place between them. Mattingly handed him a long dagger.

"We'll hurry," the high priestess promised. In truth, there was little the three could do to defend the vicinity; they served best as watchers.

The interior of the inn was marked by the body of a stout human who was likely a patron of the establishment. He sat in a chair, arms dangling at his side. His expression was contorted into such a look of horror that the night elves could not help but stop in their tracks.

Broll leaned close. The human was murmuring something. His brow tightened.

"We must go on." Tyrande strode up a set of wooden stairs two steps at a time.

Broll eyed the man a moment more, for some reason finding this victim of particular interest. Then, still dissatisfied, the druid followed after Tyrande.

He reached the upper floor to find several doors already flung open. Far ahead, Tyrande shoved aside the one at the end.

"This is it . . ." the high priestess said.

But as Broll joined her, he saw nothing but a nearly empty chamber with several flowering plants—still fresh and well-cared for—and a bed that was covered with a woven green blanket.

"She's gone . . ." the druid muttered. "They said she was asleep, like the others."

Tyrande wordlessly stalked into the chamber, seeking the wooden wardrobe at the far end. She flung open one of the two doors, the creaking sound echoing ominously.

The high priestess prayed. The light of Elune came down and spread over the interior . . . but then focused most on one empty corner. Tyrande reached to that area.

She clutched something unseen. As the high priestess raised it up, the light restored the object to visibility.

It was the hearthstone.

"It looks old," Broll commented.

"Brought by a survivor from Zin-Azshari," Tyrande said with some distaste. "I would have had it destroyed merely because of its original ties to that accursed place, but creating a new hearthstone is even more monumental than changing an old one's spell patterns . . ."

Long, oval and crystalline, it was covered with soft blue runes that glowed. Those runes were particular to the location to which it was tied and the one to whom the hearthstone had been given. With it, they could travel instantaneously from any distance to the hearthstone's origin point . . . in this case, Darnassus.

"Why did the ambassador have this?" the druid asked.

"To escape from here, if necessary."

"Hmmph. Worked well for her, didn't it?"

The high priestess said nothing, instead intent on the artifact. Originally, it had been crafted by arcane means, but the Mother Moon had provided her with the power to alter it once already. She clutched the stone in both hands and began a prayer, hoping that the deity would grant her the ability to do it a second time.

"There's something wrong here," Broll whispered, looking around. "Something very wrong—"

Tyrande paid no attention. "The hearthstone is resisting. The ambassador is still alive, wherever she is . . ."

From the wardrobe there came a terrible howl.

Tyrande turned, but not in time to keep from being seized by a gaunt form that had somehow been hidden where even the light of Elune could not penetrate. It brought the high priestess to the floor. The hearthstone went rolling free.

The maniacal creature lunged toward Broll. She was clad in the ruins of the robes of a high-ranking night elf, but it was a pendant tangled in her robes that definitively marked her as the missing ambassador.

"You'll not take my children, demons!" she screamed. "You'll not take them!"

Her eyes seized Broll's attention, for they could *not* be seen. The ambassador's lids were squeezed tightly shut.

"She's dreaming!" he warned.

And as the druid shouted, from without came a warning call from the major. There also came other screams that to the night elves were far too reminiscent of their attacker.

Tyrande prayed. Silver light from above bathed the other frenzied female before her. The ambassador seemed to calm—

But then a shadow passed over her face. Her mouth twisted and she began to scream anew.

On each side of her peeled away shadow creatures such as had attacked the high priestess in her tent. They lunged at Tyrande and would have seized her if not for the moonlight still near her. The light shifted as if of its own accord, coming between Elune's servant and her new attackers. The two shadows recoiled.

Struggling away from the ambassador, Tyrande called, "Broll! The hearthstone! Take it up!"

He did as bade, but when he prepared to toss it to her, she shook her head. "You can use it now! It should be able to send you to Darnassus!"

"You want me to abandon you?"

"No! I want you to help us all by finding Malfurion! Go! I command it!"

She had never commanded the druid and he knew that she did not like ruling in such an imperious manner. Broll understood the necessity of what she wanted, though it pained him to leave her and the others in such straits.

"I'll find him! We'll stop this!"

He held the hearthstone and concentrated. The stone began to glow.

The shadow creatures focused on him. The line between nightmare and reality was slipping more and more and the druid had no doubt that these fiends were now capable of true and deadly violence. Broll knew that he had to keep his focus on the hearthstone and the location to which it was tied.

Silver light swallowed up the nearest of his attackers. The shadow let out a pained hiss and twisted into itself before fading.

The second turned to Tyrande, who struggled with the unfortunate ambassador. Broll almost pursued the creature, but Tyrande glared at the druid.

The hearthstone flared.

Broll vanished from the room—

—And materialized in Darnassus.

A Darnassus in the midst of a horror all its own. Broll was tossed up and down. He lost his grip on the hearthstone, which tumbled out of sight.

At first the druid thought that Darnassus was suffering an earthquake, but that was very unlikely here atop Teldrassil. Then his heightened senses revealed the terrible truth; it was Teldrassil itself that attacked the night elves. Branches assailed every structure. The huge ones upon which the city had been built were shaking, the cause of the quake. Everywhere, black, thorned leaves stormed down on the citizenry, piercing their flesh or leaving long, vicious cuts. Several bodies lay sprawled over the once beautiful terrain.

Yet the inhabitants of the capital were not without their defenders. The Sisters of Elune stood at the forefront, protecting as best they could those around them. Their light hindered, if not held back, the evil.

But the very grass at their feet was as devious a foe as the dark leaves or the shadow creatures that formed from those leaves. Anything that was a part of Teldrassil had now turned on Broll's people.

And only now could Broll sense just how horribly tainted the World

Tree was. Yet just as disconcerting was a powerful force that not only fed Teldrassil, but fueled that taint.

Druids were aiding the terror. Their spells were adding to the World Tree in a manner that he could not believe they understood.

Broll rushed in the direction of the portal that would take him down to where he could feel the druids at work. They had to be warned and warned quickly.

But as he ran, the leaves took special interest in him. Broll spread a glowing light purple fire before him that burned the leaves before they could touch. The way momentarily cleared, he shifted to cat form for better swiftness.

The portal came into sight. Broll did not hesitate to leap through. Once he reached the others, they could help put an end to this awful attack.

The world swirled about him. It was a different sensation than that he had experienced using the hearthstone. The druid felt as if he were thrust forward.

Indeed, barely a breath later, Broll leapt out of the portal at the base of Teldrassil. The great cat surveyed the vicinity and was not surprised to find no one there. The druids were still gathered further on.

With four strong limbs, Broll tore along the edge of Teldrassil, seeking the convocation. *How could they be so unwary?* he wondered. *At the very least, Fandral and the other archdruids should sense what's happening—*

Fandral.

Foreboding filled Broll. He recalled how close Fandral was to Teldrassil. The World Tree was like the lead archdruid's own child. Fandral truly should have sensed what was happening.

Unless—

A rain of thorns struck the great cat. Broll roared in pain, lost his footing, and tumbled forward. He felt dizziness, an unsettling dizziness that could not be normal.

The thorns were drugged. His experienced mind quickly calculated which herbs with which they had been tipped. To his relief, none were poisonous. They were designed to incapacitate.

Broll could feel his muscles growing slack. He was semiconscious, but unable to move. Broll felt himself slipping back into his true form, but that brought him no relief.

A hand roughly gripped his arm. Broll was unceremoniously rolled onto his back. Through blurred eyes, he made out at least four druids leaning over him, but not the details of their faces.

"Someone should tell Fandral," one of them said. "Someone should tell him we've got the traitor . . ."

22

THE TAINTED

The victims of Stormwind City were coming for them. Lucan, Thura, and the major were surrounded by the bedraggled, slumbering figures. Each was screaming about some dire event that they somehow blamed on the three. Worse, they all moved unerringly toward the defenders with their eyes tightly shut.

"What do we do?" Lucan asked.

"We fight them!" growled the orc, the ax ready. "We fight them or they tear us apart, fool!"

"They are innocents!" Major Mattingly countered reprovingly. "Would you do this if they were your own people?"

"Yes . . . because it must be done."

The look on the officer's face when she said that was proof enough that Mattingly understood her logic. Yet he still shook his head at the thought.

"Foxblood! Take her and see what has happened to the night elves!" Mattingly finally ordered.

"But that'll leave you alone here . . ."

The two humans eyed one another for a moment. Lucan finally understood. Mattingly was trying to spare the innocents from Thura, who would surely take a terrible toll on them even if she was eventually overwhelmed. The major was also obviously hoping for some miracle to come from Tyrande's and Broll's efforts.

"Come!" the cartographer ordered the orc. As surprised as she was at his commanding tone, Thura reluctantly followed, while the major swept his sword across the shrinking gap between him and the sleep-walking locals.

But no sooner had they entered when a stout figure wielding a work ax charged Lucan.

" 'Tis my farm!" the man shouted. "I won't let ya burn it!"

The ax would have buried deep into Lucan's chest if not for Thura. She blocked the strike with the shaft of her weapon. The sleepwalker turned to face her, his shut eyes disconcerting. The rage in his face was overwhelming.

He swung at the orc. She parried the attack, then struck.

"No!" But Lucan could not stop her.

Her enchanted ax cut a red line across the possessed man's chest. He dropped his own weapon, then fell to the floor.

The cartographer was furious. "He couldn't help himself!"

Thura did not look happy with her own actions, but she asked, "What would you have done?"

Lucan had no answer. From above there came the sounds of strug-gle and more screaming. The pair ran upstairs.

They were met at the top by Tyrande, who struggled with a wild fig-ure who could only have been the night elf ambassador. Lucan raced to help the high priestess, only to be confronted by a shadow creature.

"Go to her!" roared Thura. The orc thrust past Lucan. Although her ax did not reach the shadow, it recoiled at the nearness.

The way cleared, the cartographer joined Tyrande. He seized one of the screaming figure's arms, enabling Tyrande to focus better.

The high priestess touched the sleepwalker's chest. A faint silver glow covered the flesh.

The sleepwalker let out a gasp and crumpled into their arms. Lucan and Tyrande gently laid her down.

As they did, the orc thrust. The ax cut through the shadow, which hissed . . . then faded.

But though there was a moment of calm where the trio stood, the same could not be said for without. The screams grew louder, more terrifying. One briefly rose above the rest before abruptly cutting off.

"That was the major!" Lucan gasped. He tried to go to a window, but Tyrande pulled him back.

"It is too late for him." The high priestess looked into Lucan's eyes. "Too late for so many. But there is still hope for Azeroth and hope for us . . . if you take us from here."

He nodded. "I can't promise that we might not end up by that green dragon again . . ."

"Eranikus is the least of our problems . . . indeed, Eranikus is his own worst problem."

Lucan concentrated. Tyrande extended a hand to Thura, who took it.

The world took on an emerald hue.

And then a darker one. Mad shrieks assailed their ears and the landscape was covered in the familiar, cloying mist in which half-seen, grotesque shapes moved about. Vertigo shook each of them, heightening a growing sense of anxiety and disorientation that they knew was far from natural.

They were back in the Nightmare.

"No . . ." Lucan muttered. "Let me—"

The shadow of a massive, skeletal tree stretched over them, its silhouette obvious even despite the darkness.

Welcome . . . came a dread voice in their heads. *And, especially, welcome to you, Tyrande Whisperwind* . . .

The high priestess turned as pale as death. Even the orc shivered at the dire tone in the night elf's denial.

"No . . ." Tyrande shook her head. "No . . ."

Yes . . . oh yes . . . the voice answered.

"Think, Fandral, think!" Malfurion called. "Is this truly all as you want it to be? Did you create Teldrassil to destroy your people?"

"I am not destroying us; I am saving us from you and others who betray our world!" As he spoke, Fandral leaned his head toward the shadow he believed his son. The crazed archdruid nodded, then added to Malfurion, "You spoke against Teldrassil's birth! You knew that it would restore our people to their glory and return to them the immortality that was stripped away!"

Malfurion dodged as a flower bloomed in front of him. It was a black lily and from it shot forth a white pollen. He had no idea what that pollen would do, but any plant tainted by the Nightmare was surely a threat.

The pollen landed short. The area upon which Malfurion had stood burned and withered.

There was a sharp pain on his left hand. A single grain had landed near the thumb. That one grain was enough to make Malfurion grit his teeth. Had a thousand touched him . . .

A pressure built in his chest. Malfurion fell to his knees. The pressure increased. It became impossible to breathe.

The archdruid quickly searched his body, seeking what assailed him. It proved all too easy.

The pollen had been a ploy, albeit a dangerous one. Too late Malfurion realized that Fandral had utilized a more subtle druidic attack. While Malfurion had been evading the lily, he had also been inhaling the altered plant's tiny spores. They now filled his lungs.

But as he had done with the morrowgrain poison, Malfurion forced the spores from his body. It was not as simple and gradual a feat as he had utilized in his barrow den; after all, time was not on his side. Malfurion ejected the spores with one fierce exhalation, sending them toward their caster.

The effort caused a brief sense of lightheadedness during which Fandral might have been able to attack him if not for the fact that the other night elf had to deflect the all but invisible spores. Fandral gestured and the wind scattered the counterattack before it could reach him.

Yet though Malfurion had saved himself, he knew that every second that he was forced to combat Fandral only worked in the Nightmare's favor. Fandral was lost; his madness consumed him.

Unless . . .

Palms turned skyward, Malfurion concentrated.

A calm settled over the enclave. The trees stilled and the other plants grew calm. Malfurion smiled grimly. The taint might infest Teldrassil, but not all of Teldrassil had been consumed by it. He had called out to that which was still whole to listen to him, to remember what it was.

But a mere breath later, the terror returned. Fandral stood with arms outstretched and the shadow at his side.

"I will not permit you to take my son from me again!" he cried.

Malfurion no longer listened to Fandral's incoherent words. He focused again on drawing that which was still good in Teldrassil. It was not as great as what was tainted, but with his guidance it held, at least for the moment.

And that was all Malfurion could ask.

But it was no longer merely the enclave that he affected. Malfurion strained as he spread his spell to encompass all of Darnassus. There were still screams and shouts of struggle, but they were less and he sensed that it was because his plan was working.

His body, his very soul, ached. Malfurion was fighting not one foe, but two. Somewhere deep in the World Tree was a touch of the Nightmare Lord, a physical presence. He wanted to seek it out, the better to combat it, but that would leave him defenseless against Fandral.

The strain grew. Malfurion felt his power waning. It was not that Fandral was stronger; it was that Malfurion was at the same time seeking to protect the citizenry as well.

It must happen soon! They must understand! he thought.

Then he felt the presence of others in the enclave, and both his hopes and his concerns rose. How they reacted meant the difference between victory and defeat.

Fandral lessened his attack, maintaining it only enough to keep Malfurion on edge. Malfurion had assumed that. He, in turn, dropped his hands and cut off his spellwork.

For a moment he was buffeted, but then Fandral followed suit. Now was not the time for either to look the aggressor. They were about to be judged.

The other archdruids and druids gathered around them, most with wary or uncertain looks. Malfurion met the gaze of each, letting them see into his soul. He had nothing to hide, whereas Fandral did.

And one thing that Fandral hid was the shadow creature he

believed was Valstann come back to him. The other archdruid stood before his brethren bearing a pious smile, as if he had been the one to summon the rest here. However, that responsibility lay with two unlikely figures—perhaps *three*, Malfurion saw—who now stepped into the center of the fray.

Fandral could not help but glance behind him. Hamuul Runetotem and Shandris Feathermoon were no longer his prisoners.

Malfurion's attack had involved many subtle aspects. In addition to fighting the other archdruid's efforts, Malfurion had used the distraction of the struggle to also manipulate the sinister vines holding the trio.

Malfurion tried to revive Naralex, but the other male night elf remained unconscious. He had better success with Hamuul and Shandris. Placing Naralex in Hamuul's care, he then sent them off to the portal, all the while hoping that Fandral's madness would keep the other night elf from noticing what was happening.

Malfurion had succeeded, but it was still a question as to whether the pair had come with aid for him—or more support for Fandral. The third member of the party gave indication of the latter, for he all but growled at several druids. How Broll Bearmantle had come to be here, Malfurion desperately wanted to know, but the answer to that had to wait.

"Very good!" Fandral proclaimed to the newcomers. "The traitors are rounded up! Excellent work!"

"They claim that you are the traitor, Master Fandral," one druid cautiously responded.

Broll stepped toward the speaker. "And he is, though even I was slow in understanding that he was forcing you to feed that which taints Teldrassil rather than curing the World Tree!" To Malfurion, he explained, "When I went to warn them, a group captured me! Fortunately, before they could do much else, Hamuul and Shandris came along and managed to talk *some* reason into them . . ."

"We did what we believed right!" the druid who had spoken countered. Some of the druids looked ready to fight with Broll. Hamuul Runetotem joined the night elf. Shandris started toward them, but then looked to Malfurion.

Nodding to her, he said to the gathered throng, "You know me. Most of you were trained by me. Look into yourselves and see if you still have faith in my word."

"The Nightmare has seduced him!" Fandral interjected. "You know how long he has been missing! Great though our shan'do once was, he is now an emissary of the darkness! Heed not his words!"

"And why should they heed yours, Fandral?" Broll countered. "You promised Teldrassil would restore our people, but now all they have to do is truly seek with their senses to see what it's become!"

Malfurion looked on with approval at Broll. "Always you underestimate yourself. You know what lurks within the World Tree, don't you, Broll?" He turned to the tauren. "And you, also, Hamuul . . ."

"I sensed it, but could not believe, Malfurion Stormrage. I came here with Naralex, who felt the same, and we found the general also in search of the truth—"

"Naralex?" Malfurion looked around, but there was no sign of the night elf.

"He is still unconscious," the tauren clarified dourly. "He was the most injured of us. I have done what I can for him . . . but there needs to be more—"

Many among those assembled stirred, clearly upset by these revelations. Naralex was a powerful druid well-liked by many. They looked upon Fandral with new understanding . . . and dismay.

Fandral defiantly stared down those in the crowd who were now clearly against him. "Naralex is another traitor! He gave me no choice! They are all traitors!"

His arrogant words only further inflamed his audience against him. Several of the remaining druids joined Broll and the others who had already taken Malfurion's side. Malfurion pushed to the forefront, determined that he would take responsibility for any and all of Fandral's actions.

"How many more must suffer or die?" Malfurion asked. "All Azeroth is falling, Fandral!" To the assembled druids, he explained, "While he kept you here, claiming to heal the World Tree, the rest of the world was attacked. See into yourselves and feel Azeroth's pain . . ."

They did as he bade. Almost immediately, several druids gasped in horror.

"The Moonglade!" blurted one. "Even the Moonglade! But where's Keeper Remulos? He'd surely not abandon it?"

It was an excellent question whose answer worried Malfurion. He knew that the other archdruid was not by himself either powerful or cunning enough to have taken down the keeper. However, the malevolent force behind the insane night elf certainly might have been. "Well, Fandral? Where is Remulos?"

"He is a traitor, also! He will be held until he sees the truth!" The mad archdruid gestured at everyone before him. "You will all be made to see the truth!"

Dropping all pretense, Fandral gestured. Many of the druids suddenly clutched their chests.

From out of one burst a long vine that swayed back and forth like a serpent. Despite his terrible wound, the druid grabbed it—only to reveal to the rest that other wicked vines were sprouting from various places on his hands, his arms, *everywhere*.

"I have prepared for treachery from any of you," Fandral explained, his eyes unblinking. "One way or another . . . you will all serve Teldrassil and its purpose!"

The first victim was joined by more and more. Malfurion reacted immediately, seeking to stem the growth of Fandral's malevolent seeds. He could only imagine that they had been inhaled just like the spores that had but recently attacked him. Fandral was willing to kill every other druid for his desires.

But not all were affected. In fact, there were those who moved to join Fandral, druids who had become his followers. That his calling had itself become so tainted sorrowed Malfurion, but he had no time to wonder why any would choose such a path. What mattered was saving the afflicted.

However, neither Fandral nor the Nightmare Lord intended to give him that time. The taint in Teldrassil surged again. Darnassus was once more put under siege as more shadow creatures sprouted from the World Tree's blackened leaves.

Malfurion needed to deal with Fandral and his master, but to do so meant to sacrifice his brethren. The first druid was already lost, what remained of his body devoured by the parasitic vines' explosive growth.

There was one hope, one other with the strength . . . if he believed. "Broll! Look into me! See what must be done!"

"These mean nothing!" Broll bitterly shouted back, indicating his great antlers. "I'm not like you, Shan'do!"

"You are!" Malfurion insisted, the strain in his voice growing. "Feel your tie to Azeroth! You can stop this! Or will you just let them all die horribly?"

It was a cold question and Malfurion despised himself for having to ask it, but he could no longer hold off. The rest of the night elf race—the rest of Azeroth—had little more time left than the druids did.

Malfurion focused on Fandral. As he stared at his rival, he saw the shadow creature behind and yet also a part of the mad archdruid. It was guiding Fandral's thoughts for its true master.

Malfurion understood what he had to do, though it risked much.

He threw himself at Fandral, transforming to cat semblance as he did. Fandral reacted as expected, drawing a handful of tiny thorns from a pouch and flinging them toward the giant feline.

Malfurion changed back, casting another spell as he did. For most druids, even those of Malfurion's skill, the odds of success would have been minimal. However, Malfurion had been the first trained by the demigod Cenarius. He had also learned his craft with the first invasion of the Burning Legion, and honed those skills well over the past ten thousand years.

The hurricane wind caught up the thorns and threw them back at Fandral, who cast a spell of his own. The vines that had held Hamuul and Shandris spat hundreds of drops of sticky sap at the thorns, sealing the deadly missiles inside and causing them to all land short of Malfurion's nemesis.

"Hardly worthy of—" Fandral started.

Fire that glowed like the stars—Malfurion's true attack—struck the shadow creature behind Fandral.

The murky figure twisted into itself as the fire engulfed it. It hissed and howled. Bits of burning shadow fluttered off in the wind.

"Valstann!" Fandral desperately clutched at the shadow. He tried in vain to douse the fire, but only succeeded in becoming caught up in it. Even then, the archdruid paid the agony no mind as he grabbed at the fiend he believed his lost child.

A hand spun Fandral around. Before he could react, Malfurion struck him in the jaw. It was the least of attacks that he could have used against the other archdruid and Malfurion's choice for many reasons.

Fandral tumbled back.

There was little left of the shadow creature. Like Fandral before him, Malfurion reached for what remained. The fire even burned him, but he knew how to lessen the sense of pain from it. It was vital that he make contact with the shadow.

Only fragments remained. Malfurion had tried to temper his attack in order to give him this necessary moment, but still he was nearly too late.

One hand thrust into the shadow. Instantly, a horrific chill enveloped his soul. Malfurion steeled himself and drove his mind into the shadow.

And what he sensed verified the dread that had been building up in him since first he was captured by the Nightmare Lord.

The last of the shadow burned away and with it went the fire. Malfurion took a breath as he regained his equilibrium. He turned to Fandral, but the other night elf lay sprawled where he had left him, Fandral's eyes open but not seeing. The second loss of his "son" had been too much.

Malfurion turned to Broll—and his eyes widened.

Broll Bearmantle stood among the suffering druids, his hands raised above his head and the energies of Azeroth swirling around him. His formerly silver eyes now blazed nearly as gold as Malfurion's. From his hands, tendrils of energy stretched out to each of the other druids.

Two riddled bodies lay on the ground—the first of Fandral's victims—but for the other druids, there appeared hope. Hamuul

Runetotem stood with Broll, giving what aid he could, but the effort was truly the night elf's.

You are as you were destined to be, Malfurion thought with relief and pride.

Belatedly, he realized that there was no sign of Shandris. Knowing her as he did, Malfurion felt certain that she had gone to direct Darnassus's defenders.

Malfurion transformed. Once again the great cat, he raced from the enclave and into central Darnassus. Around him, he registered the struggle still going on. Even without Fandral, Darnassus was in terrible danger, but Malfurion could only help them by continuing on.

Out into the forest beyond the capital he ran. Immediately, the branches and leaves of the nearby trees sought to bar his path. Malfurion lithely dodged them when he could, tore through them with his claws and teeth when he could not. His thick fur kept his body from much harm, but still more than a score of bloody slashes marked him before he reached the deep interior of Teldrassil's crown.

A savage, towering figure emerged from the tree, so much a part of it that even the archdruid barely noticed it in time. The ancient moved to take into account evasion by Malfurion, so Malfurion instead lunged directly toward it.

The corrupted forest guardian tried to recover, but Malfurion dove under the creature's legs. More swift and agile, the cat eluded the gigantic ancient.

The World Tree's crown both thickened and darkened. Thorns grew everywhere. No true cat the size of Malfurion could have wended its way as he did; the night elf made use of reflexes honed over century upon century.

But just as he neared where he sensed his goal lay, a small, furred form leapt upon his muzzle and scratched at his eyes. It was only a squirrel, one of the many denizens of the tree, but even it had been corrupted by the taint.

The squirrel was a foe easily discarded by a shake of the head, but that was not the true danger. Malfurion tried to compensate for whatever was to follow. When a smaller branch snagged one paw and nearly made him tumble, the archdruid immediately reverted to his normal form and caught himself before he could be snared by waiting branches from other surrounding trees.

Shadow creatures whose outlines he recognized dropped from the branches above. The fiends piled upon the spot where Malfurion had stood. They tore at both Malfurion's body and soul—

A savage roar from within sent the shadows sprawling back. Huge, glowing claws swiped at the creatures, reducing several to shreds. Once more in his feline form, Malfurion utilized its inherent abilities to decimate his murky attackers.

They fell to his claws as grass fell to a reaper. Within seconds, there remained only Malfurion the cat, a victor who unleashed one last powerful roar, then lunged the last few yards toward that which he sought.

It thrust up from the World Tree's trunk, and though on the one hand it was shaped like one of many massive tree branches spread throughout Teldrassil, its color marked it starkly. It was a color that Malfurion associated with something other than a tree, tainted or not. Indeed, as he shifted back to night elf, he had only to gaze at his hand to see skin of a like hue.

Even without touching it, the archdruid could sense how expertly it had been grafted into what had at the time surely been a much less mature Teldrassil. Malfurion could tell Fandral's work and knew that the other archdruid must have returned several times to assist his addition in its foul growth. It now stretched more than eight feet in height, its sub-branches all at least three to four feet themselves and covered with scores of the dark, thorned leaves. There was also pale fruit vaguely shaped like skulls.

Malfurion approached the grafting. The fruits glistened and one of them fell near the night elf. It cracked open upon impact with the branch upon which the archdruid stood. A thick, ivory substance poured from it, the stench accompanying the substance like that from a field of rotting corpses.

Malfurion edged away from it, though that also put him a step farther from the grafting. He knew that was what the Nightmare Lord had in mind, but could do nothing else.

Another fruit dropped. As it cracked open, the ivory substance became hundreds of bone-colored millipedes with heads resembling fleshless night elf skulls.

Malfurion Stormrage . . . they called as they converged on him. *Malfurion Stormrage . . . time you came to join us . . .*

He recognized those voices. Each was different, yet he knew every single last one of them. There was Lord Ravencrest, who had commanded the night elf forces until assassinated by an agent of Queen Azshara's Highborne; the high priestess Dejahna—Tyrande's predecessor; the evil Captain Varo'then—Azshara's devoted servant—and so many, many others who had haunted both his and surely Tyrande's thoughts over the millennia.

Malfurion . . . we have waited so long . . . come join us in our long rest . . .

He wavered, standing without doing anything as the monstrous millipedes reached his feet. The first crawled atop his foot, its skeletal jaws opening wide—

The archdruid reached down and seized it. He squeezed tight.

The millipede wailed like a dying night elf. Its ghastly outer shell peeled away to reveal a beautiful rose sprouting upward.

The others in the swarm also began to wail. Each suffered as the one in Malfurion's hand did.

"Let this be their legacy," he intoned to the grafting as roses sprouted everywhere. "Let this honor those who stood in defense of Azeroth . . . not traded their world for ultimate power . . ."

Teldrassil's crown shook as if a massive wind blew through it. The shaking leaves of the hundreds of smaller trees atop it created what to Malfurion's ears was an angry, bitter roar.

He used that moment of the Nightmare Lord's anger to shift form again, but this time into a huge bear, a dire bear. With its tremendous strength, Malfurion seized the grafting and *tore* it from Teldrassil. He dug into the very trunk, ripping even the "roots" out.

The World Tree trembled. Huge trees astride it broke free.

Malfurion the bear pressed against the trunk as the upheaval grew. He could only hope that those in Darnassus were protecting themselves.

The shaking subsided. The druid immediately sought out with his mind the extent of the damage and was shocked. Despite the brevity of the tremor, the intensity had been enough to leave the forests of Teldrassil in ruins. Entire mighty oaks had snapped in two. Much of the crown was a tangle of dangerous refuse.

Darnassus must be abandoned, the archdruid determined. Until the extent of the damage to the World Tree itself was known, everyone was at risk.

Even as Malfurion thought that, a great mass of ruined trees suddenly proved too much for those supporting their weight. With a sound like reverberating thunder, the holding branches cracked and tons of wood and dirt dropped with a resounding crash. There, their momentum wreaked havoc on other gigantic trees and the stunning sight repeated.

Then, even despite the World Tree's woes, the archdruid looked to the lone branch that he had ripped free. It had paled much and now something dripped from it. It was a thick substance with the consistency of tree sap, but was hardly the color. In fact, Malfurion's ursine senses picked up a scent to it, one that stirred an incredible fury within him.

It was the source of the taint that had spread through Teldrassil. Malfurion let out a bestial growl. He knew what it was . . . and thus, how it had come to be.

It was *blood.* Thick though it was, it was fresh and looked otherwise exactly like that which flowed through his or any other night elf's body.

Blood . . . from a tree.

The druid reverted to his true shape as the realization struck him. There was only one such tree. Millennia ago, Malfurion had caused that tree to come into being. He had done so to put an end to an evil and bring from it some good . . . but evidently had merely set into motion a more terrible darkness.

The branch was from the tree that cast the shadow of the Nightmare Lord.

A tree that had once been the dread counselor to foul Queen Azshara. The name was as poison on Malfurion's lips. *"Xavius . . ."*

23

TELDRASSIL REDEEMED

Xavius. How well Malfurion still recalled the queen's malicious confidante. It had been Lord Xavius who had fueled the spellwork by Azshara's Highborne sorcerers that had opened the path for the Burning Legion. Rather than be repelled by what he discovered, Xavius had ever been there to assist his insidious queen as she welcomed the demons through.

Twice, Malfurion had thought him no more. That first time had been during a desperate struggle atop the very tower where the portal for the demons had been opened. Malfurion, his druidic powers strong, had raised a storm that had first set Xavius aflame by lightning, then melted him by rain, and finally unleashed a roar of thunder that had literally *shattered* the villain. Malfurion could still recall Xavius's contorted face—especially the sinister, magically crafted eyes of black with the streak of ruby running across each. The archdruid especially remembered the counselor's last, nerve-wracking shriek.

And then, Xavius had ceased to exist.

But he and the defenders had all underestimated the power of the evil titan Sargeras. After snaring what little remained of Xavius's disembodied spirit and torturing it long for the counselor's failures, Sargeras had remolded it into something more terrible. Xavius had been reborn as a satyr—the first of the goatlike monsters now so long the enemies of the night elves—and his malevolence had only grown with his new, hideous aspect.

Malfurion had nearly lost Tyrande to Xavius and his fellow corrupted Highborne. In the end, unable to risk Xavius escaping death again, Malfurion had called upon Azeroth's power to transform the satyr. Despite Xavius's struggling, the young druid had turned his foe into a harmless tree.

Or so he had believed for the past ten millennia. The evil had been festering upon Azeroth all that time and Malfurion had never known.

All this Malfurion reflected upon with anger at himself as, once more in cat form, the branch clamped in his teeth, he rushed back to Darnassus. He blamed himself for what was happening now, yet he also pondered how Xavius had survived so long to become the Nightmare Lord.

But that thought was shoved aside as he entered the capital and transformed. Darnassus was in ruins and much of that was due to the collapse of other limbs from the vast tree. Victims of the Nightmare's servants also lay everywhere. The Sisters of Elune and the Sentinels were seeking to help those they could.

He spotted Shandris Feathermoon giving commands to both groups. The general looked weary, but in her element. Unfortunately, she did not realize the danger still surrounding their people.

"Shandris!" At his voice, she whirled.

"Malfurion . . ." the general said, saluting him respectfully and looking much relieved. "Praise be that you're all right." She noticed the unsettling branch that he now hefted in both hands and her brow furrowed. "By the Mother Moon! What foulness has afflicted that?"

"This is the taint that spread through Teldrassil," the archdruid hurriedly answered. "But we must not concern ourselves with that at the moment! Darnassus must be cleared! The World Tree has suffered greatly; the ruined trees you see around you are only a fraction! For everyone's safety, they must leave!"

As if to emphasize this, another thundering crack echoed through Darnassus. The city shook. Teldrassil would stand, but the same could not necessarily be said for the capital.

"I'll see that it's done!" Shandris promised.

"I will see to the druids," Malfurion told her as they separated. "We may be able to do something to stave it off . . . but I cannot promise it . . ."

"Understood!"

An agonized cry erupted from elsewhere, a voice full of loss. It did not come from any of the victims to which Malfurion looked, but rather from an unexpected direction.

He turned toward the enclave to find the other druids already streaming from there. Broll had the lead, with Hamuul close behind.

The source of the never-ending cry was Fandral. Eyes unseeing, the archdruid shouted his son's name over and over. He pleaded for Valstann to come back to him.

Two other druids guided him by hand as he stumbled along, calling to his son. Behind them, other druids guarded a small band . . . those who had chosen Fandral's madness over all else. It was already obvious to Malfurion what would have to be done with them. The Moonglade had places that could hold the sick or corrupted of mind. For those who had followed Fandral, there was hope that they could be redeemed.

But as he studied Valstann's father, Malfurion wondered if Fandral would ever be cured. Between the Nightmare and his personal loss, the mad archdruid looked as if he had lost himself forever.

Malfurion met with Broll, giving him the same warning that he had Shandris. Broll nodded his understanding, but his eyes kept shifting to the macabre branch. Malfurion finally informed him of what he had divined.

"Xavius . . ." Broll did not know the name, but had felt the immense anger and dread in his shan'do's voice when Malfurion had spoken it.

"The druids must help the people leave, then be prepared to hear from me. It will not be very long, so they must hurry!"

"What do you hope to do?"

Malfurion seized a smaller branch thrusting out near the top. He snapped it off. The same thick, foul liquid slowly dripped from it.

"What I must. What *we* must."

That said, Malfurion quickly called for a torch. Secreting the smaller branch upon his person, the archdruid set the larger branch afire. In just the blink of an eye, it burnt to ash, which he let the wind carry away.

"Be ready," he asked Broll.

"Of course, Shan'do! I—"

But Malfurion had already transformed and taken to the sky.

Tyrande knew who spoke even though she had been unconscious during their previous encounter. She knew because Malfurion had later told her the terrifying facts . . . and what he had done to her captor.

"You cannot be . . ." she protested.

The shadow of the giant, skeletal tree twisted around the trio. The high priestess felt her chest tighten, although when she brought her hand to it, there was nothing to pull away. Tyrande noted that Lucan and Thura acted the same.

I can and always will be . . . Tyrande Whisperwind . . . I am the Nightmare and the Nightmare is me . . . we are eternal . . . and soon Azeroth will be but a part of us . . .

"Never!" She prayed to Elune and the Mother Moon's light filled her. Tyrande immediately focused that light upon the shadow.

In the light, the tree all but faded. Tyrande felt the pressure on her chest ease.

Then the shadow darkened again, growing more distinct than before. The high priestess could not breathe. She struggled to remain on her feet. The others also suffered.

The light faded, leaving only the foul dark green illumination of the Nightmare . . . and the shadow of the tree that was the night elf Xavius.

I am beyond your petty deity now . . . the Mistress of Dreams is mine . . . as is her sister the Life-Binder . . . behold them both and tremble at your lost hopes . . .

The mists parted . . . and behind the shadow stood revealed the mistress of the Emerald Dream. She was snared tight in tendrils of shadow that also appeared to originate from their captor. Ysera's head was pointed skyward as if she looked for something, but her eyes were shut. Her wings and limbs were stretched apart in what was surely an agonizing manner.

An emerald aura emanated from Ysera, but barely inches from her, it altered into the foul, decaying green of the Nightmare. It was all too clear that the Aspect's power was being twisted to Xavius's desires.

And behind her, folded almost in two, hovered Alexstrasza. Her eyes stared unseeing and her jaw was slack. She looked withered, more dead than alive. Her vibrant red coloring had faded and she barely looked to be breathing.

The mists enshrouded the two huge dragons again. Tyrande was crushed by the sight. She remembered that Alexstrasza had been in some terrible danger when last they had seen her, but she had believed that somehow the Aspect would evade capture.

There was the flapping of wings. A massive green form materialized from the mist. At first Tyrande thought that Eranikus had flown to their rescue, but then the dragon that alighted between the Nightmare Lord and the trio revealed himself a dreadful creature whose very expression was enough to reveal the depths of his corruption.

Lethon bowed his head to the tree. *"I have come as you summoned . . ."*

Prepare them . . . it will come soon . . . and with its coming . . . the Nightmare's hold will be complete . . .

The green dragon grinned evilly at the three. *"Come, my little pets . . . Emeriss is waiting for us . . ."*

They were swept up in the dragon's magic.

Malfurion rose up into the sky, which was now as mist-enshrouded around the island as everywhere else. The Nightmare Lord no longer had reason to keep Darnassus ignorant of the extent of their danger now that Fandral was lost.

The archdruid banked. Teldrassil spread below him. He could not see its entire grand canopy, but he saw the central part, which was his focus.

By this time, the other druids needed to be ready. They *had* to be ready . . .

Hamuul . . . Broll . . . Though he named the two, Malfurion then touched each and every one of the druids on or around the World Tree. They quickly responded.

We are going to heal Teldrassil, he informed them.

Many were stunned, especially after Fandral's betrayal, but because it was Malfurion, they did not hesitate to follow his instructions.

Malfurion dove, then alighted on what he knew was the center point of the canopy. There, he transformed. The air was chill here, for he was even above the forests that grew at the top. Still, he was unconcerned, his plan all that mattered at the moment.

Stretching forth his hands as if to encompass the vast crown, the archdruid strengthened his bond with the others.

Let us guide that which is the life of Azeroth into eradicating the taint . . .

In his mind, he could see the other druids imitating his actions. Malfurion reached out now to Teldrassil. The World Tree was full of corruption, but it was not beyond saving. He sought out the core of its remaining health, a place buried not in its towering trunk, but far down in its roots.

Malfurion encouraged those roots to grow, to dig deeper. They sank far below, reaching the most primeval parts of Azeroth . . . and the most pure.

Feed and heal . . . he told the World Tree. *Feed and heal . . .*

The reaction was sluggish, as he expected. Malfurion continued to urge. Sick so long, Teldrassil needed to be prodded.

At last, he felt Teldrassil begin to stir. With the druids aiding it, the World Tree began to feed as it needed. Azeroth gave forth that sustenance, as it did in one form or another to all life upon it. Teldrassil grew stronger.

The effort was taxing on the druids, though. Malfurion sweated despite the cold air and he knew his followers were likewise suffering. Yet, no one gave hint of quitting, which filled him with pride for each of them.

What would have taken many years—what even they had believed was beyond the original World Tree, Nordrassil—now took place all over Teldrassil. It suddenly came in a wonderful rush of life . . .

From the crown came a cacophony of ear-splitting cracks. Malfurion feared at first that the druids' efforts had been too much for the stressed tree after all and that all the ruined branches were about to go tumbling. But no branches fell. In fact, those within sight, even the most damaged, began to *heal*. Breaks sealed seamlessly. What Malfurion had heard was the branches moving back *into* place.

And wherever the branches healed, new growth instantly followed. Buds sprouted everywhere, then, without hesitation, blossomed into beautiful draping leaves.

The healing was not merely on the surface, however. The archdruid felt a surge of energy throughout Teldrassil that originated from the roots and rose all the way to the top and into every branch. The World Tree in turn fed the many smaller trees and other plants growing atop it . . . until all were healed.

It all seemed finished, but the druids did not lessen their efforts, for Malfurion had not given them the word. Though he and the rest were already well exhausted, Malfurion searched the World Tree with his heightened senses.

He came across no lingering sign of the taint. With relief, he gave the other druids permission to end their spellwork.

Malfurion broke the link after telling the others to take a moment's respite. Despite what else was happening, the druids would be of no use if they did not recoup. Even he dared take a deep, cold breath of air before transforming to storm crow form and once more taking flight.

The swift and wonderful success of their task also gave him new strength. The archdruid rose high in order to better view what he could of the renewed canopy for a moment . . . then hesitated as a great reptilian shape emerged from the thickening mist. For a moment, he thought that perhaps Ysera had escaped and had come to him.

Yet though it was a dragon of immense proportions, he immediately registered that it was not green . . . but crimson.

There was only one red dragon so huge . . .

"Archdruid!" the leviathan, a female, roared. "I know you despite that form! You are Malfurion Stormrage!" The dragon cocked her head. "I had thought you lost!"

The archdruid dropped down to the World Tree's crown, alighting. Shifting back to night elf, Malfurion called, "Alexstrasza! Great Life-Binder! Sister of Ysera! Do you bring news of Ysera's escape?"

Her arresting visage twisted into one of sadness. "No, mortal, I do not! That she struggles even captive is all I have to keep heart! I come because I sensed some great flourishing of life in a time of peril! It was such that I could not help but come and see . . . and it seems that you are the source of it!" Alexstrasza peered at Teldrassil. "And what a feat, Malfurion Stormrage!"

"Teldrassil had to be healed, Life-Binder! Even though it was raised up against our wishes, it now stands as one of Azeroth's strongest remaining forces!"

"So it does . . . so it does . . ." the Aspect's expression was guarded. There were clearly many thoughts racing through her head. Finally, "Even though this was fashioned without the blessings of any Aspect, it was still a beautiful and proud sight, I will admit—"

At that moment, the archdruid suddenly felt light-headed. It was all he could do to keep from falling off.

The great dragon peered close at the tiny figure. "Malfurion Stormrage, while you have been seeking to help everyone else, have you taken no respite?"

"There—there is not time enough—"

The red dragon briefly looked from him to the canopy, and then back again. After a moment, she stated, "There must be time for this."

Alexstrasza reached out and took up the archdruid in one palm. She then rose higher and higher, so high that the entire crown was at last visible. Malfurion, still clutching the small branch, shook his head in disbelief at seeing such a height. He could not have flown so high himself.

"I have come to a decision," the Aspect declared in a booming voice. "Though I and the others did not bless this tree at the beginning, a blessing is needed now!"

She spread her wings wide and a glorious, warm glow radiated from her. The Life-Binder smiled down upon Teldrassil as she would have any of her children.

"Let this blessing touch Teldrassil and all upon it!" the red dragon commanded. "And let it create for us a new hope and a new beginning, also!"

The golden-red glow spread from Alexstrasza to the crown. With astounding speed, it continued down toward the trunk and then below beyond Malfurion's view.

And with that . . . it was done. Teldrassil was not only healed . . . it was now blessed, if only by the Life-Binder. Still, that single blessing meant very much.

Alexstrasza circled high above the World Tree. The transformation was complete. The glorious glow muted, but did not vanish from Teldrassil.

"It is done . . ." she declared, "and not a moment too soon!"

"Why? What is happening now?"

"You have not felt it? The Nightmare is sealing all paths into it! Now that it can reach out into Azeroth, it is preventing any from physically reaching it! You as a druid should be able to sense it! The portals are being shut one after another!"

"The portals—" Malfurion shut his eyes for a moment and sensed that it was true. That brought something else to mind. "What of the green dragons? Would not Ysera's dragonflight stop this from happening?"

"They still fight in the Nightmare, but their chances are waning, as are those of the few left fighting with them! They have no time or numbers to deal with this . . ."

The night elf gaped. "Darnassus!"

The Aspect eyed him. "Darnassus?"

"The portal there! It was open when I left! It may—"

Without another word, the Life-Binder veered toward the capital. Her speed was such that in moments the city came into sight. Alexstrasza tilted to her left, then headed toward what was left of the Temple Gardens.

She landed, then released the archdruid. Quickly looking around, Malfurion discovered Broll, Hamuul, and some of the other druids rushing toward him. In addition to them, a handful of Sentinels, including Shandris, also remained. Stunned stares took in the sight of the dragon.

"Shan'do!" Broll called as he ran. "Teldrassil is—is whole!"

"Would that the same could be said for Darnassus," Shandris muttered as she joined those gathering around Malfurion. "Or the rest of Azeroth."

The archdruid waved off further comment. "The portal? Is everyone through? Is it still function—"

As he spoke, Malfurion once again felt light-headed. The rush of adrenaline was fading. Broll and Hamuul had to grab hold of him.

But as Malfurion fought to recover, he suddenly felt a comforting presence nearby, one that he had never known before. It had a similarity to something that the archdruid had thought lost forever . . . and that was what allowed him to identify it.

Teldrassil was reaching out to him. As it had been healed, so did it offer healing to Malfurion. Gone was not only the taint, but also *Fandral's* touch. The World Tree was nearly as it would have been had it been Malfurion who had guided its creation.

"You know, then?" He heard Shandris growl. "It sealed just as the tree healed! We thought it at first something you'd done, but—"

"The Nightmare is sealing off all physical routes to the Dream," the red dragon informed them. "So, it is too late here, as well."

Malfurion said nothing as his head cleared somewhat. In touching him, Teldrassil had also revealed to the archdruid something of great interest.

Malfurion straightened. "The enclave . . . we must go there."

Without waiting, the Aspect seized up not only him, but, as they stood with him, Broll and Hamuul, too. It was a simple thing for her to carry them the short distance to the enclave and then land again.

Fandral's sanctum lay in ruins, the vines that had guarded his abode dead. There had been nothing to salvage in them; they had been the result of the mad archdruid's work combined with the evil of the Nightmare.

"Is this where Fandral has always made his home?"

"Nay," replied Broll. "He originally chose the top chamber in the largest tree. That tree there." The other night elf pointed to an area not far away to the right. "But a short time back, he suddenly had this created."

Malfurion nodded. "That verifies what I thought. I need but a moment." He handed the small branch to Broll. "Watch this for me, but be wary of it."

"I understand, Shan'do," Broll murmured.

Malfurion stood with arms raised in the middle of the enclave. Time was of the essence, and he prayed that what he attempted would not take long. He also prayed that he was not wrong in his assumption.

Though he stood, the night elf set himself into the beginnings of a meditative trance. Long experience enabled him to swiftly reach the state he desired, a place between the physical and dream worlds. It risked leaving him vulnerable to the Nightmare and Xavius, but it also opened him up to what Teldrassil offered.

He reached out with his mind and soul to the World Tree . . . and the tree welcomed him. Feeling its gentle touch both thrilled and saddened the archdruid. He prayed for Teldrassil's recovery, for all of Azeroth's recovery, should the world survive this assault.

Teldrassil prayed with him.

The night elf opened up his defenses to the tree. If there still remained any hidden hint of Xavius's evil, Malfurion also opened himself up to his foe.

But all he felt was Teldrassil's wondrous warmth. All the suffering, all the lack of food and rest, began to diminish. Malfurion smiled.

A primitive part of Malfurion wanted to escape into Teldrassil, become part of it and abandon his mortal existence. That was always a risk for druids, becoming so caught up in the glory of the natural world that their own existence paled.

But then the face that always pulled Malfurion's heart and soul even more than this desire brought him back to harsh reality.

"Tyrande . . ." he whispered to himself.

Teldrassil seemed to echo his sentiment, for its leaves shook even though there was no wind and Malfurion swore that the sound they made was akin to the high priestess's name.

Malfurion did not know how he could succeed in saving Tyrande. He could only fathom one possible course.

The Life-Binder was the only one remaining with him, Malfurion never daring to ask an Aspect to leave. Yet, Alexstrasza remained patiently silent, apparently deciding that the night elf was the one whose actions meant most at the moment.

He crouched, setting one hand on the ground before the sanctum. As he did, Malfurion spoke with Teldrassil, asking it to help him reveal the truth.

The power flowed from both the archdruid and the tree. The damaged structure trembled. The once-deadly vines became ash and the artifices set in place by Fandral fell away. The sanctum reshaped, becoming something familiar yet astounding.

"Impossible!" Broll muttered.

Rising, Malfurion stepped toward his discovery. He had sensed its presence. He had known it would be here, despite the fact that it should not.

Fandral had in secret created his own portal to the Emerald Dream.

It was simple, its round form shaped by winding branches and stonework. Powerful spells had masked it from the others.

"It is still open . . ." Alexstrasza said.

Malfurion nodded, then reached out with his thoughts to the other druids. *My friends . . . come to the enclave . . .*

The other druids came but moments later. All gaped at what Fandral had wrought, but Malfurion could not give them time to digest its presence.

"It is all up to us," Malfurion said to the others. "We must make the final stand against the Nightmare. This is what our calling has prepared us for. A taint seeks Azeroth; as those who tend the forests, plains, and other lands that are its gardens, encourage the bounty of life that is its fruit . . . we must end this infestation . . ."

The gathered druids went down on one knee before him and even

when he gestured that they should rise, they remained in the respectful position.

"What would you have of us?" Broll, who seemed to be speaker for
the rest, solemnly inquired.

"What I should not ask. I need you—and, yes, all those we can still
summon to come together be they druids or not—to march upon the
Nightmare itself through this, possibly the last portal on Azeroth . . ."

24

GATHERING THE HOST

Tyrande, Lucan, and Thura found themselves deposited in a murky valley. Around them, they heard the incessant shrieks and cries as the Nightmare's victims both suffered and served at Xavius's will. The ground crawled with the dark vermin of the Nightmare.

"See what I've brought you . . ." Lethon said to the mist.

A huge portion of the mist melted into the putrefying figure of Emeriss. The other dragon grinned at the prisoners he displayed.

"So wholesome . . . so untouched . . ." she cooed. *"Won't it be fun twisting them?"*

"You know what the master desires."

Emeriss did not look pleased with being reprimanded. *"Of course I do!"*

Tyrande listened to all this with growing dismay. Yet her concern was more for the others and for Malfurion, wherever he now was. She was certain that he was doing what he could to battle the Nightmare, although with Alexstrasza now also a slave to Xavius, the chance of victory seemed nil.

Or *was* the Life-Binder truly a slave? Tyrande recalled the image and also recalled the deviousness of the Nightmare. The vision had been too fleeting. Why hide it from them? Why quickly obscure Alexstrasza from their sight?

Unless . . . the image of the imprisoned red dragon had been an illusion designed to drain her and the others of hope?

The high priestess clenched her fist. Not for the first time, she had fallen prey to the Nightmare.

"The ax first," Lethon ordered.

The corrupted dragon's words caught Tyrande's attention and she found herself wondering why the weapon had remained in the orc's hands this long. More important, surely Xavius should have taken it from Thura as soon as the group stood before his shadow. After all, being what he now was, the Nightmare Lord would surely not want any of his foes to wield it near him.

Again, Tyrande thought of the vision of Alexstrasza. Everything was designed to create despair in the defenders . . . perhaps in great part because of this very weapon.

Emeriss stared at the orc. Thura tightly gripped the ax, clearly unwilling to part with it. She brandished the blade at the dragon, who, it was interesting for Tyrande to note, made certain not to come within striking distance.

It has to be! the high priestess decided.

"That little plaything will not help you!" Emeriss hissed. The dragon continued to eye Thura, whose hands began to shake.

"The ax is mine!" the warrior growled.

"No longer . . ." Lethon interjected, joining Emeriss in staring at Thura.

The orc's eyes shut. Trembling, she dropped to one knee. Her hands shook violently, but still she did not release the ax.

The high priestess knew what they were doing to Thura. They were assailing her with the dream-based abilities of their kind. Thura was suffering personal nightmares over and over, all in an attempt to get her to release the weapon.

The weapon . . .

"Lucan . . . the ax . . ." Tyrande quietly urged.

He glanced at her, saw the direction of her gaze and, despite a hint of uncertainty, moved.

Tyrande reached into her heart and prayed to Elune, touching upon what had made her first desire to become one of the Mother Moon's aco-lytes. She remembered the softness, the beauty of the moon's light upon her and how she knew that with it she might be able to help others.

The silver glow materialized above her.

"Little fool!" Emeriss hissed at her. Lethon snarled and also turned to the night elf.

Lucan grabbed Thura. The orc understood immediately what the human intended.

Man and orc faded away as Lucan pulled them both from the Night-mare to Azeroth. Yet, just before they did, the shadow of a branch passed over them. None, not even the high priestess, noticed it.

Tyrande still remained. She had never had any notion of escap-ing with the others. She had needed to remain the distraction for the other two. The dragons had been too confident in their power and too focused in their desire to strip Thura of the ax. Those had both been in her favor in seeking freedom for the orc and Lucan.

But a terrible force struck her. Tyrande fell among the bugs, who quickly swarmed over her. She batted them away, only to then find Emeriss's pus-covered head looming before her.

"Thank you for doing your part..." the monstrous behemoth chuckled.

Lethon joined her in their sinister merriment. As Tyrande pushed herself up, she saw that while her companions had indeed made good their flight, something had been left behind.

"Your effort was invaluable!" Lethon mocked. *"The distraction broke the orc's concentration and loosened her grip just enough at the right mo-ment... when she and the human were between realms..."*

Half-covered in eager vermin, the ax that had once belonged to Brox lay a few yards ahead of Tyrande.

And over it hung the shadow of a skeletal branch.

No one protested Malfurion's decision. All trusted in him. What they did not entirely trust was that which lay before them, that which had been crafted at their ignorance.

The portal rose from what had been the back of Fandral's lair. It was not as huge nor as intricate as those others created to reach the Emerald Dream, but the fantastic energies swirling within marked it as functional . . . and thus a ray of hope as far as Malfurion was concerned.

"How could he have had this made without us knowing?" demanded one druid.

"There was much to distract all of you," Malfurion said with apology, thinking of all that his search in the Emerald Dream had caused. "But be thankful for one thing; the portal is still open . . ."

Broll eyed it warily. "But will it stay open for what you intend?"

"I—will see—to it, that it does."

Even Malfurion was astounded to hear the Life-Binder announce this. Even more surprising was how Alexstrasza now appeared. She strode among the druids in her elven form, small licks of flames darting from her long, crimson tresses. She walked as a queen and as a mother, giving looks of trust and faith to the druids as she passed among them. Though Ysera was their patron, Malfurion and the rest acknowledged without hesitation their respect for Alexstrasza.

"Great Life-Binder, this is not—" Malfurion began.

"Do not question." The fiery figure stepped toward the portal. "Even now, the Nightmare senses that the portal of its pawn is discovered."

Alexstrasza did not stop until she stood before the swirling energies. The Life-Binder stared into the portal.

The fiery glow about her body intensified. It shot forth into the portal. There was a flash of flame within and all there were aware that if something had stood on the other side, it would have been utterly incinerated.

"Nothing will come through and nothing will seal up this last portal from the other side," she declared in a tone that did not brook disagreement. "The portal *will* stay open, Malfurion Stormrage . . . I will see to it. It is that important."

The archdruid nodded grimly. "Then, there's no more reason to hesitate! Hamuul! Your help—and yours, also, Broll—I think I'll need! As for you others, you know what you must do . . ."

The druids began dividing up for their appointed tasks. Many gathered near the portal. Others took to swifter forms and quickly departed the enclave.

Malfurion sat down in the midst of the druids' grove, with Hamuul and Broll kneeling on each side of him. Malfurion shut his eyes, but before he began his meditation, he said to the pair, "I will need all your strength and your wariness. I apologize for the danger I may put you through."

The tauren snorted and Broll growled, "I fought as a gladiator for years, but rather would I fight at your side like this!"

Grateful for their loyalty and sacrifice, Malfurion withdrew into himself. He needed to reach out to some of those others who might stand with them—assuming any were left. It would demand another tremendous sacrifice from each and possibly only make the Nightmare's victory that much more complete.

But there were no choices left now.

It was not difficult for Malfurion to reach the state he needed, despite the stresses upon him. The archdruid felt the ties between his dreamform and his physical body all but unbind. There was little strain when he pushed free his mortal form and rose up above Broll and Hamuul.

Although they could not see him, by instinct the two gazed up. Malfurion reached out with his thoughts, informing them of what he intended and seeking what guidance that they could give him about certain aspects.

Then Malfurion tried something that he had never done before. It was his best hope of reaching all those still able to help Azeroth. The archdruid reached into Teldrassil and through Teldrassil into Azeroth, using the fact that, no matter where someone could be found, it would be a part of the world.

And Teldrassil and Azeroth gave him what he sought.

Malfurion let out a tremendous gasp as he suddenly saw *everywhere* in the world at the same time. It was almost too much. Had it been any other mortal than him, Malfurion understood that they would have gone insane as their mind fragmented into a million bits and more.

There were things he had never known existed and things on the periphery that filled him with dread, ancient evils locked deep within the world that had a familiar hint to them but were pushed back as thousands of other things demanded his attention. With so much from the great to the very tiny assailing him, even he had to fight at first to maintain both his focus and his sanity.

Again, it was the World Tree and Azeroth from which he drew his strength. The danger of becoming forever lost faded. Malfurion looked upon his besieged world and found those for whom he was seeking.

They were not nearly as many as he hoped, but among them, he found those essential to his plan.

Varian eyed his beleaguered force. He knew that there were still pockets here and there throughout the capital and possibly beyond, but they were shrinking fast. That came as no surprise to him, for weapons were useless. Mostly, he and his men had to flee, an ignoble course, if necessary.

Fire seemed to slow the horrific throngs—at least somewhat. The newest wave of terror—the sleepwalkers—on the one hand presented an even greater shock to the mind, but they were also a foe that could be physically battled. The only trouble was that there remained the inherent hesitation to do harm to an innocent, even if that innocent was wildly attacking.

But desperation had caused more than one of Varian's dwindling force to bloody their weapons and he himself had had to strike hard blows.

Varian . . . king of Stormwind . . .

It was only due to the calm and comforting tone of the voice that Varian knew he was not falling to the Nightmare's power. The Nightmare offered no reassurance; it seemed to drag its victims immediately into their fears.

Varian . . . comrade to Broll Bearmantle . . . I am Malfurion Stormrage . . .

He immediately straightened. Although Varian had not met the famed archdruid, like many leaders in both the Alliance and Horde he knew of Malfurion's role as leader of the druids. The efforts of the druids had been critical in winning the Battle of Mount Hyjal and, consequently, the Third War. Varian had not been on Kalimdor at the time, but had heard the tale in great depth.

That the archdruid now spoke in the king's head was not so surprising. However, as welcome as Malfurion's presence was in some regards, Varian had little time to give him. Matters were becoming even *more* desperate.

"Whatever you want, better speak it fast . . ." the lord of Stormwind muttered low so as not to have his soldiers worry that he was talking to shadows.

Varian, I need you to lead those that will attack the Nightmare where it is most vulnerable . . . to attack it within the Emerald Dream . . .

"I won't abandon Stormwind!" Without realizing it, Varian raised his voice. Some of his soldiers glanced at him, then went back to their frantic struggles.

Everyone must abandon what they cherish, if they hope to save it . . .

Varian gritted his teeth. "Damn you . . . but how do we get out of here and where do we go even if we make it?"

There is no need to leave . . . all you have to do is simply follow my instructions . . .

A screaming figure lunged at the king. It was one of his personal servants. The man's eyes were shut and his face was drawn in such a terrible cry that it looked as if his jaw had become unhinged. What he was screaming about, Varian did not pay attention. The sleepwalkers all suffered individual nightmares in which they tried to strike back at their tormentors—who were always the defenders.

Varian attempted to strike the wild-maned man on the side of the head with the flat of the blade. The sleepwalkers *could* be downed that way, although it generally took more than one blow.

But the servitor suddenly shifted position. Rather than the flat, Varian cut him deep with the edge.

Blood poured from the wound. The stricken sleepwalker collapsed onto the king. One of the soldiers immediately tore the dying man from Varian, but the lord of Stormwind did not notice. All he knew was that he had finally slain one of his subjects, another nightmare to add to those he already suffered.

"Whatever you want to do, do it, then!" he snarled at the unseen Malfurion. "And do it quick!"

The archdruid told him what to do. Varian looked incredulous, then surrendered to Malfurion's suggestions.

"Lay down your arms!" he shouted to others. "Sound the call to stand down!"

I will have to use some force . . . Malfurion added. *I will need to start with you, the better so that you can touch the rest . . .*

"I hope you know what you're doing! We've been taking a potion to keep from—"

That will not matter. My work will override all . . .

The king grunted. As his stunned supporters watched, Varian reluctantly shut his eyes . . .

And immediately went to sleep.

High above the rest of northern Mulgore—situated on the high bluffs near the Stonetalon Mountains—lay the chief city of the tauren. Until the building of Thunder Bluff, all tauren had lived a nomadic life. Only in recent times, with the expulsion of the centaur marauders from their lands, had Hamuul's people finally established a settlement comparable to Orgrimmar, Stormwind City, and other capitals of Azeroth.

Four mesas made up Thunder Bluff, with the largest and most populated in the center. The great totems of the tauren stood tall over structures that drew much from the race's past as perpetual wanderers. Even the great houses were built like the long, wooden structures once used by the tribes for the winter seasons, while the smaller domiciles surrounding them were fashioned after the pointed, wood-and-animal-skin tents which had for generations served the daily purposes of the nomads.

The tauren had chosen the location for strategic means, the mesas giving them great defense against most enemies. However, even the bluffs were of no protection against an enemy that was much a part of oneself . . .

This, Baine Bloodhoof, son of the great tauren chieftain, Cairne, understood too well . . . now. Ax in one hand and a short, thrusting spear in the other, he stood at the forefront of a band of warriors blocking the bridge leading to Middle Rise, where the tradeskill area had, until recently, thrived. Middle Rise was all that was left somewhat defended in the northern and eastern part of Thunder Bluff. The horrors had overtaken the rest, though there were a few tiny spots of resistance.

Cairne's son thrust with the spear at a staggering figure just a few feet ahead, trying to fend him off without killing him. Baine knew the other tauren, a former comrade named Gam. They had fought centaur side by side. Now Gam, eyes shut tight and mutterings concerning the four-legged marauders slipping from his mouth, tried to kill Cairne's son as if *he* were a centaur.

Gam kept coming. In the end, Baine had no choice. His dark brown coat and black mane already matted with blood despite the protective leather over his shoulders, hump, and arms, Baine drove the spear into Gam's chest.

With a grunt, the sleepwalking tauren dropped his weapon, then fell off the rope bridge. His body plummeted to the plains below, fortunately disappearing into the accursed mists and thus saving Baine from watching his friend's body shatter.

The lifts were not far, but there was no point in descending. The scouts that Baine had sent earlier had not returned, even though they should have reported long ago. That likely meant that they had been taken and were now part of the threat.

The bridge shook as more sleepwalkers surged forward.

"What do we do?" one of his warriors asked. Tauren were stoic of nature, but this struggle had them all staring worried and wide-eyed . . . which only served to better show the redness due to a lack of sleep.

Would that you could guide me in this, Father, Baine thought. But elderly Cairne had been among the first of the sleepers and Baine could not help but think that had happened for a reason. Most tauren could not imagine life without their venerable chieftain, especially Baine.

Snorting, Cairne's son came to a decision. It only bought a little time, but there was no other true choice. He said a prayer for the innocents whom he was about to send to death.

"Cut the ropes!" Baine commanded.

"The ropes?" The other tauren looked dismayed.

"Cut them!" Baine repeated, raising his ax above the rope nearest to him.

At that moment, a voice touched his thoughts.

Baine Bloodhoof . . . I am the archdruid Malfurion Stormrage, friend to Hamuul Runetotem . . . I offer a chance of hope . . . for us . . .

Baine thanked his ancestors, then, without care what the others might think, spoke to the voice. "Tell me . . . and hurry . . ."

A question that had long bothered Malfurion was also explained in his reaching out to the far recesses of Azeroth, the question of what was happening in Dalaran. His first glimpse of the realm of the magi startled him, for the entire kingdom of Dalaran was not where it should have been. Rather, it now *floated* in the sky.

Night elves in general did not hold magi and other arcane casters in the most favorable light, but Malfurion, who knew the magi better than many of his kind, had in the past dealt with them with cautious trust. Encouraged by this display of their incredible abilities, he sought to reach those within—especially Rhonin, whom he had known some ten thousand years past—only to discover that even Dalaran had fallen prey to the Nightmare.

In fact, Dalaran had *particularly* fallen to it. Malfurion's first glances at the grand, magically illuminated streets of the flying city revealed nothing but emptiness shrouded in mist. As he entered the various oddly shaped structures, he came upon the first of the sleepers. They lay there by the scores, some in their beds, others where exhaustion had taken them.

And in one of those beds he found not only Rhonin, but the

archmage's mate, the high elf Vereesa. Though Malfurion had not met her, he knew of her through Rhonin's words. They had been caught in their slumber. Their faces even now revealed that their sleep was, like those of all the other victims, caught up in the horrors of the Nightmare.

There were no sleepwalkers, though Malfurion sensed that many of the victims were at the edge of doing so. But some spell held them where they were . . . and finally he found its source in the Violet Citadel.

The mighty structure rose above all else. Its basic form was a huge tower with cone-shaped additions flanking its lower sides. Far above the rest of the city, the sharply pointed tip was surrounded by a circular array kept in place by powerful magic spells.

Ignoring this and the countless purple-tipped spires below, Malfurion touched those within. One name came to mind immediately, an elder female mage by the name of Modera. The image of a strong-willed figure with short, gray hair and a faint, perpetual frown came to Malfurion. She was clad not in the elaborate blue and violet robes that marked the ruling committee, the Kirin Tor, but rather gray and blue armor.

The archdruid . . . she responded back with much exhaustion. *So, not all of Azeroth is fallen* . . .

His admiration for her immediate identification of him was tempered by her second statement. The magi in the chamber were utterly cut off from the outside world.

It is all that enables us to keep our brethren from rising again . . . we barely caught it in time . . . we lost several of those left in our band when the first sleepwalkers appeared . . .

She had answered his question before he could ask it. Those magi left in Dalaran could not join his plan. They were doing all they could to contain the greatest of their kind from joining the Nightmare's army of darkness.

Malfurion let Modera know as much as he had Varian. Modera nodded, though she did not appear overly confident in him. *You've spoken to other magi beyond Dalaran?*

I have.

She nodded. Modera was clearly very exhausted, as were the few dozen spellcasters with her or in other parts of the citadel. *May they be of some assistance . . . and may good fortune guide your efforts . . . I fear what you plan is our last chance . . .*

Malfurion broke contact with her. He hoped that he had not betrayed himself. Modera might have wondered at his hubris if she had known what he truly intended for her fellow magi and all the others he was gathering . . .

And as Malfurion spoke to Varian, spoke to Baine, spoke to Modera, he also spoke to scores of others. He spoke to the orc shaman Zor Lonetree in Orgrimmar, to King Magni's counselor in Ironforge, to the troll scout Rokhan—now forced to lead a band of his people trapped outside the orc capital to safety—and many, many more. Like the trolls, several were of races with enmity toward Malfurion's race, but he sought to convince them nonetheless. With some he succeeded; with others he did not.

He could not blame any who rejected his offer of aid. He asked them to leave themselves defenseless before the Nightmare.

And among those who accepted, Malfurion still sensed wariness and concern . . . until they found what many thought their spirits but what were in truth their dreamforms materializing in a place most could not even imagine.

The Emerald Dream.

What is this place? Varian asked for all of them.

Also in dreamform, Malfurion explained, *This is the place where dreams and the waking meet . . . once a place of gentle communion, but now all but overrun by the Nightmare . . .*

Then . . . what point is there in bringing us here? At least we should fall in our own lands? Many agreed.

Because only here can you make the difference . . . only here will your weapons find use . . .

That was the encouragement they needed. Yet, even then, many began to divide up by race and treaty. That would not do. Malfurion needed them as one, not many.

Varian will lead you . . . he stated flatly.

But the king looked outraged at the sight of the orcs. *I won't lead this filth! Let the Nightmare take them and be damned—*

As it took your son and so many others in Stormwind City? Only by defeating the Nightmare can you ever hope to have Anduin returned to you . . . and that can only happen if we all work together . . .

I— Varian visibly struggled between his hatred and his love.

Love won out. *Very well . . . let it happen . . .*

Now, though, many of the Horde looked reluctant to join any force led by Varian. But then the tauren leader Baine took up a place by the human. *I will trust that this one chosen by a friend of my people will act with honor toward all . . .*

The tauren's declaration shattered resistance. Malfurion gave thanks, then concentrated. He found those that had been from the start seeking to stem the Nightmare. Their numbers were fewer yet, which raised his concern. He reached out and touched the spirit of Zaetar.

Malfurion Stormrage? Remulos's brother asked in surprise and desperate hope.

The night elf let him touch his memories, instantly giving the spirit all he needed to know. Zaetar's hopes swelled, then dropped. *My brother?*

I have no news of him.

Zaetar let this pass, though the lack of news clearly bothered him. He accepted Malfurion's plan as the archdruid had revealed to him, but asked one last question, *And these, all of these whom you have brought to us . . . they suspect nothing of your true intentions?*

No . . . and if they do not . . . the Nightmare Lord may not . . .

The spirit said no more on the subject. Instead, Zaetar reached out to Varian. The king did well in concealing his surprise when he felt Zaetar's distant presence.

We're coming, he promised Remulos's brother.

The king of Stormwind raised his sword—what was actually a part of his dreamform—and led his host forward.

The archdruid stared at Varian as the king moved on. Just for a moment, Varian's countenance had seemed to change to something else. A *wolf*'s. A name came to mind, an ancient spirit revered by many races, including the night elves.

Goldrinn . . . Malfurion thought, recalling the legendary Ancient. The white wolf had slaughtered hundreds of demons during the War of the Ancients before falling to their great numbers. Yet, his spirit was said to live on, watching over those he favored.

May you be one of those, the archdruid concluded, aware that he had likely imagined what he had seen. *May Goldrinn watch over you and all those marching to meet our enemy . . .*

And as the dreamform army moved on the Nightmare, others called by Malfurion and aided in their journey by the other druids began to join them. From his multiple viewpoint, Malfurion saw the coming of not just ancients whose calling was war, but those of others. Their shapes were as myriad as the species of trees of Azeroth and though many were tenders of learned paths, they were all ferocious defenders of the natural world. Some were winged, others clawed, and though their numbers were not great, each represented a mighty force in themselves.

They were far from alone, though. With them came the treants. Even more resembling the forests they guarded, the treants were smaller and less powerful than the ancients, but were by no means only a slight presence. More numerous than the ancients, they were a force Malfurion welcomed, as were the dryads, also forest protectors and the powerful daughters of vanished Remulos.

Flying hippogryphs by the scores came, joined in aerial endeavor by other denizens of the sky, including gryphons, gargantuan moths, carrion birds, dragonhawks, and, foremost, the remaining dragons of the red, green, and even blue flights. Though led by others than their respective Aspects, the dragons were well versed in combat. The three dragonflights flew separate from one another, for each had its own method of battle, in addition to their mighty jaws and claws. The blue wielded magic spells of incredible power, the red breathed searing fire, and the green, of course, touched upon their dream abilities.

Kobolds and other creatures with great enmity toward all else also had agreed to at least join the mighty throng. Fearsome ursine furbolgs, more comfortable among wild animals than as part of Varian's force, let out howls of anticipation at final combat. Giant panthers, tusked boars, fearsome basilisks, crocolisks, hyenas, and other animals, many of them in part herded by the more sentient, reptilian raptors, were just a part of the animal legions that followed. The druids and others also guided the beasts, who, if they did not know what the ultimate reason was for this struggle, they knew that their lives and their progeny were endangered.

Malfurion gave thanks to all of them, realizing more and more that each had a crucial role, that he needed them as much as they needed him.

Though even fewer in number than ever and among the last to join, the Forsaken were eager to lend their monstrous might as well. They stood with their allies in the Horde, awaiting their chance to strike back.

Malfurion watched all happen and felt both gratitude and regret. Only Zaetar understood the truth. Only Zaetar understood that all this might be for nothing if what else the archdruid intended failed.

Thinking of the spirit caused the night elf to think also of Remulos. Cenarius's son was nowhere to be sensed. Malfurion had hoped to find Remulos during this spell and the fact that he had not boded ill. Only where the Nightmare stood ascendant in the Dream were things shielded from the archdruid . . . and if Remulos was there—

Malfurion could not concern himself with the missing keeper, no matter how great his power would have enhanced their chances. Indeed, the son of Cenarius was not even the first of his concerns. That was and would always be Tyrande, whom once more he had utterly let down.

Tyrande . . .

No sooner had he thought of her than a brief, ever so brief presence touched his mind. He knew without hesitation that it was *her,* that it could only be her. Just as some ten thousand years earlier, Tyrande had always stood with him. She had done so even though he had forsaken her time and time again for the druidic path. If she perished now . . . the years lost to them would that much more burn at his soul. He was the foremost—in his mind, the *only*—reason for their separations.

Malfurion could not help but shiver at such thoughts, for he also knew that she stood in the shadow of the tree that was his nemesis . . . and that even the Mother Moon's gifts were not the reason that she had been able to manage that momentary link.

The Nightmare Lord was inviting him.

The archdruid willed himself back into his body. He felt the tremendous relief on the part of both Broll and Hamuul at his return.

He also felt another near them . . . someone who should not be there.

Malfurion sprang to his feet the moment he had control. Broll and the tauren pulled back in surprise.

"Are you all right, Shan'do? Did something happen?"

But Malfurion did not answer them, instead steeling himself to face an unexpected danger to all of them.

The figure overshadowed the trio. He did not smile, but grimly nodded to Malfurion. In one hand, he held a long spear made from a single branch. In his other hand—

His other hand—and the arm to which it was attached—was a twisted, withered mass now more resembling a rotted tree limb.

Remulos stood before them, the woodland guardian, the son of Cenarius, trodding forward on his four hooved feet. Where once the sense of spring pervaded his very being, now it was as if chill winter was the mantle the forest guardian wore. His skin was grayer and the leaves in his hair brown and dry.

"Glad I am to find you here, Malfurion." Remulos displayed the mutilated limb, then rumbled, "I have been to the heart of the Nightmare . . . and if you have the strength and spirit, you and I must return to it *immediately* . . . or all is lost . . ."

25

A Choice Made

They were on Azeroth again, though no part that Lucan recognized. The only thing familiar about it was that which *all* the world now seemed to have in common . . . the cloying mist of the Nightmare.

A powerful hand gripped his collar. Thura leaned close, the angry orc's breath hot and odorous. "The ax! What did you do with the ax?"

"I don't know what you're talking about!"

Thura showed him her other hand, now formed in a threatening fist. "The ax of Broxigar! It didn't come with us! It was in my hand—and then it wasn't!"

"Are you certain you didn't let go?" The expression with which the orc replied quickly made him retract the question. "Then it should've remained with you! It did before!"

Releasing him, the female warrior furiously gazed around. "Then where is it, human?"

Lucan no more knew that than where they stood. The hilly landscape was full of treacherous ravines and equally desolate terrain. There were some shrubs and, on one hill, a huge, ugly tree—

The cartographer swallowed. The tree was not in keeping with the lack of life around it. Indeed, of all the vegetation around, it was the only one that seemed to be thriving. Even then, it bore hardly any leaves.

But that was not what so disturbed Lucan about the tree. It was the outline it cast even in the haze.

Like a giant skeletal hand.

Now he felt he understood how and why the ax had been left behind. Something else had *wanted* it to stay, something with the power to do so.

"We've got to leave!" he blurted.

"I will have the ax back!" Thura insisted, unaware of what Lucan had discovered.

A crackling sound all around them made both pause.

The ground beneath their feet began to move as if something huge was burrowing its way up. As that happened, shadows that seemed half night elf, half goat formed in the mists.

A root shot out of one of the cracks, seeking Lucan's ankle. However, Thura seized it first, cracking off a large part of the pointed tip. What looked like congealed blood dripped from both broken ends.

The root pulled back, but others darted up. The orc brandished the root at the oncoming shadow satyrs.

One lunged. Thura thrust the point into the murky form.

The shadow hissed, then melted.

But there were more and more coming. Thura looked to Lucan. "There're too many! If I had the ax—"

She stopped as she saw the human's expression. Lucan was staring into one of the fissures created by the roots. His face was, if possible, more pale than ever.

The orc grabbed his arm, which seemed to break whatever fascination he had with the fissure. Lucan seized her in turn.

"I can't promise where we'll end up in the Nightmare!"

Thura stabbed another shadow, watching with no satisfaction as it faded. "Just take us!"

They vanished . . . and reappeared in all-too-familiar emerald-tinted surroundings.

But they were not alone.

"*Again?*" Eranikus roared. His fury caused their surroundings, a cave, to quiver. The green dragon unfurled his wings, shattering several stalactites. "I want no part of this insanity! I warned you about that!"

"I couldn't help it!" Lucan responded. "We had to escape them— and I wanted to go somewhere safe! I didn't know it would bring me back to you again and again!"

"Around me, you are hardly safe, little bite!" Eranikus's head dropped down near the pair. "And neither are you, orc, even with that magical weapon . . ."

"I no longer have the ax," Thura growled, thrusting her open hands toward the huge head. "It seems it was somehow lost when the high priestess bravely sacrificed herself to enable us to escape from the corrupted ones!"

" 'Corrupted ones'? You speak of Lethon and Emeriss? The night elf left herself with that odious pair . . . and the ax also is theirs?"

"It couldn't be helped—" Lucan began, but Ysera's consort was no longer listening to him.

"It will not end . . . until . . . but I can't . . ." The green leviathan hissed as he muttered to himself. "I cannot sleep . . . I cannot forget . . . she was lost . . ."

A wailing roar escaped the distraught dragon. Thura and Lucan sought cover as Eranikus's frustration with himself erupted fully.

As the last echoes of his cry finished reverberating, the dragon returned his attention to the tiny pair. His expression was unreadable.

"It seems there is only one way to be permanently rid of your intrusions . . ."

Eranikus reached for them.

"Your arm . . ." Malfurion quietly answered. "What happened to your arm?"

Remulos glanced at it. His eyes grew troubled. "The least of injuries, you may believe me."

"He appeared out of nowhere just before you awoke," Broll explained. "We almost lost our concentration, so surprised were we."

"And it is a credit to your teaching that neither did." The son of

Cenarius pointed his spear at Malfurion. "But we've no time to discuss that further, my father's favored thero'shan—his prized student! There is one chance to help turn matters around, but we need to depart at once!"

Malfurion eyed the others. "I cannot leave now—"

"Archdruid, you know that the Nightmare has your Tyrande . . ."

"I know too well—"

"And you know the true name of the Nightmare Lord." Remulos spoke the title with all the dread that Malfurion kept hidden deep in his soul. "A diabolical creature once named Xavius! The same Xavius—as you related to me later—who served your Queen Azshara in aiding the Burning Legion to come to Azeroth, and thus having a part in causing my own blood much grief . . ."

Even after millennia, Malfurion recalled all too well Cenarius's near death in battle and how it had also cost the life of Malorne—the White Stag—at the hands of the demon Archimonde. Malorne had been the sire of Cenarius and, thus, the grandsire of Remulos.

"Xavius has Tyrande . . ." Remulos continued. ". . . and he also has the ax fashioned by my father for the brave orc Broxigar . . ."

The news struck Malfurion harder than even Broll or Hamuul likely realized. He knew what he had to do, though it threatened everything.

Turning to Broll, the archdruid ordered, "Broll, I must ask you to help guide the druids and the others while I am gone. Hamuul, I have given you much to do, but you must also help him, if you can. Can I rely on both of you?" When both had bowed their heads in acceptance, Malfurion said to Remulos, "Tyrande and the ax are in the same place? You are certain?"

"I am. Deep in the Nightmare."

"Then we need to enter through Fandral's portal."

The forest guardian shook his great antlered head. "No, I have another method."

Malfurion's brow arched. "You do?"

"The manner by which I came here." Remulos drew a huge circle with the spear tip. As he completed it, the circle flared into being, the edge a searing dark green.

The hooved forest lord muttered something that Malfurion could not make out. The circle swelled, expanding enough for both of them to enter it side by side.

"Come!" Remulos insisted.

A concerned Broll reached toward Malfurion. "Shan'do—"

"All will be well." The archdruid pointed toward Fandral's portal. "Do what must be done."

With that said, he joined Remulos in stepping through the forest lord's circle.

A chill swept over him as they entered the Nightmare. Malfurion sensed that they were very near where the sinister shadow had kept his dreamform imprisoned and reshaped. The thought of what Xavius might do to Tyrande stirred a struggle within the night elf that he kept secret from his companion.

"Beware . . ." Remulos whispered. "One of the dragons is near . . . I think it Emeriss . . ."

Malfurion felt something nearby and trusted that Cenarius's son had rightly identified the threat. But then the night elf sensed something more. In addition to the dragon, there was someone else nearby. His heart pounded as he realized just whose presence he felt.

Tyrande . . .

However, Remulos was not heading in that direction. "The ax of Broxigar is this way. We must hurry! If the Nightmare succeeds in gaining its power, it'll become an additional threat, but if we regain it, we may be able to use it to free Ysera before she can no longer prevent the Nightmare from using her power . . ."

Malfurion frowned. "You were not able to take it yourself?"

"This hand is the result of that last attempt. It'll take the two of us to deal with the dragon and take the ax . . . and also rescue your Tyrande, my friend . . ."

Nodding solemnly, the archdruid let the forest guardian continue to lead. Malfurion studied their surroundings—or lack thereof—as they moved.

"It is very silent . . . why?"

"The Nightmare Lord is likely more concerned with your valiant army now," Remulos replied without looking back. "And with Emeriss to guard both the weapon and the high priestess, of what concern is there here?"

"If the ax is of such importance to the Nightmare, there should be more than merely one dragon to watch over both it and Tyrande," Malfurion commented. "I know I would not leave them so lightly guarded . . . especially her . . ."

"Your faith in your love is laudable, but do not underestimate the power the corrupted dragon wields! Moreover, the Nightmare has many plots in play and its servants must attend to those as well . . ."

The archdruid did not answer, for at that moment they heard the sound of heavy breathing. Malfurion's heart began to match the sinister breathing, which he knew must be from Emeriss.

"Be prepared!" Remulos murmured. "Between the two of us, we should be able to at least ward her off . . ."

The murky outline of a huge, winged form began to coalesce ahead. Emeriss appeared to be fixated upon something on the ground near her forepaws . . . very likely the fabled ax.

Malfurion chose that moment to glance behind him, but almost immediately Remulos demanded his attention. "Look there to the side! Not all that far from the dragon! The high priestess!"

Indeed, the shadowy outline further on was that of a female night elf clad much like Tyrande had been. Malfurion gritted his teeth at the half-seen sight; Tyrande hung several feet off the ground as if bound to some invisible post or perhaps *tree*. Her arms and legs were pulled tight behind her. Worse, there were more than a dozen of the shadow satyrs clawing at the air below her. Their talons just barely missed her.

"Fend off Emeriss and the curs will flee," the son of Cenarius assured him. "Be ready."

Remulos raised the spear. The tip flared green.

A similar glow flared to life around the dragon. In its light, Emeriss's disease-ravaged form looked even more hideous.

As his companion struck, Malfurion gestured at the ground. The Emerald Dream had itself been much corrupted, but, unlike the foul behemoth, there was still inherent in it some of its true nature.

Fresh tendrils—vines—instantly grew up under Emeriss. The moment they made contact, the dragon reacted as if they burned her. Some attempted to ensnare her legs and tail. She hissed and howled, batting with her paws at both the vegetation and the glow.

In what was apparent desperation, Emeriss exhaled on the tendrils. The vines yellowed, then withered.

Malfurion thought of Remulos's ruined limb and felt a pang of remorse. Then he strengthened his spell.

The tendrils grew higher, the blades sharper. Emeriss howled again. The glow also grew stronger.

With a furious roar, the dragon took to the sky and fled. Remulos's spell still surrounded her.

As the dragon vanished into the mist, the shadow satyrs turned to the pair. However, Remulos pointed his spear at their ranks and a similar glow surrounded the fiends. Unlike Emeriss, however, they simply melted to nothing.

Malfurion started toward Tyrande, but Remulos reared up in front of him.

"The ax! Take it quickly!"

The weapon lay as if abandoned, though Malfurion knew that Thura would have never given it up willingly. What had happened and whether she was dead or alive were questions to which the archdruid would have liked an immediate answer.

The sickly green taint of the Nightmare surrounded Brox's former weapon, but there was also another, lighter green aura in between, one that seemed to radiate from the ax.

"We're in time," Remulos said with much relief. "The ax has not been turned."

"No . . ." Malfurion knelt down near it. Setting his palms over the weapon, he tried to sense what was happening. The archdruid could feel the innate magic used so long ago by Cenarius, magic that had drawn upon Azeroth's most primal energies. "What should we do?"

"You must draw the ax's energies out. Reshape them to their original state."

Looking up, the night elf commented, "That might weaken the ax, even cause it to disintegrate."

"I will stand ready to reclaim the energies and see to it that they're shaped as needed."

Frowning, Malfurion rose. "Perhaps it might be better if you did the first, I the second. I fear that I might fail you."

Remulos's hoof scraped impatiently on the ground. "You won't, Malfurion! Now hurry! There's still Tyrande, remember?"

"I have never forgotten." The archdruid started to turn toward where the shadowed figure hung. "I will attend to her first."

"You will do as I command!"

Having expected what was about to happen, Malfurion leapt. In his wake, the green glow that Remulos had used on both the dragon and the satyrs struck where he had been standing. However, now there was a strong dark touch to it, one very much akin to the evil aura surrounding the ax.

Malfurion faced Remulos . . . but not the Remulos he knew. The limb was still withered, no doubt, as the forest guardian had said, the result of having confronted Emeriss earlier . . . but Cenarius's son was now a vile, twisted version of himself. The foliage in his beard and hair consisted of thistles and black weeds. His face and form had a skeletal semblance to them. His skin was now the white of death, and his eyes were the macabre, madly shifting colors of the Nightmare.

He had been corrupted. His new master had clearly worked very hard to shield the keeper's transformation and for a few seconds after Malfurion had spoken with Remulos in the enclave, the archdruid had thought that his old friend had indeed returned injured but with mind intact.

But Remulos had been too eager to separate him from his companions, too eager to focus only on the ax and not so much on Tyrande.

The Remulos that Malfurion recalled would have been greatly concerned for her, even before dealing with retrieving the ax.

Corrupted, it appeared that Remulos could no more wield the ax than his master. The Nightmare was everything unnatural, the opposite of Cenarius's creation. That was why Malfurion had been needed, and why only Emeriss and the shadow satyrs had been here to guard the weapon and Tyrande.

As for Tyrande, she had been bait to ensure that the archdruid would come this far, just in case the ax proved insufficient.

Malfurion had come to understand the truth shortly after arriving. Too many things seemed too convenient. Xavius and the Nightmare had underestimated him this time.

They had also underestimated his deep bond with his beloved.

All this flashed through his thoughts in but the space of a single breath. At the same time, the archdruid prepared to meet his former friend in battle. The hooved figure charged Malfurion, who shifted into the form of a dire bear. Claws clashed with talons. The natural energies flowed around the archdruid, but the foulness of the Nightmare fueled Remulos. Their battle became a standstill that Malfurion could ill afford.

Then Remulos's expression shifted. His voice changed. Worse, his eyes became the deep, black orbs with the ruby streaks running across them that, after ten millennia, were still all too familiar to Malfurion.

"There is no hope for your struggle this time . . ."

The voice sent a shiver through Malfurion. He knew it very, very well. Almost without thinking, the archdruid reverted to his true form. "I was too kind to you, Xavius . . ."

" 'Kind'? I lived trapped, tortured for more than ten millennia!" Xavius/Remulos roared, spitting on his foe. "Watching and waiting and screaming for release! I burned when the land burned, only to have my bark heal and my branches grow anew! What you suffered was but a minute expression of what I lived through over and over and over!"

"I'm sorry, then . . ." Malfurion replied, truly meaning it. He had done his work too well. Xavius the Nightmare Lord was as much his creation as the counselor's. "I would go back and change it, if I could . . ."

Xavius/Remulos laughed harshly. "But I no longer desire it changed! All that suffering, all that waiting . . . now it has all been worth it! Azeroth will be remade anew and everyone will suffer agonies only my own long, endless torment could have allowed any to conceive! It will be glorious!"

The talons raked Malfurion's chest. The night elf cried out in pain but did not falter. He sought out Remulos in his foe.

But there was nothing to find of the keeper within the menacing figure before Malfurion. Cenarius's son had either been utterly consumed by the Nightmare or was buried so deep within his soul that there was no hope of freeing him.

"I'm sorry," Malfurion murmured.

"Still the mournful fool!" Xavius mocked through his host.

But the archdruid was not apologizing to him. Reaching into a pouch, Malfurion drew out what he sought. He immediately rubbed the contents of his hand against the body of Remulos.

Cenarius's son roared. His skin began to harden, to take on the appearance of thick bark.

It was a unique variation of a spell used to strengthen a druid's own skin against attacks. Malfurion had developed it to use against the Burning Legion. Long ago, he had come to the realization that every spell could have a reverse—and, in this case, *adverse*—reaction from that originally intended. The powder had been ground from the hardest of barks.

Remulos stiffened. He now was more statue than living. The rage still in his eyes was clearly that of the Nightmare Lord. The irony of the spell was not lost on Malfurion; he had transformed Xavius into a tree and now he did virtually the same to poor Remulos. A part of the archdruid wanted to stop what he was doing, but a tearful Malfurion knew he had no choice but to complete the horrific spell.

A wordless cry escaped Remulos before even his mouth would not work. One hand sought to throw the spear, but failed.

Stumbling back, Malfurion ignored his handiwork. He took one short glance at the ax, knew it could not be touched by his foes, and then raced not toward the shadowed figure of his love, but rather to the place where he had originally sensed her.

That, more than anything, had verified his suspicions concerning Remulos's "quest." He had realized that he was being led away from her, that the false image existed purely to lead him toward the ax.

Shadow satyrs jumped from the mists, flinging themselves upon him. Malfurion shifted to cat form and tore through them.

He came upon Tyrande at last. Both a thrill and a stirring of tremendous fear filled him as he stared at her. She hung in a position identical to what the false image had displayed. Her eyes were shut. That she was alive, he had known; whether she was at all corrupted, the archdruid could not yet tell.

Still a cat, Malfurion leaped. Although Tyrande hung some distance in the air, it was but a small gap for his powerful form. As he neared her, the archdruid shifted into his true shape. At the same time, he saw that her body glowed a slight but consistent silver. There was no doubt of the purity of Elune's power covering her. Captured she had been, but they had not yet had the chance to corrupt her.

She fell free as soon as he touched her. Malfurion briefly shifted to dire bear form, catching the high priestess in his mighty arms as they landed.

Reverting, Malfurion openly wept as he caressed her cheek and her hand, so grateful was he for the knowledge that she was alive and whole . . .

But he also finally noted that she still lay motionless, almost as frozen as he had left Remulos.

The clatter of hooves made him straighten. Worse, in their wake Malfurion also heard the beating of wings.

He had failed to stop the corrupted keeper . . . and now Malfurion suspected that Emeriss, made aware that the trap had not worked, was returning, too.

Remulos reared up before him. Parts of his body were still encased in bark, but he moved with great swiftness nonetheless. He glared down at the night elf and threw the spear.

Malfurion quickly cast a spell, but one aimed at himself. He not only felt his own defenses heighten, but his strength and agility also increased. The druids called it the mark of the wild, and Malfurion had learned it from Cenarius. Now he was forced to use it to protect himself against his shan'do's son.

Although he also did his best to evade the spear, Malfurion was only partially successful. The physical weapon but grazed him, yet that was enough for its potent energies to sear the archdruid to the very bone despite his spellwork. Still, he managed to use his own power to knock the spear to the ground beside him.

Struggling with the pain, Malfurion dropped to his knees. The act was all that saved him from Remulos's flashing hooves. The edge of one struck the tip of Malfurion's antler. The tip cracked off, flying away.

The night elf looked up into the scowling visage. He could not sense Xavius inside, anymore, but neither could he yet find the true Remulos.

Again the hooves came at him. Like the spear, they flared with tremendous dark energies. Malfurion spun to avoid them and saw that the broken tip from his antler was now a twisted, bony mass. He could well imagine what would happen to him if those hooves struck directly.

Reaching into another pouch, Malfurion sought out a particular powder. He prayed to the spirit of Cenarius to forgive him for what he intended.

With expert aim, he threw the powder at the keeper's face.

Remulos's hand thrust toward the flying powder. Most of the powder burned black, then vanished. A few bits managed to get through.

The keeper sneezed.

"A last, truly desperate attempt—"

But Remulos's arrogant remark transformed into a howl of pain. He looked down at where Malfurion now shoved the point of the keeper's own magical spear into his chest. The night elf had merely sought the least of distractions in order to obtain the spear from where he had knocked it.

The weapon burned his palms even despite his protections, but Malfurion did not release his hold. He shoved the spear deeper.

Remulos clawed at both him and the weapon. His chest was afire with crackling veins of energy.

Then, the corrupted keeper finally let out a gasp . . . and collapsed.

Malfurion pulled the spear free. Remulos still breathed, but whether he would recover was another question.

"I'm so sorry . . ." the archdruid whispered. "So—"

He was buffeted by a tremendous force. A monstrous roar filled his ears.

Emeriss picked him up in her paw as if he were some tiny plaything. The corrupted leviathan flew up into the air.

"One way or another . . . you will serve us!" she hissed. *"You'll unbind the ax from Azeroth and give it to us—"*

A blinding silver light materializing from the sky above enveloped both. Malfurion experienced a wondrous sense of rejuvenation. All his injuries and pain—save the emotional pain of having had to fight Remulos—faded away.

But for Emeriss, it seemed to do just the opposite. She roared. Her body violently contorted.

In obvious pain, the dragon lost her hold on Malfurion. The archdruid immediately shifted into storm crow form. Wings spread wide, he descended.

And there he saw Tyrande, her face screwed up in concentration. The high priestess's legs wavered, but she stood determined as Elune's light surrounded the huge beast.

Emeriss veered around. The corrupted green dragon exhaled in Tyrande's direction, but the light caused her deadly breath to dissipate. A look of incomprehension spread over the dragon's ghastly countenance.

"What are you doing? What are you doing?" she shrieked at Tyrande. *"I feel—I feel—"*

Her body grew translucent and without definition. Emeriss became a vaguely seen thing, almost as if she had become a part of the mist itself.

Malfurion alighted near Tyrande. Changing form, he ran to her. Just as her knees finally buckled, the archdruid gave her the necessary support. He choked up inside, relieved to have again not lost her.

Above them, Emeriss let out a gasp. She was now barely identifiable as a dragon. Before Malfurion's eyes, the last of the behemoth dispersed.

Exhaling deeply, the high priestess let her hands drop.

"I did not know if it would . . . would work . . . and certainly not . . . not like this . . ."

"If *what* would work, Tyrande?"

She steadied herself. "I thought of what the corrupted had become and I hoped to try a different tact; I pushed Elune's healing power to its utmost, seeking to strip away the taint . . ."

Malfurion looked up where Emeriss had last hovered. "I understand."

"Yes . . . there was nothing left *but* the corruption . . . and when I tried to heal that . . . it left only emptiness . . ."

The archdruid would have replied, but he sensed renewed danger. "Xavius's shadows come. Too many of them, I suspect. I need to take you from here."

"But the ax!" She clutched his arm. "Thura lost the ax here—"

"We can't worry about it," he curtly answered. Instead, he ran to where the spear lay and, despite being aware of the pain it would cause, plucked it up. Then, with Tyrande near and the unmoving Remulos between them, Malfurion did as the corrupted forest guardian had.

A gap opened up right before them. Shifting to ursine form, the archdruid continued to hold the spear as he took hold of the heavy Remulos.

"Mal, think what you're doing! We need to retrieve the ax! I know now! I know what—"

He roared for her to go through. With great reluctance, she finally obeyed.

Dragging Remulos with him, Malfurion followed.

The gap vanished.

The shadow satyrs faded away the moment that the gap did. For a time, there was silence. Then the shadow of the tree stretched over the area where the ax lay.

The silhouettes of the skeletal branches draped over the weapon but could not seize it. There was no hint of frustration on the part of the Nightmare Lord, though. Xavius could not touch it, but, where it lay, neither could it be of harm.

The low laugh of the Nightmare Lord echoed over the shrouded region. The shadow of the tree withdrew . . . and the mists covered the ax.

26

NIGHTMARE WITHIN THE NIGHTMARE

King Varian stood with the host, watching as the Nightmare flowed forth. There were things both distinct and indistinct within its murky airs, some recognizable, others not.

The gathered host awaited not only his signal, but that of Broll. Varian was not so vain that he thought his command of the situation absolute; indeed, he thought just the opposite. Like everyone, he had expected Malfurion Stormrage to be the one through whom the druids and their allies would coordinate with his army.

But when Broll had briefly touched his mind, telling him that it was he who was to be Varian's contact, the lord of Stormwind had not very much minded. The two had shared savage lives as gladiators and knew one another's ways well. Thus, when Broll finally warned that the moment had come, the pair easily slipped into their old roles as comrades in war.

The dreamform army surged forward to meet the darkness. As the Nightmare converged on them, shadow satyrs formed in multitudes, their claws sprouting more than a foot long.

Yet just before the first of the fiends could strike, the druids and other spellcasters gathered began their own assault. The druids led the efforts, for they knew the Dream and the Nightmare best. Silver fire lit the landscape, sweeping across the infernal ranks. Shadow satyrs by the scores burned to nothing.

In the chaos, Varian's followers struck. Their dreamform blades cut through satyr after satyr, but, unlike in the mortal world, the creatures did not re-form. Rather, like ribbons of sliced silk, they fell in tatters that were crushed underneath the encouraged defenders' feet, hooves, and paws.

The druids worked with what still thrived in the little part of the Dream remaining. The seeds of trees became a rain of furious missiles that landed within the Nightmare, then sprouted. Within seconds, new trees molded by efforts led by Broll and the druids grew tall among the satyrs.

One satyr slashed at the nearest trunk. The tree spurted a thick sap. The shadowy fiend pulled back with a hiss as the sap splattered it, despite the satyr's supposed incorporeality.

But it did not end there, for the areas touched by the droplets spread and as they did, they burned away the satyr. The shadow sought to flee what it could not. Within a few scant seconds, the sap had entirely eaten away at it.

The trees began to extrude sap from everywhere, especially their branches high above. A rain of searing droplets guided by the druids fell upon a vast swath of terrain. Shadow satyrs burned.

The collapse of the Nightmare's first lines energized the defenders. Though they suffered losses, there seemed hope after all. Bitter enemies willingly fought side by side with one another, even shielding those left open. Not since the War of the Ancients had so many diverse forces come together. Indeed, coupled with the addition of the creatures summoned by Malfurion and the rest of the druids, it could be said that Azeroth was even better represented as one in this moment than ever before.

But Varian and Broll were concerned over what seemed too simple a battle. Remaining linked through Broll's efforts, they passed on their wariness, their suspicions that the Nightmare was not to be so easily crushed.

And moments later their apprehension was vindicated. From the mist flowed the nightmare forms, as Broll had come to think of them . . . the hideous, cursed dream selves of the Nightmare's thousands of victims multiplied many times over. Drawn from the sleepers' subconscious, they came in macabre versions of the innocents, which made them all the more horrific to the defenders.

"We must not let what they appear to be slow us!" Broll urged Varian. *"They are only dreams!"*

"I know . . ." replied the king grimly, already seeing multiple versions of both his son and the nightmare of his dead wife. Varian thrust forward with his sword and led the way, cutting at the first image of his son. Even though the visions of his wife helped remind him that this was not the true Anduin, he still cringed as Shalamayne cleaved through and the figure vanished.

And that, they all knew, was also a part of the Nightmare's insidious intentions. Strip away the defenders' morale.

But under the king's guidance, the dreamform legions continued to press. There were costly hesitations along the way, but they could not be helped. Varian and Broll could only pray that seeing one's loved one madly attacking them over and over would not wear down the brave souls.

Then, a garbled cry arose from one of the defenders. Varian glanced to his side in time to see one of his own soldiers from Stormwind—his dreamform a paling green—clutch at his own throat. The stricken fighter dropped his weapon, which, also being a dreamform representation, faded away. With a last gasp, the soldier keeled over.

His dreamform dissipated before it could even strike the ground. There was no doubt in Varian's mind that the man had not simply woken up, but rather died . . .

A second fighter, a gruff orc warrior, grabbed at his stomach, then, like the human, tumbled over and faded away.

As a third perished, Varian desperately reached out for answers from Broll. To his surprise, however, a different voice, a different creature, touched his thoughts.

I am Hamuul, King Varian Wrynn . . . you must beware . . . the Nightmare now strikes against us in Azeroth in a manner that should not be possible . . .

What do you mean? the lord of Stormwind demanded. Two more of his army dropped. The others were beginning to take notice of the mysterious, debilitating threat in their very midst.

The sleepwalkers are attacking the slumbering bodies of those who make up your host . . . and somehow are causing your fighters' dreamforms to perish at the same time as their physical shells . . . again, it should not happen so! The dreamforms should remain "alive" . . .

The king bitterly recalled the nightmarish figures assaulting his men prior to Malfurion Stormrage's summons. He had feared that they would turn upon the still, helpless bodies of the defenders and now *that* nightmare had come to pass, with results even more terrible than he had imagined.

What do you suggest?

We must continue to fight . . . replied Hamuul. *We must continue to fight . . .*

Where is Broll? Varian asked . . . but the tauren did not say.

Another orc warrior collapsed and vanished. Varian let out a growl of exasperation and did as Hamuul bade. He had no choice. None of them had a choice.

Where is Broll? he continued to wonder as he desperately slashed again at his son and wife. *And* where *is Malfurion Stormrage?*

They stepped out into what was clearly not any land near Teldrassil and Darnassus. A corrupted Remulos had used his new master's power to drag himself and Malfurion far through the Dream/Nightmare.

Tyrande peered around, stunned. "Mal, where are we? Where is this desolation?"

The archdruid did not immediately answer, instead seeing to the unconscious Remulos first. When it was clear that the forest guardian was still out, Malfurion shifted to his true form, then surveyed what he could of their surroundings. The mists of the Nightmare were strong here, but there was something vaguely familiar about where they had stepped out. He was not surprised to find them near this place, considering that it coincided with the area Remulos had brought him, and had actually wanted to reach it . . . but like Tyrande, the desolation struck him hard.

"Close to where we must be, unfortunately," the archdruid cryptically replied. Indeed, now was the moment he had been waiting for, but not all those he needed—whether they wished to be a part of his plan or not—were where they had to be.

He looked again to Remulos. The catatonic presence of Cenarius's son was something for which he had not planned. "Tyrande, can you see that he is protected? We may have to leave him here for a time . . ."

Malfurion did not add that the last was based on the assumption that they survived what was to come. If not . . . it would not matter where Remulos lay.

The high priestess bowed her head and prayed. A moment later, Elune's soft light came down, piercing the mists. It settled on Remulos, draping him like a protective blanket. The forest guardian was completely covered.

"This will do him as good as anything," she solemnly promised.

At that moment, a voice he had been anxiously waiting to hear from briefly touched his thoughts. *I have a pair of roving fools for you . . .*

They are not fools . . . any more than you, Eranikus . . .

The green dragon's tone radiated his disagreement with Malfurion. *I was a fool long before you contacted me in secret while the cartographer rode upon my back! I was a fool to agree to any plan . . . and yet, I could not refuse . . . if only on the slim chance it could help rescue her . . .*

The archdruid had to push beyond Eranikus's self-recriminations and fast. Each moment meant that Xavius might divine his plan. *You have both Lucan and Thura with you . . . see now where I need them to go . . .*

After a moment Eranikus responded with a mocking grunt, *Ah, the irony! They were very near where you desired . . . indeed, the human still babbles about the "thing" in some fissure—*

No more! Malfurion warned. *I will speak with them . . .*

The archdruid reached out to the pair simultaneously. They were both startled, though Thura only momentarily. There was much bitterness in her mind at how he had used her. Though he had not had any choice, Malfurion radiated his sorrow for not only doing that, but being forced to demand more of them now. He quickly explained what he desired, incorporating factors both good and ill that his original plan had not contained.

They accepted his words in part for the same reason that Eranikus had . . . because to not accept was to welcome the Nightmare's victory. Still, there was courage behind that acceptance and Malfurion was grateful for it.

Only the green dragon was any question to the archdruid. Yet Eranikus promised to do his part . . . so long as the night elf proved himself able to do his own.

That left only Broll. It had taken mere seconds for all to pass between Malfurion and the others. Now he reached out to Broll, pulling him from the battle and leaving Hamuul in his place as guide between the Alliance and Horde elements that made up those led by King Varian and Azeroth's druidic defenders.

I hear you, my shan'do . . . Broll replied.

You are beyond being my student anymore, Malfurion reprimanded. *No student could I dare ask what I must ask you now!*

I'll do whatever you say.

Another who believed so much in Malfurion that it made the archdruid sad. Many had already died because of what needed to be done and many more likely would.

He explained what he needed and received immediate assurance from Broll. Hamuul could be trusted to keep matters coordinated with King Varian and the others. The tauren would make certain that the efforts by the defenders would not flag.

They dared not . . . not even though it was very likely that, by themselves, all those whom Malfurion had gathered would prove insufficient to stop the evil tide.

And so, with the others hopefully soon where he needed them, Malfurion at last knew that he had to tell Tyrande where they were. "This region looks much different now, but you must recall it."

The high priestess had been studying their surroundings during his brief contact with the others. Her expression had grown more and more troubled.

"I cannot shake a feeling . . ." Tyrande looked into his eyes, her own growing as wide as saucers. "Malfurion, this is not where—but Suramar was taken—"

"Yes," he murmured. "We are in Azshara . . . at the edge of what was once Zin-Azshari."

The high priestess shuddered, then her resolve steeled. "Where do we go?"

The archdruid pointed to her right. There, some jagged hills could just be made out in the mist. The smell of the sea—the Coral Sea, they both knew—permeated the air and in the distance they could hear the crash of waves against the great cliffs overlooking the dark expanse of waters. Waters where far in the past the legendary night elf capital and the Well of Eternity had existed.

Tyrande nodded, then frowned. "He should have been pulled into the sea with the rest of it, Malfurion . . ."

The archdruid's gaze narrowed in thought. "Yes . . . he should have been."

Expression grimly set, she started toward the hills. However, Malfurion seized her arm. "No, Tyrande . . . this must be done differently." ·

He threw aside the spear. Then, from his belt, the night elf removed what little bit remained of the branch that he had broken off. Malfurion had placed it there just before following Remulos.

To her surprise, he then sat down.

"Mal! Have you gone mad?"

"Listen to me," he urged. "Watch me close. I must do something that may put me at great risk, but it needs to be done if the others are to play their part. Be wary . . . he could easily choose that time to strike us down."

She eyed the mist. "It's very quiet here."

"And that is when the danger is greatest." Setting himself into a meditative position, Malfurion shut his eyes. "If I do this right, it will take only a moment."

Exhaling, the archdruid concentrated. Despite his concerns, he quickly began to sink into the state he required.

That which had once been the glorious Emerald Dream greeted him. Malfurion darted forward. His goal lay just ahead.

A shadow moved. It was not one of the satyrs, however, but rather that of the huge, wicked tree with the skeletal branches.

I have awaited your return . . .

He said nothing to the Nightmare Lord. Only a few yards remained—

The ground erupted. Malfurion's dreamform was thrown back. He kept his one hand tightly closed as he battled for balance.

The shadow limbs grabbed for him. Simultaneously, from the ground there issued forth grotesque figures, all of whom were recognizable to the archdruid as those whom he had known during the War of the Ancients.

Come join us . . . come join us . . . they echoed in his head.

Although he knew that they were phantasms, such was the power of his adversary that Malfurion had to struggle to remember that. Such visions had been what had initially set the night elf off guard enough for Xavius to capture him.

"Not this time," Malfurion muttered. The archdruid clamped both hands together and molded what he held in his palms.

From Malfurion's hands sprouted a long, silver staff. The shadow tree recoiled. Yet it was not the staff alone that caused the archdruid's foe to be taken aback, it was that the staff had been formed from the very essence of the true tree that was Xavius, the Nightmare Lord. Malfurion, with his ancient knowledge and long practice, had brought a part of the physical world with him when he had entered by dreamform. It had taken much strain, but the need was there.

Raising the staff above his head, Malfurion spun it around and around. Emerald and gold streaks of energy flew from the tips. The streaks ate away at the mist.

"From what has stolen the Dream will come its salvation!" the archdruid proclaimed.

The macabre branches of the shadow tree receded further into the mist. Malfurion pressed toward it.

The ghastly visions of his past swarmed him, but the staff cut through them as if they were air. They vanished with terrible sighs.

He came within sight of the ax but did not go near it. Rather, Malfurion continued after the shadow of the tree.

But the Nightmare Lord was no longer retreating. Xavius perhaps sensed what Malfurion had known from the beginning.

One long, bony shadow darted forth from the tree. The shadow limb sought the archdruid's chest. Malfurion had no choice but to defend. Staff and shade met in a brief, dark flash.

A tiny bit of the shadow fell away from the limb, immediately dissipating. Yet in the night elf's head, Xavius chuckled. The Nightmare Lord knew that he could not destroy what had been drawn from his physical essence, but neither was it sufficient to cause him harm.

The end of this little drama draws near, Xavius mocked. *And all you can do is fail and fail and fail, Malfurion Stormrage . . .*

The shadow suddenly expanded over the archdruid's view. The silhouettes of the skeletal branches again raked at Malfurion. One drew near the night elf's chest.

Malfurion took the staff and drove it point first down upon the shadow. However, his strike missed and instead he buried the tip in the ground.

The branches sought to crush him in their grip. They failed, but Malfurion released his grip on the staff.

Xavius's laughter came from everywhere. The shadows surrounded the archdruid.

Malfurion vanished—and woke.

But it was to find that the situation on Azeroth was little better.

"Mal! Praise Elune!" Tyrande cried.

All around them dark, massive tendrils thrust from the parched ground, racing toward where Tyrande had watched over a meditating Malfurion. They sought the archdruid and the high priestess like hungry leeches. Malfurion counted more than a dozen, with others adding to their number from the great fissures that now opened up.

Tyrande fended them off as best she could, the light of Elune having been shaped into a weapon resembling her favored glaive. The agile warrior leapt between the seeking tendrils—some as thick as the trunks of oaks—and threw the deadly weapon. It sliced at whatever drew too near her and Malfurion, then returned to her for another expert toss. In seconds, several severed pieces lay scattered around her, yet the archdruid noted that none of the main tendrils looked impaired.

He saw why a moment later when she managed to cut off another piece. The tendril immediately sealed over its wound and regrew its tip.

"Pull back!" Malfurion shouted to Tyrande.

But in her determination to protect both of them, the high priestess finally made a misstep. One of the tendrils seized her leg and sought to drag her toward a steaming fissure.

Malfurion threw himself to her side, but the tendril proved stronger than both combined. Tyrande's legs slipped into the fissure. She clutched at Malfurion as he tried to keep her from being pulled into the dark depths.

Slipping one hand to the offending tendril, the archdruid discovered that though it was of the plant world, it was also something more. He could not help but glance up in what he thought the direction of its true source. Even now it was impossible to see from whence what were not tendrils, but rather *roots* originated.

When Malfurion had been a prisoner of the Nightmare Lord, he had used his captivity to create roots that had stretched long enough to serve his purpose. Xavius, trapped as a tree for ten thousand years, had evidently done the same, only on a far more elaborate scale.

His roots stretched for miles around. Moreover, their mobility gave some hint as to how the tree could be where it was, instead of at the bottom of the sea where it belonged.

There was no time to cast a proper spell, no time to push against Xavius from a distance. Malfurion sought for assistance from Azeroth itself, but at first found only dead soil. There was nothing in it, no insects, no plant life . . . nothing. Xavius had fed on everything living in order to grow stronger, deadlier. The final, most visible part of the devastation had surely taken place only recently, though, for someone would have noted the dead land. The Nightmare Lord had been clever, likely eating his way up from beneath through his deadly roots, then finishing the rest when finally ready to strike.

And Xavius had been able to do all this in great part because of what he had been made into by Malfurion.

Both he and Tyrande struggled to keep her from not only being dragged under, but from the pair also being assailed by more roots. Malfurion managed to deflect them, but knew that the Nightmare Lord was inexorably pulling the high priestess deeper.

The archdruid thrust deeper with his mind, seeking the life that had to be somewhere. He refused to believe that Xavius had made a wasteland of this entire region, especially having done so slowly and in secret.

But what Malfurion found instead was something even more shocking than what Xavius had done to their surroundings. It was an evil so intense, so monstrous, that it nearly caused him to lose his grip on Tyrande. Only his love for her kept the archdruid from failing. Yet another piece of the puzzle fell into place. Now it was clear how Xavius's location had come to change.

Something welled up inside Malfurion. He sought again for Azeroth's life forces and finally found them. The archdruid drew upon them.

Thunder roiled. The ground shook anew.

Lightning suddenly flashed farther ahead, in the direction the Nightmare Lord truly lay.

The roots released Tyrande. However, the ground began to seal shut. Malfurion barely tugged her free before her legs would have been crushed by the fissure's sealing.

The pair half-dragged one another from the region of the tremor. The ground shook and high hills were created by colliding ground and rock.

"What is happening?" Tyrande shouted.

"There are two forces battering against one another! One comes from the Nightmare!"

"And the other?"

He did not answer her, though he knew the truth. Somehow, Malfurion had stirred up Azeroth as he never had before. It was fighting back against the evil that was Xavius.

No . . . the archdruid frowned. That was *more* than Xavius.

They ran until they could run no more. Behind them, great upheavals of land continued. Now it was not merely the mists that obscured much of what lay ahead, but immense clouds of dust and vapor.

And still it went on.

But though Malfurion had raised up a force that astounded even him, he felt no sense of hope. In delving deep near the fissures, Malfurion had gone farther than he had thought. He had not only touched near Azeroth's core, but also touched the place from which Xavius truly drew his sinister power. A place beyond both the mortal world and the Emerald Dream, but infesting both of them.

And in that foul place, he sensed something incredibly ancient— and somehow *familiar*—to him. The hardened archdruid shuddered.

There was another, darker force behind the Nightmare Lord . . .

27

Into the Eye

Humans, elves of different natures, orcs, dwarves, trolls, tauren, gnomes, draenei, undead, and more continued to struggle against a tide that proved relentless. Warriors, druids, magi, priests—they and those of other callings added each of those skills that made their particular path a worthy addition to the defenders' force.

Varian's dreamform army continued to sacrifice itself at the forefront, striking down the endless enemy and perishing not only by the satyrs' claws but also the increasing deaths of their physical hosts. Hamuul, who monitored all this, pondered hard on why the dreamforms did not live on despite the deaths of their physical bodies—as happened with druids—and could only assume that the Nightmare's terrible magic flowed from those killing blows back in Azeroth into the dreamforms by the inherent link between the two parts of each victim.

The druids fed their spells into the onslaught. Here, seeds exploded into cleansing silver fire. There, other druids in bear, cat, or other fearsome shapes used their magic-enhanced claws, teeth, and even roars to wreak what havoc they could on the servants of the darkness.

But still the tide slowed, stalled . . . and began to shift.

And then both those who remained on Azeroth or fought in the other realm discovered the next wave of evil. From the mists in either plane marched armies composed of shadow-possessed drakonid, lesser drakes . . . and other corrupted dragons.

Then . . . then came something that no druid, not even Malfurion could have expected.

The barrier between the Emerald Dream/Nightmare and Azeroth began to break down . . . and the two slowly started to meld into *one*.

The seemingly impossible melding caught Eranikus by surprise. He briefly lost control, then battled to both regain it and keep Thura and Lucan with him.

But as the dragon struggled, Lucan heard a voice calling out. It was not necessarily to him, but to anyone who would listen. There was something familiar about it, something that reminded him of those lost days when his slumber and his dreams had been gentle. He was drawn to it . . .

And, without thinking, he slipped from Eranikus's back. Yet he did not fall. Instead, Lucan dropped only a foot or two in the air, then felt as if something invisible tugged him along. Eranikus and Thura vanished—

And a moment later, the cartographer reappeared in an area most definitely part of the Nightmare. The shrieks and gibbering assailed his ears. Horrific shapes moved in the mists around him . . . yet they no longer disturbed Lucan so much. He picked himself up off the vermin-infested ground—ground that should have been hundreds of feet below the dragon and his riders and yet now was not.

Then . . . Lucan realized that there was something just ahead of him in the mists, something that, even though it lay in the midst of the Nightmare, still inexplicably filled him with some hope.

Daring the dangers of the Nightmare, he ran toward the sight. As he neared, he marveled at his find. The structures—an arrangement of vast domes—had not been built by men. They were too perfect. While he could not be certain from his angle, the "smaller" domes seemed to flank or surround an even greater one that, despite the foulness of the Nightmare, retained a wondrous golden color that strangely comforted him.

The cartographer was drawn to the golden dome. Despite his previous weariness, he picked up his pace. Lucan became so focused on the golden dome that he now barely even noticed the Nightmare. He only knew that he *had* to reach the structure.

How long it took him to reach it, the cartographer could not say nor did he care. A few minutes, hours . . . time meant nothing. All that mattered was that at last he came to the entrance . . . only to find it sealed by a darkness that he recognized as from the Nightmare.

The foul discovery brought him back to his true circumstances and almost made Lucan turn and run away again . . . but then he sensed that what had drawn him to this ethereal place was *inside*.

And it needed him . . .

The beating of wings from another direction made him suddenly dart around to the side of the structure. No sooner had he done so than a massive shape loomed overhead.

Though Lucan would have thought it impossible for him to identify any dragon by face, he was certain that it was the one called Lethon. The dark-scaled leviathan, his ghostly form shimmering with the same sickly green glow of the Nightmare, peered around as if suspicious.

The black, bottomless pits that were Lethon's eyes turned in Lucan's direction. The gaze stopped just short of where the human hid.

Lethon snorted, then departed the area.

The dragon vanished in the distance. Letting out a sigh, the harried cartographer leaned against the wall.

The wall shimmered.

He fell through.

Yet it was not into a room that he ended up, but rather a swirling mass of constantly bombarding magical forces that left him spinning out of control as he flew through it. Worse, Lucan felt his strength also beginning to fail him. He knew that soon he would not even have enough to stay conscious.

Be at ease, young Lucan . . . I will stave off the effects long enough . . . I hope . . .

He knew the voice, knew it even before his body turned in the direction of the source.

As with the human, the great dragon Ysera floated in the midst of the churning forces, albeit clearly more assailed by them. Her wings were spread wide and she was surrounded by a very thin emerald-green aura that constantly flickered, as if seeking to vanish. The long sleek dragon's eyes were shut tight, but she seemed to see him nonetheless.

Lucan sensed that the dragon was far from helpless, despite her captivity. She was still fighting—

But that was wrong. He had seen her utterly defeated. The Nightmare had taken her, bent her to its will . . .

Trust only lies to come from the Nightmare and its lord, Ysera answered to his unspoken question. *I am a prisoner, yes, but with some resistance . . . though fading, I admit . . .*

What is this place? he silently asked.

Her head twisted to the side. *Long ago, when Azeroth was new and we were first sent to protect it and the Emerald Dream, those of my flight honored me by naming the field and that created within it the Eye of Ysera . . . this became the place from which we watched over everything . . .* Her expression saddened. *Now, through Lethon's betrayal . . . it has become my prison . . .*

The Great Aspect suddenly rumbled in pain. Her body shook and for a breath became as that of a ghost.

Though the effort was futile, Lucan yet reached out a hand to try to comfort Ysera.

The line between the embattled Dream and Azeroth is blurring! she proclaimed in terrible worry. *Though I still fight, they are quicker and quicker leeching my will and adding my powers to the destruction of all!*

What can we do? the cartographer pleaded.

Drawing from what strength remained to her, Ysera replied, *Know the truth, Lucan Foxblood . . . I have been aware of you since Eranikus found you when you were an infant . . . I decided to see what could become of your unique birth . . . if anything . . . even Eranikus did not know . . . he simply acted as I knew his heart would make him . . .*

Lucan gaped. To his tired mind, the Aspect could have prevented all his troubles, kept him from this ability he had—

There was nothing I could do to change the circumstances of your birth, but perhaps . . . I acted with hubris in not giving you some . . . some sort of protection from early on . . . Ysera gasped again, then continued, *But there is no time for thinking of the past . . . I have been attempting to . . . to contact another . . . and nearly given up hope . . . but your very uniqueness may help me to reach him after all . . .*

Me? What can I do?

Again, the dragon suffered great agony and all but faded. *We are— reaching the point of no return!* she managed at last. *You may be the way to circumvent the Nightmare's spells that keep me from communicating with Malfurion Stormrage . . .*

Malfurion? I'll do anything, if it can help, even if it costs me my own life! the cartographer responded. He realized that he meant it. What was his life, if all else fell to the Nightmare?

Let us hope it does not come to that, the Aspect commented, again appearing to read his thoughts. Eyes still shut, she added, *Are you certain, Lucan Foxblood? Are you certain you understand the risk to you?*

He nodded.

I will seek to be as gentle as possible . . .

Ysera opened her eyes. Her gaze met the human's.

To the human, it was as if every dream that he had ever had began again. The eyes of Ysera carried within them a kaleidoscope of images all tied to Lucan . . . and every other creature that dreamed. He became a part of each one of those dreams and by doing so opened up the most hidden parts of his subconscious to the dragon . . .

Lucan Foxblood stared in awe as he was engulfed by the Aspect's will.

· · ·

We must return to Azeroth, Varian warned Hamuul. *Tell Malfurion Stormrage it must be so! They strike our bodies down even as we fight them here!*

The tauren acknowledged his words but did not otherwise reply. However, he immediately sought for Malfurion, seeking to warn him of the looming disaster.

Hamuul's concern reached Malfurion even as the night elf came to grips with the truth behind Xavius's astounding power. He had felt that ancient evil before and could never forget it. Small wonder that Xavius had accomplished so much; an even greater darkness worked through him.

But Malfurion still kept his wits about him, aware that to lose all hope was to lose everything. He listened as Varian's demand was relayed through Hamuul to him. The archdruid understood what the king desired and why. Malfurion cursed himself for having allowed it to happen; he had feared that Xavius would do just what he had— strike the unprotected mortal forms of the defenders.

As he drew Tyrande back, he told her what was happening and what he had to do. She nodded understanding, though her face filled with dread for all of them and pity for all that Malfurion had taken upon his own shoulders.

"Are we lost, then?" the high priestess bluntly asked, clearly having considered matters as he had. "Is all Azeroth lost?"

Before he could answer, another voice touched his thoughts, a voice he had prayed constantly that he would hear before it was too late.

Malfurion Stormrage . . . can you hear my words?

Mistress?

Yes . . . it is Ysera . . . listen to me . . . see me . . .

A living image suddenly filled his mind. He saw Ysera in her confinement, the Aspect struggling to hold back her full abilities from being utilized by Xavius and his secret master.

And in seeing that, Malfurion came to a realization about his foes and their nature. He understood that he had been about to make a critical mistake.

You see the truth, then . . .

Malfurion did . . . he also sensed that he was not alone with her in this conversation. There were two others. One was the human, Lucan, who somehow acted as Ysera's means by which to at least bypass her imprisonment enough to speak.

The other—the other was not supposed to be a part of this, but he had somehow sensed the communication . . . sensed it and been driven to fury by the discovery.

It is you! I felt it immediately! They keep you at the Eye! I should've known! The audacity . . . and the foolishness of them in the end . . .

Eranikus. Malfurion sensed that he had just set Thura down near where Broll would find her. Now, though, having sensed his queen's desperate contact with the archdruid, there was but one pressing thought in the male dragon's head . . . to free her.

Heed me, my mate, Ysera pleaded, seeking to stop him. *Your place is with the efforts of Malfurion—*

No! I will save you! Eranikus interrupted, his words coming so forcefully that they gave Malfurion and Lucan pounding heads. *I swear so!*

Ysera forbade him, but Eranikus refused to listen. Malfurion, caught between conflicting choices in the matter, started to speak with the male. However, before he could, a hand violently shook him, breaking contact.

"Mal! Beware!" Tyrande cried.

He focused on his surroundings again.

Shadow satyrs were everywhere.

No . . . these were not shadows. They were very solid, very real. These were living satyrs, including those of Queen Azshara's Highborne servants who had followed Xavius into damnation. Seduced by the power the reborn Xavius had wielded, they had given up their handsome forms for these monstrous ones, all to serve the ultimate cause of the Burning Legion's lord, Sargeras.

And their numbers seemed endless. Malfurion was stunned. Clearly, all this time, the satyrs had been hiding the truth, no doubt gathering in long preparation for these dire events.

My children have awaited their chance for glory! the Nightmare Lord gleefully mocked. *I have deigned to grant them such . . .*

The satyrs had horns and though their faces retained most of their original features from before their corruption, there was a bestial touch to the demons' expression. Savage grins revealed sharp teeth. Coarse brown fur covered their arms, backs, and hooved legs. They had shaggy manes and beards that added to their grotesque appearance and their eyes had a foul green cast.

It is him, indeed! Xavius declared to the oncoming satyrs. *The cursed Malfurion Stormrage . . .*

Several of the satyrs let out howls of anticipation as they charged the pair.

Tyrande took up a stand in front of the archdruid and threw the moonlight glaive.

"I know that you must focus on the true battle!" The high priestess shouted as the spinning weapon slashed through the first of the satyrs. The three sharp blades cut deep into two of the sinister creatures before returning to her. The glaive's victims fell, the upper halves of their torsos nearly severed from the bottoms.

The merciless and efficient strike caused the satyrs to falter somewhat as they tried to divine how best to get around Tyrande and the deadly blades.

But Malfurion did not want to leave her to face them by herself. "You can't hold them all off!"

"With the others' help, perhaps I can at least delay long enough!"

Before Malfurion could ask who she meant, Tyrande brought the glaive up in a salute and murmured something in the hidden tongue of the Sisterhood. At that moment, the satyrs regained their courage and charged.

The Mother Moon's light shone down in front of Malfurion, bathing both Tyrande and the areas to each side. As Malfurion stared, a line of glowing figures somewhat resembling priestesses in battle garb took up a stand with Tyrande. Indeed, each even bore some resemblance to her.

Tyrande had prayed to Elune for aid and it had come as she needed it, in the forms of guardians created from the moonlight. With glaives, bows, swords, lances, maces, staves, and other weapons, the gleaming line decimated the foremost satyrs. Yet more continued to pour forward.

Malfurion did not remain idle while Tyrande and those she summoned defended him. Aware that she was correct in her assumption that he had to focus on the true battle, Malfurion turned his attention on two things.

The first was to reinforce his original decision upon Varian and Hamuul. *The Nightmare must be fought in the Dream!* he pressed. *The core of the Nightmare's strength comes from the sleeping and from what it has thus far managed to tear from Ysera! Force it to draw its power there to defend itself!*

To their credit, they acquiesced. Still feeling guilty that so many would likely perish despite this being the best hope, Malfurion then reached out to Broll.

Have you found Thura?

Broll Bearmantle's response was immediate. *Yes, Shan'do! But she's not able to fight effectively here! Let's return her to Azeroth, then—*

No . . . you know what I need her to do.

As with Hamuul and King Varian, Broll agreed.

Malfurion looked to Tyrande again. She stood defiant against the odds, just as she had so often during the War of the Ancients. Face so very dark—the night elf version of being flushed—she threw the glaive again and again. The gleaming weapon severed limbs, cut deep into chests, and even removed the head of one satyr.

But the archdruid noted that the moonlight around her had grown slightly dimmer and as it did, so dimmed Elune's guardians beside her. It was not merely physical foes that the high priestess battled; Xavius was feeding his gathered power into the satyrs, strengthening especially those that fought Tyrande. She was the nexus around which the guardians drew their substance. If she fell, they would quickly dissipate.

Malfurion turned to the second of his problems. He quickly sought out the mind of the male dragon. *Eranikus! Think this through!*

No! I will not leave the Eye without her!

The night elf's view shifted. Malfurion saw through Eranikus's gaze as the Aspect's consort descended. The dragon was nearly at his destination.

The Eye was not as the archdruid recalled it. Even as Eranikus approached, its appearance wavered. The structures became jagged, toothy things that looked ready to impale the dragon. The buildings began to change places with one another.

They can't fool me! Eranikus said to him. *Hide her in a thousand such places and they will fail! She and I are linked again and this time nothing will ever sever the bond! I will always find her!*

Be wary! Malfurion called futilely.

Eranikus dove toward the least impressive of the structures. As he did, it suddenly began to grow.

You see? he said triumphantly. *She is in the great building, though they tried their best to make it look other—*

Malfurion, paying more attention to matters in the Eye beyond that of Ysera, noted a shift in the Nightmare. *Eranikus—*

Lethon materialized above the fixated dragon, then dropped upon him.

Welcome back, brother Eranikus! he mocked as his talons dug into the other leviathan. The corrupted dragon sent entrails of dark green energy into Ysera's consort.

Eranikus shrieked as his body pulsated madly. His scaled hide twisted and shifted as if some great worm bore through flesh and bone and sought to now burst to the surface.

Your greatest nightmare comes true . . . Lethon cooed. *Welcome back to the fold . . .*

Malfurion sought to maintain a link to Eranikus's mind, but although he managed to do that, the link was so weak that he could not sense what, if anything, the dragon thought. Moreover, none of his attempts to make Eranikus understand him succeeded, either. The archdruid feared that Lethon spoke true; Malfurion was well aware of Eranikus's dread concerning once more becoming one of the corrupted.

Indeed, the dragon moaned loudly as the foul energies of the Nightmare sank into him. Although still aloft, Eranikus curled as much as possible into a ball.

And then, with a raging roar, let loose his own power upon Lethon.

Caught overconfident, the corrupted behemoth hurtled back as the attack struck. With a painful roar of his own, Lethon went spiraling from the Eye of Ysera.

Again without hesitation, Eranikus returned his attention to where his queen was imprisoned. He sank all four sets of claws into the structure.

The prison shimmered. The green dragon was assailed by more of the Nightmare's taint. Eranikus's shape twisted, perverted, as the corruption sought to overwhelm him. Yet he steadfastly held on, pouring his own might into the edifice.

Already focused on so many directions, Malfurion could do little, but he gave Ysera's consort what support he could. Between the two of them, the spread of the taint toward the male dragon halted.

The prison shook. The attack on Eranikus abruptly ceased. The leviathan let out a triumphant growl.

But then a powerful force ripped him from Ysera's prison. Lethon, aglow with the Nightmare's awful energies, swooped down to batter his adversary.

Malfurion tried to help Eranikus regain his momentum, but the dragon now refused his aid, shouting in the archdruid's head, *No! She's nearly free! I'll hold him off while you finish it!*

The night elf could not argue. Freeing Ysera was far more important. She was the mistress of the Emerald Dream, bound to it and versed in its very essence. The Nightmare needed her to strengthen its connection to the Emerald Dream in order to manipulate its magic even more. Whatever the cost, Ysera had to be freed; the act would surely weaken the Nightmare's hold and, thus, further the defenders' chances. Indeed, Malfurion could now sense the Aspect herself testing her weakened cell. Eranikus was correct; there was far greater hope now of success.

Concentrating, the archdruid attempted to draw from both Azeroth and the stricken Emerald Dream as much as he could. He was surprised at how easy those forces, especially from the latter realm, came at his request. Then Malfurion decided that it could not be by his doing alone; Ysera had to be assisting somehow.

As he struggled alongside the Aspect to free her, Malfurion felt Eranikus's battle continue. The two dragons grappled, their power washing over one another. Neither at first seemed to have the upper hand, though the night elf feared that before long their surroundings would finally grant that to the corrupted beast.

He felt Ysera pushing harder from within. Yet her concern was not for herself, but rather her consort, Malfurion, and Lucan.

Save him first, for he is not bound by any of the Nightmare's spells as I am, she commanded of Malfurion, indicating the human. Although he had been able to enter the golden dome, it seemed that now Lucan was too exhausted to make use of his odd abilities. His rescue was the least of problems for Malfurion, who was able to bring the cartographer back to Azeroth and near where Hamuul stood.

Ysera pressed harder. The barrier weakened. Malfurion could feel it straining . . .

No . . . not quite! Lethon, manipulating the powers of his master, nearly crushed the efforts of the pair. Malfurion's mind became awash in fear-stirring images of all his actions creating greater disaster for those he sought to protect. The archdruid knew that they were nightmares raised up by the darkness, but it took tremendous effort to not only deny them but still maintain the assault on the Aspect's cell.

Lethon abruptly cried out. Through his own thoughts, Malfurion caught images of a very scarred, half-distorted Eranikus gripping his corrupted counterpart through both claw and magic. Eranikus had clearly been much ravaged by the other, but sheer determination for the moment swayed the fight to his direction.

But that could surely not last long. Reluctantly, Malfurion started to abandon the efforts to free Ysera.

NO!! Eranikus thundered in his head. *She must be saved! I will finish with Lethon!*

Lethon apparently caught this, for the tainted behemoth laughed at such hubris. The power of the Nightmare filled him. He was now larger than the consort.

It is you who are finished, Eranikus! Give in to the Nightmare! Let it embrace you! The walls between Azeroth and here are also weakening! Soon, I and the others like me will be able to fly Azeroth's skies unimpeded . . .

Azeroth's skies . . . Eranikus repeated.

A glow suddenly surrounded Ysera's mate. The dragon's face bore a grim aspect. At the same time, Lethon's expression grew uncertain.

What do you do? he demanded of Eranikus.

But the other dragon said nothing. Instead, Malfurion sensed him drawing upon other energies. Only then did the archdruid understand Eranikus's ploy.

And as both titanic figures began to fade, so, too, did Lethon understand . . . but much too late. *You can't! Do this and you'll destroy yourself, too! I swear! The instability will take you with me!*

So be it, then, Malfurion heard Eranikus reply.

My mate! Ysera called . . . but too late.

The Nightmare sought to make both this realm and Azeroth one. Then the power of this realm would be impossible to overcome.

But that shift had not yet completed . . . and here, in the vicinity of the Eye, a nexus of the Emerald Dream, Malfurion saw that the shredding boundaries between the two realms were so unstable that to be at the center was to invite annihilation.

Eranikus refused to release the corrupted creature. The pair crossed into the instability suddenly existing between the two realms.

As Lethon had warned and Malfurion and Ysera feared, the desperate villain drew the power of his master into himself in a futile attempt to avoid the inevitable, but it was too late.

The monster howled as he was torn asunder. The fearsome forces that he in turn had been summoning were unleashed.

A fiery maelstrom erupted where Lethon had been. That maelstrom swallowed up Eranikus, who made no move to escape it.

The wild forces struck out everywhere. Malfurion felt Ysera urge him to do something to contain them. Not certain what she expected of him, the archdruid nevertheless tried.

A desperate plan came to him. He managed to steer those energies to a chosen spot.

They struck Ysera's prison, reducing the center of the Eye to nothing but vapor . . . and freeing at last Ysera.

Roaring her relief at her release, the mistress of the Emerald Dream rose above what remained of the place of her confinement. An emerald aura surrounded her, an aura that briefly brightened the entire Eye.

But mists began converging on her, seeking to recapture. Ysera let out another roar and the aura trebled in scope. Whatever it touched suddenly returned to the full, lush life and beauty for which the Emerald Dream was known. The mists immediately retreated—

And in that precious moment, the Aspect vanished.

Malfurion no longer sensed her in the other realm. Instead, Ysera had retreated to Azeroth. Aware more than any how the bonds between the two places worked, she materialized near the druids fighting out of Darnassus.

Thank you . . . Malfurion Stormrage . . . she said with much sadness. *You . . . and Eranikus . . .*

He did what he had to, the archdruid replied quickly, honoring the male dragon's sacrifice but aware of so many other sacrifices taking place even now. Still, his hopes were high, now that the mistress of the Emerald Dream was free, Xavius had no powerful captive. With Ysera's power to guide them—

No—Malfurion—I fear—I fear that there is little I can offer you . . . the effort to keep the Nightmare from utterly using me has drained me more than—I—imagined . . .

The words so stunned Malfurion that he almost lost his link to the others. He had waited for this hope! What power was greater than hers when it came to the Emerald Dream and the taint spreading through it? The only reason that she had not been able to vanquish the Nightmare before had been due to his own foolish capture. If not for Xavius being able to draw upon his meager abilities, none of this chaos would have happened—

Un-untrue, Malfurion! It was clearly an effort for Ysera to stay conscious. *You know the forces at work here and how long that they have been in play!*

But what does it matter? he retorted. *If even you are not able to put an end to this, we are lost!*

The Aspect was losing consciousness. It was all she could do simply to protect herself. *There is hope . . . I am . . . I am of the Emerald Dream . . . but you . . . you are of the Emerald Dream . . . and Azeroth! In that . . . there is a chance—*

What do you—

She broke contact. The Aspect had failed in her battle to remain conscious. The strain had been too much.

And as her thoughts vanished, the Nightmare Lord's laugh seemed to echo in Malfurion's head.

Ysera had left the fate of both realms to Malfurion . . . who had no idea what he could do.

28

BEFORE THE TREE

Broll Bearmantle struggled to keep Thura from racing ahead of him. The orc insisted that she had to push on, even though they were in possibly one of the worst places of all.

The night elf was here because Malfurion needed him here. Malfurion had not said exactly why, but Broll trusted in his shan'do. Still, he wished he knew why the orc was also desired. Thura had no useful weapon and her headstrong ways were going to get her taken by the Nightmare.

"It's this way!" she snarled, not for the first time. "This way!"

They had not been impeded other than by the cloying tendency of the mists. Broll did not think that good fortune. The Nightmare likely did not believe them much of a threat by themselves, and the druid was inclined to share that opinion.

What are you planning, Malfurion? Broll wanted to know. *What?*

Ahead, the mist suddenly did a new and disturbing thing. It receded. Not all of it, but a fairly wide path more than sufficient for the pair to move side by side.

And Thura, of course, headed right into it.

"Hold back!" the druid called.

But she ignored him, instead picking up her pace. "There it is!"

Broll, more concerned with their lives—and their spirits, should the Nightmare take them—did not at first understand what she wanted. Then he saw the ax.

The magical ax. Small wonder that Thura wanted it. With the weapon, she could confront the shadows and nightmares.

But the druid doubted that regaining the ax would prove so simple as merely picking it back up.

Thura reached for it . . . and the ax flared emerald green.

At the same time there was a sound of rage. Broll spun, for the rage came from all around them. At first he feared it some new manifestation of his own, old rage, the raw fury that he had fought and defeated only by great effort during a previous journey into the Emerald Dream. However, almost immediately, the druid knew that the rage had a different, more terrible source. The Nightmare Lord was angry.

He could not understand why. The orc appeared either unable or unwilling to touch the ax now. That surely benefited the unseen evil.

"What's wrong, Thura?" he muttered. "Is it that you can't pick it up? You won't?"

The orc shook her head. She glanced back at the night elf, revealing an expression of deep confusion. "I—I don't know, druid . . . I don't . . . know . . ."

And even as she revealed that, the mist closed about them. Broll sensed the Nightmare Lord's anger focus upon them. Even though it had clearly been able earlier to strip the ax from Thura, it evidently could not use it. Thus, it had waited for someone it had expected *would* be able to do so.

"You will wield it yet, orc," came a voice that made the druid shudder, for he knew who spoke. *"And through you, this ax will become our weapon instead . . ."*

A great fist materialized out of the mists, a thing covered in festering bark. Carrion bugs crawled over and into it. It struck Broll hard in the side. He went tumbling from the orc.

Gnarl stepped forth from the hungry fog. The corrupted ancient grinned. His eyes were the madly shifting colors of the Nightmare. Jagged branch growths jutted all over his body and the wicked leaves that Broll had seen in his early visions—Malfurion's attempts to reach out—now covered much of the creature.

"I won't use such a weapon for you!" Thura roared defiantly.

"*You will . . .*" he responded, in a voice that was as much the Nightmare Lord's as it was Gnarl's.

The ancient reached for her. Thura sought to move, but the ground was again awash in the carrion bugs and the orc lost her footing. As she fell, what first appeared to be black worms burst from the ruined ground. Yet they were not worms but, rather, the shadows of roots.

The roots of a skeletal tree.

But even though shadow, they sought to bind the orc as if strong rope. She struggled.

Broll rose. He had constantly been expecting attack, though not from Gnarl. That had enabled him to be in part ready. Still, the strike had momentarily knocked the air out of him.

He threw himself at the ancient, transforming in his leap to cat shape. Even still, he was a small foe against Gnarl.

The corrupted ancient sought to swat him again, but Broll was more dexterous. He twisted as he approached, sending himself lower than the huge fist. Simultaneously, the druid raked his foe's nearest leg.

Gnarl bellowed in pain and anger. Forgetting Thura, he turned to where the cat landed.

"*The Dream and Azeroth will soon belong to the Nightmare . . .*" Gnarl/ the Nightmare Lord rumbled. "*And for you, night elf, there will come a particularly dread, eternal vision . . .*"

Shadow figures began to converge on the cat from all directions. Broll peered past them to Thura. She kept one hand free, a hand that was just within reach of the ax. If she could only take it—

No! Broll would have realized the truth then even if he had not just witnessed one shadow root *avoid* the lone free hand. *The Nightmare wants her to seize it without thinking!*

The Nightmare could not for some reason take the weapon itself, nor could any of its corrupted. However, it clearly thought that it *could* make use of the ax through Thura once she had it.

He tried to warn her, but the shadows became satyrs who swarmed him. Broll was buried under their evil. His last view was of Gnarl turning to watch what Thura would do.

Shan'do! the druid called out in his thoughts. *Malfurion!*

But there was no answer.

Malfurion heard Broll's warning and tried to respond, but only a terrible emptiness greeted his attempt. At first, he feared that Broll was dead . . . or, worse . . . but then the archdruid understood that the Nightmare Lord was seeking to keep the two from contact. That could only mean that Xavius had divined much of Malfurion's original intentions, which put what was left of the night elf's ultimate plan in jeopardy.

But then, Malfurion was not even certain if what remained had ever had any hope. It had relied in part on the assumption that Ysera would be there to coordinate it. As a student of the druidic teachings and a seeker in the Emerald Dream, Malfurion had been like the rest of his brethren in seeing in the Mistress of Dreams the ultimate guiding force when it came to the intertwined natures of the two realms.

Ysera was still unconscious, though, and Malfurion knew that it was not by any fault of her own.

Tyrande and the guardians continued to present an impenetrable defense against the satyrs, whose bodies lay piled three high in some places. Yet both she and the guardians glowed far less now and some of the ethereal priestesses were very transparent.

She was relying on him to save them. They were all relying on him to save them. And though they did not understand it, he was relying on them every bit as much. They were all needed if he was to succeed, if he was to save Azeroth. Malfurion gritted his teeth and reached out to one last hope.

He touched Alexstrasza's thoughts, but any hope that she might be of aid faded immediately. The dragon was under siege. Fearsome energies assailed the portal from the other side, and for brief moments a part of it sealed off, only to be opened anew by the straining dragon's efforts as she fought back the attempt by the Nightmare Lord.

Malfurion wondered why sealing this last portal still mattered so much to Xavius. It seemed a small thing now . . .

The Life-Binder all but threw her thoughts at the night elf. *The attack here has come with more and more fury! The Nightmare Lord needs the portal sealed! It takes all my power to keep it from succeeding! I can do nothing more for you!*

He had not yet even asked, but she had known why he had reached out to her. Confronted by yet another setback, Malfurion's resolve weakened.

The red dragon said something more, but now other voices in his head were demanding to be heard. King Varian and his army were in terrible straits, their physical selves falling more and more prey to the Nightmare's slaves on Azeroth. Broll's fate was still a mystery, and Hamuul managed only a brief alert that corrupted servants of nature—ancients, dryads, and more—were pressing the druids and Lucan, who stood willing to fight under the tauren's guidance.

Xavius—and the true lord of the Nightmare—were poised for triumph.

And a more immediate aspect to that horrific possibility was represented in Tyrande, who, in seeking to protect the one she not only loved but believed was essential to Azeroth's survival, was now harried as never before. The high priestess dropped to one knee as she fought to keep three satyrs from ripping her to shreds. As she struggled, first one, then a second of the moonlight guardians faded like so many of Malfurion's hopes.

With savage abandon, the satyrs surged forth to take both Tyrande and Malfurion.

The catastrophe overwhelming Azeroth and the Emerald Dream was forgotten. Malfurion saw only that Tyrande was doomed unless he did something. Nothing else mattered. In fact, at that moment, he cared not a whit whether Azeroth, whether *everything* survived, if it meant that she who he loved perished.

Guilt swelled up within him, guilt such as he had not felt before. Not for the first time, Malfurion saw in his mind all the trials through which he had put Tyrande and how over and over she had stood steadfast in her support of him. He also recalled those few precious times when they had been allowed peace and seclusion. Malfurion especially treasured the building of the night elves' first new capital after the War of the Ancients. Through his druidic skills and her prayers to Elune, they had fashioned a great, living pergola at the center outwardly honoring their peoples' new beginning, but also secretly marking their own deep relationship. The oaks had been encouraged to grow intertwining with flowered vines circling around each part, then Elune's power, through her high priestess, had gifted them with a soft, white-blue glow that made the pergola radiate a sense of calm to whoever passed underneath it.

It was a small thing, a minor thing in the measure of their titanic struggles through the ages, but perhaps that was why Malfurion cherished it so much. It was something they had done together for simple, pure reasons. They could have done much, much more together, if not for him. She should have forever rejected him for all the long absences he had so callously taken over the many millennia . . . but she had not. Despite all her other duties—and they were extraordinary—Tyrande had always been there waiting.

And now she would die because once again *his* duties had taken precedence over her.

"Not this time . . ." the archdruid rumbled. "Never again!"

Hands clenched, Malfurion summoned up as best he could the innate forces that he and Ysera had together gathered to help her escape. A maelstrom of energies rose up from the ground, while others descended from the hidden sky.

The ground swelled. A forest of green burst up, enveloping both the front lines of the satyrs and Tyrande. However, where the fiends were swallowed up, the high priestess was softly carried aloft by the sudden growth, then guided by sprouting branches toward her love.

In devouring all he could from the land around him, Xavius had left small dried seeds from his many victims, things so inconsequential that the Nightmare Lord had not even noticed them. But Malfurion's druidic powers had found them, no matter how deep or long they had been buried. The archdruid had not only resurrected their potential, he had unleashed it.

Where the forest had been gentle with Tyrande, it had dealt sharp, harsh death to many of the satyrs. Dozens hung pierced, impaled, for Malfurion had no time for niceties. They had perished swiftly; that was the best he could give them.

Yet still more came and Malfurion, fearing that they would still reach his beloved, asked of Azeroth more of its power. He reached out to Teldrassil and even Nordrassil and, to both his relief and tremendous gratitude, they, in turn, gave as he needed . . . even though Nordrassil still struggled to recover from the last war with the Burning Legion.

Trebling in intensity, the wind shrieked loud and long. A score of satyrs were blown into the deadly forest, joining their fellows. At last their ranks hesitated. This was not the easy victim that their "god" had promised; this was the accursed one in strength as they could not believe.

But in Malfurion's eyes, this hesitation was not enough. They had threatened Tyrande. He swept them back from where they stood and brought Tyrande nearer.

But at that point the high priestess called to him, "Worry not about me! The others need you more!"

Malfurion did not lessen his efforts to protect her, but he understood her meaning. Indeed, the very fact that he had considered her life and hers alone of the most importance filled him with a renewed sense of his own life, not the one that he had dedicated to his world. He had found new strength in protecting that thing most precious to Malfurion Stormrage the night elf, not the great archdruid of legend.

As he had done with Azeroth, a steeled Malfurion now extended his will into the Emerald Dream and sought to draw more of its essence in order to help stave off the Nightmare. When the Emerald Dream gave to him as he asked, he was relieved. With its added energies, the archdruid swept back the mists before Varian's dreamform army. The green fields grew anew.

Yet, of more significance, not only did the shadow creatures fighting Varian's force fade as the mist did, but so, too, did the *dream* slaves. No longer did the defenders also battle the images of their former comrades and loved ones. Like the shadows, it was as if they had never existed.

A sensation coursed through Malfurion as the last happened, a sensation of utter calm. He knew its source, knew that Tyrande prayed to Elune to let the high priestess's love in turn act as not only shield for Malfurion, but also new resolve to aid him further. The calm and the love with which Tyrande touched his heart gave Malfurion the impetus to push even further beyond what he had expected to be his limits. This time the archdruid extended his will into Azeroth and the Emerald Dream simultaneously.

It worked. With Tyrande's presence and power reassuring him within, rather than feel overwhelmed, the night elf actually found himself *stronger* and more refreshed as the two realms added more to his attack.

He could not also help but finally turn his thoughts to Ysera, certain that she also remained an integral part in enabling him to cope with such power. But, to his astonishment, the gargantuan dragon was still in a dangerous state of exhaustion and pain and certainly not *aware* enough to have been of any aid.

The discovery jolted Malfurion. The revelation meant that it was only he and Tyrande who kept the Nightmare at bay here. That should have been impossible—

The thought vanished as the ground under his forest churned. The new trees and other remarkable plants that he had urged to fruition were undermined.

Gargantuan red roots tore at the area, heaving up trees and satyrs alike. Several of the trees went flying toward the archdruid.

Transforming to cat form, Malfurion nimbly leapt to avoid the deadly rain. As he moved past Tyrande, she jumped atop. Although the high priestess was very weary, she continued to use Elune's gift to protect them as best she could. Moonlight blinded the satyrs pouring through the gaps made by the roots and kept the nearest of the roots themselves at bay, if for a few critical moments.

The archdruid brought her to a place of temporary safety, then reverted. "You need to leave."

"Be sensible! Where would I go? All Azeroth is under siege! If the end is to come, then, by Elune, I will be with you at the last! We have lost too much time together!"

"And all of it my doing," agreed Malfurion.

"That's not what I—"

The ground thundered again. More roots shot up near their feet. Tyrande quickly threw her glaive, which sliced the nearest root. The effort left her gasping, but she did not falter.

Malfurion reached into his dwindling stock of herbs and powders. He cast a fine spray of green spores at the encroaching roots.

As the spores touched, the archdruid encouraged their activity. Small, burrowing tendrils blossomed from each. The spores began drilling into the roots.

The roots writhed as hundreds of holes developed. One root dropped. From several of the holes dripped the thick, bloodlike fluid.

But that same fluid filled the holes in the remaining roots. The tiny, parasitic plants were cast out, their forms now shriveled.

Futile . . . it is all futile . . . Xavius echoed in his head. *Everything is becoming Nightmare . . .*

It was true. No matter where Malfurion sought out some hope, some help, he found none. King Varian's army was losing. Broll could not be found, and lost with him was the orc. Ysera was unconscious, and Alexstrasza's control over the one portal was slipping. The Nightmare was everywhere, both in the Emerald Dream and Azeroth. It was all lost—

Malfurion let out a roar . . . but one of anger, not despair.

"You nearly had me again, Xavius!" he shouted at his devious foe. Despair and fear were the greatest weapons of the Nightmare. Xavius—no doubt with the power of the ancient evil to reinforce his will—had fed Malfurion's uncertainties well. "But no more!"

Tyrande gripped his shoulder. Her love amplified Elune's gifts to him. Glaring at his unseen foe, the archdruid called upon the two realms, seeing if they could grant him just a bit more strength.

He felt the additional energies flow into him. Malfurion focused his will.

The sky crackled with lightning, which struck the upturned soil. The roots slithered back into their holes . . .

In Stormwind City, Orgrimmar, and other embattled capitals, the winds picked up with a directed force, striking those that were a threat and leaving untouched the sleeping fighters made defenseless by Malfurion's need for them in the Emerald Dream. Yet the arch-druid did what he could to protect those victims of the Nightmare who now unwittingly served it. They were buffeted together, packed so tight that they could bring no harm to each other.

Yet the shadow satyrs, the mists, and the corrupted still assailed the dwindling defenders. And even though the living puppets had been pushed back, their nightmares had substance in the Emerald Dream and even upon the mortal plane. Xavius's power had grown that terrible.

Sweating from effort, Malfurion fought against all those aspects of his foe. Winds arose everywhere, even the Emerald Dream. Whether shadow or corrupted, the Nightmare's servants were held from advance.

But still it was not quite enough.

"It will never end unless I go to him!" Malfurion informed Tyrande. "I must strike at the heart of the darkness . . . Xavius is the key . . . without him, even the ancient evil behind his foul work cannot hold the Nightmare together . . ."

The high priestess eyed the satyrs and the roots, which had not given up their attempts to reach them. Only Malfurion's constant efforts kept them at bay. Tyrande hefted her weapon of moonlight. "Very well . . . let us begin . . ."

"You are not coming with—"

"I will follow you. You cannot do this alone and you know that. It is beyond merely you."

She had the truth of it. It was not for him alone to either save the world or fail. Surrendering, Malfurion turned to face their enemies. "I do not deserve you."

"No, you don't," she replied with a forced chuckle.

Inhaling, the archdruid stretched forth a single hand.

Wind and lightning attacked. Now rain also joined them.

The satyrs retreated. The roots sought in vain to avoid the lightning and three were left burning hulks.

A way opened.

"Now!" Malfurion became a cat again. Tyrande mounted. The archdruid raced on at breakneck speed, leaping atop and over the ruined landscape. Satyrs lunged, only to have claws, entire limbs, and even heads lopped off by the skilled priestess's flying glaive. Malfurion trampled others who sought to bar his path, clawed those who stood their ground, and bit through the torsos of yet more.

Roots constantly sought for his legs or to snag Tyrande from his back. Malfurion twisted out of their reach and Tyrande severed more than one grasping tip. The path grew slick, but his claws better caught purchase than the satyrs' cloven hooves. The landscape sped by.

And, finally, something ominously familiar broke through the mist ahead. It was still far from the pair and yet so gigantic. Indeed, Malfurion realized that it was far taller than most normal trees and that its branches, seemingly empty of life from this distance, stretched along the horizon. It was not Teldrassil nor any of the Great Trees . . . but it was a thing of titanic proportions.

And as twisted as the shadow had been, it failed to fully reveal the dread majesty of the true tree. There were hundreds, thousands of smaller branches, all as wicked as the great ones and as the pair approached, they were at last able to perceive that there *were* leaves. Yet unlike the World Tree's corrupted leaves, these were long, arched, and to Malfurion's heightened gaze, very much shaped like a reaper's sharp sickle. Moreover, as Malfurion brought himself and Tyrande nearer yet, it became evident that both the leaves and the tree itself were not black, as first it had seemed . . . but the same deep red color of the "sap" that flowed through.

It was not the tree into which a much younger Malfurion had

transformed his adversary thousands of years ago. That one had been a symbol of renewal, something that would bring life where Xavius sought death. Malfurion had meant to return to it after the war in order to see to its growth, but then had thought it lost with Zin-Azshari.

But how did this abomination remain hidden from us? Malfurion wondered, then thought of the ancient evil lurking behind Xavius. It surely had extended much of whatever power it had in Azeroth to shield the tree from everyone's senses.

The dark force behind the Nightmare Lord must have been able to reach Xavius shortly after Malfurion had left the new tree, for what it had become had surely taken many millennia. It showed the insidious patience of not only the former counselor, but his monstrous master. Only when it had been powerful enough, dread enough, had there been no more concern for hiding the truth of its presence.

As if a tremendous wind gusted, the branches suddenly moved as one toward where the pair raced. Despite the great distance still separating the tree from them, the branches stretched closer and closer . . .

And were nearly upon them.

Malfurion sensed the ground move again. Growling a warning to Tyrande, he threw them to the side. The roots shot up just where they had been, spearing so high that they nearly collided with the foremost branches.

A sinister swishing sound cut through the air. The archdruid twisted in mid-jump. More than a dozen smaller branches passed within inches of them, each covered in the long sickle leaves. Malfurion did his best to avoid all, but two caught him.

The leaves sliced into his skin and he heard Tyrande gasp.

The cat spun. The path behind briefly filled his gaze. There was now a wall of roots cutting off the two from any escape and satyrs were eagerly spilling through the one gap left.

Xavius had wanted them to come to him.

"Beware!" Tyrande shouted. Her glaive sliced through three branches before the deadly leaves could touch the duo.

Malfurion made a decision. He was still in contact with the others, still trying to guide them. The strain was tremendous, but the archdruid knew that he needed to do even more.

With a growl, he warned Tyrande of his need to change form again. The high priestess expertly slipped off while still using her whirling glaive to cut at whatever branch snagged at them.

Once again himself, Malfurion looked into both Azeroth and the Emerald Dream. He had to seek deeper this time, both within the two realms and himself.

The sky roared. It roared not just above them, but *all* over Azeroth, *all* over the Emerald Dream/Nightmare. Malfurion straining more, paid it little mind.

Yet his attack was not focused on his enemy, not directly. Rather, Malfurion concentrated on the ones he needed most.

Broll . . . Thura . . .

This time, he could sense them. This time, he could feel the other druid's struggle to keep them from falling to the Nightmare.

Shan . . . do . . . came the weak but still determined response.

The time is now . . . the tools are in place . . . the branch I gave you, this is the truth about its origins and what we need to do . . . Malfurion showed him.

Broll drank in what was revealed and to his credit accepted it immediately. He trusted in the archdruid completely. *I am . . . ready . . .*

It was all Malfurion needed to hear. Over the continuous rumble, he shouted to Tyrande, "Take yourself from here! I must end it now! I cannot promise—"

"No! We live or die together!"

He knew better than to argue. The archdruid looked within himself one last time.

And suddenly . . . the storm stirred again.

29

THE TWO TREES

Broll had expected to fall, but somehow he had been able to stave off the attack not only on his physical body, but also, more insidiously, his mind. The Nightmare sought him for its own, aware that he was one prized by Malfurion. Cries assailed him and his thoughts filled with visions of his dying daughter and his own guilt over her demise. It was a well-calculated assault, for Anessa had always been his weak point.

But no more. Having witnessed the horrors of the Nightmare, Broll condemned himself for having fallen prey to it through her death. He did not honor her memory by doing so. Broll had not seen that until he had seen so many others suffering because of their lost loved ones. The Nightmare had been particularly good at twisting its victims' minds and turning love into torture.

The druid cast a handful of powder mixed from plants known for their fiery qualities. As the powder touched his dark foes, it sizzled. The shadows burned away, their vanishing accompanied by tormented hisses. Broll looked for Thura, expecting the worst, but the orc squatted next to him, her eyes closed, but otherwise well.

"I have an oath to fulfill . . ." she said flatly. "I will fill it . . ."

Broll scattered the mist from them and for the first time saw that there was not only the ax, but another, odder object nearby. It was a thing that had once been alive but no more, and the one who had brought it to this place had planted it carefully, though not with any hope or desire of seeing it bloom.

It was a branch. A foul thing that Broll instantly knew well. He also understood why it had been placed here. The plan still had a chance.

And even as he thought that, the storm swept over their area. Yet Broll felt no fear from it, no concern whatsoever. He knew its source and that it existed to protect, not harry, him and the others.

The druid seized the branch. To that from which it had originally been plucked—so that it could then be grafted on Teldrassil—the branch was nothing anymore. Dead.

But it was still of the Nightmare Lord's essence. "Thura! You must grab the ax at the same moment as I strike!"

To her credit, the orc warrior understood immediately. Broll then began a distasteful spell. It was possible for those who were strong to nurture from seemingly dead plants, even trees, some measure of life. For any true plant, Broll would have had no qualms trying, though he also understood the limits.

But now he sought to revive something monstrous. His shan'do had revealed all concerning the truth about the branch and the tree from which it had originally come. Broll could sense the wrongness, the demonic essence, even in this tiny piece. This was not a thing of nature anymore; this was an atrocity.

But as he began his spell, Broll also sensed the other, more ancient evil of which Malfurion had also warned him, the ancient horror that had added its own infernal influence into the creation of the Nightmare Lord.

The spark he sought was there. Broll urged it on, even though the wrongness magnified.

The branch shook, fighting his grip.

"Now!" the druid called, raising the branch.

Thura grabbed for the ax, which still glowed both from its own good power and the Nightmare's malevolent forces.

The orc's hand and the branch touched the glow at the same moment. That was what was needed for the defenders. It broke what hold the Nightmare had on the weapon, strong enough to keep the ax there, but not enough to corrupt the enchanted artifact. Cenarius had forged the ax that pure and Brox, by his deeds, had made it more so.

And Thura, chosen in part by Malfurion, was an apt successor.

She took up the weapon. Broll tossed aside the branch, which, bereft of his spell, could not survive. He shifted form, becoming a cat.

Thura leapt atop. He carried her forward. The shadow of the tree stretched to take them, but the storm struck hard, bending back the smoky branches and washing away the foul mists. Lightning burned away shadow creatures and even set some of the intangible branches aflame.

Broll marveled at what he saw. He had witnessed large convocations create storms when rain was necessary, but none so huge or so directed. *Surely, Malfurion must have all the other druids focused on this!*

However his shan'do had managed this, it behooved Broll and Thura to reach the shadow tree. The fiendish silhouette rose over them—

A huge hand swatted both aside. Gnarl seized a stunned Thura, who still held tight the ax.

"All will be nightmare . . ." the corrupted ancient grated.

As Broll rolled to a halt, he became a night elf again. Teeth clamped from pain, he managed to cast a spell.

The ancient was a plant in nature. Even corrupted, he was covered in tremendous if now malignant growth. Still, that growth was yet susceptible to a skilled student of the druidic arts.

Stunted growths became thick, curling vines that within seconds ensnared the ancient's limbs. Those near the hand that clutched Thura tightened, forcing Gnarl's hand to open.

The orc dropped to the ground, landing on her feet. She wavered, but then steadied.

Gnarl struggled. Some of the vines holding his legs and one arm snapped. He reached again for Thura—

Grunting, Broll increased his efforts. The vines strengthened, thickened.

Just before the thick fingers could reach the orc again, the vines bound the corrupted ancient so tightly that he could no longer move. Broll did not let up. He had the vines continue to grow, continue to tighten.

The ancient tumbled to the ground, unable to move in the least. The night elf marveled at his own effort, aware that there had been a time not that long ago when he would have thought his skills insufficient to capture one such as Gnarl without being forced to slay him in the process.

Thura, meanwhile, had not wasted her time. She was almost upon the shadow. She hefted the ax—

The storm faltered. The winds lessened.

The tree moved.

One shadow branch thrust into the orc's chest. Although it had no substance, it impaled her. Thura stood frozen, the ax still raised high.

The other branches reached for Broll . . .

You are too weak . . . our foothold too strong . . . you have failed, my dear Malfurion . . .

Malfurion refused to listen to such words, even though they had some merit. He knew that even with Tyrande standing with him, he was fast approaching his limits.

See how they all fall now . . . offered the Nightmare Lord.

Before the archdruid's eyes, visions of all those who depended upon him came anew. Thura transfixed. King Varian leading a shrinking army. The other druids—Hamuul yet urging them on—trying to do what they could against an unstoppable foe transforming both realms . . .

He had been shown this before, had felt it before, but the crushing weight of having come so close just to fail again was too much. Perhaps if he had been a hundred Malfurions, a thousand, he might have succeeded . . . but he was only one.

Despair . . . and know that as you do . . . I have only shown you what is happening . . . this time, you know your failings yourself . . .

Xavius laughed loud.

The storm all but faded. What his adversary said was so true. Xavius was not doing anything; he merely showed Malfurion what Malfurion already understood . . . that the archdruid had let everyone down.

Then, just as the darkness seemed about to close about his heart, a cool, soothing light touched him from within. He knew its source instantly.

"Malfurion!" Tyrande called in his ear. Her voice was haggard, yet still somehow unyielding to her own pain. "Please! Do not . . . give in! He plays on your mind . . ."

The archdruid stirred . . . and found both of them caught up in the wicked branches. Only the fact that Tyrande had evidently been holding on to him at the time of their being seized had kept them together.

All is the Nightmare! Xavius the tree intoned. *You . . . she . . . all . . . How I have waited for this . . . trapped so long in the darkness beneath the waves, waiting and growing in strength with its guidance . . . growing until the time was right and then rising from the depths to set down roots here upon the eastern cliffs overlooking my lost Zin-Azshari! Here, where once my queen ruled all, where once I was power, how more appropriate that here you fall and the Nightmare covers all . . . how fitting!*

All . . . that one word most of all struck a chord with Malfurion.

I have made a terrible mistake . . . he knew what he needed to do to finally finish this. Victory or defeat was not dependent on him and him alone nor even him and Tyrande, though together they had stemmed the tide.

It depended upon *everyone* working in concert as never before.

Strengthened by this last revelation, lightning guided by Malfurion struck the foremost branch involved in holding them. The two night elves were flung into the air. Malfurion transformed into storm crow form and caught Tyrande in his talons. He brought her to the ground just beyond the grasping branches, then became himself again.

"I made a mistake!" he informed her. "I know the truth now!"

She nodded. Tyrande knew what he expected of her. Without waiting, the high priestess began a prayer to Elune.

Malfurion reached out to the other druids . . . every druid left in either realm save Broll. *Let me show you what we—together—may accomplish . . .*

To do what he needed, Malfurion had to ask the other druids to leave themselves defenseless. He was surprised, grateful, and fearful when all accepted without hesitation.

He showed them what they already knew, but did not fully understand even now. They were druids. They were Azeroth's caretakers and guardians. They also served as the same for the Emerald Dream. Yet, though they understood that as such their bonds with the essence of nature in both was powerful, they did not realize that they had, as a group, believed that they were more limited than they actually were.

But the two realms themselves were intertwined in a manner that even the druids had never fully comprehended and thus, the bond was more complex, and potentially far more powerful. The others marveled at what their shan'do revealed, but Malfurion could not let them dwell upon this amazing discovery. Guiding them on, he had them turn their spellwork to his intention.

The storm. His storm. The other druids were essential to its crafting, to its growth, but it was through Malfurion—with Tyrande's prayers to the Mother Moon helping to keep his mind clear of the Nightmare's presence—that it truly swelled, truly took on the epic proportions he needed.

A deep rumble shook both Azeroth *and* the Emerald Dream. King Varian kept order among his fighters, aware that they could not make the assumption that this brought new hope. As the lord of Stormwind led the fighting, at times the image of the wolf would again superimpose itself upon his face, a sight that gave further encouragement to those who knew of the spirit's favor.

The Life-Binder, standing at the one gate that prevented the Nightmare's own efforts, smiled grimly in recognition of what Malfurion was accomplishing. She threw her last efforts into making certain she did not fail in her part.

Malfurion sensed it all come together. The druids became as one under his leadership. He felt an understanding of his world and the

Emerald Dream that he could never have imagined. Yet it was his bond with Tyrande that enabled him to most make use of that understanding.

The storm unleashed.

It struck with a fury with which no tempest ever before had done. Azeroth trembled. The Emerald Dream shimmered. They were two that were one, but not as Xavius desired. He had wanted one realm perverted into an evil mirroring his own and that of the force behind him.

But Malfurion instead gave them the purity and strength of nature.

The wind roared. It set the mists swirling. Its force made the nightmarish figures and shadow satyrs ripple, then dissipate like so much dust. Stormwind City, Orgrimmar . . . every embattled place upon Azeroth was suddenly cleared.

The rain poured, rivers spilling over the landscape wherever the evil had spread. The pristine waters not only washed away more of the Nightmare's shadows and other horrific servants, but brought new life, new growth, where the Nightmare had stunted or manipulated it.

The carrion bugs melted in the rain, their foulness unable to withstand its force. Those too corrupted by the Nightmare to be saved fled from the cleansing, retreating with the melting mists that represented the darkness's dwindling hold.

But the Nightmare still held sway over its many victims and the power that their fears brought was yet tremendous. The sleepwalkers rose in vast numbers, driven by their terrifying dreams to strike out at those living.

Malfurion had known, though, that this would come. He called forth the thunder, stirring it to a rumble.

There had been on Azeroth no sound like it. A hundred volcanoes could not match it. All the combined storms throughout history could not come even close to its fantastic power.

And no creature, no matter how deeply asleep, deeply hidden in the lowest recesses of any cave or high up in some mountain or behind thick stone walls . . . could avoid hearing it.

The thunder roiled.

The sleepers awoke.

The hold of the Nightmare shattered.

Xavius's outrage echoed in Malfurion's mind a moment after, a piti-ful sound in comparison to the majesty of the storm. However, the archdruid did not assume his victory assured or imminent. Arms out-stretched, hands clenched, Malfurion threw his will into what he and the druids had created, then threw it at the Nightmare Lord.

The storm raged.

Wherever the taint resisted, lightning flashed, burning away the darkness. The bolts were not white or yellow, as normal, but the bril-liant green of nature in its most lush growth. The ground where they struck was not scorched, but *bloomed*.

Malfurion did not let up in either realm, aware that to do so would possibly give the Nightmare a new foothold. Indeed, as the evil was pressed further and further back, its resistance grew. Malfurion felt some of the druids flagging and out of concern for them took on a larger burden. Tyrande reinforced him throughout it all, her determi-nation matching his. This *would* end here . . .

But in the midst of it, Malfurion felt the evil behind Xavius for the first time exerting itself . . . and succeeding in pushing back.

It took a moment for the archdruid to understand why. The truth lay in the sleepers. They were now awake, but the horrors of their dread dreams were with them. Their fear still fed the Nightmare.

Malfurion and Tyrande sensed at the same time what had to be done. His left hand arced. The rain covering Azeroth altered, grow-ing finer, warmer. It even took on a reddish hue, such as a rose might have. As this happened, Tyrande asked of Elune her help. The silver light of the Mother Moon came down, joining in concert with the rain.

As the astonishing rain touched the Nightmare's victims, a sense of calm instantly overtook them. They began to forget much of what they had suffered or made others suffer as slaves of Xavius.

The resistance against Malfurion's spell weakened. Encouraged, he pushed . . . pushed until it reached the tree and its shadow.

Until it reached Xavius and could go no farther.

I will always be with you, the Nightmare Lord mocked. *I am you, Malfurion Stormrage . . .*

The archdruid made no response. He summoned up the energies of Azeroth and the Emerald Dream and cast them at the great and terrible tree.

They did nothing.

Malfurion turned his gaze to the Emerald Dream and the shadow of Xavius. There he saw what he already knew: Thura impaled and Broll fighting to keep from being snared by the smoky limbs.

The gathered energies struck at the shadow . . . with as little result as against the true tree.

So, this is what you want of me . . . Malfurion thought to his enemies. *Very well . . .*

Focusing within himself and utilizing the tremendous forces gathered from both realms, Malfurion separated his dreamform from his physical body in a manner that even he once would have never thought possible. Malfurion now stood as two separate beings, but still the same person. His physical body was not dormant. He stood and acted in both the Emerald Dream and Azeroth, something no druid had ever done before and what should have been impossible. Indeed, it was in part because of what the Nightmare had caused in trying to bring the two realms together that enabled Malfurion to accomplish this unique feat.

It was the only way by which his attack could be focused at precisely the same instant on both the tree and the shadow. He had to be of equal part to each, enough that they then became very susceptible to his powers.

But it was also what Xavius desired, for, by the same reasoning, Malfurion was now doubly susceptible to threats occurring in both realms. The shadow limbs assailed his dreamform. The wicked tree attacked with renewed effort his physical body.

However, as the Nightmare Lord attacked, Malfurion touched the mind of another. *Broll . . . we must strike . . .*

The druid gave a brief acknowledgment. Seen now as inconsequential, he gained that one second to bring his own powers into play.

Transforming into cat form, Broll used his mouth and seized Thura from the shadow's grip. Her skin was cold to the touch, but the moment contact with the shadow was broken, her body warmed.

The orc stirred. Broll threw her forward.

A thousand shadowy branches plunged into Malfurion's dreamform. On Azeroth, Tyrande clutched the archdruid as more agony than he had ever suffered as a tree himself tore through his system. The high priestess cried out as she took his pain and made it her own so that he could better concentrate on his own attack.

Malfurion gritted his teeth. The night elf now condensed the massive storm's fury on but two places, one in Azeroth, the other the Emerald Dream. The Nightmare Lord's tree and shadow bent under the added onslaught. The branches buried in the chest of Malfurion's dreamform were at last ripped away by the wind. Those of the true tree were scorched by lightning. New ones sprouted in their place as the Nightmare Lord sought in turn to seize his foe, but Malfurion's spell held sway.

And in the Emerald Dream, Thura reached the shadowed trunk. She raised the ax, which glowed with the glory of the energies that the demigod Cenarius had ten thousand years earlier imbued in it for Broxigar.

Strike here! Malfurion told her, revealing in her thoughts an image of the critical spot.

With a crooked grin, the orc caught the shadow at the very point.

A shriek echoed over the Emerald Dream, a shriek whose twin erupted from Azeroth. The ax sank deep, as if biting into something solid.

The shadow wavered.

As Thura struck there, Malfurion increased his attack on the physical tree by a thousandfold. Emerald lightning hit true time and time again, setting vicious branch after branch ablaze.

My lord! Xavius abruptly shouted. *Hear me!*

But Malfurion felt the ancient darkness abandon its vile servant. Although he wondered at that, the archdruid dared not lessen his efforts against Xavius; he knew too well that if any spark remained, Xavius's evil would rise again . . . and in a form likely even more terrible. The entire terrible ordeal would begin anew.

Thura struck the shadow a second time and some of its outline faded. Malfurion continued to assail the true tree with lightning bolts, creating an inferno.

Xavius threw those flames back at his foes. Even though Tyrande did her best to protect Malfurion as he worked, the archdruid's flesh burned.

Thura struck a third time. The fabled ax sank so deep into shadow that the head briefly vanished.

And then . . . as she pulled the magical weapon free . . . the shadow tree simply faded to nothing.

The Nightmare Lord shrieked.

On Azeroth, the true tree shook. It began to rapidly wither. The branches slumped. The great roots curled and shriveled.

The bitter, angry voice of Xavius, of the Nightmare Lord, thundered in the archdruid's thoughts. *Malfurion Stormrage! I will never leave you! I will ever be your nightmare! I—*

The crown of the horrific tree crumbled.

Black ash marked its fall. The lower branches cracked off, powdering as they struck the hard ground. Even the trunk collapsed, huge pieces breaking away and scattering across the landscape. Malfurion deflected those that would have struck him and Tyrande. The blackened bark decayed rapidly.

In the end, only a rotted trunk—seemingly already centuries dead—remained when the last of the dust settled.

Xavius, once counselor to Queen Azshara, once first among the satyrs, once the Nightmare Lord . . . was at last no more.

Malfurion did not wallow in his victory. Rather, he pushed on, crushing what remained of the Nightmare, seeking to utterly eradicate it. The grafting from Xavius's tree, worked into Teldrassil by Fandral, had given Xavius a tie to both realms—allowing the evil behind

the Nightmare Lord to touch Azeroth and the Emerald Dream simultaneously. However, Xavius's physical form had remained most domi-
nant in Azeroth and without the tree to sustain that link, what was
left of the Nightmare could not hold.

And when Azeroth was free of the taint, Malfurion—Tyrande
standing with him throughout—focused then completely on the Emerald Dream, determined that it, too, should be cleansed. The Nightmare dwindled, receded . . .

But in one small corner of the Emerald Dream, in a vast, deep fissure, known to the druids as the Rift of Aln and believed to be where
the magical realm itself first originated, even the combined efforts of
the archdruid and the high priestess could not entirely end the struggle. The Nightmare held firmly in that place, which those of Malfurion's calling believed bled into the Twisting Nether and the Great Dark
Beyond. Gazing into it, Malfurion saw it as a bottomless chasm which
radiated with primeval energies that even he dared not investigate. Indeed, the very rift itself seemed half-dream, for it had a surreal quality
to its expanse and to the archdruid now and then seemed to ripple as
if ready to fade or change.

Curiously, only then did Malfurion truly sense that the ancient
evil, though it fought to keep its grip there, did so from somewhere
deep in the depths of Azeroth's own seas. Bereft of Xavius's link to the
dream realm, it was still powerful enough somehow to keep that one
place under its horrific sway.

At last it became clear that there was nothing more to be gained by
pressing. Aware of those yet needing them, Malfurion sealed off the
vicinity around the rift. There was silent agreement between Tyrande
and him. The day had been saved . . . this other war would have to
wait for another, a better, time.

With the danger passing, the night elf felt his hold on the incredible energies slipping away. He was not bothered, but still had matters with which he had to deal before they fully vanished. Sweeping
across both realms, he sought out any surviving corrupted. There
were few, and of those only a handful could he salvage. Gnarl was
one of those, for he had been but recently taken. Remulos was already

cleansed. However, many, regretfully, were like Lethon and Emeriss and could not survive without the Nightmare; they melted away as the shadow satyrs had. For what and who they once had been, Malfurion mourned them.

Next, he restored to their bodies those surviving members of Varian's dreamform army, no matter from where they had been summoned. Night elves, of course, and orcs, trolls, draenei, blood elves, tauren, dwarves, gnomes, goblins, humans . . . they had all done their part, even some among the undead. He savored briefly one sight, that of the king rushing to his son and the pair holding one another tight. For those defenders who had no physical forms to which to return, the archdruid attuned them better to the Emerald Dream, so that their lives there would be at the fullest possible.

Of those who had been his closest allies in this, he found special time. Thura he delivered back to her people, letting their leader, Thrall, know of her significance in the struggle. Lucan Foxblood, the human of unique abilities, became the charge of Hamuul Runetotem. The tauren agreed to stay in the Moonglade for a time to teach the cartographer how best to control his unique abilities. The two were oddly suited to one another's company and Malfurion had great hopes that the teaching would go well.

And even as Malfurion did this, he sensed Tyrande summon forth the Sisters of Elune to go forth into the Alliance-held lands and do what else could be done to bring further calm and order to those victims at least. Shaman and druids also lent their skills to the Nightmare's former slaves, tending to those with whom their particular race had ties so as to avoid any chance of further conflict. It was impossible for all the wounds to be healed, even by the forces guided by the archdruid. Too many had died for any power to be able to erase all the memories. Though banished to the Rift of Aln—where Malfurion prayed it would stay—the Nightmare's legacy would haunt the world for years to come.

Malfurion saw many other things for which he would have liked to have utilized the gifts of Azeroth and the Emerald Dream, but knew that it was time for him to end his efforts. With much gratitude, he let the other druids break from the spell first. They had given much, more than he should have asked. He was proud of all.

And finally, Malfurion reluctantly separated himself from the spell, returning to the two realms the bounty that they had given him. The archdruid refocused upon the real world. His gaze settled upon she who had been with him from the beginning to the very end despite the great faults that had eventually led to his capture and torture and despite the travails through which she had gone through because of his failings. Malfurion saw the love within her and, though he knew he was not worthy of it, was determined that they would not be parted again.

He put a gentle hand to Tyrande's cheek.

Exhaustion overtook him.

Malfurion collapsed in her arms.

30

A Gathering of Hope

Broll Bearmantle took the news of Malfurion's awaking with
an exuberance rarely seen in most night elves, much less
druids. He let out a hearty yell that echoed throughout the
enclave and rushed to the Temple of the Moon. He raced past those
taking a more solemn approach to the home of the Sisterhood, only
caring that his shan'do appeared to be well.

Two armed Sisters briefly blocked his path until one recognized
him. "Our orders are to allow only a select few in," she explained,
"lest the temple be overwhelmed with those concerned for the archdruid's health."

Broll nodded, grateful that he was one of those Tyrande had permitted to enter. Aware where they had brought Malfurion, Broll
needed no directions. He rushed through the temple, giving homage
and thanks to the Mother Moon's image more than once during the
trek.

They had made a place for Malfurion underneath the great statue,
where moonlight ever shone. The high priestess had insisted that he
be brought to the temple, though the first notion of the druids had
been to take their esteemed shan'do to the Moonglade. However,
Tyrande had refused to be swayed and as she was not only ruler of
the night elves but also Malfurion's beloved, in the end none could refuse her.

Eyes shut, Malfurion lay on a mat of woven leaves and herbs—an offering of the druids. Tyrande knelt beside him, a soft, moist cloth in her hand. She had been tending to him as if she were a novice, not head of the order. Behind her, and standing guard, was an equally quiet Shandris Feathermoon. The general wore a look Broll would have more expected of a child concerned over her parents than that of a seasoned warrior.

"My lady," Broll murmured to Tyrande as he neared. Shandris gave him a cursory glance; she had registered his presence much earlier and thus was not concerned. "I had heard that he was . . . that he was awake . . ."

"And so . . . and so I am . . ." Malfurion responded, his eyes slowly opening. The archdruid's orbs still shone like the sun . . . and always would, it seemed. He gave the other male a brief smile. "But she"— with his gaze, he indicated Tyrande—"insists I rest some more . . . a command with which, after a failed . . . failed attempt to rise . . . I must agree . . ." Malfurion's smile grew. "But I'm remiss. I see that the struggle has changed you as well, Broll . . ."

That to which the archdruid referred was Broll's own eyes, which, while not as resplendent as those of his shan'do, now also gleamed gold. In reaching into himself and into Azeroth, Broll had finally broken the final barrier—a self-imposed barrier—and truly become the great druid so many had believed he was. More important, the change went deep within. Gone was Broll's uncertainty; he himself knew at last that he was as he had always been meant to be and his every movement radiated his great confidence in his calling.

But that was not of interest to him at the moment. Only one thing mattered. "But . . . you are truly well?"

The high priestess paused in her ministrations to stare at Broll as if he were mad. "He is in the house of Elune and I am her hand in this world . . . do you think he would be otherwise?"

"Forgive me," the druid returned with a chuckle. "I clearly wasn't thinking."

Malfurion put a hand on her knee. Tyrande's expression softened. To Broll, the archdruid replied, "She is rather protective. I've made her a promise she intends I keep."

" 'Promise'?"

"It is fortuitous that you are here, Broll, for I can think of no other I would have stand with me when I and Tyrande take our vows."

It took Broll a moment to register what he meant. Shandris laughed lightly at his delayed reaction.

"You two—you are to marry?"

"Please do not sound so shocked." The high priestess smiled. "I believe that I have waited long enough for him to come to his senses."

"And I believe you should have long found someone with more sense than me," Malfurion, sounding stronger, returned. Now holding her free hand, he said to the other male, "Well, Broll Bearmantle, will you stand with me?"

"There are surely others—"

"Many good souls, but I choose you."

The druid bowed his head. "Then, I'm honored. I only pray that I will not make a mistake."

His shan'do laughed. "You can make no greater mistake than I did by leaving her so often throughout the millennia, my friend."

"When will the ceremony take place?"

Without meaning to, both Malfurion and Tyrande answered simultaneously. "As soon as possible."

Although Darnassus did not in some regards present the most practical of places to hold such a ceremony, there was no other place that would have been more appropriate. With Malfurion Stormrage leader of the druids and Tyrande Whisperwind not only high priestess of Elune but monarch of the night elves, they could only choose the capital.

Long before the eve of the ceremony, the two had already quickly settled any question as to their roles—or rather, Tyrande had. Malfurion knew Tyrande was the best leader his people could have and made no claims in that direction. However, she insisted that there could be no other choice but for the two to rule side-by-side, equal in all things where their race was concerned. She remained high priestess of the Temple of Elune and he the lead archdruid, but now those two stations would have closer ties, which would only benefit the night elves in general.

The ceremony took place in the Temple of Elune, of course. Granted, that meant arranging the audience involved some maneuvering, but General Shandris proved as adept at organizing guests as she was in battle. There were some who said, not in earshot, of course, that she seemed to enjoy it more than her normal duties.

Still, in addition to the Sisters, the Sentinels were well in attendance, ensuring that no one would cause trouble . . . a necessary point since, in addition to their own people, Malfurion and Tyrande had as guests King Varian, Archmage Rhonin, and other leaders. Naturally, each also came with the prerequisite attendants and personal guards. Even with the vast recovery taking place throughout Azeroth, Varian and the others had seen it as an absolute priority to acknowledge this seminal event concerning the one most responsible for there still even being an Azeroth. Even the independent-minded dwarves of the Wildhammer clan—the famed gryphon riders from Aerie Peak—had come, led by their high thane, Falstad.

Words of well wishes for Malfurion and Tyrande came from Thrall, representing the Horde. The fragile partnership between the Horde and the Alliance was already falling apart as personal hatreds seized control now that the main threat was gone. It was all the pair could have hoped, aware of how quickly peace could vanish. The only other benefit of the message was that the bearer was none other than Thura, who had asked of her warchief to be the one to carry it. To her, the archdruid, the high priestess, and those others beside whom she had fought were blood comrades.

Although the time of the ceremony was of course set for when the White Lady—the great silver moon that to the night elves was Elune herself—was at its zenith, other illumination existed that both added to the splendor and eased those visitors who were not of a nocturnal nature. Fireflies by the thousands decorated the trees, and small silver-blue orbs of moonlight hovered over the people themselves.

At the offering of Rhonin—who had in a unique manner known the pair longer than nearly anyone else there—the magi created a series of magnificent rainbows that, set against the dark sky, marked the ten millennia of Malfurion and Tyrande's relationship.

Near Rhonin stood his wife, Vereesa Windrunner—leader of the high elves of the Silver Covenant, itself created to oppose the inclusion of blood elves in the Kirin Tor—and their twin sons. The two boys bore a subdued look. They had their father's crimson hair and strong, clean jaw, but were somewhat more lithe in appearance and with slightly longer ears. The combination of elf and human could have proven unfortunate, but both were handsome offspring.

Triumphant horns announced the entrance of the wedding party. An honor guard of Sentinels bearing lances topped alternately by the lunar banner of the Sisterhood and the tabard of the Cenarion Circle—a great leaf from which majestic antlers sprouted—led the way. The honor guard was followed by a stately procession of druids and members of the Sisterhood. Behind them solemnly marched senior officers of the Sentinels hand chosen by General Shandris.

And then . . . came Malfurion and Tyrande.

Malfurion, chin high and antlers thrusting skyward, wore a long, draping cloak of forest leaves and a breastplate crafted from fallen wood. On it had been shaped the World Tree with the sign of the Cenarion Circle above it. In addition, the archdruid wore a knee-length green kilt and sandals.

Tyrande glowed with the love of Elune, the Mother Moon clearly giving her blessing to this union. As she passed, many night elves instinctively knelt. Tyrande was dressed as high priestess. She was also adorned with a grand cape of silver-and-blue light that flowed long past the end of her mount. Her midnight-blue hair was loose and long and though she looked as wise as all thought their ruler to be, there was also an added youth to her tremendous beauty that many were certain came from the joy of the moment.

Shandris and Broll strode behind the pair, both also adorned with long cloaks akin to those of the archdruid and the high priestess, but not quite as grand. Their task was to stand as witness and strength for their respective companions, a task of which they were clearly proud.

At the center of the great chamber, the party came to a halt. Malfurion and Tyrande held each other's hands forward, then solemnly walked on ahead. Broll and Shandris moved to the side and back of the pair, with the druid near his mentor and the general near her ruler.

The honor guard, the druids, and the Sisters divided into two columns that departed in opposite directions.

There had been great question as to who would perform the ceremony. Had matters been otherwise, many believed that Remulos would have done so. However, the forest guardian, now recovered but weak, was part of the audience, as were others such as Elerethe Renferal, who assisted Naralex beside her. Even up to this point, only the high priestess and the archdruid knew who it was to be. Not even Broll and Shandris were aware of the truth.

Malfurion and Tyrande stood ready. Together, they looked up.

The light of Elune suddenly shone down most upon the pair. Yet this was not what seemed to attract their attention.

A great flapping of wings resounded from above. The audience, which included among its members Lucan, Hamuul, and Thura, followed Malfurion and Tyrande's pleased gaze. The tauren looked up with eyes not only strongly gold, but with a unique hint of emerald green at the edges; he, too, had given so much of himself in helping to guide Malfurion's efforts that he had been likewise marked. Lucan, now not only Hamuul's student but newly appointed chief cartographer of Stormwind by King Varian—who had heard much of his subject's part in the struggle from Malfurion and Broll—especially radiated pleasure at the fantastic sight high up. Though it made some glance aghast at him, he waved as if sighting a friend among the giants now circling.

Red and green dragons filled the air above Darnassus.

"Be at ease," Malfurion calmly commanded before chaos could erupt. "They are here as friends and guests . . ."

Most of the dragons hovered, but the four largest descended. As they did, the two smaller—and clearly male—alighted onto some of the greatest branches.

A chuckle escaped Archmage Rhonin, who, along with the couple, knew the red male. Korialstrasz was his name and he was chief consort to Alexstrasza. Awakened with the rest of the sleepers, he had been active in helping restore calm to Azeroth.

But to the trio and Rhonin's mate, Vereesa, he was also the mysterious mage Krasus. As with Rhonin, it was quite clear from Korialstrasz's expression that the dragon would not have missed this pivotal moment for anything.

And, naturally, Korialstrasz had come in the company of his queen. Alexstrasza hovered just above the columns, next to her none other than Ysera.

The green dragon looked worn and thinner, her titanic struggle having taken much out of her. Yet there was also a tremendous expression of pride from her, that pride directed at Malfurion Stormrage.

The dragons hovered a moment more, then, before the startled eyes of the audience, the two leviathans landed and transformed. Wings shrank and bodies contorted. The dragons dwindled to the size of night elves and took on shapes akin to theirs.

Alexstrasza became as Broll and the others had met her, a glorious, fiery figure. Ysera was no less astounding, though in an ethereal manner. Clad in a gossamer gown of emerald, the cowled female was otherwise very much a twin in face, save that her skin was of a pale green and her eyes were, as usual, shut.

The two Aspects smiled at the high priestess and the archdruid. Ysera took up a place near Malfurion while Alexstrasza did so by Tyrande.

"We are honored to have been asked to be the ones to perform this intertwining of two spirits," they sang in unison. "But in truth, these spirits have been one since the beginning . . ."

The two females brought the pair's other hands together, then placed their own atop and underneath.

"Though this ceremony shall be brief, let it forever mark the culmination of ten thousand years of love, of destiny," Alexstrasza and Ysera continued.

"Let there be peace for this pair, who have brought it to all others, who have sacrificed for all others . . ."

The moonlight shining upon the wedding couple grew stronger. At the same time, a beautiful crimson aura arose around Alexstrasza, while an emerald one did so about Ysera.

The auras blended with the moonlight, bathing the high priestess and the archdruid.

"The blessing of our kind upon you, Tyrande Whisperwind, high priestess of Elune and ruler of the night elven people and you, Malfurion Stormrage, archdruid and leader of the Cenarion Circle . . ."

Now Malfurion and Tyrande glowed so very brightly. Their radiance would have been blinding, if it had also not been so *soothing* to the onlookers.

"This is a day to be well-marked by all Azeroth!" The Aspects pulled their hands away. The fantastic blending of auras and moonlight continued around the newly married duo. *"But, most of all, this is a day well-deserved for these two here! Tyrande Whisperwind . . . Malfurion Stormrage . . . we bless this union . . . and, as our gift . . . we also do something else this glorious day . . ."*

The expressions of the two night elves indicated that they were as ignorant of what this meant as the rest of the audience. In response, Ysera and Alexstrasza gestured toward the direction of Teldrassil's vast crown.

"This tree was born without our blessing . . . it has been cleansed by the druids and blessed by one of us, but a more special blessing shall now be made . . . let it now receive through both us our hopes for a world and a future of which we can all be proud . . ."

Following their direction, the couple faced Teldrassil's center. The Aspects each stretched a hand that direction. Malfurion and Tyrande smiled in understanding.

From the two transformed dragons, there shot forth a wondrous light that flowed to the archdruid and the high priestess, then outward.

It washed over the entire crown in a mere heartbeat, then spread down through the branches to the trunk and quickly beyond sight. What was visible to the onlookers clearly strengthened, flourished.

No one there could deny that Teldrassil was obviously stronger, more vibrant.

The moment swept over Malfurion. His people, his world, was safe. Teldrassil was purified.

Most of all, he was at last one with his beloved.

A sense of fulfillment rose up within him. The archdruid smiled.

There were gasps from many in the audience.

"Mal!" Tyrande blurted. "What are you doing?"

He suddenly realized that he glowed and that glow now touched Teldrassil in a manner much as had the dragons' blessing.

The assembled guests peered around in awe as even the surface beneath their feet was transformed.

The glow around Malfurion faded, but Teldrassil remained illuminated. In that light, its leaves grew even more lush than when Malfurion had cleared it of the Nightmare's taint. Huge, multicolored fruit blossomed from the branches and, after reaching a thickness akin to the largest of apples, began to softly rain down. Those assembled laughed with delight as they caught the fruit and dared taste them.

"Like the sweetest nectar!" Elerethe Renferal blurted.

"Have to admit, nothin' like this in the Aerie," Falstad rumbled as he all but swallowed one of the two he had procured.

Tyrande tasted one, then also smiled. "Mal . . . this is amazing . . ."

He looked deep into her eyes. "This is because of you . . ."

She flushed.

"May your life be as full of life as Teldrassil is now," Alexstrasza murmured to the bride and groom as she and Ysera stepped further back.

"Our time at these festivities is at an end," She of the Dreaming added. "Congratulations to you, my child," the mistress of the Emerald Dream said to Malfurion. "Be worthy of her . . ."

"I will always try to be."

Ysera became more serious. "This is only your beginning, both of you . . . but you, most of all, my Malfurion, have entered a new stage. When there is time . . . and I say *when* . . . you have a complex level of training to start, one which no other has faced before."

"I look forward to your teachings, great one . . ."

The Aspect cocked her head. "This is not something that I can teach you . . . this is something that must be learned by yourself. You have done what no other, not even I, could do." After a pause, the dragon added, "But I will be happy to offer advice, though if I were Malfurion Stormrage, I would listen most to she next to you . . ."

Malfurion squeezed Tyrande's hand. "Oh, I will."

Alexstrasza and Ysera nodded, then, without further words, transformed. They rose into the air, again the great behemoths.

The two night elves glanced at one another. Tyrande quickly nodded.

To Ysera, the archdruid called, "Ysera . . . great one . . . we give our condolences for brave Eranikus!"

"And they are welcomed . . ." She of the Dreaming bowed her head, sadness and gratitude vying in her tone. "From this happy place, I go to mourn! His sacrifice I will honor forever . . ."

"As do we all," Alexstrasza added.

With that, the two soared high into the sky. Korialstrasz and the green male joined them, the red briefly giving the night elves a knowing nod.

"Thank you, my good friends . . ." he rumbled before departing.

The party of dragons circled over Darnassus. Most expected them to simply depart, but then, as one, the huge beasts issued a triumphant roar . . . their final homage to Malfurion and his bride.

And as Ysera and Alexstrasza led their kind away, the archdruid and the high priestess turned back to those who had come to honor them. Malfurion looked upon the assembly and wondered if Azeroth might have any chance not only to completely recover from the Nightmare, but even move beyond it, to that future that might have hope.

Then Malfurion recalled what still held sway over the Rift of Aln and grew troubled. It was not a threat that could be left untouched for long. The archdruid began pondering what they would have to do—

He felt Tyrande squeeze his hand. She leaned and kissed him.

"Enjoy today, Mal . . . that's all we can ever ask . . . today *together* . . ." She kissed him again, then added more strongly, "And then we shall begin dealing in earnest with the foulness that guided Xavius's evil . . ."

The archdruid nodded, accepting her wisdom. He *would* enjoy today—and all his time with Tyrande—and knew that he could indeed ask for no more than that. Still, both of them could not also help but have some hope for the future . . .

And Malfurion Stormrage was well aware that great things had been successfully built upon far less than *that* . . .

ABOUT THE AUTHOR

Richard A. Knaak is a *New York Times* bestselling author of some forty novels and numerous short stories, including works in such series as Warcraft, Diablo, Dragonlance, Age of Conan, and his own Dragonrealm. He has scripted a number of Warcraft manga with Tokyopop, including the top-selling Sunwell trilogy and the upcoming Dragons of Outland trilogy, and has also written background material for games. His works have been published worldwide in many languages.

Recent releases include *Legends of the Dragonrealm,* an omnibus featuring the first three novels of his original epic fantasy series; *Beastmaster: Myth,* a heroic tale that brings the classic film and television character back to his roots in an all-new adventure; and *The Gargoyle King*—the third in his Ogre Titans trilogy for Dragonlance. He is presently at work on several other projects.

Currently splitting his time between Chicago and Arkansas, he can be reached through his website: http://www.richardaknaak.com. While he is unable to respond to every e-mail, he does read them. Join his mailing list for e-announcements of upcoming releases and appearances.

The story you've just read is based in part on characters, situations, and settings from Blizzard Entertainment's computer game *World of Warcraft*, an online role-playing experience set in the award-winning Warcraft universe. In *World of Warcraft*, players create their own heroes and explore, adventure, and quest across a vast world shared with thousands of other players. The rich and expansive game also allows players to interact with and fight against or alongside many of the powerful and intriguing characters featured in this novel.

Since launching in November 2004, *World of Warcraft* has become the world's most popular subscription-based massively multiplayer online role-playing game. The game's second and most recent expansion, *Wrath of the Lich King*, sold more than 2.8 million copies within its first 24 hours of availability and more than 4 million copies in its first month, breaking records to become the fastest-selling PC game of all time. The next expansion planned for *World of Warcraft* is titled *Cataclysm*, and more information on it can be found on worldofwarcraft.com.

FURTHER READING

If you'd like to read more about the characters and circumstances that shaped Azeroth and led to the events of *World of Warcraft: Stormrage*, the sources listed below provide additional pieces of the story.

- You can find more information about Malfurion Stormrage's past, including his valiant struggle against the Burning Legion and its agents, in *Warcraft: The Well of Eternity*, *Warcraft: The Demon Soul*, and *Warcraft: The Sundering*, books one, two, and three of the War of the Ancients trilogy by Richard A. Knaak. These three novels also explore Malfurion's relationship with Tyrande Whisperwind.

- Broll Bearmantle plays a key role in the monthly *World of Warcraft* comic book by Walter and Louise Simonson, Ludo Lullabi, Jon Buran, Mike Bowden, Sandra Hope, and Tony Washington. The comic also reveals influential moments from Broll's past, such as the tragic death of his daughter, Anessa, in issue #4 and the battle against his own rage inside the Emerald Dream in issue #5.

- Tyrande Whisperwind's history with Malfurion Stormrage and her rise to the rank of high priestess of Elune are chronicled in the War of the Ancients trilogy by Richard A. Knaak. More than 10,000 years after the War of the Ancients, Tyrande encounters Broll Bearmantle and Varian Wrynn in issue #6 of the monthly *World of Warcraft* comic by Walter Simonson, Ludo Lullabi, and Sandra Hope.

- The creation of Broxigar's enchanted ax is portrayed in *Warcraft: The Well of Eternity,* book one of the War of the Ancients trilogy by Richard A. Knaak. Broxigar goes on to slay many demons with the powerful weapon, and he even uses it to face the malevolent Dark Titan, Sargeras, in *Warcraft: The Sundering*, book three of the War of the Ancients trilogy.

- The mysterious Idol of Remulos's history and the reasons why the idol was gifted to Broll Bearmantle are revealed in issue #4 of the monthly *World of Warcraft* comic by Walter Simonson, Ludo Lullabi, and Sandra Hope.

- Archdruid Fandral Staghelm witnesses the horrific death of his son Valstann during a battle with the qiraji and the silithid in "Warcraft: The War of the Shifting Sands" by Micky Neilson (on worldofwarcraft.com). The archdruid also makes an appearance when Broll Bearmantle gives him the Idol of Remulos in issue #6 of the monthly *World of Warcraft* comic by Walter Simonson, Ludo Lullabi, and Sandra Hope.

- Sargeras's corruption of Lord Xavius, counselor to Queen Azshara, is portrayed in *Warcraft: The Well of Eternity* and *Warcraft: The Demon Soul*, books one and two of the War of the Ancients trilogy by Richard A. Knaak. These novels also recount Xavius's bitter history with Malfurion, including the brutal final showdown between the satyr and the druid.

- Further details about Ysera the Dreamer are revealed in the War of the Ancients trilogy by Richard A. Knaak. Ysera also plays a role in stopping the vile schemes of the black Dragon Aspect, Neltharion, in *Warcraft: Day of the Dragon* by Richard A. Knaak.

- Other tales of Alexstrasza the Life-Binder and her struggle to safeguard Azeroth are told in the War of the Ancients trilogy by Richard A. Knaak, *Warcraft: Day of the Dragon* by Richard A. Knaak, and *World of Warcraft: Tides of Darkness* by Aaron Rosenberg.

- Prior to the events of *World of Warcraft: Stormrage*, the wise archdruid Hamuul Runetotem aided Broll Bearmantle and Varian Wrynn in issue #3 and issues #23–25 of the monthly *World of Warcraft* comic by Walter and Louise Simonson, Ludo Lullabi, Sandra Hope, Mike Bowden, and Tony Washington. Hamuul will also be featured in the upcoming Christie Golden novel *World of Warcraft: The Shattering: Prelude to Cataclysm*.

- Before she was taken under Tyrande Whisperwind's wing, Shandris Feathermoon was orphaned during the War of the Ancients. Shandris's first encounter with Tyrande and subsequent role in fighting the Burning Legion are depicted in *Warcraft: The Demon Soul* and *Warcraft: The Sundering*, books two and three of the War of the Ancients trilogy by Richard A. Knaak.

- Although King Varian Wrynn leads the people of Stormwind in *World of Warcraft: Stormrage*, his path to becoming king was long and difficult. His early years are detailed in World of Warcraft: Arthas: Rise of the Lich King by Christie Golden, World of Warcraft: Tides of Darkness by Aaron Rosenberg, and World of Warcraft: Beyond the Dark Portal by Aaron Rosenberg and Christie Golden. Varian's more recent struggles are depicted in the monthly World of Warcraft comic book by Walter and Louise Simonson, Ludo Lullabi, Jon Buran, Sandra Hope, Mike Bowden, and Tony Washington. Varian will also appear in the upcoming novel World of Warcraft: The Shattering: Prelude to Cataclysm by Christie Golden.

- Tales of the foul nightmares tormenting three of Azeroth's most important figures—Warchief Thrall, Lady Jaina Proudmoore, and King Magni Bronzebeard—are told in Warcraft: Legends Volume 5 "Nightmares" by Richard A. Knaak and Rob Ten Pas.

- In this volume, the once-beloved queen of the night elves, Azshara, haunts Tyrande Whisperwind in the Emerald Nightmare. The details of Azshara's corrupt past are recounted in Warcraft: The Well of Eternity, Warcraft: The Demon Soul, and Warcraft: The Sundering, books one, two, and three of the War of the Ancients trilogy by Richard A. Knaak.

- Sylvanas Windrunner's torturous transformation into a banshee—an event that plagues her dreams in World of Warcraft: Stormrage—is portrayed in World of Warcraft: Arthas: Rise of the Lich King by Christie Golden.

THE BATTLE RAGES ON

For now, Malfurion and his allies have defeated the insidious evil that took hold of the Emerald Dream—an evil so powerful and corrupting that even two of Azeroth's great Dragon Aspects, Ysera and Alexstrasza, could not defend against it without help. Yet another evils still persist on Azeroth, evils that seek to transform the world into a place of chaos and suffering . . . and you can play a part in stopping them in World of Warcraft.

World of Warcraft's first two expansions, *The Burning Crusade* and *Wrath of the Lich King*, take players to the alien world of Outland and the icy wastes of Northrend. In the upcoming third expansion, *Cataclysm*, players will witness the face of Azeroth being altered forever, as the corrupted Dragon Aspect Deathwing awakens from his subterranean slumber and erupts onto the surface, leaving ruin and destruction in his wake. As the Horde and Alliance race to the epicenter of the cataclysm, the kingdoms of Azeroth will witness seismic shifts in power, the kindling of a war of the elements, and the emergence of unlikely heroes who will rise up to protect their scarred and broken world from utter devastation.

To discover the ever-expanding world that has entertained millions around the globe, go to worldofwarcraft.com and download the free trial version. Live the story.

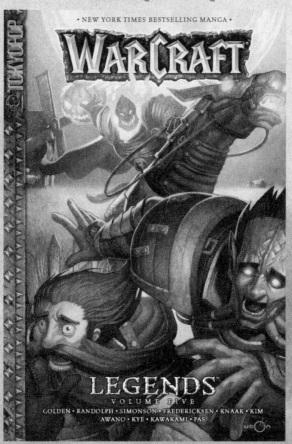

A MESSAGE FROM RICHARD A. KNAAK, AUTHOR OF NIGHTMARES

Greetings!

I hope you enjoyed reading *Stormrage* as much as I enjoyed writing it. Working in the *Warcraft* universe is always an immense pleasure, as Azeroth is populated with so many interesting characters (and stories), that often the possibilities seem limitless.

But, as with any work of literature, some tales simply can't be told in one book, no matter how epic the storyline (and lengthy the novel). Much like how a film director cuts scenes, a novelist must make some tough cuts as well. No matter how enticing side stories may be, if they don't push the central story forward, the fat must be trimmed.

However, I was given a unique opportunity to further explore the *Stormrage* saga outside the confines of the novel you now hold in your hands. TOKYOPOP publishes many *Warcraft* manga, including *Warcraft: Legends,* an anthology series set in the *Warcraft* universe. For *Warcraft: Legends* Volume 5, I was given the opportunity to write a *Stormrage* "prelude." In the short manga story "Nightmares," we are given a glimpse into the nightmares of the dwarven king Magni Bronzebeard, the orc warchief Thrall, and the human sorceress Lady Jaina Proudmoore. It's always exciting to see your written work brought to life with art, and *Legends* 5 is no exception.

So if you enjoyed *Stormrage,* be sure to complete the journey by picking up *Warcraft: Legends* Volume 5, available now at bookstores everywhere.

Until then, please enjoy this exclusive preview of "Nightmares"...

Richard A. Knaak

IT IS SAID THAT THE WORLD OF AZEROTH CANNOT EXIST WITHOUT THE DRAGONS...JUST AS THE DRAGONS CANNOT EXIST WITHOUT IT...

AFTER RESHAPING AZEROTH, THE STAR-SPANNING TITANS CHOSE THE DRAGONS--GREATEST OF THE YOUNG WORLD'S CREATURES--AS ITS GUARDIANS.

EACH REPRESENTED A POWERFUL FORCE: RED BEING LIFE, BRONZE TIME, BLUE MAGIC, BLACK THE EARTH, STONE AND DEEP PLACES...

AND FOR GREEN...WHOSE MISTRESS WAS THE GREAT LEVIATHAN YSERA...THERE WAS NOT ONLY SOVEREIGNTY OVER THE LUSH WILDS OF THE WORLD...

...BUT THE WATCHING OVER OF ALL AZEROTH FROM A MYSTICAL PLACE THAT WAS ITSELF CALLED THE EMERALD DREAM.

A PLACE BARELY TOUCHED BY MOST OF THOSE OF THE MORTAL WORLD, SAVE THROUGH THEIR OWN SLEEP-MANIFESTED IMAGININGS.

...AS IF WITH INTENTIONS OF THEIR OWN...

DREAMS MUCH DARKER THAN EVER BEFORE...DREAMS NOW SPREADING...

UNTIL OF LATE, THAT IS...UNTIL THE SUDDEN COMING OF DEEPER, MORE VIVID DREAMS...

...ACROSS AN UNSUSPECTING WORLD...

TOUCHING ANY SLEEPER...

HUMAN, ORC, TAUREN, DWARF...INDEED, ALL CREATURES...

AND IN THAT...LIES THE GREATEST DANGER.

FOR THERE ARE SOME DREAMS FROM WHICH EVEN THE BRAVEST WOULD RUN...

MMMPH!

NIGHTMARES

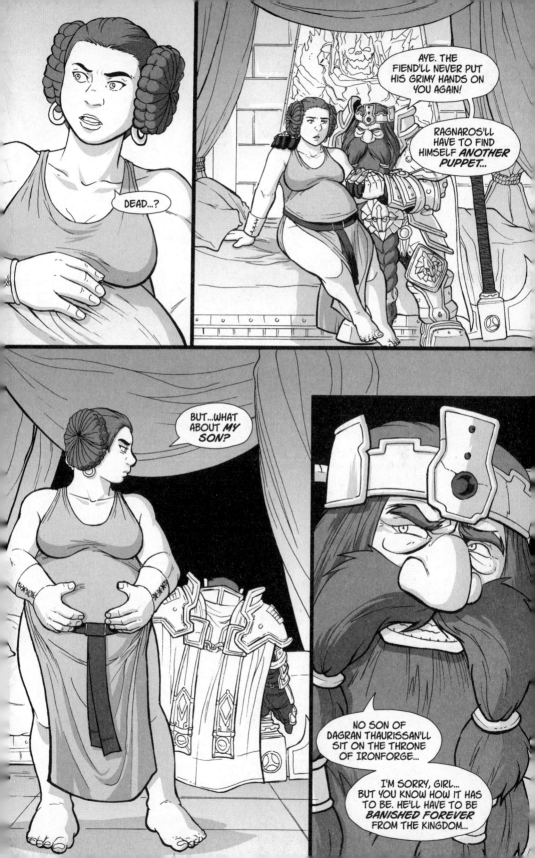

CONTINUED IN WARCRAFT: LEGENDS VOL.